OUTLAW MAGE

The Dageian Puppetmaster Book One

K. S. VILLOSO

Snowy Wings
PUBLISHING

Copyright © 2023 by K. S. Villoso

Cover illustration by Merilliza Chan

Edited by Amanda Bohannan

Published by Snowy Wings Publishing, Turner, Oregon

Cover and map design by Liam's Vigil

Interior art by Trish Isiderio

Author photo copyright © 2022 by Mikhail Villoso

978-1-958051-20-7 (hardcover)

978-1-958051-21-4 (paperback)

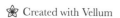 Created with Vellum

CONTENTS

MAGES ARE EXPERTS AT SUBTERFUGE

"HOW'D YOU GET TO BE SO SMART, TAB'ELIAN?"

"YOU'RE SWIMMING IN AGAN AND YOU CAN'T EVEN SEEM TO
CONTROL IT."

THE OCEAN SWELLED AROUND ME. I FELT A RUSH LIKE NOTHING I'D EVER KNOWN BEFORE .

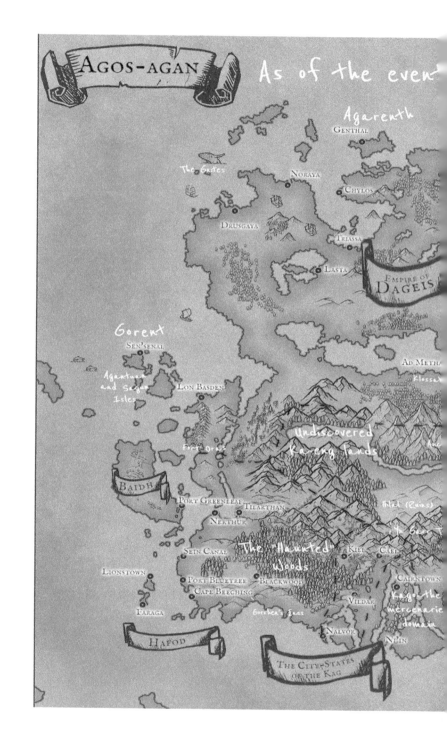

Don't be ridiculous.

— SAPPHIRE ORSALIAN AT THE BATTLE FOR
DRUSGAYA

For my daughters

ACT ONE

CHAPTER 1

THE FINAL TEST

I dropped out of magical school during my final exams. Sleepless nights spent cramming valuable knowledge into my brain, hundreds of evaluations which shot me up to the top of my classes —in short, thousands of hours of hard work, sweat, and tears— vanished like a speck of dust in a windstorm. It felt as if I had stabbed an infant the night of its birth. All of it gone, in an instant.

This is what they teach of the *agan*: it is the blood on which both the living and the dead run. It flows with the nourishing touch of water, connecting us to what was once and what is and maybe a touch of what could yet be. Those who can see the flow are gifted. What you can see, you can manipulate. Draw a line between your fingertips to your chest. Now pull, like a fisherman reeling the day's catch to shore. Let it burrow deep into your very own veins and heart. Let the touch turn into fire, let the fire burn your skin, let it spread through your flesh and your veins and your bones until you can't tell yourself apart from pure power. Your past, your name, the very breath in your lungs become meaningless in the face of what you can accomplish with a flick of your fingers.

Mages are experts at subterfuge and tricks. Most of us are pompous, arrogant, know-it-alls. Eheldeth, the most prestigious magical school in all the empire, has it more than most. The tuition fees mean that only the wealthiest, or those lucky enough to have a rich sponsor, can afford to send their children there. Even where they teach of the lifeblood that connects all of us, the true power still lies in the clink of coin. Children whose guardians cannot afford such schools are doomed to a life of servitude, bound to the will of masters born with better luck. In the

Empire of Dageis, magic is a commodity, and people like me must obey rules that keep the few above the rest.

I knew all that, and more. I knew the only path towards a promising career was to submit myself to the strictures of the school and therefore, by extension, the mage council who run both the school and the empire. I knew without its blessings, I was ruined.

And yet I left, like a fool. I didn't once look back.

It began like an itch.

Exams started right at the cusp of dawn, staggered in such a way that every student got the chance to be evaluated by the givers thoroughly. Every day they gave one written test on the histories and theories of various spells, and one practical test conjuring the same spell in front of an audience. Time slots were drawn at random—you might be asked to form the spell first and then write the test later on, or the other way around. Every student was on their own; there was no way to piggyback off your classmates' hard work, because most students didn't get the same spells on the same day.

I'd been hoping to draw morning slots for all my practical tests. Conjuring spells were easier when you had had a full night's rest. Most people preferred the other way around—the written exams gave them time to think over the steps of the spells and ensure they didn't embarrass themselves in front of the instructors. I didn't need the crutch. I'd committed every spell, every step, every theory in my mind as if it had been burned on my skull with a branding iron. The first day was an easy one for me, as I got exactly what I wanted: create balls of fire under the morning light and lob them at targets. Child's play: I hit everything on the first try. The written test? I knew I got a perfect score; how the *agan* could be manipulated to shift the temperature in your palms, how you drew on the air and fashioned it into a weapon of choice—

The second day arrived.

I woke up before anyone else in the dormitory did, sweating and itching underneath the flannel covers. I'd barely gotten more than a couple of hours of sleep. One simple spell out of the way meant everything else would be much harder. My eyes fell on the open book next to my mattress, my last vain attempt at a refresher even though I already knew everything by heart. I was pretty sure I could recite the damn thing back-to-back.

"Portals," I whispered under my breath, counting the lines on my fingers. "Please, don't let it be portals today."

"You nervous, Tar'elian?" my bunkmate grumbled. "Let the rest of us sleep before you continue muttering to yourself, yeah?"

I didn't answer. Instead, I picked up the book, stuffed it in my pack, and walked outside. It was still so early that the servants had yet to arrive to light the lanterns. I flicked my fingers, hoping to light one myself.

"Tar'elian!" someone yelled, before I could connect to the stream.

I turned to see who it was, and then turned away almost at once. Ivasus placed a hand on my shoulder, his fingers gripping through my robes in a gesture that seemed almost friendly at first glance. But by then, I trusted none of my classmates' intentions, and I trusted him even less.

"Our last week in this hellhole," he said with a grin. "And talk of your performance yesterday is already making rounds as we speak. How'd you get to be so smart, Tar'elian?"

I shrugged away from him and began walking down to the end of the hall. I didn't get far before I realized he was following me.

"We can have a few minutes in the library before anyone else is up. Come on, Tar'elian. You know you want to. Loosen up a bit."

I turned the next corner. He wasn't going to touch me. He needed to graduate as much as I did. A boy as talentless as Ivasus had nowhere else to go, and he wouldn't risk expulsion in the final week.

"Look at the high and mighty *princess*," he continued, as if his insults were enough to catch my attention. "You can't fool me. It's lonely where you plan to go. It doesn't help the instructors barely tolerate you, and you have no friends. All the perfect marks in the world won't make up for what you don't have: a beating heart."

We reached the courtyard. He finally stopped at the door, letting me walk out into the cold air all by myself. I suppose he liked watching how his words were enough to drive me barefoot into the frozen field. Maybe it gave him a sense of power. He wasn't the first classmate to taunt me for all the things I wasn't: friendly, warm, and not of old Dageian stock. I might as well have painted a target on my back. But as I continued to walk through the grass, my toes sinking into the frozen grass, I wondered if he would be the last. It would soon be over. I briefly allowed myself to wonder what it would be like to live without the looming presence of the school over me. To cast spells on a whim like I did when I was child, without instructors telling me it wasn't allowed—to be able to walk without anyone staring at me like I had an extra head...—For the first time since I walked into Eheldeth, I was eager to shake off its shadow.

It's almost over. Just be patient, Rosha. I turned to my books. My one comfort in all of this was how easily studying came to me. How *did* I get to be so smart? If Ivasus ever cracked a book open in his life, he would know.

I flipped to the *Portals* page. I could feel the cold air on my cheeks and underneath the soles of my feet. The book outlined the procedure for the test word for word—never let it be said that Eheldeth prized ambiguity. The school's fame came about because it produced students that remained consistent in the face of ambiguity. Mages who graduate from Eheldeth were all cut from the same cloth.

You were supposed to build a portal from the classroom all the way to the yard, where you were to leave a unique token provided during the exam before returning. Simple. Difficult. To do it effortlessly was the ultimate mark of the Eheldeth-trained mage—no other mages on earth are as capable of portals as Eheldeth students. For a perfect score, the keeper overseeing the exam must honestly believe the student didn't leave the classroom at all.

I'd spent all of the last six months preparing for this one. My nervousness didn't come from a lack of faith in my abilities. It came from the edge of anger. Last week, I had applied for a chance to use spell alteration items, which were perfectly acceptable to use during exams. Every mage was different, special, and it was the mark of a great mage to know how to prepare oneself in advance. Some items helped students with wandering attentions to focus; others caught loose strands of the *agan* for those who couldn't walk without spilling power everywhere. There were even items that could help amplify weak connections. Using such items didn't affect your grades, either, as long as you wrote an accompanying essay justifying their use. If you went into detail on how the items affected your performance, even better.

The lineup for the supply store was over a hallway long. When I finally got to the door, the keeper on duty took one look at me and shook her head. "You're unauthorized."

I took a deep breath. "You've said this before," I replied. "Over the years, your excuses change. Last time, the other keeper said someone like me can only request these enchantments for the finals. Well, it's the finals now. Let me in."

She looked unamused. "You're unauthorized," she repeated, emphasizing each syllable, as if I was incapable of understanding her. "These resources are earmarked for students who need them. I don't know what the other keeper told you, but this is the truth." Then, in a vain attempt to soften the blow, she made a great show of smiling at me. "And you don't *need* them, do you, Kirosha Tar'elian? We know your reputation here. One of the top two students in your class for your first six years, and *the* top student for the last three. I think you'll do just fine."

The memory burned like salt in a wound I'd been nursing for years. It really wasn't the first time they'd denied me something in the guise of *you don't really need it, anyway.* It was unfair. You didn't get where I was by napping your way through it. And yet everyone else that I knew of used the extra resources wherever possible—whether it was spell alteration items or weighted staffs or tutors, or a pass to the special section of the library, where you could read books outside of the assigned texts. Everyone in the top ten of our class got there with a bit of help—everyone but me. It was as if they'd all conspired to make sure I didn't go another step further.

I closed the book with a sigh. Overthinking it wasn't going to help my case, and neither was self-pity. All I had to do was trust myself.

I returned to the dormitory for my shoes, dropped by the cafeteria for a sweet roll—a light breakfast was all my nerves would tolerate—and then went straight to the main hall to draw my tests for the day. My heart sank the moment I unrolled the piece of paper.

Portals: written before noon, practical in the evening.

Sometimes I felt as if the gods were toying with me on purpose.

I did a fair job of keeping myself calm for most of the day. I blew through the written test with time to spare, though not as well as I did the day before. I wasn't even worrying about *perfect* this time around—I didn't want to obsess over the answers more than was necessary. You could say as much as you could about portals, but once all was said and done, the basics remained the same. Rip a hole through the *agan.* Step through. Close everything behind you, pray to the gods your body parts stay attached when you reach your destination, and try not to land on your face.

It didn't do a thing for my nerves, of course. If anything, it made it worse. I went back to bed as soon as I handed my test over and napped for the better part of an hour. I woke up to blinding nausea—bad enough that I had to find a bucket to puke in. Afterwards, I returned to the cafeteria and forced my way through a bowl of thin corn soup and a plate of fried potatoes. *It's just your nerves,* I told myself. *You've spent the entire week obsessing over this spell—of course it's going to make you sick.*

"You don't look well, Tar'elian," one girl called from across the table. "Maybe you should sit out the rest of the week—you don't want to work *too* hard."

Directed towards me, it couldn't be anything but an insult. I kept my face to my meal, resisting the urge to walk away. I needed food in my belly. In my experience, you didn't try portal spells on an empty stomach, or else you'd spend the whole day in bed, doubled up in pain.

"She looks worried," the girl's friend chimed in. She sneered.

"What's she so worried about?" the first girl asked. "Felan's gone. We all know there's no one else who can beat her."

"Felan's only gone because she went and offed the competition," a third broke in.

Laughter all around followed. I even caught Ivasus amongst the crowd, waving for their attention. They turned to him, and he lowered his head, his eyes sparkling. "They say if you go to the field at midnight, you can find his headless ghost pointing out where she buried him," he said in a low voice. "*Don't get in her way,* he'll moan. *She won't stop at anything to get what she wants.*"

There were pretend gasps, and then more laughter. I drained what remained of my soup and walked out of the cafeteria with my hands at my sides. Everyone was looking at me, waiting for me to say something, anything, to defend myself. But I didn't want to give them the satisfaction. I had long stopped trying to escape their torment, which in my experience only intensified if I ever tried to fight back. Letting it wash over me was the fastest, safest way to get it over with, and I had less than a week of this hellhole left.

I went to the lavatory first, where a connection to an icy stream left a basin constantly running with cold water. I dunked my head in and opened my eyes, letting the shock of freezing water course through my body. *You can do this. You've done this a hundred times before. Remember what your parents used to tell you. Remember why they brought you all the way out here. You are born with a rare gift; with power most mages can only dream of. You were born to make a difference. How can you not pass?*

I came up for air, gasping for breath. Of *course* I was going to pass. But the question remained whether I would make a fool of myself in doing so. I'd set a reputation for myself. Any mistake, any flaw in my process, would make the whole damn school turn their heads and laugh. It wasn't enough that I graduate. I had to make a mark, the sort that would go down in the annals of history forever. A hundred years from now, wide-eyed students entering Eheldeth for the first time would know my name. Kirosha Tar'elian, the first ever Gorenten to ever be honoured in its halls…

I struck my forehead with my palm, twice. None of that was going to happen if I bungled up a damned portal spell.

The bells rang, marking the moment of truth. I gathered my courage. *Do this, and the rest will follow.* The portal spell was the hardest. It made sense to get the hardest spell over with.

I walked into the assigned classroom as the perfect picture of calm. *No one will laugh at you today,* I thought. A stupid thought. Ivasus was there the moment I walked in. He crossed his arms and gave a grim smile. *Show me,* that smile said. *Show me what you killed your rival for.* The truth didn't matter. My failure was all he cared for.

The keeper started writing on the chalkboard. His assistant passed tokens around. Mine was a small jade figure of a tiger, a creature found in lands across the eastern sea. I scraped my thumb over its eyes. It stared back at me in judgment. *You don't deserve to sit there. Leave now, before you embarrass yourself.*

Ivasus went first. He had a jeweled necklace for amplification, and golden gauntlets engraved with runes that glowed blue, and a weighted staff that kept him grounded—to ensure his spells didn't go out of hand. The boy was practically relying on the items to cast the spell for him. If life was fair, he would pass and then get a note on his file, penned in red ink, saying *Desk Duty Only.* But he was a rich man's son, and I was willing to bet they would have him leading armies or some other job that put the public at risk within five years.

"And—begin!" the keeper said.

Ivasus cast his spell. A hole appeared in thin air. A neat circle, clean. And why not? Those damn gauntlets kept his hands still. Naturally made tears were jagged along the edges. They were easier to stitch shut, which meant they caused less leakage over time. A straight-edged hole like this was detrimental over time. Not that people like Ivasus cared. Even the keeper hardly seemed to blink.

Ivasus stepped through his portal, which disappeared about five breaths later. Sloppy work. Leaving portals open too long meant others could cross them. Another body, another soul, in the same channel you occupied defied the laws of nature. An unexpected one could be catastrophic. I saw the keeper scribbling in his notebook. Rich man's son or not, he was going to get deductions for that.

A few minutes passed. Ivasus returned through a second portal, sweating heavily.

"You didn't use the same one," the keeper exclaimed.

"I couldn't find it," Ivasus gasped. He fell to his knees even before the portal behind him closed. I could see vomit in the corners of his mouth—he must have heaved out on the grass somewhere, or else tried to swallow it down.

7

The keeper grunted, unconvinced. Another deduction. If you were going back to the same place, using the same portal was more efficient. You had to shut it behind you to keep it protected from intruders, but detecting where it was in the fabric *should* be easy enough if you knew what you were doing, which Ivasus clearly didn't. I took another deep breath. His mistakes were making me feel better about my chances.

He crawled just till he got near my feet. He looked up, as if expecting me to help.

I ignored him and strode up to the keeper. "I *was* just about to call you," he said. "Very well. Begin the exercise."

I curled my fist around the jade tiger, tightening my hands until my knuckles turned white. My wrists itched, followed by a burning sensation. One breath, two breaths, and then...

A blow, like a kick to the face. I ignored the pain and focused on drawing the jagged edges of the hole through the fabric. Blue light flashed all around me like uncontained wildfire. I finished tearing through the hole and quickly pushed my body through the portal, which I at once shut behind me. *Show them how it's done, Rosha. Show them what you're made of. You're everything you believed you were, and more.*

I heard a roar.

I couldn't believe my ears at first. Had I internalized the image of the tiger so much that I was hearing it inside my head? But no—it was coming from somewhere in the portal. I stepped back. It wasn't a tiger at all, but a dog, or what had once been a dog. An unprotected creature, an unwanted body, in a well of *agan* could make short work out of anything, and it had done its damage on the poor beast. Its eyes popped out of its head. Its limbs were warped. And its mouth was full of razor-sharp teeth.

My first thought wasn't to save myself. What was the creature doing there? There weren't any dogs in the classroom, and even if there were, I'd closed the portal so quickly nothing could have gotten through. Which could only mean...

I glanced up, noticing the clean circle behind me. I could have sworn I *tore* into this portal. And yet—

No. I'd been so focused on making sure I cast the spell well in the first place that I'd neglected to check my surroundings. It shouldn't have been necessary if I'd gone after a competent mage, which Ivasus was clearly the furthest thing from. The idiot hadn't sealed his portal going back, and I'd foolishly created mine right where his had been. The dog must have come from the field.

There was no time to defend myself. I burst back into the classroom with the dog's snapping jaws behind. I sealed the portal just as its teeth snapped on my robes.

The monster's decapitated head lay in a puddle of blood on the floor, its teeth still snapping away.

Ivasus got up, looking well all of a sudden. The smile on his face turned cruel.

My eyes blurred as I stared at the blood. I couldn't even focus on what the keeper was saying. His words were incomprehensible as he screamed, pointing at me as if I was the one who did this. Why couldn't he see the truth? Ivasus had played a trick—he'd kept his first portal open on purpose, probably because he saw the dog and knew I would make my portal right where I did. But his expression and the keeper's accusations were the last straw. I'd spent the whole morning...no, the whole *month* worrying about this exam, and now...it seemed as if it was all for nothing. The outrage on the keeper's face told me I couldn't just waltz through the rest of the week the way I'd hoped. There was going to be an inquiry, and if I was going to retake this exam, I would have to defend myself a dozen times over even though it was another student who started it. What chance did I, the daughter of some social-climbing Gorenten merchant, have against the son from an old family? I could hear *his* defense already, too. *I made a mistake, dear keepers. How could I have known she would be so careless?* And then the inquiries would turn into a discussion of my competence. They would tear apart everything I had done and could do, my grades, my history in the school, my parents. *Everything.*

I was sent here to learn not to make noise and here I was, creating chaos already.

I stepped back. The keeper was still yelling. I suddenly understood what he was saying, and painful as they were, they made sense. And then, only then, did I decide it was over.

CHAPTER 2

THE WOODS

The decision wasn't made lightly. I knew what I was throwing away. Behind the polished hardwood doors and underneath the arched rooftops lay all the knowledge a mage could ever hope for. The key to my dreams and everything I had ever wanted. But they didn't want me. They never wanted me. It was as if the last few years had only been spent in tolerance of my existence and they couldn't wait for an excuse to get rid of me. Now it was here. Why prolong the wait? Why force myself to perform tricks for people who didn't care?

I went to the dormitories first, to get a change of clothes and whatever money I had left for the season. A blanket of calm had descended over me. My actions were as deliberate and precise as if I was on the cusp of performing a major spell. Once I'd bundled all my things, I strode into the fading sunlight.

"Your exams are down the other way, Rosha," Keeper Soa said as I headed for the main gates. "Did you forget something?"

I ignored her and kept walking. The anger throbbed from my heart to my palms. I kept it there. You don't throw a tantrum right in the home of thousands of skilled mages. There weren't just students there—you had bearers tasked with researching every magical aberration from one end of the empire to the other, alumni who hadn't been assigned jobs yet, and keepers who maintained it all. And of course, you had guards at every corner. One mage alone was dangerous enough already. A multitude of unskilled youths in a single building was a recipe for disaster.

I held it in. Eyes were on me everywhere I went. *Smug, assuming faces just waiting for me to make a scene. What do you expect from a Gorenten?* Even tears in my eyes would be enough to spread rumours that I was unstable. They already saw me as a talentless hack, not worth the money my father spent to keep me here, allowed in only because it made the school look good to be generous to the people its empire harmed a long time ago. Nothing I was capable of had made them think I was worth anything; they would be less generous in the face of my greatest mistakes.

Conflicting emotions, raging with every step. There was a sliver of relief that I didn't have to play by their rules anymore, that I didn't have to waste nights lying awake, wondering how their minds worked and how I could bend myself to fit their demands. But also anger—so much anger, enough to burn an entire forest down. I had been ready to bend since day one. Eheldeth was the only place in the known world that could have seen me as something beyond a freak of nature. In there, I could belong. In there, I could dream again. What was I outside those walls?

"It's cold out there, Rosha," another keeper called. "You're not wearing enough cloaks."

I didn't reply, and she chose not to stop me. It wasn't illegal to leave Eheldeth. Students did it all the time.

The keeper was right about one thing. Past the gilded gates of Eheldeth, the world was wet and dreary. I stared into the biting wind so long my eyes watered. I could feel the tall building behind me, with its promise of warmth and belonging. I kept the image in my head without having to glance back. Eheldeth would be there long after I was gone, and I didn't want to give it the satisfaction of one last, longing look. It had taken my entire youth already.

Clarity began when I found myself in the first village in the valley. I knew I had to find a place to stay, a place where I could sit in silence and nurse my injured pride. As soon as I reached the marketplace, I fished around in my pockets for coins.

"Are you a mage, sweetie?" a vendor called. He was selling baskets of fresh apples.

I froze before shaking my head. It felt heavy, a rock on my shoulders.

"But your clothes—" the vendor began. He pointed.

I glanced down. I realized, belatedly, that I wasn't thinking as straight as I would have liked. The robes were Eheldeth-issued.

I nodded, placing a finger on my lips. "All right, maybe I am. Do you know where I can get an inn?"

"Mages never stay here," the man said. "Eheldeth is only an hour away."

"I came from Eheldeth. I need a room."

"My sister has a place, as it happens…" he began, doubt filling his expression.

I threw him a coin. "For your troubles."

He gave a gap-toothed grin and left his stall for his daughter to watch while he led me to his sister's place. It wasn't the sort of inn I was used to—travelling back and forth between my parents and Eheldeth had gotten me acquainted with the kind of place built above pubs, where food and drink flowed as freely as conversation. This was simply a quiet house with many rooms, bigger than the usual, with a bakery downstairs. A woman in the yard took me out of the vendor's hands and led me to a small room beside a closet.

It was bare, with nothing but a straw mattress on one side, and smelled faintly of wet dog. It reminded me of the dog in the portal, and I turned my head in disgust. I closed the door and placed my belongings on the floor. I slumped next to it and stared at the dirty window, where the sun was still sinking on the horizon. It couldn't have been over two hours since the test, and yet I felt as if I'd aged years since. A grain of truth there, perhaps. In Eheldeth, I was a child subjected to the whims of adults. Out here…

I looked at my bare hands. If I wasn't a mage, what else could I be? I'd trained for years to be nothing but. And yet you weren't supposed to be one without the blessing of the mage council.

Someone knocked from the hallway.

"Mama told me to bring you food," a girl's voice spoke from the other side. "May I come in?"

I got up to open the door slightly. A girl with greasy hair and in an unkempt woolen skirt pushed herself through the narrow crack. She was holding a tray with a piece of bread and a bowl of stew, which she placed on the mattress before turning around to face me. I got the impression she had no intentions of leaving. Her fingers played with a loose thread on her shirt before she blurted out, "Mother said Uncle said you were a mage."

I knew where this was going. "I don't have time for questions," I said, curtly. "Thank you for the food." I moved to let her out.

She grabbed my wrist with hands so filthy she looked like she had been digging ditches all morning. "Help me. Please."

"I'm not—"

"My sister…I can't tell our mother, but she's…we're in trouble. Just come and look. Only a mage can help, and you're the only mage who's come through the village today."

I glanced at the mattress. I really wanted to sleep again, to drown out the last dredges of my failure in blackness. But the girl's fingers tightened around my arm. "Please," she repeated. "I don't know what else to do. You're nearly our age. The older mages will call the guards on us, I just know it. I'm begging you." Her eyes watered. She couldn't have looked more pathetic if she'd tried.

"Lead the way," I grumbled.

The cold evening air played symphonies on my skin as we took a small dirt road to the south. The girl carried a lantern, which told me she expected to be there far beyond sundown. We entered the woods, and in the back of my mind, I remembered warnings often uttered by my class-mates trying to scare each other into leaving the school grounds. Of stray monsters and thieves and brigands, of people who knew what we were on first sight: children with parents who could cough up a year's worth of wages in ransom on the spot.

But I wasn't a child anymore, and I was confident I could defend myself in a tight corner. If I could be honest, part of me was looking forward to setting someone's hair on fire. The humiliation I felt in that exam room had yet to leave. The insults the keeper had hurled over my head came back, so clear it felt like it was the first time I was hearing them. *"What did we expect when we let someone like you to learn with the rest of us?"* He'd said *us* as if I wasn't one of them. Not that it came as a surprise. No one in the last few years had ever voiced what I long suspected quite as succinctly as he did. More than an affront, his words felt like permission. After all this time, I could finally stop playing by the rules.

The dirt road ended. We were at the foot of some ruins, a broken-down temple of some sort. I had a sudden flare of memory. Ruins and I don't mix very well. I remembered the boy Felan, the one whose name they had thrown at my face for most of my senior year. If he was still alive, he would feel the same way.

"Maria?" the girl called out, interrupting my thoughts.

The wind brushed past the treetops. I felt a tightening in the air, as if lightning had been dancing through it all day long. And yet the sky remained clear. I held out my arm to stop the girl from taking another step further. "Tell me what happened here," I said.

She pressed her hands together. "I—"

"You don't send a mage on an errand unprepared," I snapped. "Speak up, girl!"

She fell to her knees, sobbing. I turned my head away in distaste. Fear I could understand, but allowing it to control you? In Eheldeth, they trained you to be prepared for anything, because if there was one thing consistent about the *agan*, it was its ability to surprise even its best scholars. Students who couldn't control their fear grew up to be capable of nothing more than parlour tricks. If you were to be capable of more, you needed to learn how to face down your own death without screaming.

And so I kept myself steady when the ear-splitting, animal-like howl sounded through the shadows. I tore my attention away from my racing heart to the ruins, where I could see a dark shape shuffle forward, one agonizing step after another. I allowed a ball of fire to settle in my right palm. The substantial heat was comforting. The easiest spell, under the right circumstances, could also be the most devastating. My gut said this was an animal, some sort of beast or monster who had taken the girl's sister. Most could easily be frightened by a bit of flame, and if this Maria was already dead, well…there was time for mourning later.

The figure lurched forward. I prepared to throw the fireball.

"Stop!" the girl screamed.

I didn't know if she meant *me* or the beast. But then I realized my mistake. The figure wasn't a beast at all. It was a girl in a dress even filthier than her sister's. Maria—because it could only be Maria—stood on all fours, tears dripping down her face. She opened her mouth, and…

Flowers sprouted out, like a bubble of vomit.

My trepidations dissipated. I felt like laughing, though I tried not to show it. The girl was clearly distressed as the flowers continued to grow, as if they'd all taken root on her tongue. She fell on the dust right next to me, her hands gripping my ankle. "Help," she coughed out, her voice muffled over the petals. "Help me!"

I placed a hand on her head to placate her. She tried to scream. The flowers turned grey and wilted, only to be replaced by more. "What happened here?" I repeated, turning to her sister.

"Maria and I were going through the ruins," the girl blurted out. "We're…we're not supposed to. The elders have warned us. But we finally thought they were being overly cautious. The other children had been here already, picking through the wreckage over the years. Some mages came by a few weeks ago and set up camp here, so we thought maybe they've left stuff behind…pretty baubles, trinkets. You mages are rich…"

"A misconception," I corrected. "What mages *do* have is the capability to create spells and stamp them on things. You walked right into one, didn't you?"

She started sobbing again. I sighed. Between her and her sister, it was looking like I wouldn't get any useful information at all, unless I somehow frightened them into a stupor. I had no desire to work up a temper, anyway. Maria wasn't dead or witless yet, which meant it couldn't have been a terribly complicated spell.

I left them near the road to venture in the ruins myself, taking great care not to trip another spell. Easier said than done—skilled mages know just where to hide traps to catch the unsuspecting. Well-trained mages *should* be able to detect if there was a trap nearby and be able to deduce where it could have been placed, but one careless mistake was all it took. I tried to take comfort in the fact that the girls should have stumbled through all the obvious places already.

I found the runes scratched out near the foundation, next to the remains of a campfire. As I figured, the spell was almost an afterthought —someone got bored enough to scratch it out while investigating the area. It was a one-time use trap spell, as most of these tend to be. Creating spells that attacked people indefinitely required vast amounts of energy, so to conserve their reserves (and sanity), most mages were trained to form ones that could just be re-armed when needed. Boredom was also why the spell's effects seemed relatively benign. I thought about the order of events unfolding if I wasn't there. The girls would be forced to return home the way they were, which meant the village would then have to file a request for the mage council to come and investigate—for a fee. A tug-of-war would then follow, particularly if the villagers didn't have the funds. They could file a complaint at the nearest city in an attempt to force the local government to go up against the mage council, which might only happen if the villagers could prove they *weren't* at fault to begin with. Were the girls going through property that wasn't theirs? Yes? Well, too bad.

If Maria died, and someone higher up actually cared, they might continue to put pressure on the mage council. Eventually, the heads of it —which included the Firekeeper of Eheldeth, a woman who held more power in the mage council than the rest put together—would have to decide if protecting some small-time mage who didn't even have the funds for a night at the inn was worth all the trouble. The investigation would probably happen after all, because the mage council, as one of the two guilds that formed the backbone of the great Empire of Dageis, couldn't afford to have the merchant guild—the other side of the coin—

start investigating themselves. Why risk giving your rival a reason to chip away at your own power, after all? Both guilds had been at odds which each other for centuries, vying to be closer to the emperor's ear than the other—a back and forth that kept the balance in those lands.

So either the mage who scratched out an almost childish glyph was unaware of the repercussions or stupid enough to risk it, or...

I took my chances and slammed a spell of undoing on the runes. It shattered like glass struck with the end of a spear.

Or it was just a practical joke. I gave a grim smile. I could make a wager that I wasn't needed here at all. The spell would have faded within the next day or so, and the girl would be fine, if a little shattered. Her parents would blame something she ate, or their own eyesight, and whatever the mage council would receive would amount to nothing more than gusts of wind, to be forgotten with the rest. Such was the price you paid to live in a land run by magic, no matter how much the mage council pretended they had it under control.

I returned to the girls. Maria was lying in a puddle of her own spit, her mouth flower-free. There wasn't even a touch of fragrance left in it —her breath smelled as rotten as anyone's would after hours heaving out bile. She looked up. I sensed, among other things, jealousy in her expression, mixed with gratitude. "Thank you," she gasped. "Thank you so much! You—"

"I'm going to bed," I declared. I glanced at the sister. "I trust you'll find a suitable excuse for all of this." I turned away and walked back to the inn on my own. I didn't want them to force me to stand there and make small talk. People who weren't mages, I had found, always needed some sort of explanation for what just occurred, as if saying "It's just magic," wasn't enough. How, where, when—and always, *why*? Why did this have to happen? Why did the gods bless you to see things no ordinary person can't?

Why have the gods wasted their blessings on *you*, Rosha?

CHAPTER 3

THE BALL

I can never figure out how to respond when people start with such nonsense. Most, I've found, come from non-mage families who don't understand a thing about the complexities of living with an affliction that others see as a weapon. They think being a mage means everything ought to come easier for me. I could, with the snap of my fingers, conjure all the things I need or get rid of my problems. Never mind that you can't really do the former (no matter what the books say, magic—at least, the magic I've known—can't create something out of nothing), and the latter is ridiculous if you break it down a bit more. We all have problems, some of us more than others. Sure, I could probably chase away a rampaging bear, but could I magic away the fact that my father is a fraud?

I suppose the act of *knowing* what I was born into makes me one of the luckier ones. It is better to know fool's gold for what it is—to understand the nature of lies before they get the chance to make you believe you are something you are not. I learned what he wasn't, and so knew early on what I could never be. A castle built on sand cannot hope to outlast the waves.

I crawled onto the thin, hard mattress, closed my eyes, and had a memory of the month before my eleventh birthday, a month before I was sent away to Eheldeth. In those days, the weather offered little respite from the pelting rains typical of the western coast of the continent. The leaves of the cherry trees along the streets drooped from a perpetual wet sheen, and every street gutter ran full. A dreary month for children who liked to be outside, but I welcomed it. At nearly eleven, I

17

didn't have anything to do that could be interrupted by rain. My life back then was solidly behind walls—an existence made bearable by long hours of reading and not having to deal with any other children.

It should have been the right sort of age not to be surprised. My father acted as if the world revolved on his whim, and until then I thought he at least deserved every bit of his arrogance. A merchant with a title in the Empire of Dageis, the most powerful empire in the world, carried weight. I never thought much of him as a father, but I thought he had that, at least. I thought he had power, money, and prestige. I believed his name could shelter me the way he couldn't when I was an infant wailing at my mother's breast.

Not that the man ever cared what I thought about him. He first came into my life when I was eight, far too old to think much of the words *my real father* as anything but a sign that the people in my life had done nothing but lie to me. Since then, he had made every effort to show me my opinion counted for very little in his everyday. A child was a burden, one he never expected he would have to deal with in his extremely calculated, precise, grand scheme of things. Which is astounding, considering the revolving door of women in his life. He started affairs in nearly every city or town he visited, very often with more than one woman at a time. At his age, he must have sired enough children to fill an entire nation, the kind of man who could introduce half a dozen wailing infants as his firstborn.

But there I was, his only one. A daughter, bearing all his gifts and then a little bit more. I've heard people say it was his punishment, which seemed like an odd thing for the gods to do. You punished a man like that with itchy loins and rotten teeth, not a girl who would bear equal weight for his sins. At nearly eleven, I should have been blissfully unaware.

There was a party. A ball, one of the many my father began funding since his bankruptcy from years ago. As a businessman, my father used to be the sort who thought himself so smart the only person he could trust was himself. This led to a series of poor decisions, each one worse than the last. One of these—an ill-conceived alliance with nobility where it turned out they needed him more than he could use them—resulted in the loss of a remarkable amount of money overnight. Yet where most people would have given up, my father seemed to regard it as nothing but a challenge. He borrowed money, begged his creditors, made inane deals that somehow pulled through and gave him back everything he'd lost and then some. Years later, there he was, spending a good deal of it on fizzy wine, smelly cheese, and half-moldy ham. The vast array of rich food never ceased to make me dizzy. You could spend all night picking at it and never once feel full.

As his daughter, I had to sit through every single one of his shallow introductions with potential business partners and associates and pretend they had interesting things to say. They never did. "Just smile and nod, Rosha," he'd remind me, right before each one. "Smile and nod. You don't have to do more than that." There was always an element of pleading in his voice, like he was asking for such a simple request that I —stubborn, selfish daughter of his—adamantly refused to give.

Which was always a lie, because the topic would inevitably turn to me and my gifts.

One mention is like a few drops of wine in a glass—enough to fill the room with an intoxicating haze. They would all fall silent, mouths agape, white teeth flashing. They all wanted to see the unexpected: to marvel at the sight of a Gorenten child crafting magic tricks in front of a whole crowd...and not be taken away.

To this crowd, I was a novelty. A caged little songbird. The Dageians had subjugated my people for centuries, taken their ancestral lands, forced them to barren islands with nothing but the clothes on their back and their pride. The ones they didn't leave alone they took back to the empire, harnessed like oxen to their ships or drained for the use of their mages or whatever menial, back-breaking task Dageian citizens refused to do for themselves. Now here they were, pretending none of that ever happened or happens still. The Empire of Dageis is a land of opportunity for those who can afford it, and anyone can be a citizen if you just have the right amount of coin. And my father had plenty of that, if nothing else.

But few Gorenten do. It still seems to come as a shock to them that we would be here at all. It starts when they meet my father, with his sun-touched hair and brown skin. Even his fine robes can't erase the look of surprise on their faces—the wonder, the confusion, the anger. Like they were looking at a monkey in a suit and couldn't comprehend how they were supposed to react. Do you feign indifference? Do you talk to it? Do you ask how it can speak your tongue so well? *We know two other languages on top of yours, citizen. Why do you look so surprised?* And then my father would shake hands, exchanging courtesies that would bring a modicum of normalcy. They would try to adjust; in a land of progress and magic, there is only so much disbelief people could take, at least for a moment. They would turn to talk of the weather and economy and how well our fine emperor was doing these days.

But then my father would introduce me. "My daughter, Rosha," he would say, as if presenting a rare item, an object he was lucky enough to obtain. "She's being tutored right now, but in a few years she will enter Eheldeth. They've already approved her application."

You would think he told them I turned water to wine. "No!" most would almost always gasp. "Her?" Reaching for words, many failing, most of them afraid their feeble minds would drum up an insult for their generous host and not realizing the silence itself was insult enough. Some would manage a small, "But how fantastic!" Fake excitement, masking what many really think. *How vile. How unexpected. How...dangerous.*

No other school has the reputation Eheldeth has, and the name alone invoked a sense of hearing the clink of coin in your skull. Which meant that when my father said these things, they almost always never believed him. A Gorenten, in *Eheldeth*, of all places? Not any of the smaller schools strewn throughout the land, the ones that teach would-be mages to control their powers and nothing else? But how? *Why?*

They'd ask for the tricks then, as if it is a thing they needed to see with their very eyes. As if they needed proof.

In the mighty Empire of Dageis, the magic that is feared in other places is embraced without a second thought. Everything runs on magic. The trams, the airships, the sewage. The Empire of Dageis, mighty conqueror, the bastion of civilization, envy of the world. And yet its people cannot grasp how a mere Gorenten child could make a pebble float in mid-air. I think they would have been just as surprised if I had told them I could read.

On that night, I counted four of my father's so-called honoured guests. Three women, each old enough to be my grandmother, which somehow didn't stop them from pawing my father and his fine clothes. I couldn't tell if they were listening to the words falling out of his lips, but they seemed to find him fascinating nonetheless, and would nod with fake acknowledgement even if it was clear to me he was merely making things up as he went along. "How wise," they crooned, touching his arm without permission. "How so very insightful of you, Count Tar'elian! Truly, the gods have blessed you with a gift for words." They wore enough perfume to make my eyes water, and I wondered how much they would pay to take my father to bed.

There was also one man, old, wrinkled, and yet with the proud, haughty air of someone who probably thought he was thirty years younger. "My daughter, Rosha," my father said, right on cue, and they clapped their hands and drew me closer at almost the same time my father pushed me forward.

"She's just been—"

"Yes, Eheldeth, so I've heard!" a woman almost squealed. "How lovely, and what an honour for such a fine gentleman as yourself, Count Tar'elian. Truly something to be proud of."

"Eheldeth?" the man asked, in a voice that made it sound as if *we* were mistaken, and could we please make sure we rectified it immediately?

"Yes, Eheldeth," Father said, beaming. He had the kind of smile that made women's hearts beat faster and the men turn their heads, and I thought for sure the women's knees all buckled. At the same time, I could see him clinking his teacup with the nail of his little finger, as if he was counting the clicks it made against the porcelain. Outside of Dageis, it could have been a spell. Here in the empire, however, where heavier magic was regulated and charms could cause trouble if you cast it on the wrong person, I chalked it up to nothing more than a nervous tic. These people bored him out of his mind.

"A marvellous honour," the man exclaimed. His expression changed slightly—not enough for anyone else to notice. But I saw it. And my father knew I saw it, because he gave me that quick look, that quick darting of eyes that told me I had to keep my mouth shut. I hated that look. He used it knowing I had no choice but to obey. Because to say something would be to jeopardize the precarious position our family was in here in the Dageian Empire. The precarious position *I* put them in. If I wasn't a novelty, then Dageian law demanded I be a mage-thrall, the lowest of the low, sworn to a mage body and soul with no agency or life to call my own. I would be beholden to my master for life. My father had paid good money to stop that from happening.

But still, I hated it. I hated the reminder of what I owed him.

"Do you know that every Firekeeper in the Mage Council has been a graduate of Eheldeth?" the old lord continued, oblivious to the high-pitched chatter he was suddenly involved in. "Even Adherent Orsalian, hero of the Battle of Drusgaya, was a scholar there!"

Father's unbreakable smile faltered just a little. "I am...*was* acquainted with Adherent Orsalian," he said. "A remarkable woman."

They crowded around him, champagne glasses tinkling. "You don't say!" one of the women, the same one who had been squeezing my father's bicep all night long, exclaimed. "I thought I heard something like that—but truly, you knew her?" Her fawning made me ill.

The irritation on Father's brow was visible to me now. I had seen it often enough myself—whenever I would place a glass of water without a coaster on the wooden table, or take any of his books without permission, or let the dogs out so that they would bark all night.

"I did," Father said, drawing his brows together in an expression that was almost—but not quite—like grief. "I knew her very well, in fact. I'm sorry—I said acquaintance out of respect for her. I'm not sure she would have liked me saying we were close when we weren't."

It was a rare moment of honesty for my father.

"It must feel surreal," the old man said. "To have been in the presence of such greatness. This woman's sacrifice ensured our great empire's continued survival. Do you know, they're thinking of creating a day to commemorate her life? I've heard the inner council has been in talks."

"The empire would," Father replied. The grief had turned to irritation. "It knows how to give empty praise when they should have done more. Adherent Orsalian died because the empire failed to protect its people. She gave up her life because others wouldn't."

Silence fell across the room. The old man scowled now, his wrinkly, liver-spotted brow furrowing. "Such defiance of the empire who was kind enough to nurture you and your daughter, Lord Tar'elian, is unbecoming for a...for a..."

"Lord Talos!" the women gasped. "Control yourself!"

"Enosh Tar'elian is Gorenten," the old man continued, gaining courage. "His people serve the empire, not the other way around." He turned back to my father, pointing a finger straight at his face. "I don't even know what *you're* doing here. Shouldn't you be in the sewers, cleaning the refuse with the rest of the help? And your little piss pot half breed daughter here—"

"You won't insult my daughter to her face."

"I just did," Lord Talos sneered. He turned to the crowd. "Has anyone even seen the girl's mother? Who's to say he didn't just pick her up from an orphanage, snatching her from a destitute life as a mage-thrall so he could pass her off as his own? You are a fraud, *my lord*, and if I had known better, I wouldn't have graced your despicable festivities with my presence!" He dropped the champagne in his hand. It shattered on the floor like a spray of water, all crystal shards and spines. He stepped on the glass, gnashing his teeth in satisfaction as he grounded it under his boot.

The crowd fell silent, but not because of his wanton display. I turned my head in time to see a woman descend from the staircase—a beautiful woman in a silver-laced gown, her hair bound above the nape of her neck. My father stepped aside with a smile, taking the woman's hand as she held it out for him. He kissed the top of it, his lips lingering on her skin longer than it had any right to.

"You were looking for the girl's mother?" the woman asked.

"My lady," Enosh said. "This was unnecessary. You needed your rest."

"I believe my lord was just being insulted," the woman continued, gazing at the crowd. "Nevertheless, I am pleased to make all your acquaintances. I am Sume Tar'elian. Dear Rosha here..." She gestured, all but dragging me to her for a brief embrace. "Rosha is our only daughter. I'm afraid we haven't made it all that clear, though you *must* see her resemblance to my dear husband's face."

Enosh gave a small, crooked smile, and bowed briefly.

That was all it took. The crowd buzzed again, drifting amongst each other like bees. I looked around for Lord Talos, but he had already left. All the better, because the woman's embrace was becoming too tight. I pushed away and she let me go at last.

"Lady Sume," one guest called. "Is it true you came from the far south, from the dragon-lands of Jin-Sayeng?"

"I did," the woman tittered. "I much prefer it out here. My people are such barbarians. Everything is so much more cultured. Why, I—"

"Stop," I said.

Enosh stepped between us. "Rosha," he said, "I believe it may be getting a little too late for you. I'll escort you to bed myself, shall I?"

"No," I replied. "You won't." I pointed at the woman. "That's not my mother. That's just some dolled-up harlot—"

"Rosha!" Enosh reprimanded.

"This is why people don't believe you about me," I retorted. "You lie about everything else! You want a trick? Look!"

I threw my hands up, sending a force strong enough to shake the paintings from the wall. Drawing a deep breath, I tugged at them with invisible strings I made in the air, pulling them apart slowly, all the way down to the expensive wallpaper. I could feel my eyes burning, but I didn't want to stop. I wanted to show them. I—

Enosh slapped me.

I dropped the paintings and stared at him, hot tears gathering at the edge of my eyes.

"That child needs to be controlled," my supposed mother said under her breath. "You've let her get away with too much."

"You're not my mother," I hissed. "You don't get to have *any* say in what I do." I turned to glare at my father. "I'm going to send myself to bed." And then I regarded the crowd, who looked scandalized beyond belief. It made me wish I had done more. Scandal was nothing—I should have frightened them where they stood. "Good night, everyone. I hope you enjoyed the show."

"Get back here and apologize, Rosha," Enosh said.

I turned on my heel and walked away.

I didn't need my father's love, nor his approval. Before I knew of his existence, I had my stepfather and a different life, one far simpler than anything that gilded cage had to offer. But the magic showed itself and my panicked parents didn't know what to do. I was sent from place to place, hounded by those who desired my power. Some were just people —mortals who craved to turn something so precious and untouched into theirs. Others were far more insidious.

Most of those days feel like a bad dream. I was so young and being surrounded by so much magic has a way of dulling your memories. *Agan* does that—it is tricky, that substance that allows those like me to make spells and possess power the likes of which normal people can only dream of. Energy does not discriminate, and flesh can only do so much. And when you pound so much of it into one person, especially one as young as I was, it can do things to you. The lucky ones lose parts of their memory. The unlucky die. The unluckiest lose their souls.

That I was stuck with a man like Enosh Tar'elian as my blood father makes me wonder if I am in that third group. There is a price attached to everything; I'm just not sure what it is I gained.

People tell me I exaggerate. That night was no different. I wasn't halfway across the hall to my bedroom when the door opened. My mother walked out. My real mother, not the primped-up, painted-faced, perfumed woman downstairs. "What are you doing?" she asked. "I heard the commotion down there."

I didn't say anything. It was hard to get my mother to understand. She grew up poor, and she always thought I needed to be more grateful for the gifts the gods had bestowed upon me, Enosh included. He could be worse, she would say. He could have decided amends were beyond him and simply not cared. Her own father was a merchant, too, one who *couldn't* turn his fortunes around. The man's failing business became a tragedy that beget more tragedy and took away most of the people she loved. I've always wanted to ask her why she thought I could change her past. Loving my father wouldn't bring hers back.

"Rosha," she continued. "Look at me."

I obeyed. A habit, nothing more. I don't know if I hated her as much as I hated my father, but I knew, even then, that I couldn't stand to be around her anymore. She sold me to this life. She sold me to it by marrying that man, putting shackles on both our necks.

"He picked the worst actress to be you tonight," I said.

"You know I'm no good with people," she replied. "It's better this way. The last thing I'd want is to embarrass him."

"Why doesn't he hire an actress as his daughter, too? I'm even worse than you are. I know. He *says* so."

"A touch of authenticity. If everything is too perfect, people will be suspicious. Besides, in time, they'll be seeing more of you."

"How can you say that?" I asked. "How can you pretend everything is all right?"

She drew in a quick breath. Sume liked to pretend she was patient; I think that's what allowed her to tolerate Enosh for as long as she did. "It isn't," she said, at length. "But we do what we must, my dear."

"What for?" I asked. "I never asked to come here. We could be back in Jin-Sayeng. We were happy there."

"You were so little. Surely you don't remember how miserable we were, too. How difficult it was to put food on the table. With the warlords constantly on the edge, it wasn't safe—especially not for someone like you."

"It was miserable, but it was still *home*."

"So is this."

"But it's not."

She placed a hand on my cheek. "It could be if you gave it a chance."

I pulled away. "I've been here four years and I hate every minute of it. Everything is so clean and perfect and rigid, with all these rules that don't seem to be enough to stop anyone from being pricks—"

"Rosha."

I glared at her. "This place is going to drive me mad. *He's* going to drive me mad."

"You owe him your life."

"So you love to remind me," I said. "I find it hard to believe. We're here for *him*, because it makes it a whole lot easier for him to get things done when people believe he's a loving father and devoted husband. Tell me that's not true, Mother. I dare you."

"We're here because Jin-Sayeng can never accept you," Sume said. "That part is as true as it can get. I still get nightmares over what the warlords might have done to you if they knew. They would have killed you or they would have used you. Or the *agan* itself might have swallowed you where you stood. I don't need to remind you, Rosha, that you are not indiscriminate about your gifts. I almost think you take it for granted. Children less powerful than you have gotten themselves killed."

I decided I wasn't going back to my room, then. Not if she was just going to follow and lecture me further. Truth was a bitter pill. In my mind, there were a thousand ways she could have protected me, none of which involved returning to the man who abandoned us in the first place. She didn't stop me as I made the turn to the main hall, leading to the back door. That was one good thing about Mother, at least. She respected my space.

My father, on the other hand...I think the man believed he owned me. He believed everything I did reflected off him, and he expected I made sure his image was as clean as possible. I could have told him it was a lost cause; he had done more than enough to tarnish it himself. Even at an early age, I knew what he was doing out there. I tried to imagine what he was telling his guests now—probably some sort of excuse about how tired I was, or maybe how uncouth my Jinsein upbringing had been. As if being Gorenten somehow absolved him. The Dageians can't even tell the difference. As much as I detested him, I look like my father—dark skin, light brown eyes, dark hair with a touch of brown. In Dageis, I was only Gorenten, my Jinsein blood nothing but a blur in the background. And it made no difference.

I reached the gardens and heard someone cough. I turned to see Lord Talos sitting on the stone benches right beside the fountain. Enosh had neglected to hire someone to fix it and it wasn't doing much more than dribble water like a little boy spitting. Lord Talos sucked on the pipe in his hand and sent out small white puffs from his mouth. "That whole show doesn't sit well with you either, does it, child?" the old man asked. His skin was very red under his beard.

"You should probably leave," I said.

He waved his pipe in the air. "Probably. I was hoping I could catch your father alone."

"You don't want that. You've made him angry. He'll never talk to you if he's angry. So unless you want more trouble, I suggest you leave now."

"You've got a lot of fire for a little girl."

The air around us hummed, and the rocks shook. I couldn't make them stop. I tried not to get angry, but words like that always cut me to the bone. My father treated me the same way—as if I was nothing to be afraid of, despite all the power they said I had. As if I was just a little dog that yapped too much and got underfoot.

He noticed that, too, because he smiled. "And your powers *are* there. He wasn't lying about that. But look at you. You're swimming in *agan* and you can't even seem to control it. That—" He indicated the air around me. "That's not normal. I'm surprised you've lived this long. Have the mages checked on you yet?"

"I have a tutor," I replied.

"Tutors can't do much. If you're what they say you are, you need more than that. You need chains, girl. To make sure you don't hurt anyone. I mean, that's why you're here, right? That's why your father risked himself to go out here."

"He risked nothing," I said. "He *wanted* to go here. For money."

"Lots of places you can get money, girl. Not sure if it's the best place for a wanted man." He blew smoke into the air. "You don't look concerned."

"Should I be?"

"Because it will make all the difference between whether or not your family can stay here legally," he said, with the confidence of a man who didn't *care* what I thought. "Count Enosh Tar'elian may *pretend* he is an up-and-coming young merchant with a newly acquired fortune from a distant relative, but he's done business here before under another name. Lord Hertra Ylir yn Ferral, if I'm not mistaken. That ring any bells, child?"

In my deepest memories, the name seemed familiar. An echo, a ghost, the source of which was so faint I didn't think I could ease it out of my *agan*-drenched mind even if I wanted to. But I didn't want to give it away. I wasn't going to let this man intimidate me. "I don't know anything," I said. "You're talking to the wrong person."

"Perhaps," Lord Talos said. "As it happens, your father is also the wrong person. Everything your father owns, the money he used to pay for your Dageian citizenship, was stolen from someone else. Stolen from the real Lord Ylir. I wanted to give your father a chance to come clean, but as it is—"

I didn't wait for him to finish. I didn't care about the insult to my father, but even at a young age, I knew a dangerous man when I saw one.

I didn't kill Lord Talos, if you must know. Perhaps not for a lack of trying. The spell I threw at him *could* have killed him if he had been caught unaware. But we were in Dageis, and many of its citizens knew the basics of protecting against magic, even if they lacked the necessary connections to the *agan*. He had a ward around his neck, a small neck-lace with a pink-red orb in the middle, which burst into flames as soon as my spell touched him. The flames spread straight onto his perfumed clothes, which filled the air with the scent of rotten eggs and blood. But the malfunctioning ward hurt him the most; you could see the long, grey lines spreading from where it touched his chest, long webs of thick blood and crystallized *agan* pressing under his skin. He should've returned it to the store he bought it from and gotten a refund for his trouble.

He couldn't, of course. The injury left him speechless, unable to form words, unresponsive to his surroundings. Not that his tongue stopped working. The mages who came to arrest me said he screamed for days afterwards, as if haunted by something he couldn't explain. I don't know what for. All I did was show him a fraction of the terrors a little girl had to face all her life.

What merely bends some of us can break others.

CHAPTER 4

WHEN THE FATES DECIDE

I woke up in the middle of the night to the distinct sensation that something was very wrong. At first, I tried to convince myself I was only tired. The exams, the spells, the hours I spent thinking about my father in particular, would wear anyone down, and the pounding headache I'd felt all night had yet to go away.

But then I heard the knocking on the main doors below.

I glanced at the sky. It was still dark, and the stars were still out. The sky was a greyish blue, and I guessed we were still in the early hours of dawn. I got up from bed and parted the curtains. Three hooded figures stood along the road, waiting for the innkeeper to answer the door.

I gathered my things. The people down below were mages. Not Eheldeth instructors, either, but mages of a distinct rank: bearers. Bearers were officers tasked by the council to carry out important tasks across the empire and beyond, often with a circle of mages at the adherent level or lower at their beck and call. Three bearers together in the middle of nowhere signaled an anomaly. I wondered if they'd just come to seek shelter in the early hours of dawn. The vendor said most mages just went straight to Eheldeth, where the facilities and food were much better (and free), but that couldn't be true all the time. *I* was here, wasn't I? I couldn't very well risk arousing their suspicion by making hasty decisions, either. If they thought I had something to hide, then they were probably going to investigate further.

More pounding on the door, and then the innkeeper finally cracked it open. "What is it?"

"I am called Bearer Lontas and we're here looking for someone," the closest bearer said.

No instructor in Eheldeth had that name, and I was pretty sure I knew all of them. You didn't navigate the rigors of schoolwork like I did without an idea of who to deal with and how, even if they weren't my direct instructors. Remembering people's names and faces was a pastime of mine, one made possible because I hardly did any socializing amongst my peers.

This man was a stranger. I needed to go—now. But where? Through the window, and out on the roof? I wasn't insane. And yet it was the only escape route. Could I fashion the bedsheets into a rope to get me down? It was only two floors. I glanced at the mattress—there was only one ratty blanket, and no bedsheets at all. Of course—that was why I felt so worn out. I'd tossed and turned all night from the itching.

"She abandoned her studies in Eheldeth," Bearer Lontas continued. "Working with the *agan* when you when you don't know what you're doing is dangerous, and leaving one's studies unfinished at Eheldeth is even worse. Eheldeth holds some of the most coveted knowledge on the *agan* in the whole world and if she has gone rogue after taking this knowledge, well—I'll let your imagination decide on what her fate will be, *and* the fates of those who help her."

There was a long pause.

Bearer Lontas wasn't done yet. "We hear she's around her somewhere, representing herself as a mage. You people should know such claims is illegal. The mage council is aptly named. We represent only mages who have *fully* graduated from formal education, which means an outlaw—"

I closed my eyes. A mage gone errant, a rogue, an outlaw…I thought such words were only reserved for people who caused destruction against the mage council's orders. The entire empire was full of people gifted in the *agan* who *didn't* go through the expensive mage schools. It was true they weren't technically supposed to call themselves mages, but surely the council ought to know such mistakes were made all the time, especially in a small village full of ignorant people. And it was true such people needed to be documented by the mage council in other ways—usually because they were indentured as a mage-thrall to assist an actual mage—but that was only something that came up if an official took notice.

I didn't expect bearers to come looking for me in the middle of the night. Was it because I had a record? They came when I harmed Lord Talos, but they knew that was an accident then. What did I do this time?

Would they have been happier if I pushed through with my exams, knowing I'd failed one already? I just gave up. That was *all*. Why were they acting as if I had done something unforgiveable?

"We received reports that a spell was cast in the vicinity," Lontas continued. "The imprint matches our records of her."

"How are you so sure it's her?"

"We've watched these children since they first enter Eheldeth's gates, madam," Lontas replied. "Their spells, their flesh, their blood—everything they do, we can find. And we've been looking all night. She can't cast a spell anywhere in the empire without leaving a whiff of her for us to track down. If she's hiding here, we'll know."

I can't cast spells without alerting them. Is that what he's saying? I tried to remain calm. No—he's saying if I cast a spell, I would leave a mark, and if they're looking for me specifically in the area, they'd be able to trace it. But such marks fade; the *agan* rights itself everywhere in time. I just needed to be careful. I was hanging on to anything that would give me a bit of hope, a chance to escape and keep on escaping. The thought of returning to Eheldeth was suddenly more than I could bear. If they were to bring me back there, they would have to drag me through the mud.

The door opened. One of the innkeepers' girls peered through.

"Maria and I are here to help you," the girl who'd first asked for my help said.

"Mother's entertaining them in the dining hall now," Maria added. "She gave me and Vera time to let you escape. She'll fetch you in a few minutes. You need to be on your way then." She grabbed my hands, clasping them to her chest. "I'd be dead if not for you."

You'd be alive, actually, I thought. *That spell couldn't have killed you.* But as much as I detested the thought of tricking them, my tongue wouldn't say the words. I swallowed and watched as Vera cranked open the window before pushing the bed against it. She unrolled a rope ladder she was holding under her arm, tying it firmly to the bedposts. It looked like it would hold my weight.

They helped me get over the window and on the ladder. As I was climbing down, Maria glanced over and gave a small smile. "Be careful out there," she said. "The mage was saying what you did was illegal."

"It's not," I gasped. "I just decided I wasn't going to finish my exams. My family paid the tuition already. This is all on me."

"He said you're not supposed to get all that education and knowledge, and then abandon it," Vera added. "It's dangerous." She looked at me wistfully. "Couldn't you have stayed? What's so bad about being a rich girl with talents? He said if you'd failed your exams, they would just ask you to write them again."

I reached the ground and jumped off the ladder. I didn't know what to tell her. It would look like a rich girl like me hadn't thought it through, and maybe they were right.

I tightened the straps on my bag and took off into the woods. I hadn't gone much farther than the first stream around the bend before I heard the distinct baying of hounds behind me. Taking a deep breath, I plunged deeper into the shadows.

The girls weren't exactly mistaken. Eheldeth might not have held Ivasus accountable for the incident, but they would have made me write the rest of my exams for the week and then redo portals if my parents were willing to fork over added fees. Come to think of it, I don't remember anyone ever actually failing them before—at least not to the extent that they couldn't just take another year or be sent away to another school. One way or another, you ended up right where the mage council wanted you: a pawn in the palm of their hands.

If all I ever cared for was to have school over with, if my future wasn't something to be bargained for in exchange for near-perfect grades and a record unheard of in Eheldeth history, I would have gone back on my own, even without bearers at my tail. But this wasn't about *passing* the damn exams. This wasn't about graduating. If I could be damned to think it over with a clear head and a full stomach, I would have said it was a matter of pride. I *was* the best student Eheldeth had seen in years. I shouldn't have to beg for scraps.

Well, there I was then: the best student Eheldeth had seen in years, running through mud on two hours of sleep. I had no place to go, with no plans at all on how to get there if I did. In the back of my mind, I knew I was being stupid. I knew that no matter how much I rationalized my actions, I *was* reacting badly. Emotion fuelled my flight. I was angry, and the anger had turned to stubbornness, which meant even if all I knew was that I would not return, I remained committed. Even if I didn't know what I wanted to do with my life, I knew what I *didn't* want. I didn't want to prove myself anymore. I didn't want someone else dictating my worth, when I knew they were just waiting for an excuse to prove me worthless.

I kept running.

Darkness turned to light, and morning eased its way across the skies. Orange, as if paint spilled by a brush, lit up the clouds. I thought I'd heard the last of the dogs and decided I might have actually succeeded in outrunning them. I slowed down to catch my breath. I could see a wagon on the road up ahead. Perhaps if I begged the driver, I might catch a ride to the next town. Perhaps the farther I got from Eheldeth, the less heated these pursuits might be. Surely bearers had more important things to worry about.

I reached the wagon. A shaggy, butter-coloured dog with cropped ears crawled out from under the wheels and began barking non-stop. I realized I'd made another mistake.

I had walked right into the mages' carriage.

The dog shuffled forward as I stood there in shock, its hackles raised. As it continued barking, I noticed there was no one else there. No human, at least—there was just the dog and a horse attached to the wagon, its bridle tied to a tree. The mages must have left the dog to guard the carriage before carrying on into the inn. My eyes skipped to the bed rolls and what looked to be sacks of food supplies in the back. These bearers were probably passing by Eheldeth before being sent on this errand, and likely had a long way to go after they'd brought me in. Maybe I could make their journey even longer.

"Easy, there," I told the dog, who seemed to be perturbed by my lack of reaction to its bravado. Or at least what seemed to be a display of bravado—since I chose not to react to its barking, the intensity had dropped to something resembling a question. *Should* I be near its carriage? Could I just walk away now so it didn't have to decide whether I was a threat? I glanced at the horse, who was clearly unamused by the dog's racket and was doing its best to show the whites of its eyes. I untied the horse from the tree before giving a quick whistle, directed at the dog. "There's a good dog." I reached into my pockets. "Do you want a treat?"

It started barking again, lips curled into a half-growl. I put my hand away. "I guess you've been taught not to accept treats from strangers." I glanced away so I didn't have to look it in the eyes. "Good dog," I repeated. "What about scratches?" I made a wiggling motion with my fingers.

The barking slowed down again, and turned into a small, half-hearted whine.

There, I thought. It had been alone all night, and I could sense a deep loneliness within the creature. "I know," I said, though I still kept my eyes on the ground. "I know what that feels like. You keep to yourself, so they think you don't really need the company. You don't say much, so they think it's fine to let you sit alone when all you really need is someone who knows just to sit with you in silence."

The dog whined again, before unexpectedly lifting its paw to touch my arm. It felt like it wanted to pull me closer to it. Even though I knew it couldn't possibly understand me, I wondered. It *was* a mage's dog.

Remembering that, I got up to turn my attention to the wagon. "Will you let me inspect it?" I asked.

The dog barked, all the rage and froth gone from its voice. It wagged its tail.

Making a wide berth around the suspicious horse, I quickly walked around the wagon to make sure the mages didn't leave any trap-spells on the thing. I wanted to look underneath it, too, but I knew I had little time. The mages and the other hounds would be right behind me, and I couldn't risk missing the opportunity to get ahead of them *and* slow them down a bit. I had to take a chance.

I pulled out a dagger and cut off the dog's tether before it even knew what was happening. It lunged forward, bolting to the middle of the road. "You can go back to your masters." I hopped onto the driver's seat. I picked up the reins and patted the horse's backside. "Or you could—"

It jumped into the wagon and placed one paw on my shoulder. It nuzzled my ear.

"Guess that means we're travelling together." I clicked my tongue and directed the horse down the road.

I had never been the sort of person who follows a path just because I happened to be on it. I used to wonder about such people—those who could carry on as if it was enough to rely on the goodwill of fate. Was it faith in their gods, or something equally powerful? How could you not plan out every detail of your life to prepare for the unexpected so that nothing truly caught you off guard? Surprise quizzes never bothered me, for instance. I used to think there was no room for uncertainty in my life. More than most people, my path had always been clear. I would blaze through my studies, graduate with flying colours, and become a prestigious scholar assigned as an adherent to a high-ranking mage before moving up the ranks myself. With enough effort, I could drown out the emptiness of this strange land and my homesickness with accomplishment.

And yet here I was, without even a roof over my head. The words *outlaw mage* throbbed like a sore wound in my head, and I was afraid if I thought about it any further, I'd turn the carriage around and force the horse to gallop back to Eheldeth. The single road from the village led to an intersection that split into two main roads: Meruse to the right, and

Ad Methas to the left. I knew nothing about either city except that I would be a stranger to both. Knowing my pursuers could be on me at any moment, I decided, on a whim, to take the left fork. Ad Methas was farther away. The journey would give me time to think. It was the one thing I could never get enough of.

The dog didn't seem to care either way. He just seemed content to finally get some attention at last. As the afternoon wore on, I decided to call him Daisy, just because. He responded to the name as if he'd had it since he was a pup.

The mages' equipment gave me a good reason to avoid the villages along the road. When evening fell, I led the horse into the woods and made camp on a dark hillside overlooking a lake. Based on my knowledge of the empire's geography, I figured it was one of the southern lakes that fringed the border. I made no fire and simply ate cold food under a blanket next to the dog. Jerky, ham, and cheese, all of a quality finer than what we were given in the cafeteria—these bearers were no joke. I traded bites with Daisy and then later dropped on the grass next to him to stare at the stars.

"I wonder if they sent a letter to my parents," I said out loud.

He grunted before curling into a ball, as if to say he didn't know my parents. I ran my fingers through the sandy fur above his brows.

"On one hand, it's their responsibility," I continued. "Imagine the scandal if it's discovered that a student simply walked out of the school, and they failed to inform her family. On the other hand, if that Bearer Lontas's words were correct, letting me walk out in the first place sounds like a mistake. The keepers would be punished, and the school might try to cover it up."

I sighed, allowing my arm to curl over the dog's neck. He licked my cheek in return. His breath smelled like sawdust. "I always knew the answers," I told him. "*Always*. But I don't have one now. I would feel a lot better if I'd planned this. But until that moment—until that keeper started yelling at me, I didn't know I was going to walk out. All I know is that *this*—" I gestured at the expanse, and the stars up above. "*This* makes more sense than all those years in Eheldeth. And I don't know what that says about me. Does that mean I've been lying to myself the whole time? I really *am* a nobody, just like they said I was. I'm a nobody who will never amount to anything, just another wasted talent. I'm a nobody who can't even go back home."

The finality of my words stung like salt in a wound. Daisy sighed, as if he dared not to disagree.

I slept another few hours before harnessing the horse back to the wagon and returning to the road. Early hours, long, slow days...I had no idea if it created enough distance between me and the bearers. But if uncertainty frightened me, stillness was worse. I had to keep moving, even if it was futile.

Days later, we pulled into Ad Methas without trouble. By then, my supplies were running low, and the horse was more than exhausted. Knowing it would be cruel to subject her to another day on the road, I sold her at the stables to a man who promised to take good care of her. Judging by the condition of the rest of his stock, I believed him, and said my goodbyes. I sold the wagon, too, and whatever supplies I couldn't carry on my back.

That left me and Daisy, standing in the middle of that sleepy city, thousands and thousands of miles away from everyone I had ever known and cared for. I placed a hand on his head. His presence was so warm and cozy it made me want to cry. "Now what?" I asked.

Daisy whined. He didn't know, either. I couldn't blame him. He'd left his masters for a friendly face and the promise of ear scratches—a failure of a guard dog if there ever was one. He reminded me of myself. Maybe that was why our paths crossed. Maybe that was a sign fate wasn't done with me yet.

"You a mage, miss?" someone called.

I stiffened, one hand on Daisy's collar. Drawing from my feelings, he began to growl.

A young man with a thin, brown beard approached us, hands held up. He was tall and muscular, with the kind of face you'd quickly forget in a crowd, until he smiled. And he did it now—a warm, inviting smile that gave a slight crease on his forehead. "I mean nothing by it," he said. "Only your robes—"

"I stole them," I blurted. "They're just robes."

He looked confused. I glanced down and realized it was because my robes looked like they'd been washed in mud. I didn't look much better —I'd been sleeping in the woods and tromping about on the road for nearly a week. I probably reeked.

"I'm not a mage," I repeated. "If I was, would I look like this?"

He rubbed his jaw. "Do grooming spells exist?"

"Glamour does," I snapped.

"Ah," he replied. "And you'd know, even if you're...not a mage?"

I swallowed. Walked right into that one, didn't I? "What do you want?" I asked. "Surely you don't just walk up to every stranger to the city to ask if they're a mage or not."

He puffed up his chest and pointed at the necklace he wore. "I do, actually," he said. "Or rather—I walk up to every strange face I see to check if they belong. It's part of my duties as a town guard of Klossaka."

"And Klossaka is…?"

"A village an hour's ride from here," he replied.

"Why is a town guard from a village patrolling the city? Don't you have a city watch?"

He crossed his arms. "That's partly why I asked if you're a mage. We're in dire need of people around here."

"What do you mean?"

He pointed at the airship tower in the distance. "The airship here stopped working since the war ten years ago. We're short of people these days. No one wants to live and work in a city weeks removed from the rest of the empire. They contract out patrol duties, and town guards from the various villages all contribute to the effort."

Weeks removed from the empire. I tried not to let excitement show on my face. "Does that mean there's plenty of work here?" I asked.

"If you're a mage," he said with a grin.

"What do you mean?"

"This is as much as I know: the *agan* fabric around Ad Methas is unstable. Has been since the war. Something about the connections becoming all dysfunctional…" He made a face, as if reciting a remembered word. "We need mages to do just about everything, but the last time the mage council sent them out was three years ago. As far as this region is concerned, we've been forgotten."

My ears were ringing. What he was actually saying was no scheduled inspections, no systems to fix. No officials to run into. "So you were hoping Eheldeth sent me," I said.

"Yes? Maybe?" He threw his hands up. "We've been hiring anyone with any knowledge of the *agan*—merchants, travellers, *witches*, we don't care. Like I said—the land here is unstable, and things just crop up here and there. Even if it's just someone who can tell us to rope an area off and keep the kids out, we need them. The problem is nobody wants to stick around here for long. After a few months or years, they just get up and leave."

"I won't," I blurted out.

He lifted an eyebrow. "What?"

"I'm looking to settle down," I said. "And I know…about the *agan*. If there's a place for me to stay…a quiet place, far away from everyone…"

His smile widened.

CHAPTER 5

THE WITCH'S COTTAGE

"What do you think?" the young man, Jehar, asked. There was a grimace on his face, as if he knew already and just wanted to go through the courtesy of pretending to hear me out. The cottage was cramped, with just enough wall space for maybe one or two bookcases. A wooden table, two rickety chairs, no curtains on the windows. The floor was made of hardened earth, polished to a fine sheen, which did nothing to lighten the drab appearance of the rest of its furnishings. I could only imagine what all their other guests would have said. Many mages are born from nobility and end up accepting work in remote areas of the empire only to bring honour to their family name; the humble cottage in the middle of nowhere would have seemed like an insult.

But it looked like heaven.

I refrained from asking, "All this, just for me?" if only because my excitement would be embarrassing. And yet that was exactly what I felt. An empty living space, all mine to decorate. Those bookcases could be filled with books I chose for myself. I could leave books on the floor if I wanted to! No keepers to tell me to tidy up, no mother who would make thinly veiled commentary about the hobbies a young woman ought to indulge in, and most importantly, no father who would scream about shaming my ancestors if I looked like I lived in a rat's nest.

Maybe I stared at all of this in silence a little too long, because Jehar turned red and tugged at his collar. "I know it doesn't look like much, and it can get chilly in the winter. But a rug and a steady of supply of firewood can go a long way. Anyway, you don't have to decide right now.

Let's go meet the mayor first. She'll be having lunch with my mother at around this time."

A village where the mayor had lunch with its inhabitants was as small as they went. I managed to nod and felt a twinge of impatience—and maybe a touch of anguish—as he shut the door to the cottage. I don't remember wanting anything half as much as I wanted that empty room.

The mayor was a cheerful middle-aged woman with grey hair; Jehar's mother, Ivy, was also a cheerful middle-aged woman with grey hair. I wasn't sure who I was talking to for at least a good hour after he made the introductions. They also had a habit of talking over me, mostly about whether I looked like the kind of mage who would drop the village as soon as a better opportunity arose. As soon as I could, I stepped outside for a breather.

"You the new mage?" a woman called from the street.

I managed a small shrug. Evidently, she took this as an enthusiastic sign and jumped over the fence to take a closer look.

"You're *really* the new mage," she remarked. "I don't think I've ever seen them up close before. Felt like you're all an endangered species, or something. Everyone's always been too ashamed to be seen out in the open." She laughed before rubbing her hand on her pant leg, which she then stuck out. "Wren, at your service."

I shook her hand. "Rosha."

"Amazing. You're even telling us your *name*. You really don't mind charity work, do you?"

"I don't understand."

"Every mage that's come through here sees us as nothing else. People don't help people because they want to, you know. They only care if it's good for them, too."

I felt my cheeks flush. If that was the case, then I was as bad as the rest. But I only nodded. Wren narrowed her eyes, as if my moral compass was something I carried about my neck. "If you must know," she said, after giving a small sniff, "the village folk *can* pay you. Not much, but we still have our pride. I don't know what sort of stipend the empire offers you to get you out to these places, but—"

"None," I replied.

She smiled. "Well, then."

"I mean, I'll be happy to accept what you can pay me," I continued. *Beggars can't be choosers, after all.*

Wren squinted. "And now I'm starting to question if you're even qualified. Really. Why are you here? You can tell me."

"I…" I swallowed. I needed to find a lie that straddled the truth. "I barely passed exams."

She laughed. "All right."

"All right?"

"I believe you. You look like the sort. Tumbling about the hay with the boys, weren't you?"

"I'm sorry, what?"

"Or the girls, because I'm sure there's some gorgeous lookers in your classes." She winked coyly. "Don't worry. Never went to school, but I always thought I was the type to do everything they told me *not* to do, and then some."

"I didn't…tumble with anyone…" My cheeks were burning like lava now.

"Making trouble again, Wren?" Jehar called from his mother's doorstep.

"Trouble always finds me first," Wren said wryly, drawing away from me.

He crossed his arms. "She's new. Be nice."

"I *am* nice." Wren made a graceful bow. "In case it wasn't obvious, I bid you welcome to our humble village, your majesty. Now, I have a pig with a weird growth on his back, if you want to get started on something. It wasn't there yesterday."

Jehar clicked his tongue. "Wren—"

"It's true," she said. Her eyes flashed. "Unless farm work is somehow *beneath* her highness?"

"Show me," I replied.

The *growth*, it turned out, was a mass of warts the poor thing picked up after escaping its pen and snuffling around in an *agan*-soaked stream. It wasn't the worst thing that could have happened to it, and the affliction —which ceased to be magical the moment it became a physical thing— could have been cut away by anyone with a knife and was brave enough to look at it. I glanced left and right, still feeling Eheldeth's mages breathing down my neck, before I dared myself to cast a small fire-spell to burn it all off. The villagers likely weren't going to let me have the house without showing I was capable of magic somehow.

A small spell, and yet you would have thought I conjured a castle out of nowhere. Jehar stepped out to bellow my accomplishments to everyone down the street, and suddenly I was being handed a list of tasks to keep myself busy for a week. Five tainted fields, a barren sow, a dog that walked funny, a windmill that insisted on turning the wrong way…all things that made life inconvenient for simple folk only looking to feed themselves. All unglamourous work that I could have never imagined doing a month ago. No, Wren wasn't entirely wrong. There was a time I would have thought such things beneath me.

But right after the crowd had wandered away, Wren came up to place a coin in my hand. It was, as she said, not much, but I felt a flush of pride. I'd earned this. When she walked away, I held my palm up to look at the coin closer. It glinted in the sunset.

"Let me walk you back to your cottage," Jehar offered.

I pocketed the money. "Is it really *mine*?" I asked.

"You're welcome to use it for as long as you're staying here for a monthly fee. As you saw earlier, there isn't much in it yet. They figure we can get you started with a bed from Hansett, the furniture-maker. He's happy to be paid in installments."

"Is there…no bed there already?"

"The last mage had an unfortunate run in with…" He turned red and made several hand movements. "Let's just say fire was involved, and one not half as controlled as yours was earlier. Wren told me you *barely* passed exams. Unbelievable. We've had at least one mage claim he was the top of his class, and he would have made roast pig out of poor Sammy."

"There's more to the exams than just casting spells."

Jehar gave me a look that told me he didn't quite believe me. "On second thought, maybe it's still too early. Do you want to come by the tavern with me? You can meet more people. Well, you'll know them soon enough, but why not have some beer and a hunk of chicken with it?"

"No, thank you," I said. "I can walk on my own, too."

He glanced at the lonely road. "Are you sure?"

"Daisy will be with me." I pointed at the dog.

Jehar looked like he wanted to argue that a dog wasn't much company, which was when I made the speediest of exits. Being alone again on the road, for the first time in hours, was a breath of fresh air. Even more than that, though, was seeing the silhouette of the hut in the distance with its dark windows, hungry for a candle to shine through.

"Mine," I said out loud.

Daisy barked.

"Let's go home," I told him. We strode through the gate, which was so rickety a small child could probably rip it off the hinges. Using the key the mayor had given me, I unlocked the door, and stepped inside.

I didn't appreciate the musty, moldy scent of the cottage before, but now I got a whole lungful.

I flicked the coin in my hand. "Maybe I should have taken the tavern offer," I told Daisy. "He might have paid, and I'm not sure we have enough here to buy us food. Rent alone will kill us."

He whined.

"I know. I wasn't thinking. I've never been out by myself before. Food just magically appeared in the dining halls. Not by magic, you know, but it's something I've never had to ever worry about." I shuffled indoors and looked around. "Should have asked for blankets, too. What's this?"

Daisy had found a basket on the table, one that wasn't there before. My stomach grumbled. It was pathetic to wish it was food, and yet...

There was a whole meat pie inside. My mind jumped to Ivy, because she'd been baking something when I first arrived. A note said, *Welcome to Klossaka. Make yourself at home.*

I closed my eyes. I wasn't convinced this place *could* be home, but I wanted so very badly to believe it.

I heard snuffling. Daisy was licking the edges of the tray.

"Share. We need to save enough for breakfast too, you know." I cut a whole slab just for him and then a slightly smaller one for myself. I didn't trust the chairs, which shook too much when I put weight on them, so I sat in the corner and ate the meat pie with my dog. It had steak and peas and leeks and mushrooms. I practically inhaled it.

Afterwards, belly full of pie, I lay on the floor with the dog in my arms and slept like the dead.

I woke up to the sound of somebody pounding on the door. "Mage!" someone screamed. "Open up! Mage!"

Daisy charged, barking. I grabbed him by the collar.

"Mage! We need you right now!"

It was the booming voice of a man. I pressed my ear against the door. If there was any way for me to tell if this was one of the mages from Eheldeth pretending to be a villager, it must be in the villager's rural drawl. I couldn't imagine any mage from Eheldeth stooping to that level; even the ones from rural towns altered their speech so they could blend in with the mages from the big cities.

I opened the door. A bearded man, red-cheeked from the icy wind, stood outside. He stared down at me with a look of disappointment. "You're the mage," he declared.

"Is there a problem with that?"

"You're…" He trailed off, probably trying to decide between *young* and *inexperienced-looking* and *short*. He settled on, "Not what I expected."

I started shutting the door to his face. Eventually, and probably because he remembered there were no other mages available in the village, he stuck his foot through the crack. "I didn't mean to offend you, Mistress Mage," he said. "But it's just…a delicate situation. I don't know if you could help."

"You can start by telling me the problem."

He swallowed. "My baby was taken from its bassinet."

"Perhaps you are in the wrong place. Shouldn't you have alerted the guards? The mayor?"

"It would probably be easier if I showed you," he replied.

I followed him down to a house right at the edge of the meadows. It stood in a clearing formed between five trees with branches laced together, as if they sprouted from a single seed. The moon shone right above. A group of people stood under the shadows formed by the branches. I recognized the mayor, along with Jehar.

"I told you not to call her," the mayor said. She took my arm almost gently. "She's had a long night, and this—"

"—is exactly the kind of thing we need mages for," Jehar interjected.

"Not always," the mayor said gently. She coughed and patted my arm. "Take no offense, child. It's one thing to help us out with troubles and another thing for you to write a report to the council on what you've seen here. We'd rather not have them decide that Klossaka is unlivable and must be evacuated."

"Isn't it?" Jehar snapped. "What do you call that, then?"

He gestured above. I cast my eyes upward and spotted a lone figure swinging from the branches. At first, I thought it was an unusually thin, long-limbed man. But then the moonlight shone on it, and I saw its green skin from which stringy vines and leaves sprouted. Its hands were fronds; its head was a flower bulb, laced with sharp teeth. More vines sprouted from its torso, from which hung a bundle that wailed into the night.

"That plant is alive," I said, calmly.

My tone of voice must have struck a nerve. A woman—the mother, I guessed from the tears in her eyes—screamed. Someone came up to the mayor to gesture at me. "You see? These outsiders just come here to make fun of our problems. It's amusing, isn't it, mage? Plants coming alive. Animals growing extra appendages. Things we should have all learned how to protect ourselves against, living in this empire! If we could afford to pay mages properly!"

"Shut up," Jehar snapped. "She didn't come here to judge us."

"You don't know a thing, Jehar," the man said. "Hoping for the empire to take pity on us—like it ever cared. You know mages like these grow up in luxury. That mage school is nothing but a dumping ground for the rich. They only go to hamlets like these because they don't have a choice. But in the meantime…"

The child continued to cry. "In the meantime, that thing may drop the child or stuff it in its mouth," I replied. "Save your accusations for later."

"We don't need you," the man said. "Bloody islander. Don't you have enough problems where you're from?" He pointed at the baby's father. "That thing is made of magic already, Mathir! Do you want more magic in the air? What happens if she strikes your child? We'll have an abomination running around! I say we cut down the trees and tear it limb from limb. It's about time we spit at the empire's rules and take matters into our own hands!"

The despair in his voice was palpable. I wasn't surprised. Magical rules confused ordinary people, and most distrusted it. Why trust in something you couldn't see, when violence offered the illusion of a quick and easy solution?

I stepped forward. The townsfolk drew away. No—they couldn't see what I could. The blue strings around the creature's vines, the flow of *agan* that was giving it the appearance of life. A puppet, being jerked by an unseen puppetmaster. I followed the strings, which led away from the trees and straight to the field beyond. The child's wail faded.

I heard Jehar's heavy breathing nearby as he followed. "What do you see, mage?" he asked.

"I have a name," I said. "I'd prefer if you used it."

"Rosha. Please." He held out his hand to take my elbow. "I hope you didn't take offense to all of that. The townspeople are…well, we don't know our manners anymore. It's been so long since we've actually had anyone around to help."

"I thought you needed mages."

"We do." He nodded. "This is an old village, one that's always looked at magic with distrust. People don't want to admit we need mages. And the more it falls apart, the less they want help. A matter of pride. People like you…"

I stared at him. "Me?"

"Smart. Educated. Someone who has brushed elbows with the wider world." He coloured a little. "And an outsider."

"What do you mean by that?"

Jehar scratched the back of his head. "We've only gotten mages from old mage families before…" He coughed.

"I see." I strode ahead. I had no desire to listen to his excuses. I knew what *old mage families* meant. Few Gorenten probably ventured this deep into the empire. And people like that had long forgotten that once before, they, too, were the outsiders.

I found the source of the *agan* powering the plant-creature. It was in the pond, a fissure no wider than my arm. I took my shoes off and waded in with no regard for the state of my dress. Jehar watched, open-mouthed, as I removed the surrounding rocks to get a better look at the opening. All he could see was a woman shuffling rocks around; to the naked eye, it would seem as if I'd had gone mad.

I inspected the fissure. It didn't need magic to close it, which was a relief. I kicked sand over it before returning the rocks, which I used to seal the hole. The bright blue glow dissipated.

I returned to the shore, drenched in water from my chest down. Jehar was still staring.

I coughed, and he suddenly seemed to remember. He unclasped his cape and offered it to me. As I huddled under the warmth of it, we heard a cry. We rushed back to the crowd just in time to see the leaf-thing crumple to a heap, dropping the infant.

Jehar reached out to catch it. The baby landed in his arms and laughed.

There was a general outcry as people rushed to his side, blocking him from my view. I heard murmurs of relief, and at least one instance of someone criticizing me for having taken care of the creature too fast without giving them time to prepare. Which was, admittedly, my mistake, but I had been hoping the thing would stand by itself a lot longer than it did. *Agan* was unpredictable, and to stand there and explain that to the crowd was to risk inviting more anger my way.

I made my way back to the house. Daisy was waiting for me there and did a little dance as soon as I stepped indoors. "You *could* have stayed with me for moral support," I said, rubbing his head. And then I sneezed. "But I guess I don't blame you. It's a lot warmer in here. And it'll be a lot warmer if we can get a fire going, eh?"

He barked.

I grabbed firewood from the shed and went down to start it. I resisted the urge to light it with my fingers and took the time to find paper and matches. As soon as the smell of burning wood touched my nostrils, my stomach grumbled again. Surprising, as I hadn't really cast any spells and I hadn't done too much walking. Maybe dealing with people now made me hungry. I wandered over to the kitchen. The cupboards were mostly bare save for a cast iron pan. A neat find, since I'd sold the mages' cookware in town. I used it to cook the last hunk of bacon from my pack.

The smell of frying meat filled the cottage, and then someone knocked on the door.

I closed my eyes and swore under my breath.

Mathir and Jehar were standing outside, baskets in hand.

"We never got the chance to thank you, my wife and I," Mathir stammered. "You saved our baby. Forget what the others are saying—none of them were brave enough to. Thank you." He bowed before indicating the baskets. "We brought jam and cheese from our larder, and a change of clothes—you're just my eldest daughter's size, you see, and—"

"What we're saying is that we're hoping you stay," Jehar interjected. "Please. "We have our problems, and I know we're not much, but…" He, too, bowed.

I didn't have the honesty to tell him we deserved each other. I wasn't much, either. And this small village at the edge of the world might be all it could ever be for a Gorenten girl who dared hope for more.

Instead, I took the baskets, and let them think I was happy there.

ACT TWO

CHAPTER 6

THE VILLAGE AT THE EDGE OF THE WORLD

In the following months, I occasionally indulged in how my father would have reacted to the inevitable news of my abrupt—and apparently *illegal*—departure from Eheldeth.

Ever since the incident with Lord Talos, I'd done what I could to create a reputation as anything but a delinquent child. As far as my father was concerned, the fate of Lord Talos was a bad childhood memory no one in the family ever needed to talk about, ever. But of course, certain things were out of my control, and I figured that last one wasn't exactly my fault, either.

But I knew dropping out of that very expensive school would be the last nail on the coffin of our relationship, so I made no effort to reach out to inform him of my whereabouts. Imagining his reaction kept me amused, though. He must have read the letter from the Firekeeper. He must have tried to act calm for a good few minutes before giving in to his rage—a hapless cup or vase might have taken the brunt of it. Perhaps he then demanded my mother to go and find me. He was perfectly capable of finding me himself, but I knew he wouldn't sink so low. I also knew my mother would tell him *no* to his face.

In any case, it was satisfying to think that my parents would have argued and blamed each other long into the night. A touch of fire in their unbelievably cold, needless marriage. I hoped for a while that it ended there; that my absence in their life would get them to face the truth and abandon the pretense of a rich, happy Gorenten family lucky enough to have made it out in the empire. Maybe my father was a fraud, but the rest of us didn't have to be.

48

Tough luck, I suppose. I filed an inquiry from the city a few seasons after I arrived in Klossaka and found out they were still married. So I stayed away.

The months became years, and I still heard nothing from them. I knew they had the resources to find me...the fact that they never did gave me an inkling over how angry they must have been. But I was too busy to dwell on it. I had my own life to worry about. I didn't think I'd ever find one when I left Eheldeth, but there it was.

"Tell me about these dreams again," I told the pimple-faced boy who sat across my desk. He had the kind of ears that stuck out like teapot handles and freckles that covered his nose. "Slowly, this time. It's hard to make notes when you're swallowing your words."

"It's a succubus, I'm telling you," the boy rattled on. "She comes in looking like Aniya—"

"Aniya is your neighbour, correct?"

The boy nodded. "And then she...she..." He coloured.

"She takes off her clothes," I said dryly. "Go on."

His ears turned red. "Then she rubs up against me, and..."

I placed the pen down. "Is it perhaps that these are just regular dreams, since you've been pining for this neighbour for a while?"

"That's the problem," the boy gasped. "I'm *not*. Aniya? I hate her guts!"

"Uh huh."

"There's a succubus out there! I need a charm...I need to make it stop!"

I cleared my throat. "A succubus of the nature you're describing... doesn't really exist. It's hard to make a charm against something that doesn't exist. Have you recently woken up with your pillows soaked in blood?"

"No."

"And by blood, I mean something else and by pillows, I mean your pants."

"That's not—"

"I can't help you if you're not honest with the symptoms."

The boy glanced down. "Yes," he finally mumbled.

"Might I suggest new underwear instead?"

"This isn't a joke, Mistress Rosha! I need those dreams to stop!"

"What you need is to tell this girl what you really feel about her," I said. "So you can stop wasting my time with these frivolities. I'm charging you just for the last half hour."

"That's—highway robbery! They said you were the best!"

"I am, which is why I'm letting you off easy. Unless you want me to send Aniya a batch of flowers and a love note myself?"

The boy's mouth fell open, but I could see a visible hesitation in his eyes.

"I'm not joking," I said, ripping out another piece of paper. "I can do that, too, for a price. I don't *just* solve magical problems."

We were interrupted by the sound of wind chimes as someone burst through the shop door.

"I'm busy," I said irritably. "Didn't you see the sign?"

"I did," Jehar replied. "I didn't think it applied to me."

I laughed. "Oh, it most definitely applies to you. *Especially* you."

"You made a sign just for me? I'm touched."

"I'm with a client, if you don't mind."

"That's not a client," Jehar said, placing his hands on the boy's knobby shoulders. "That's Ignus, the butcher's boy. What are you doing here, kid? It's market day."

"It's none of your business," Ignus grumbled.

Jehar gripped his shoulders tighter. "I'm sorry, what was that?"

"I said it's none of your business, Officer Jehar, sir," Ignus said in a louder voice.

Jehar slapped him on the back. "Run along now," he said. "I'll make sure she just charges for the time she spent with you."

"I was going to round down," I replied.

Ignus looked at both of us in confusion.

I sighed. "Come back when you've decided." I shoved the fresh note into his hands.

He gave a quick bow before scampering out.

"Why do you entertain those brats?" Jehar said, slumping into the first chair. He lifted his legs and placed his boots on the second.

I twisted my face in disgust. "The same reason I once entertained you, I imagine," I said. I crossed my arms. "Those are velvet chairs, sir. I'd prefer if you removed your dusty boots from them at once."

Jehar pulled his feet away and pressed them on the ground. "Entertain*ed*," he said. His expression grew sombre. "Look, can we talk about that?"

"We have nothing to talk about. I'm a busy woman, and you—"

"Just got promoted to Chief Officer," he said, pointing at the badge on his chest. He gave a proud grin, like a boy showing off his most prized possession. "Not a bad leap from just common town guard, eh? We've gone far in the last three years! You, the beloved village witch, and me, the Chief Officer…"

I squinted. "Is that what that was? I thought you mistook an acorn for a brooch."

He ignored the jibe. "Let's get married."

"What part of *it's over* do you think implies a future offer for marriage?"

"The part where you didn't give me a chance to explain things to you. You said I was too busy. I said I agreed. And then you slammed the door to my face, and I was left standing in the rain like a drenched…a drenched puppy."

"My goodness," I drawled. "*However* did you survive?"

"I've spent the last month thinking," he continued.

"Did it hurt?"

He grimaced. "No, but this does. Let's start again, Rosha. It won't be like last time. My job pays better now. I have men who can carry out my orders. I'll have more time for you, for us."

"I don't recall saying *you* were too busy," I said. "I said *I* was. I thought I'd made that perfectly clear."

He stared back at me, open-mouthed. A good-looking man, Jehar, even with that mess of brown hair and slightly crooked nose, but he couldn't seem to understand how a world functioned when it didn't revolve around him. He had been a pleasant distraction for a while, but I had a limit as far as distractions went, and he'd just about reached it.

"If you don't mind," I said, "I have a full day ahead of me."

He tried to reach for my hand. I swiftly avoided it and headed for the door. I opened it. "Good day, Jehar."

Jehar rubbed his head sheepishly. "Can't even talk you into having a cup of coffee with me, can I?"

I smiled grimly. "No, unfortunately."

He shuffled his feet and finally started walking out of my store. It took an unbearably long time. I sighed and even counted in my head. He slouched over the doorway, a tall ox of a man diminished by a few words from a small woman. It was pathetic. Surely, he had better things to do with his day.

Before I could close the door, he turned around. "I ah, there was one thing I forgot to mention."

I crossed my arms.

"I promise I'm not trying to work my way back in," he said with a laugh. "Unless—"

"It's not cute. Out with it."

"Someone's staying over at the inn asking for you. Not for the local witch and not for your store. *You*. I've never heard of that before. I told the guy this isn't the place for him—you've only been here a few years, Rosha, but you know we think of you as one of ours. I don't think he'll be back, but you never know. You watch yourself, all right?"

"Thank you, Jehar," I said.

"If there's anything you need—"

I shut the door, pressed my forehead against the wall, and sighed. *This is it*, I thought. The other shoe had finally dropped. I closed my eyes. Even after all this time, Bearer Lontas's words were as strong as ever. Simple rules, for a complicated world; for three years, they had hounded me through my nightmares. They'd found me at last.

I opened the door again, just quickly enough to switch the sign to *Closed*, before shutting it a second time. I bolted all five locks before taking a step back to look at the store.

Jars of pickled herbs, frogs, and lizard eyes lined the shelves. Half I used to treat various ailments, the other to make people think what they wanted to think—that I was a harmless eccentric who settled in the village and made money off the desperate, the ignorant, and the greedy. The small, harmless tricks I performed for the villagers were unlikely to draw attention to the fact that I was a mage with enough power to destroy everything around me if I so much as snapped my fingers. A mage living outside the council's rules. *Outlaw mage*. I felt that familiar anger, the one that had driven me out of those exam halls. There I was, with a cottage and a store of my own, and the beginning of a reputation —business was still tough, given how little the villagers paid, but this looked to be the first year that I could start making money on top of the payments to my loans. I hadn't even dared tap into the *agan* the way I used to before I learned how easily they could trace my activities back to *me*. Why were they still after me? Why, by all the gods, wouldn't they just leave me alone?

I heard a snuffling from the other end of the room. Daisy squeezed himself through the little swinging door that separated my shop from the rest of my house. When I didn't greet him, he stuck his nose into the crook of my arm and tried to flip the whole thing on his head.

"They found us, the bastards," I told him. "They can't just write us off for the failures we were."

He cocked his head to the side.

"I didn't think they'd come *here*, of all places. We're thirty miles both ways from the nearest outpost and the airship route still hasn't been fixed. I don't know where I went wrong." I got up and made my way to my desk, pushing aside the stacked papers and the ungodly number of paperweights on it. I made the mistake of mentioning to Jehar once that I could use more paperweights, and in all the time we were together he'd gotten me at least a dozen. I wanted to get rid of them, but I was sure he would know one was missing and I didn't really want to break his heart that way.

I found the map and wiped away the fresh coffee stain on one end before carefully spreading it out. Daisy clambered into one of the chairs and placed his head on the arm, his tail wiggling the way he always did when he wanted to shake his whole rear but didn't think I was in the mood to appreciate it.

"There," I said, pointing south of the city of Ad Methas. "There's just absolutely no reason someone would go all the way out here." The village was on the shore of the lake, far away enough from the half-functioning city that just getting there was an added inconvenience on top of everything else. The only people who went out here were people with elders who refused to abandon their wyrm farms—the kind of irrational pursuit you only did out of sheer stubbornness, because wyrm leather and meat weren't popular anymore.

Daisy made the sort of whining noise that told me he would love to help if he knew how.

I massaged my temples. "I mean, I just know whatever Jehar told him won't be enough. Jehar can't even scare a cat trying to steal his dinner. What chances does he have against a bearer from Eheldeth sent to take down an outlaw? You remember your master—how persistent is he, really?"

He yawned, as if to say, *persistent enough to have found you after three years.*

"Well, I suppose," I grumbled. "He *must* have just let Jehar think he scared him off to let down his guard. And then the bastard went right to my house to warn me. Because of course he did. If Bearer Lontas isn't waiting outside that door right now…" I opened the bottom drawer of the desk, removing a bag of coin and an envelope of documents—including a copy of the loan from Ad Methas I used to buy the hut and truly make it my own. I had placed it under the name Rosha Laiag.

"Don't worry," I told Daisy. "I'm not leaving you to fend for yourself. Come on." I whistled. He followed me as I went through the back door.

The air felt like a wool scarf dipped in ice water. We were in land a little higher than the rest of the valley, which meant the air was always humid. Spring snow dusted the mountains in the distance—it would be another month or two before they melted. I took just one cloak and a walking stick, and then slipped out to the forest right beside my house. Brush obscured the path, which was just as well. If I was going to be fleeing once more, I didn't really want to look back and see the house one last time. I loved that cottage, with its crooked chimney and the stream that ran through the garden, for all that it got lonely some days. It was the first thing I could ever truly call *mine*.

Whistling to Daisy, who bounded ahead, I made my way along the road, hoping the mages—Bearer Lontas wouldn't have come alone—wouldn't chance upon me there. Even though I had a reasonable grasp on the combat arts—if my grades back in Eheldeth were any sign—out in the real world, like with anything, things were different. Defending yourself when you had no idea if the other person was also skilled in the *agan* or wore protective charms all over could backfire. One of the first things they taught in school was that many mages died young from their own mistakes. Therefore, they strongly suggested that even if you thought you could solve your problems by setting them on fire, you probably shouldn't.

"Even without a connection to the *agan*, we all have the power to do harm," a keeper once said. "You can pick up a knife and stab your husband, your wife, even your own children. You can throw a pot of boiling water at someone. As a mage, the knife you think you're wielding can just as easily cut your own throat—and you wouldn't even know it until you're bleeding on the ground."

As far as I was concerned, I was helpless out there. Bearer Lontas and his mages wouldn't confront me without heavy charms and spells surrounding their person. They were dealing with an outlaw; they'd be prepared.

I glanced at Daisy, who wagged his tail at me. "Maybe you could protect me," I jested. A distant hope. I hadn't forgotten how useless of a guard he was, and against his former masters, there was a chance he would just scamper into the distance.

I had to get out of there, and fast.

The road was clear of people, at least. A light fog had come in, though it was only afternoon. I hoped bad weather would help keep Bearer Lontas off my track. We reached the edge of a small wyrm farm. In such cold weather and at that time of the day, the wingless reptiles were probably burrowed safe underneath the soil. You could smell them if you tried hard enough—they had a sort of burnt stench, like pig shit set on fire. I could hear a woman singing from her window. Daisy's ears pricked up appreciatively.

"Rosha," Ivy called before I could open the gate. She brushed back a strand of yellow hair that had yet to turn grey and greeted me with the warmest of smiles. "How lovely of you to visit me during your business hours. Judging by the look on your face, I assume my son stopped by, and you're here to complain?"

I came up the steps and cleaned my boots on the rug before opening the door. Daisy squeezed through before the door could open wide, his entire rear shaking. Ivy always kept bacon ends for him—it was already on the plate near the kitchen.

"He did," I said as I came in.

"That promotion has gotten to his head," Ivy said with a laugh. "I'm so sorry. I tried to stop him, but you know...he thought you'd have a different opinion. You didn't say *yes*, did you?"

I blanched. "Gods, Ivy, no."

"*Good.* I can think of no better daughter-in-law than you, but let's be honest here—my son isn't exactly marriage material. Not for a good few years yet. And you! You've just started getting your business up and running."

"Marriage is the last thing on my mind." I made myself comfortable on her couch.

"I told him the same thing. In fact, I told him not to bother you about it, but you know how he is. Idea gets into his head and he's off before anyone can finish saying *think it through*." She smiled as Daisy finished licking bacon grease off the bowl and returned to us, tail still wiggling.

"How are your crops?" I asked. "Have the season's piglets been born?"

"Oh, I have my hands full these days," Ivy said, fanning herself. "And you visit more than my son, so there's that. I could really use his help, but being Chief Officer is such an enormous responsibility. I can hardly blame him. He said he can afford to send a boy or two to help here."

"That'll be a good use of his new pay."

"Isn't it? To think he'd rather spend it on a *wedding* instead." She laughed.

"I didn't come here for that, Ivy," I said at last. "I might be due for a long trip soon. I was hoping you'd take care of Daisy and keep an eye on the shop while I'm away. It might be too much—you did say you're busy."

"Never busy enough not to help you," she replied, smoothing out her skirts. "Now, come. If Daisy's as hungry as he looks, that must mean you haven't eaten yet either."

Had it been anyone else who offered, I would have said no. But a sudden whiff of Ivy's beef stew made my stomach grumble. She heard it and laughed as she walked off to set the table.

"I don't want to be a bother," I said, getting up to help her. I removed the empty dishes from the table. Two, from the looks of it, still filled with remnants of bacon and egg. I could have sworn they were still warm. As I thought, Jehar didn't even wait an hour before running off to make his proposal.

"You're never a bother. I appreciate the company, dear. We women need each other, even if we don't think we do." Ivy gave me a knowing smile.

I glanced away. She *knew* how to jab, even with her honeyed words. When I'd first arrived in that small village, I made it a point not to speak to anyone at all unless it was for business. When people in the market waved, I looked down. If they drew close to me for small talk, I walked past them. It was Ivy's insistence at sending a pot of whatever she cooked that day that made me finally break my vow of silence. The smell had been too hard to resist. Later, Jehar took to sticking around my yard, which was how I learned he'd been the one bringing them over.

"My old mother thought—well, if you wanted someone to talk to, you could always go say hi," he said, by way of greeting. "She lives just up that road. You don't *have* to go if you don't want to, of course, but…"

I pushed the memory away and settled at the table while Ivy placed a piece of bread in the middle of my bowl and then ladled stew all over it. The steam felt good on my face. I murmured a soft prayer to the Goddess Sakku, out of habit—when I was little my mother made sure I gave thanks before every meal—and started to eat.

"Who will take care of you while you're away?" Ivy asked. She didn't ask *where are you going*, the way she'd never asked me where I came from or what I was doing in a village so far away from everything else. I appreciated that about her. Life without the bitterness of my past felt good, even if a part of me knew it would end someday.

"I'll get by, Ivy."

"You can't even really cook for yourself. You should learn. It's good for everyone to learn how to cook. You shouldn't have to eat pig slop when you're all by yourself."

"It's not as if I have the time."

"Ah, well."

I was about halfway through the bread when someone knocked at the door. Daisy got up, ears pricked. He didn't bark, which was odd.

Ivy started to answer it. I grabbed her wrist and shook my head.

The knocking came again, and harder now.

"Out the back," Ivy mouthed. She went towards the door to pick up a shawl and handed it to me.

I nodded. Wrapping the shawl over my head, I left.

CHAPTER 7

ON THE RUN

Ivy's back door led straight through the stone fences that separated the wymrling fences from each other. Wyrms ate their young, I was told, so one of the more excruciating tasks of caring for them was making sure you knew exactly when the eggs would hatch—you couldn't move them *before*, or you would risk addling them—and then rounding the pink, blind, mud-covered babies away from their cannibalistic parents. Jehar took me to one of their yearly roundups when we were still together, and it was exactly as unpleasant as it sounded. Shirtless men and boys all piling through the mud, wrestling with wyrms that flopped around like giant carps, all laughing with their mud-streaked faces. I wasn't even sure how he talked me into it. Something about the warm weather, or the ducks, or how reading so much in the dark when it was so nice and sunny outside would surely make me go blind.

There weren't as much wyrmlings this year as that last one. They gathered in lumps against the gates, peering through the bars like puppies in the hopes I brought food for them. I grumbled an apology and showed my empty hands. Wyrms *didn't* eat people, I was told, but I wasn't going to take my chances. I dodged out of there as soon as I could.

I climbed up a small hill of apple trees and finally reached the road again. I was panting. It was more activity than I was used to, and a part of me was starting to get angry again. There was the uncertainty, too, of whether I was going to get to go back to the home I'd built for myself.

I imagined what my father would say over such a thing. Just the thought of the smirk at the corner of his lips was enough to remind me why I made the choices I did. One thing for sure: I wasn't going to return to *his* abode.

I saw a figure on horseback and turned to flee the other way.

"Stop, Rosha!"

Jehar's voice. I recognized Roan, Jehar's grey-spotted gelding, as he came tearing down the road. He pulled to a stop right in front of me and made a great show of turning his horse in a half-circle.

"Thank the gods I found you," Jehar said. "Gods—I led him *right* to you. I didn't notice until someone told me he went straight for your house. I'm glad you went to Mother."

"He's still chasing after me," I replied.

"Get up," he said, offering his hand. "Roan can carry us both."

"Not for long."

"We can still make it to the city. Quickly."

I hesitated, and then took his hand. He swung me up the saddle, setting me front. He grabbed the reins and positioned both arms around me.

"Don't take this opportunity to get handsy," I hissed.

"No problem. If you swing too far to any one side, I'll just let you fall." He dug his heels into the horse and set him off on a gallop.

We rode in relative silence. Jehar knew I wasn't much of a talker, and this seemed to be something he had—*finally*—come to terms with. It wasn't the case when I first met him. When I met him, he seemed to almost take offense to me not wanting to have a conversation that lasted over thirty seconds. He would change topics to pique my interest and prod me about what I thought about the thing he just brought up even if it was the first time, I'd heard of it and had yet to form an opinion. Afterwards, he figured it was him—that I must find him dull and uncultured. He started trying to read books and making even more conversation than usual on topics he wouldn't have given the time of the day before. His fellow guards made fun of him for it, which only seemed to fuel his desire. It was oddly sweet, but…I was really glad when it dawned on him that I just didn't like to talk to other people. I could go days on end without speaking to anyone—the drone of conversation I am forced to take part in gives me a pounding headache. The realization seemed to kill him, but at least he stopped trying.

The next town was about an hour's ride away. We were still well within wyrm farm territory, which also happened to be hay and cranberry-field territory. More of the latter than the rest. Fields of red, as far as the eye could see, just waiting to be flooded for the harvest. Farther in the distance were windmills, powered unpredictably with wind. Which I realize is an odd thing to say, but this was Dageis. To see things *not* powered by the *agan* was as unbelievable as a third eye. If I travelled farther out in the region and told people, they would laugh.

But the *agan* fabric around Ad Methas was just that difficult. Mages put up spells but couldn't get the windmills to turn on a predictable enough schedule for the farmers. Not that wind was predictable itself, but at least they didn't just suddenly stop working, requiring a very expensive visit from a certified mage to get them running again. The farmers eventually gave up on the *agan*-powered ones and resorted to constructing more windmills instead.

We got off at an inn. Jehar tied Roan outside, removed his saddle, and began rubbing him down. A boy appeared with a big, toothy grin. "I'll do that for you for a coin, and get him some water and food besides," he said happily.

Jehar threw him two and winked. "Get him back safe and there's another in it for you."

Beaming, the boy led the horse away.

"And I'm buying *you* dinner." He turned to me with the expression that told me it was useless to argue. My traitorous stomach agreed. It grumbled again, reminding me of the unfinished stew back at Ivy's.

I sighed. "As long as you don't think it's an engagement dinner."

"I heard you loud and clear, Rosha. It's a *no*. A man's got to have some rejections in his life." He grinned sheepishly.

"I'm not sure that's anything to be proud about," I mumbled.

"Either way, you'll like it here. They have the best lettuce wraps."

"I think you've told me about this place before," I said as we strode in through the doors.

"I did. You didn't want to go."

"It's an hour's ride from home, Jehar."

"So, you need to be running for your life before you'd agree to be seen out in public with me. I can take that." He whistled to a waiter.

"Table for two?" the waiter asked.

"By the fire," Jehar said. "It's cold out there." He flashed his badge.

The waiter bowed and led us to the end of the room.

"I worry this Chief Officer thing is getting to your head," I said when we found our table. "I mean, you really should be *working* today, shouldn't you?"

"Mayor gave me the day off."

"Ah. The assumption being that we would be celebrating?"

"Of course, Rosha. But given the circumstances…" He sighed. "I'm still glad I get to spend time with you. Even, you know, as just friends."

"We *are* friends," I said, taking the menu from the waiter and flicking it open. "When did I ever say we weren't?"

"Less now than ever before, though," Jehar replied. He cleared his throat and waited for the waiter to be out of earshot. "You're leaving town, aren't you? For good?"

"I don't know."

"Be straight with me. That man. Why is he looking for you?"

I read the items on the menu first, to give myself time to think. I didn't want to lie to Jehar. It was like pretending to throw a stick for a very eager dog. Just imagining the disappointment on his face filled me with guilt. The man meant well, for the most part. He was the sort of person who made friends with everyone because he couldn't imagine a world where people hated each other and if he was going to help make it a better place, so be it. During rains, he would be the first in line to carry sandbags and stop people's houses from flooding. It didn't really come as a surprise that he would be Chief Officer after only being a village guard for five years. People loved Jehar, deservedly so. He could be a little annoying, but he was hard *not* to like.

Which made me, the woman who was about to lie to him, probably the vilest person in the entire empire. It at least made me feel like garbage. I cleared my throat, testing the story against my thoughts first before I finally opened my mouth. "I believe this might be an old class-mate who thought himself better than me."

"A him?" Jehar raised an eyebrow.

"Yes," I said. "You could say he's my rival. We competed in every class, every subject, and…"

I'm not much of a storyteller, to be honest. Nothing compared to my father, for whom making things up was second nature. He always seemed to have a ready tale on hand, something equally believable but breathtaking. He could have people's sympathies in half an hour. Enosh was quick his thoughts, knew how to make the lies flow from his tongue like water from a stream. A gift more valuable than the connection he had to the *agan*, so faint it might as well be useless.

I lacked the flair, which might very well be because I didn't enjoy it. I had to draw from my memories. I couldn't just make up an enemy on the spot without admitting the true story, so I told Jehar about a real one. Felan, my rival, as nearly everyone who went to school with us would be happy to say. He did have it out for me from the beginning. I was eleven when they finally brought me in to Eheldeth, skipping ahead of the waiting list because I *had* injured a man and the council realized I needed to be locked and chained as fast as possible. Sending me to prison would cause an outcry amongst the many (by then) friends my father had made with the merchants' guild, so they stuck me in with the thirteen-year-olds.

Felan, who was only ten, was there with them, no doubt due to some strings his own father had pulled. He was at the top of the class already. My presence threatened the little kingdom he had carved out for himself. Things became worse when he realized I didn't come from an old Dageian family—that my father, in fact, was a Gorenten merchant who just happened to know the right people (or person, as it were). I don't think I ever found out what he thought about me growing up in Jin-Sayeng, either, but I'm sure it must have added to his irritation.

He was never outright cruel; he didn't have to be. All he had to do, for instance, was question anything I did—the spells I designed, my test scores, my attitude during evaluation—and the keepers would be on me like flies on a slab of raw meat on a hot day. He *wanted* to be the best, to be the only one heralded for being unusually young and gifted. He never had to say it to my face. The arrogance wafted off him like a second layer of stench.

I was, perhaps, justified in the lie. It could have been true. He *could* have gone on to graduate before making it his life's goal to ruin my reputation. He'd done it often enough in the past, after all. But it was unfair to lie to Jehar, who listened with rapture, his hand gripping his mug of beer so tightly I thought he would actually crush it. He immediately hated this boy, this fictional man, as if he had seen these atrocities with his very eyes.

It was most definitely unfair for Felan, who never made it to those final exams. He just…disappeared one day. The keepers said he went on an indefinite vacation, with the kind of listless eyes and quivering jaw that made it clear they were lying. The others blamed me, but even though I certainly didn't bury his headless corpse in the fields, I could almost agree with them.

I do think he died.

I think it was my fault.

I stopped talking and focused on the food in front of me. "I'm sorry, Jehar," I finally said. "I don't think I can talk about it anymore. It's…too much."

"It's fine," Jehar said, reaching for my hands. He sandwiched it between his. "You don't have to say anything. I understand. Your life is in danger, and I'm here for you. I've always been here for you."

If he knew the truth, even a man as kind and honourable as Jehar would be compelled to hand me over to the authorities. Protecting me would have far-reaching consequences that would spread throughout the village, and his mother too. So, I let the lie linger in the air. Later, when the meal was over and we realized it was too dark for him to return on the road, I let him take me to bed. I let him kiss me in the dark, knowing full well we didn't see eye-to-eye about the arrangement. Love and passion were meaningless, but I could use the distraction.

I wasn't as good a liar as my father, but it grated me to know I had room to learn.

CHAPTER 8

A FATHER'S FEARS

I made it clear to Jehar that one more night together would not change my mind—not about marrying him or being with him or imagining any sort of future together. He seemed to understand. When I woke up, he was gone, leaving only a faint scent and a warm imprint on the bed we'd shared.

I prepared to leave. I figured I might get the bank on my side if I made a complaint about a harassment over a mistaken identity. You wouldn't be able to get away with it in the big cities, but Ad Methas was more a town than a city, and I knew the payments I made were more valuable than the worthless piece of lakeshore property. Perhaps I could convince them to send someone over and distract the mages long enough for me to put some distance between us. "Rosha Laiag," I was ready to say over and over again, jabbing the name on the documents. "*Not* Kirosha Tar'elian. They've got the wrong woman." It was as good a plan as any.

"Oh, you're awake," the innkeeper called as I stepped through the door. There was a tremble in her voice. "I was just about to go there and wake you myself, but your companion—your, er, man—told me not to. There was a disturbance this morning, down at the tavern. He was getting breakfast and…he saw someone. I believe they knew each other —they were arguing. Then he asked me not to wake you up and went outside with this man."

"How long ago was this?"

"Not that long. Umm—I think they're going to walk all the way to the fields for a duel. If you want to stop them, I'd go now if I were you."

A duel. Bearer Lontas had caught up to us and Jehar, somehow, had challenged him to a duel.

This is it. You can slip away undetected, and with any luck Jehar will kill him and no one will come looking for him. The Dageian Empire was one of the few places in the continent where duels were still a thing. They were proud of it, too, so as long as it wasn't a mage-fight that made things explode or ruined crops or called down monsters from the abyss. But a good old-fashioned, sword-on-sword battle, or maybe even a gunfight, between two consenting adults…

Jehar *would* kill him, too, mage or not. He was good at that sort of thing. My problem seemed to have solved itself.

But something else told me not to leave it there. *What if the mage is just as good? What if Jehar gets hurt?* An Eheldeth-sent bearer wasn't just nobody—he'd know how to fight in return. And if Jehar got hurt, Ivy would never forgive me. I didn't want to marry Jehar, but that didn't mean I wanted to see him dead. I turned back to the innkeeper. "Which fields?"

She gave what would have been vague directions in other circumstances but having just passed the three windmills in a row she indicated, I knew exactly where they'd gone. Jehar would have picked the place, too. The man was a romantic. If he thought he was going to die, he would do it right amid a field of gently wafting golden grains, drenched in blood while clasping a handkerchief with my name on it. I had never given him such a handkerchief, of course, and with his luck, he'd just as likely be floating facedown in a flooded cranberry field, pecked to bits by birds. Poor, stupid fool. I shouldn't have gotten him involved.

I ran a little faster.

The sky *was* alarmingly bright, and I saw enough people along the way that I wondered if maybe both men decided not to go through with their duel and just talk about their differences. Even if a duel wasn't illegal, people rarely liked cleaning dead bodies off their fields. They were bound to be stopped.

I reached the road shadowed by the three windmills. Annoyance had given way to worry. I wondered if I could use magic to track them. It'd lead the official to me, though, and I wasn't keen on throwing away my chances to escape, either. I wanted to save Jehar *and* get away. One or the either wasn't acceptable.

Birds started screeching in the sky. Crows, unhappy with strangers in their nesting grounds. I crossed a small wooden bridge over the ditch and reached the edge of a wheat field, exactly like I'd predicted.

The flash of sunlight glinted over the edge of a broadsword. Jehar was already engaged in a sword fight with the stranger.

I remember being in a battle once—a shard of memory from the remnants of my past, long before my parents brought me to Dageis. A fight between men intent on killing each other doesn't last very long. But a duel was different. For both parties to agree to it meant there was something else at stake—something worth risking death for. Some people want to think it's about honour; I always thought it was about humiliation. You agreed to a duel because you wanted to show what a coward your opponent was.

I saw Jehar fall back, the his tunic red from a cut along his chest. Not a deadly wound—not yet. But his opponent was more skilled—the man held the sword with the confidence of someone who had killed before. That Jehar was alive meant that he was giving him a chance to back away. Which meant that Jehar was the one who pushed him to this duel in the first place.

"Have you had enough?" the man said. That voice…

He angled his head away from the sunlight, which removed the shadows that blocked his features. I thought I felt my heart stop beating.

"Papa?" I called.

I already had a father when Enosh came into my life. Kefier was my father's only brother, younger than him by a few years. I didn't know the particular details—I didn't know why Kefier was the one who welcomed me into the world while *he* was nowhere to be found, and I never really bothered to find out. Why did it matter? Kefier was with my mother when she gave birth, the one who braved sleepless nights to change my diapers when I was an infant, who rubbed my back with liniment and sang me to sleep, who told me stories of both our people, of Gorent and Jin-Sayeng, so that I would never be alone.

The worst part about the last three years was not seeing him. I missed his company, for all that I know my concerns vexed him. I missed his face. We shared the same features with Enosh—the shape of our nose, the shape of our chins—except his hair was a touch lighter. It had a tinge more rust under the sun, nearly bronze. And his mouth different. It didn't have the sardonic turn at the edges of his lips. Even when he was angry, you could tell he wasn't waiting to drop scathing words with the sole intent of hurting. He would rage for a moment and then it would be gone, forgotten in the blink of an eye.

I had hoped my longing for his presence was just a phase. I was too old for stories, too old for lullabies, and much, much too old for a father. But seeing him now after I had maybe given up the idea of ever seeing him again had the unfortunate effect of making me choke up in tears. Why was it so hard to grow up? In the presence of the man who raised me, it seemed all too easy to turn into a little girl once more.

He turned his head at the sound of my voice, which was a mistake. Jehar recovered mid-tumble and dashed forward.

"Jehar, no!" I screamed.

Jehar slammed into Kefier's side. Kefier grimaced and dropped his sword. As the blade clattered to the ground, he balled up his fists and struck Jehar on the face—hard. Though Kefier was a smaller man, the force was enough to knock Jehar back. Jehar stumbled a second time, falling on his backside with his nose all smashed.

I rushed to them, yanking the sword out of Jehar's hand before he could recover. "Rosha," he managed. "Don't stop me now—I almost had him!"

"He was taking it easy on you, you idiot," I snapped back. I felt like punching him myself. But as terrible as he looked, he was still alive, so I stepped over him and ran up to hug Kefier.

He looked surprised. "I thought you didn't want to see me," he said ruefully, before pressing his hands on my back to return the embrace. "You made it really hard to find you, you know."

"I thought you were someone else."

"Someone come to kill you?" he asked, now looking at my face. "You know better than to deal with your problems alone."

"Papa—"

"I'm not going to yell." He hugged me a second time. "I've missed you, girl. Look at you. You're all grown up! You should have come to me first. I thought you would. I waited a very long time. But you look well— I'm glad for that. I thought the worst for a bit but then your mother said—"

"Can someone explain to me what's going on?" Jehar grumbled from the ground.

"Ah, the little shit," Kefier said, crossing his arms. "I *told* you I didn't want a duel."

"She was scared for her life," Jehar snarled. "What was I supposed to do?" Beyond his smashed-up face, I could see he was embarrassed. His great show at playing the hero had been foiled.

"Ask her what *she* wanted, maybe?"

Jehar stared at him.

Kefier rubbed the back of his head. "Let's try this again. I'm going to ignore all the blood." He held out his hand.

"This is my stepfather, Kefier," I told Jehar. "I didn't realize it was him. All of this precaution was for nothing. Couldn't you have *told* people who you were and spared us all this trouble?" I added, glaring at Kefier.

"I thought you didn't want to see me," Kefier repeated. "Then he showed up and told me to stay away from you, so I figured I was right, and you sent him to make me go away. I wasn't going to *kill* him, if that's what you were worried about."

I sighed. "He clearly didn't have the same reservations."

Kefier laughed. "He wasn't doing a great job. Better men than him have tried." He nodded at Jehar. "That footwork needs work. If you have time, I can teach you. Big man like you need to learn to control yourself better."

"No one's teaching anyone anything," I said. "Let's get him cleaned up and take him back to his mother. She'll be worried sick."

"You heard the lady." Kefier took Jehar's arm and helped him up. "I've got my horse up at the inn. Yours too, I'm guessing?"

"This has been a waste of time," I murmured as Kefier strode ahead, leaving me with the limping Jehar.

"It's good, right?" Jehar asked. "That means you're not going to leave town after all." He tried to move his head and cringed in pain. "Though your father saying he wasn't trying to kill me is a touch too far. I can't feel my toes. I think he cracked half my bones with one blow."

I stepped on his foot. He yowled. "Proved you wrong," I said.

"You're still mad at me. I get it."

"Starting a duel on my behalf—like that's going to solve anything. We could have gotten into more trouble. You could have hurt my father. If anything had happened to him, I'd have snapped your neck myself."

Jehar lowered his head. "I'm sorry, all right?"

"Anyway, if he *was* trying to kill you, you'd already be dead. What the hell did you tell him?"

"I said that as the man who loves you, I wasn't going to let him besmirch your honour…"

I sighed so loudly he stopped.

"What does your father do for a living, anyway? I didn't expect him to be so fast, or that strong." There was a note of admiration in his tone. Give it to Jehar to admire someone he wanted to kill minutes ago. The man wasn't capable of holding grudges—at least, as far as I knew. There was still the matter of how he would react to my secrets.

"He used to work at a blacksmith, but these days, he's…" I suppose I had lied enough already and decided to come clean this time. "He's a mercenary," I said, before mumbling something at the end.

"A what?"

"A mercenary commander."

Jehar's eyes looked like they would fall out of his head.

"There's a reason I don't like to talk about my family," I continued.

"Is it any mercenary company I've heard of?"

"Probably not. It's not based in Dageis."

"Most mercenary companies aren't. Dageis has too many regulations. But—" He caught the look on my face and sniffed. "Right. I'm Chief Officer now. I shouldn't talk like this."

I wiped a streak of blood off his chin. "You're a boy who just got his face beaten bloody by someone almost twice his age. You shouldn't talk at all."

He grinned. "I'll get new scars. It'll look good, won't it?"

"I'll remember how you got them. They won't."

"Are you two talking or walking?" Kefier called. "Because you know you can do both. I hear it makes you get to your destination faster." He laughed at his own joke. Hearing his voice made a cold spot in my heart grow warm again. It made me wish, for a moment, that I could tell him I missed him, too.

Later, back at home, Kefier helped himself to a cup of wine from my stash while he used Daisy as a footstool. "What a lovely dog," he said, for what was probably the tenth time. "I'm surprised you remembered our old Daisy. That dog…she was a keeper." He clicked his tongue and reached down to stroke Daisy's chin. The brown dog, already enamoured with him, wagged his bushy tail and rolled over some more.

"It was the only name I could think of at the time," I said. "He's a mage's dog. A terrible guard. I took him along when I journeyed out here, for company."

Kefier straightened himself. "They don't name their dogs in Eheldeth?"

"He's not exactly from the school. I'm not sure where to begin."

"Ah," he said. "More secrets?"

I didn't answer, and he fell silent. I could see him watching me slowly, the way he always did when I was a child. That was one of the things that made him different from Enosh. He looked at me like he was still trying to find the little girl he carried on his shoulders—always this expression of delight and disbelief. Enosh…hardly noticed me at all. "I know the years have been hard for you," he said. "We haven't really been much of a family lately, have we?"

"Not since Jin-Sayeng," I said in a low voice.

He winced, as if I'd struck him. "That was a long time ago. I wasn't expecting you'd feel that way. Haven't we tried our best? I mean, I know there were some difficulties…"

"You mean with your brother?" I sniffed. "You can say his name. I won't explode."

"I know how he could be." Kefier grimaced. "I grew up with the man. He'll treat you like gold one day and then forget you exist for weeks, even months. I've learned not to take it personally. It's not *you*…"

"Papa," I said carefully. "We've had these talks before."

His eyes gleamed. They were a greyish blue under a certain light. A touch of *agan*, though he expressed none of the gifts himself. But it was supposed to run very strongly in our family, especially along the Gorenten side. "Yes, we have."

"You're not going to make me change my mind about him, or about leaving all of this to come home. This *is* home now. This life…" I glanced at the humble cottage, at the things I'd amassed in a short three years. "This life is all I have, and it means something to me. I don't regret what I did. Eheldeth wasn't going to give me anything worth a damn."

Kefier didn't reply. He had turned to scratching Daisy's belly. Another five minutes and I wouldn't be able to peel the dog off him. It was funny how years could pass and some things remained the same. All of this could have been ripped off a page from my childhood, in any of the homes we had shared over the years. Enosh could wear a hundred glamour faces, I could change my name a thousand times, but Papa would still be the way he was, as solid and steady as a rock. Without him, our family would have been in shambles long ago.

"Do you remember when you were little and we would get those puppies from the market?" he asked, offhandedly.

"You mean the puppies *you* would get from the market to bring home for me even though I didn't like dogs?"

"She doesn't like dogs, she says," Kefier told Daisy. "Do you believe the lady? I don't. Look how fat you are."

"You're just about to compare Enosh to a dog, aren't you?"

"If only I was so eloquent with metaphors. I only meant that some-times you think you don't like someone—"

"It's not that I don't like him. I *hate* him."

"—but if they don't come back after you let them out to piddle, you're going to put on a shawl and walk out in the middle of the night to fetch them from the pig trough, anyway."

I closed my eyes for a few moments, trying to gather my thoughts. "What," I finally said, "did he do this time?"

"Who knows what Enosh ever does?" Kefier asked. "Whatever it was, he's gone. He hasn't come home in over six months."

I stared at him, wondering if this was a joke.

"We need your help, Rosha," he said. "You're the only one I haven't gone to yet. We need you to help us find him."

CHAPTER 9

A DAUGHTER'S REGRETS

I stared back at him in disbelief. He didn't come to take me home. I felt a pang of girlish impudence. Three years without trying to reach me, and he came in search of a man he detested from the bottom of his heart. I knew he meant it when he said he was afraid I didn't want to be found, but I couldn't help but see the glaring irony.

"You're joking," I said, after an unbearably long silence. "You must be. Oh, I know the part about him being *gone* has to be true. Have you and Mother paid a visit to his latest lovers?"

"We…er, we have," Kefier replied. He scratched the grizzled beard along his cheeks. "It's exactly as uncomfortable as it sounds like."

"Did you check their closets? Maybe they stuffed his body in a trunk and tossed it in the river. Maybe their husbands did. You know he has a gift for pissing people off."

"Would that they have made our job so much easier," Kefier grumbled. "There's only one at the moment, as it happens," he said in a louder voice. "Surprising, I know. Maybe he *is* getting old. She's staying with Portia. She brought it to our awareness in the first place. Enosh not coming home for weeks, months at a time—that's normal. But his lover said he missed several appointments in a row. One was a business meeting that cost him a contract. Enosh was never that sloppy, especially if money is involved."

"So, his body may very well be in the bottom of the river anyway," I said. "Good riddance, I say. I hope he didn't give the fish a stomach-ache."

Kefier's brow furrowed. "You can't possibly mean that."

72

"With all due respect, Papa—"

"No," Kefier said, growing serious. "I didn't teach you to be like this. I didn't teach you to hold grudges."

"It's not a grudge. It's a lifetime commitment."

"We need you, Rosha," Kefier repeated.

"Why?" I asked, my voice rising a little. "What in the world could you possibly need *me* for? You said it yourself. You checked everywhere. You probably have more contacts than I do."

"Not when it comes to mages." He shooed the dog away so he could look me in the eye. "As far as I can tell, he was last seen making an arrangement with a mage from Eheldeth. We don't know who or what for, but we could find out together."

"I'm not going to leave my shop and the life I've built for myself just for him."

"Do it for me," Kefier said.

My lips twitched. "That's not fair." When he didn't answer, I got up and slammed my hands on the table. "He's treated you worse than he's ever treated me and you're still—the way you are! You act like you're his second-in-command, his right hand, like that's good for anything but wiping himself with? Why, Papa? He doesn't have anything on you. I've reached the age of majority in Dageis. As far as they're concerned, I'm a citizen. You don't need him to protect me anymore. I can protect myself."

"What about your brothers?" Kefier asked.

I sat down again, breathing slowly.

"You've forgotten that Dageis recognizes them as Enosh's sons," Kefier continued.

"But they're not," I pointed out. "Are they? Take them home, Papa. The war is over in Jin-Sayeng, and they don't *need* Dageis like I did. Like you said I did."

"Jin-Sayeng is under Yeshin the Butcher's rule," Kefier said. "That is not a place I want your brothers to grow up in. Your mother agrees."

"Then take them back to Lon Basden, or further south. Take them back to our ancestral lands. That's where you'd rather be, right? Fresh air, mountains, the sea. The farms are yielding good crops, and you still have your mercenaries. By all the gods, you even have a house there!"

"We can always leave Dageis," he agreed. "But then what?"

"Then you live your life," I said. "Marry Mother. Her marriage to Enosh is only recognized here. Outside of Dageis? You're free. I know you've always wanted to be hers as much as you want her to be yours. Isn't it easier? To be able to call her your *wife* any time you wanted, to not have to deal with this farce of having another man pretend to be her husband, to stop hiding. Your sons will be yours."

"That all sounds lovely."

"Then why, Papa?"

The muscles along his jaw tightened. "Because this isn't about me or what I want." He folded his hands together. "This is about family. I have a feeling whatever Enosh had gotten himself mixed up in isn't going to end with him. You're *his* daughter. To protect your brothers, we've had them registered as *his* sons. That doesn't go away just because we leave Dageis, and if we seek shelter in the Gorenten peninsula, well...Dageis still has an interest in those lands as far as they're concerned, and nothing can stop them from going in and wreaking havoc if they want. If we don't find him first, they're going to find us, and...I don't know how I'm going to protect you all. I'm just one man, and all this mage business is beyond my comprehension." The desperation bubbled out of his voice like a dying man's cough.

"You're hiding something," I said.

Kefier made a fist, which he gently struck against the edge of the desk. "It's...three weeks ago, I was in Chylos, investigating leads on Enosh's whereabouts. He's set up a shop there last year. Small place—sells nothing but travelling clothes. I sent the staff home and was closing up when someone dropped a letter. There was no address on it, nothing except a newspaper article that ran years ago when that boy went missing. Do you remember him?"

"Felan," I said. "I remember that article. It said I bullied him to his death." I wasn't sure if it was the article that started the rumours, or the rumours that led to the article being written in the first place. I'd read it one time before forcing myself to forget everything. The story painted me as a malicious little girl who couldn't stand having someone be better than her. And poor Felan, that rich man's son, the light of his father's life and the only thing he has left of his beloved dead wife, was only doing his best to get by. The administration at Eheldeth never even tried to protect my name—when every student in the halls was reading the damn thing, it just looked away.

"Everyone knew it was a lie. Putting the blame on a fourteen-year-old girl! Enosh had the editor sacked. I bought all the copies I could find and burnt them. Do you recall?"

I gave a small smile. As far as actions went, that last one had been useless, but I remember feeling a smug sort of satisfaction watching his mercenaries light bonfires in my name. They had always cared about me more than the teachers who were supposed to guide me through the years. "So many connections…and yet he can't magic himself back out of nowhere," I mused.

"There was something scribbled in the back of the article, where your picture was. It…gave this address."

I felt myself grow cold.

"Whoever took your father knows where you are," Kefier said. "And they know the name you've gone under. From the look on your face, I'm guessing no one else is supposed to know, either. You left Eheldeth before you graduated, which makes you an outlaw. You're not supposed to be running loose in the empire, are you, let alone setting up shops?"

"No," I replied weakly.

It was annoying how well he could read me. He could play the gentle, supportive father long enough for me to cough out my secrets without a second thought. He walked up towards me now, like a hound who had just cornered his prey. "Why exactly did you leave Eheldeth, Rosha?"

"I don't know where to start, Papa," I said. "All I know is that I can never go back."

There are few things worse than admitting you don't exactly have it all together. One of those would be if I was forced to admit it all to my father's face—not that Enosh would have ever asked how I was doing at all. If things had been the other way around, he would have simply barged into my home and demanded—though he liked to pretend he didn't *demand* things, not really—I offer my assistance. Just like that.

He would have killed Jehar without blinking, too.

Maybe admitting all of this to my stepfather, who had supported me without question, even when he didn't understand half the things I had to go through. Both men could turn me back into a child at a moment's notice—two entirely different girls reacting to each man's presence in her own unique way. Father turned me into a girl who existed just to defy him. It carried me all the way through Eheldeth, that golden place, that rotten place.

But Papa was different. Papa reminded me of being helpless, relying on someone like him to protect me. Which was easier to accept if you were six and you knew nothing of life. Papa was just always there—as steady and stalwart as the sun, and even if the clouds blocked it, you knew it was only a matter of time before it shone again. To admit my weakness to him now was to accept that I had, in fact, made a mistake.

And maybe he was thinking that I needed him to fix it for me. I didn't, of course, but it filled me with shame.

I didn't speak. I stared at the fire, and he knew better than to press me. "Think on it," was all he said, followed by, "Good night." He moved to kiss me on the head, the way he always used to when I was little, but I think it caught him off-guard that I wasn't that girl anymore. He scratched the back of his head, placed a careful hand on my shoulder instead, and went straight for the guest room.

I fell asleep in my chair, one hand on Daisy's head. When I woke up, it was dawn, and a part of me thought Papa must have left already. I couldn't blame him. I'd given him the worst welcome a daughter could. I could only hope his other children—his trueborn sons—wouldn't grow up to be as much of a disappointment.

But then I heard the sound of an ax splitting firewood in half. I went out into the chilly dawn and saw him already hard at work, as if he hadn't aged a day. It brought me back to my childhood in Jin-Sayeng, where the winters weren't so cold. Even then, the stove always needed fuel, even if it was just to heat a pot of stew. Even back then, Kefier was always restless. I remember Mother telling me once that out of all the things Kefier hated, it was sitting still. Some of that must have rubbed off on me.

"Already bored?" I asked, sitting on the steps near the doorway.

"Do you know how much ribbing I get any time I gain a bit of weight around the belly?" he asked.

"From Mother, or from your mercenaries?"

"From both," he coughed. "Though your mother, especially." He paused, wiping sweat from his brow before gesturing at the woodshed. "I heard winters here can be long, so I thought I'd just get you started."

"It's still spring, Papa. Jehar always makes sure I have firewood, anyway."

"Well, I busted his nose pretty badly. Boy will be seeing double for a while."

"He's as stubborn as they come. He'll be up and about in no time."

Kefier gave a crooked smile. "Is he the reason you want to stay here?"

I rolled my eyes. "Of course not."

"Boy might have been convinced otherwise. He said something about marriage."

"You should have beaten him up some more, maybe knocked some sense into him." I rubbed my hands together, breathing warm air into them. "What do you want for breakfast? I can put together something.

Eggs, probably? If I don't burn them first. I should really learn to cook for company." I made a sound. "I...I thought you left."

"Why would I leave without saying goodbye?"

"Because I don't want to go with you, Papa. My place is here."

He nodded. "It really is a nice place. You've done well for yourself. I always knew you would." Then he gave the smallest of smiles. "But don't you think it's a little...lonely? If you're not staying for the boy, then..."

I rubbed my arms and looked away. "I needed a bit of loneliness after Eheldeth."

He got up to pick up another log. "You had that. It's why I didn't come after you when I did. Your mother wanted me to, but I knew you too well. I knew you would have never forgiven me if I didn't let you have some time alone."

"She could have come herself," I grumbled.

He made the kind of frown that told me he didn't really want to step between me and my mother if he could help it. "I know you've had a tough relationship," he said at last.

"She left us," I said. "To be with *him*. To marry *him*. And then at the last moment she decided it was all a big mistake and returned to you. As if we were dolls she could play with however she wanted. I don't know how you ever forgave her."

"I love her. It's not a hard leap."

"She ruined our life."

"She misses you. That's all that matters." He turned away, his hand on the handle of the hatchet, as if he didn't really want to look at me while he talked. "None of this is ideal. I'm sorry I couldn't protect you from it when you were little. I'm sorry I couldn't keep things the way it was before all of this. We were just trying to keep you alive. But you're not little anymore."

"I'm not," I agreed. "And I can make the decision not to be part of this mess anymore. Don't feel the need to protect her from this. Did you ask her to marry him and bring me to Dageis? You didn't. I remember how infuriated you were."

"I was, and I let it go. Your mother was terrified for you."

"She was terrified *of* me."

"Given how they treat those with mage-powers in Jin-Sayeng, I can't exactly blame her." He sighed and placed the hatchet back on the log. "Gods, I don't know if your stubbornness takes after Enosh or her."

"You've been good to me, Papa," I told him. "But I don't belong there anymore. I chose not to be a part of it anymore."

"We all miss you," he grunted, as if saying it more to himself than me. "Your brothers—they've asked for you almost every day since we heard the news. They always looked forward to your visits, you know. You won't even recognize them anymore. Haro's about this tall now—" He held his hand up to below his chest. "—and Ryo…"

Kefier paused, as if to compose himself. He quietly stacked the wood he'd chopped before walking back to the house. I got the sense that we weren't going to have breakfast after all. He lingered at the door.

"I understand you want to be alone," he continued. "Enosh—Enosh was like that, too. Didn't think he wanted or needed anyone. It's why he abandoned your mother and you when he did. Why he abandoned *me*, more often than not, when we were boys. It's not that I've forgotten, or that I'm not carrying a grudge over everything. Or that I don't know— even if I don't have all the answers—what being here in the empire has done to you. You never had to tell me how hard it was. I saw it in your eyes every time you came home for vacation. You wanted me to step in and take you away from Eheldeth, even when you'd convinced yourself you wanted nothing else. And I would have done it if I knew where to take you, if I knew how I could make it go away, if I knew another land that could give you a home without having to prove yourself."

He drew a quick breath, pausing as if to wait for me to have my say. But when I kept my silence, his voice dropped to a near-whisper. "You're not the only one who's ever had to live in his shadow, Rosha. Don't repeat the same mistakes he's made. We're family. That's not always good enough, I know, but for all how messed up we are we've never actually hurt each other, have we? There's a line we've never crossed. We've always been on the side where we may all not like one another very much but we'll do whatever it takes for each other. It's a good line. I'd like to keep it that way. But if you don't come home then you're deliberately telling me that you don't care about making amends or putting your brothers in harm's way. I don't know how I can deal with that. If this is the kind of person you've become…"

The disappointment in his voice was plain enough. Kefier always thought I could do better, even when I was sure I couldn't.

But I didn't argue. I didn't do anything at all. I listened to him pack his things while I stared at the sky, wondering if this was the end. If I let him leave, I knew he wouldn't come back. At the end of the day, he was just as stubborn as the rest of us, and in many ways perhaps more so. It wasn't Mother or Enosh I took after the most; it was him.

When he reached the door, I made up my mind.

"Wait," I said.

He turned around, a look of hope crossing his expression. There was no way I could deny him then—the man had sacrificed too much for me.

"I'll go with you," I told him. "I can't promise anything, or that I'll be able to do much, but…"

The smile on his face settled like a burst of sunlight. "That was all I ever asked for."

CHAPTER 10
TRIASSA

Kefier bought two more horses from Ad Methas to carry both me and my things, which was entirely too much, given I wasn't planning on carrying more than a change of clothes and my documents. But he was insistent that I have my luxuries, even though he blew the thought of what those were out of proportion. He'd forgotten I'd done my fair share of travelling, with all the discomforts that came with it.

Taking Daisy with us this time—that was a luxury, too. I couldn't bear the thought of telling Ivy, though, so I simply left her a note on my table, along with instructions on what to tell the bank if I missed next month's payment. She had a key to my house—she would check, eventually. But I didn't think I'd be gone that long. I'd stay a day or two, long enough to point out that Enosh really *did* just screw up his affairs and there was nothing we could do about it, and then be back on my way.

We left in the afternoon. It was strange how I really didn't feel as sorry as I was two nights before, when I thought I was being chased away from it. I wasn't running away this time. But I wasn't going *home*, either.

Home is a strange word to me. If you asked me where that was, I'd say *Jin-Sayeng* without even thinking about it. Jin-Sayeng, where I hadn't been in fifteen years. Ruled by a tyrant now, so Kefier said, and yet the knowledge that it was being run to the ground by cruel men did little to remove the memories of warmth and love and a time when I never had to ask where I truly belonged. Even as the details faded, a part of me believed I could still go back to that tiny house in the middle of that crowded street and simply pick up where we left off.

A wistful dream that could never come to pass. That house burned to the ground a long time ago. To be precise: a dragon came and set the entire city aflame, and our house was in the neighbourhood where that first rain of fire came pouring down. The irony is that if we never left, we'd all be dead. My longing was completely illogical.

Still, it was where the thought of *home* brought me. Kefier later built another house just off the coast of western Dageis, on land that used to belong to the Gorenten. He thought I could be safe there, surrounded with nothing but trees and mountains, where my magic couldn't possibly hurt anyone.

But people needed people, and my skills were just as dangerous to myself as to others. That was when my mother married my father—the man who *left* us before I was born, and whose existence I didn't know until then—so he could bring me to Dageis and send me to a proper school. I said goodbye to that other house and lived in a bunch of other houses and apartments in Lon Basden until that fateful day when the whole empire decided I needed to be locked away in Eheldeth for good.

My family moved to Triassa, a coastal city in central Dageis, not long after. It was partly so I wouldn't have to travel so far to be with them during breaks. Unlike Lon Basden, Triassa was in the mainland, which meant it had access to the airships. Enosh set up a couple of shops there, while Papa got a house just on the outskirts of the city—a sort of compromise so they could keep the appearance of a happy family. Dageian authorities were strict on the matter; Dageian citizenship was precious and too many people were faking arrangements just so they could stay in the empire. If Enosh and Sume claimed to be married, then they had to look the part.

I was surprised to learn they still lived there. A part of me always thought that running away would result in the dissolution of the whole family. I'd been expecting the divorce, of course—but I also thought Kefier, of all people, wouldn't want to stay there after all. He preferred Lon Basden, where the weather was warmer and he could visit the Gorenten towns any time he wanted to. The headquarters of his mercenary company stood there, too. Its captains did a good job of running it without him, but I was sure he would rather be close by.

All of this must've shown on my face when we left the airship dock and started walking down that familiar street. "Of course we wouldn't move," he said nonchalantly, before I could even get the chance to speak. "How would you know where to find us?"

I shook my head. "What about the Boarshind?"

"Ah, I've left most of it to my captains these last few years. They're mostly capable, and it was getting harder and harder to stay away with the boys growing up and all. Look at that." He whistled, and another dog—a big, yellow-coated beast with a fluffy white chest—came bounding down the street and began an immediate game of tag with Daisy.

"He looks familiar," I said.

"That's *your* old Daisy's grandson. Takes after his grandmother quite a bit, doesn't he?"

Seeing his dog again put him in a good mood, and he hummed a soft song to himself as we went up the hill. Me, on the other hand...I knew what waited for me in that house, and I was starting to regret coming here at all. I wasn't sure I wanted to see my mother. I could almost hear the words that would come out of her mouth, all swathed in bitter rage and even more disappointment than either of my fathers could muster.

None of those fears came to pass. A boy was playing on the ground, tracing it with chalk. Another boy watched intently from the side.

"Now, we need to find a stick," the older boy said, before he caught sight of us. His face broke into a grin. "Papa!" he screamed.

The younger boy looked startled as the older boy ran past him. He jumped into Kefier's arms.

"No fair, I wanted to greet Papa first..." the younger boy began.

Kefier, carrying one boy, bent down to pick up the other. "I've got a surprise for you two," he said in a low voice. He turned around. "Look who it is."

They looked confused.

"Haro," Kefier continued. "Don't you remember? It's your big sister, Rosha. I told you I'd bring her home."

"Rosha?" Haro repeated. He jumped back to the ground and tentatively stepped towards me. He *had* grown. The last time I saw him, he had been chubby and small, given to repeating certain words and wanting nothing but endless stories about dragons and castles and ships. Now he was growing lanky. A boy now, not a little child.

"Hello," I said, not really knowing how to talk to him anymore. A boy was different than a baby. When he was a baby, I could carry him around, blow butterflies on his belly, and tickle his toes until he fell asleep.

"I...brought a dog," I continued, before he flung himself at me, spindly arms wrapped tight around my belly. He started sobbing.

I glanced at the other boy, who didn't recognize me. He was born during my final years in Eheldeth, when I didn't have as much time to visit anymore. Funny how the years could just fly by. The older I got, the easier it was to just blink and lose track of time.

"Greet your sister," Papa said.

Ryo eventually followed his brother's lead. His hug was as awkward as I felt. I quickly counted back the years. He should be six by now, which made Haro eight, maybe nine. Looking at them made me feel old.

"Where's Mama?" Kefier asked, looking around.

"She went to the shop," Haro said. "Portia came by and said there was trouble."

"Omer?"

"She left him with us. He's inside—"

"Gods, boys, you don't leave a baby alone." Kefier ran straight up the steps.

"He's sleeping, Papa. I can hear him from here…" Haro ran after him, Ryo at heels. I was left alone in the street. Even the dogs were nowhere in sight.

I took a deep breath, gazing at the world I thought I had said goodbye to once and for all. And then, because I wasn't sure if going inside the house to see a brother I had no idea existed was worse than confronting my mother, I decided to get it all over with and started walking back to the city. Once all was said and done, it was better to pull a thorn out than push it back in.

Where do I begin about my mother?

How about I just never talk about her at all? That might be easier, surely. I was certain Kefier didn't mention the baby because my mother told him not to. It was a signal to me that she had buried me as much as I'd tried to bury her. I wasn't the only one trying to move on.

The city of Triassa itself had changed little in three years. I noticed a couple of new shops, but nothing out of the ordinary. A vendor waved at me as I passed by, and it was only then that I noticed he was calling my name. "Since when have you been back?" he yelled.

"Today," I answered, half-distracted by the crowd.

He waved happily. I kept walking, unnerved that he still remembered me. Perhaps three years wasn't that long after all.

Enosh's store was around the corner. It was closed—a rare thing that time of the day. Triassa was a tourist hub, because you could get an airship from there straight to most of the best places in the empire to visit. The family's general store sold just about everything for those tourists—clothes, walking sticks, oiled cloaks, swords that met Dageian authorities' definition of a blade you could carry with you at all times.

It was really all just a front, though. The more important stuff happened on the second floor. Risen Industries' true love affair, apart from my father's women, was investment. Enosh poured money in a series of random projects across the continent, some of them ridiculously obscure. I never had a head for how he did his business. He tried to teach me once or twice, but a good deal of it involved pretending to like people you wanted to stab in a back alley somewhere. I can think of a thousand other ways I would rather waste my time.

I went around the back, where there were stairs going up from the alley to the second floor. The door there wasn't closed. I locked it behind me as I went in, because I realized there was no one in the office.

I went down the stairs to the store and saw the dead body first. It lay in a pool of sticky blood. There were two women standing next to it, arms crossed.

"Oh my goodness," Portia exclaimed, staring at me with wide eyes. "Did we forget to lock the back door? And oh—you're home at last!" My father's secretary stepped over the body to hug me.

"Can someone explain to me what's going on?" I asked when she finally gave me the chance to breathe. "Why is there a dead man on the rug?"

"Portia killed him," Mother said.

"I didn't *mean* to," Portia exclaimed. "He just broke into the shop while I was opening up, and I…threw a chair at him. I think I broke his neck." She was near tears. "Shouldn't I have? He was trying to kill me. At least, I thought he was. He was brandishing a knife." She pointed at the rusty thing on the floor next to the dead man's hand.

"That's usually a pretty good reason to kill someone." I glanced at Mother, who was acting calmer than expected, given the daughter she hadn't spoken to in three years was right in front of her. Maybe she'd used up all her energy on the dead body. I gestured for her hand, which she grudgingly gave. I pressed the back of it to my forehead.

"At least you still know how to greet your elders," she said under her breath.

I held my tongue. I could still recall the last time we had seen each other, the summer before my final year in Eheldeth. Words were exchanged. Words I could never take back. I didn't intend it to be a goodbye. She was probably still thinking about that, too. In fact, what I couldn't remember was the last time we *hadn't* fought. Family, to me, meant walking around eggshells. It was probably a good thing there was a dead body there to break the ice.

"Is this normal these days?" I asked, pushing it with my boot. The man looked like the sort of rough-hewn brute you could buy off an alley for a few silvers. Even if he wasn't a paid assassin, he had no business barging into a store with a weapon. Especially not if the only person in there was the unassuming Portia, who fit the description of a woman who couldn't hurt a fly. "I mean, since Enosh has been missing. Are we getting assassins by the boatloads now?"

"*Father,*" Sume corrected.

"Father," I repeated, trying hard not to roll my eyes. "Papa told me some things, but he didn't tell me everything."

"This is the first, as far as I know," Sume said. "Which makes me hesitant about reporting it to the authorities. They'll want to know *why*, which means prying into our family's business..."

"And we can't have that, of course," I finished for her with a grumble. "Well. We have to get rid of it somehow."

"I was thinking the river," Mother said, as if I was just asking what we were going to have for dinner.

Portia still looked terrified. "You're not seriously suggesting...we carry him all that way..."

"No, I guess not," Sume replied. "Even if we could carry him, he'll bleed from the mouth and leave a trail on the street. Not really the sort of thing you can hide from authorities."

"Almost like you've done this before," I said, intending it as a joke.

Sume didn't even blink. "We could cut him up—"

Portia turned her head to the side and vomited.

"Blessed Sakku, Portia, you're the one who killed him," Sume sighed. "Please keep it together."

"You're not honestly blaming her, are you?" I asked.

"I'm asking her to remain calm," Sume replied.

"You could take it easy on her."

"I am," she said, her voice even. "But if we don't act soon, the body's going to start stinking. I sent everyone else home before they could see this, but they'll be back tomorrow, and we might not be able to get the store ready in time."

"I'll clean up after myself..." Portia broke in, wiping her mouth. "But I don't know if I can...hacking someone to pieces like that..." She turned her head and vomited once more. I didn't want to ask what she had for breakfast.

"Just don't think of it as someone," Sume said. "It's a slab of meat."

"Mother!"

She glanced at me. "You could make yourself useful and find a saw. I think we had one in the workroom upstairs."

She gave that tone of voice that told me it was useless to argue without inflaming her further. I retreated up the stairs, all the while wondering why on earth the office would have a saw in the first place. If the shop needed repairs, Enosh had the money to get craftsmen anytime he wanted to.

I found it in a box in the closet, along with a bunch of old work boots, an umbrella, a ridiculously oversized coat, and birdseed. The absurdity of the situation struck me.

I returned downstairs with the saw and the coat. Sume took both without comment. She laid the coat down beside the body before rolling it over. I took the man's feet to help her. It was harder than it looked. The bastard probably weighed as much as the both of us combined.

"We should get Papa down here to help," I grumbled once the body was finally off the rug.

"And risk the boys finding out? Better we do this ourselves." She wiped sweat from her forehead as she considered the saw in her hand. "There's going to be more blood if we do this," she said. "Maybe if we drag him to the alley…"

"It's nice and sunny," I replied. "We'll be seen no matter what."

She stared at the floor, almost like she agreed with me. Anyway, if she didn't, she'd say so. I was about to suggest pretending he was a customer who slipped on the floor and hit his head on the way out when three solid knocks sounded on the door.

"Ferral?" a voice called. "Is this Hertra Ferral's residence?"

I stared at my mother in silence. Hertra Ferral. The name of a ghost, of an old life, one Enosh swore he'd left behind when he married my mother. No one was supposed to know it was him. *Lord Talos wouldn't have spoken. He's incapable of speaking now, in that madhouse where they locked him in.*

"Drag it to the warehouse," Sume whispered.

Portia stumbled forward to help me. Sume wiped her hands and went up to answer the door.

CHAPTER 11

THE STRANGER

You can admire a woman without wanting to be in the same room as her. My mother's unbelievable composure set the tone. We got the body into the warehouse and slammed the door shut just as we heard her open the door. I didn't know how she planned to defend herself if it was another assassin. I should be the one out there. I knew how to set things on fire and make shields out of thin air, and if I was given the time and space, I could create a portal to get us out of the shop. Even if I could do none of those things, I wasn't a middle-aged mother of three young children. I wouldn't be missed.

Perhaps it was better, though, not to cast such huge spells in the middle of a city like Triassa. This wasn't Ad Methas—representatives of the mage council were just about everywhere here. In the guards, amongst the officials, in little shops like the one I ran—except with the proper paperwork and legitimacy their titles allowed. I'd tried to be smart the last three years. I hadn't uttered a single spell or made a spark of flame since. I kept to very minor charms for my store. Charms were benign, untraceable, and practically harmless as far as the mage council was concerned.

It wasn't easy pretending like I didn't have the power to just make our current problem go away—at least not without creating more problems in its stead. For a moment, I saw myself in that examination hall and felt like shaking that younger, ghostly image of myself before she abandoned the school. *Bear it a little longer,* I wanted to yell. *Bear it so you don't have to be an outlaw like me.* But the thought passed quickly. Even if I could go back to the past, the outcome wouldn't change.

"Our store's undergoing some renovations right now," I heard my mother greet the stranger. "I'm afraid there's been a misunderstanding. Hertra Ferral is not a name I'm familiar with."

"I was told he was here."

"Someone lied to you, sir." How my mother could say such words effortlessly in the face of a stranger attempting to intimidate us, I had no idea. I would have never stood for it. If someone had walked into my shop like that…

Beside me, I heard Portia utter a low gasp. I glanced down and noticed the body was bleeding from the mouth. "Gods," I grumbled. "What did you do to him?"

"I don't know I don't know I don't know…" Portia said.

I awkwardly placed a hand on her back. She was shaking from head to toe. I felt bad she got caught up in my family's business. They hired her not long before I left for Eheldeth to help with starting up the office here in Triassa, and amazingly enough, she stayed. Amazing, because I don't think Enosh paid her all that much, and just about every other employee had found a reason to quit a year or two down the road. Enosh needed thoroughness in everything, which got to most people really fast. Portia didn't seem to care, even if she was far from the most organized person I knew. She just seemed happy to be there.

On the other hand, she didn't sign up to work for a mortuary, either. I wondered if she was going to hand in a resignation letter soon. Probably, because it also looked like we were going to get another body if the stranger didn't stop harassing my mother. I realized the argument had stopped. I motioned for Portia to wait.

I straightened my dress and joined Mother.

The store was empty. Sume was locking the door.

"He'll be back," she greeted me.

"Was he really looking for Father?"

"You know about the name, then."

I scoffed. "I'm not stupid, Mother. I clearly remember when he used that name before we moved to the empire. He used it in all his business dealings in the south."

"He was looking for your brothers," she said calmly, ignoring my rudeness. "He didn't say it out loud, of course. But I could tell he was fishing. He knew Enosh had children—he just didn't know how many or where they live. He'll be back soon enough. For now, he's probably waiting in the alley for you or me to run back home to check on the boys."

"We're not going to do that."

"Of course not."

"What do you want us to do, then?"

"I want *you* to stay here with Portia," she said. "I'm going to lead him somewhere else. Somewhere where I can get rid of him. I don't think we can get away with killing a second man in this store—not in broad daylight, anyway."

I still didn't know how Sume could speak about death and killing like last week's laundry. It must have shown in my expression, because she squeezed my shoulder and gave a small smile. "I'm glad you're home. Even if this isn't the reunion I had in mind."

"I'm surprised you had one in mind at all," I grumbled. "Let's not mince words, Mother. You don't want me here about as much as I don't want to be here. It's only too bad we've got *this* to deal with, isn't it? Because otherwise you'd have screamed at me for my thoughtlessness already."

"I want to do that," she said easily. "More than you think. If we were in a better spot, I'd have done it already."

I sighed and started for the door. "I'll lead him away from here."

She frowned. "It's too dangerous."

"And you're out of your mind if you think you can *tell* me what to do. I'm too old for that now, Mother. I'm a grown woman."

"If you were, you wouldn't feel the need to say it."

That did it. I didn't know why, but she had a way of making me feel terrible about myself without having to raise her voice. I think she knew that, too. I think she did it deliberately. I placed my hand on the doorknob and undid the latch. "Portia's getting hysterical out back there," I said. "I'd worry about her before me. I've survived three years without you. I can go on a little longer."

She didn't try to stop me.

Outside, I took a moment to compose myself.

Judge me when you can have an argument with your parent without turning into a child once more. I knew how I was acting—I knew it was on me to not let my emotions fly off the handle like that. Especially not in front of my mother. I could get angry at my fathers and not feel an ounce of shame, but with my mother, the less she reacted to my outbursts, the worse I felt. Almost as if I wanted her to do the opposite. If she lost her temper, then she couldn't very well claim to be better than me now, could she?

I fixed my cloak and walked down the road, trying to focus on the task at hand. I didn't come here to open up my relationship with my family under broad daylight. I didn't have to deal with any of these complications in Klossaka. There was the dog, and Jehar, and Ivy, who did a better job of acting like a mother than my own mother ever did. When was the last time Sume ever made a meal that made my mouth water, or *not* offer criticism when a kind word of support would do? I was here to solve this family problem and remove that nagging seed of guilt Kefier planted in my heart, and the sooner it was over, the sooner I could go back to my life.

A few streets down, I noticed someone following me.

I'm not sure if it was my skill in the *agan* that made me acutely aware of the fact. It's not as if I had the special ability to detect things my regular senses couldn't. But there was a tingle in the air, a sort of warmth that told me I wasn't alone anymore—that same feeling when someone unwelcome steps into your house and the back of your neck prickles in response. I was annoyed I couldn't do more than that. A bit of high-level magic and the council would be on me like a hound after a bloody deer.

I had no desire to bring that on me now, not after so many years. It was the work of an amateur, after all—to be caught simply because you let your guard down. After dodging Bearer Lontas and his mages all these years, I felt a bit of pride in my ability to evade the law. Besides, I wasn't going to be so stupid where my mother could see and judge before I could get a word in to defend myself. I quickened my pace and made my way to the docks. The alleys in the houses there were tighter, easier to lose someone in.

But it wasn't really that I wanted to lose him. That would do nothing —the man knew where the store was. And knowing my family, the store wasn't going to go anywhere. They made good money here, last I remembered, and they weren't going to make a decision without Enosh around. I needed to get rid of this man permanently, preferably without killing him.

Which left one reasonable solution: I had to get him arrested. Regardless of what his business was with my family, it had to be illegal, which meant he was going to keep his mouth shut once the authorities got to him. I just had to make sure he was arrested without my family's name being brought up at all.

I led him to the docks. As luck would have it, it was market day. Ships from all across the world were unloading their wares, waiting for their turn to be inspected by authorities. It was a long, grueling process. Enosh owned two ships and I'd been forced to watch the unloading procedure a few times when I was little, as if he actually expected me to do something with my inheritance instead of wasting it on fluffy rugs and rare books. If the man wanted to make a merchant out of me, he shouldn't have sent me to mage school.

I suppose I could stand corrected now. Against my will, I knew how the authorities at the docks functioned; I knew how to trap the stranger. I gave a quick glance at the ships in the harbour and spotted a familiar one in the distance.

I went to the harbour master's office. The man was getting close—I think he was convinced I was about to lead him to Ferral's home soon. I stopped at the receptionist's table.

"How may I help you?" the man cheerfully asked.

"I'm an officer from one of the ships at the harbour," I said. "The Crying Dragon." I rattled the registry number. I hoped I was correct—it had been years since I'd last seen the thing. But it was a common sight at the docks: a narrow ship with red sails, owned by a family who lived most of the time in Sorna to the west. So common that every time I waited in one of Father's ships, bored out of my mind, I would hear the captain call out that registry number like it was a song.

The receptionist checked. It was correct. Maybe Enosh ought to be proud—I paid attention after all.

"There's a man outside who's been hanging around the ship at night," I said. "I think he's trying to sneak into one of them."

"That's a serious crime," the receptionist exclaimed.

"Isn't it? It would look terrible on the empire if we brought stowaways to Sorna. I didn't want to confront him directly. He seems dangerous. He knows I'm onto him, and I noticed him following me today. I believe he's trying to catch me alone so he can steal the keys to my cabin."

The receptionist looked shocked. "The nerve!"

" I need him arrested."

"I can take care of that," he said, rubbing his hands together. "But he might flee before the authorities get here."

This is going to take a bit more work. I smiled, trying not to show the concern in my expression. "That's what I was afraid of. Look…I can lead him down to the east, past the market. Near the log mill."

"I can send the city watch that way."

"Thank you," I said. "Do it fast. I don't know if he'll try anything funny soon."

The man nodded and started making his way to the back of the office.

I went back out front. The stranger was looking antsy, but I didn't want to betray my plans. I sidled up to the market and pretended to look at the wares. When a woman asked if she could help, I said out loud that I was trying to find a present for my brothers.

"They'll love these kites," the woman said.

I pretended to look at them. The man was getting interested.

"I'll take three," I replied, paying for them. She wrapped them in waxed paper and handed them to me, all wrapped up in cotton rope. I bowed and then made my way east. The man kept following.

We reached the edge of the mill, right below the side of a cliff. Off to my right, I could see the islands cradled underneath the setting sun.

"You're Tar'elian's child, aren't you?" the stranger following me called. "There's no need to run."

I turned around. "In case it's not obvious, I'm not a child," I said.

The man smiled.

"You know his name," I continued. "Why go there asking for someone else?"

"Sent you in a panic, didn't it?"

"What do you want?" I asked. "You know he's not here either. I don't know what you think we can give you. My family has money, but we're not that rich. You're in Dageis. You can find someone who can give you more."

"You can start," the man said, "by closing your eyes."

I felt the air around me collapse, like I'd just plunged into a pool of water. My eyes burned. I opened my mouth to scream, but all that came out was a soft exhale, like someone had come and pressed a pillow on my face.

He walked up to touch me on the forehead. I couldn't even move my fingers. He flicked his fingers, and I flew straight into the side of the building.

CHAPTER 12

FAMILY

I slammed my back against the stone so hard I thought the breath had been knocked out of my lungs. I fell to the ground and at once tried to stand up. The man walked up to me and threw me a second time, without even touching me. He wasn't just trying to hurt me. He was trying to frighten me, to make me run away. He was going to do that so I could lead him back home to my brothers. Unfortunate for him that I'd been there before—back when I first started classes in Eheldeth. What can I say? Children can be cruel, and those who think themselves above you even more so.

An old habit kicked in. I placed a hand on the ground and started the beginning of a shield-spell.

His eyes grew wide. "I heard his daughter was a mage. They said you've been away a very long time. That they were ashamed to be around you. That you became an outlaw on your last year, and it was only a matter of time before the authorities brought you in. Didn't they do that before, already? Because of that old fart, what's his name...Lord Talos! Ah."

I stopped before I could throw the spell. "If you knew that about me, why are you even here?"

"Your childish tantrums don't scare anyone. Not here. You clearly grew up around people frightened of you. Did that make you feel more intelligent? Superior? You have powers, they don't. The empire changed your perspective, didn't it? Dageis has mages everywhere. What are you here, if not average, mediocre, good-for-nothing?" He laughed. "My name is Targus. I've come with a proposition for your family. Your mother clearly wasn't going to entertain me, so I thought I would twist your proverbial arms a bit more."

He spoke like someone who studied in Eheldeth. There was a marker, you understand—a flair carried by its proudest students, those who believed the garbage they spewed long enough to internalize it. You start to notice it if you've been around the school long enough. But I'd never seen him there before. Not surprising, of course, given the size of the school, which could hold anywhere from three to four thousand mages and students at one time.

Still, he looked at me like he knew me. It was more unsettling than the idea that he wanted to get at my brothers to punish my father. No—this man knew *me*, which suddenly made his business my own. I didn't like that. It made the last three years seem like nothing. Like I wasn't even really hiding at all. They knew where I was. And they must have simply been *waiting* for me to come back, all this time.

"What do you want?" I repeated.

"For your family to leave to go back where you came from."

I wasn't sure what he meant by that. "You mean Gorent?" I asked. "Or Jin-Sayeng?"

"Don't test me. You know what I mean. Sell your properties in Dageis, go back to the lands you've reclaimed, and stay there."

"That's what this is all about?" I asked. I felt a wave of relief. If it was about my family's business, then it had nothing to do with me at all. But then I saw a flicker on his brow, and I realized we weren't done. "What if we don't?"

"You'll regret it," the man said. "You've not exactly been a model student, have you? Let's see…does the name Felan Cartos ring a bell?"

"He was an old classmate," I replied.

"Is that all?"

"He went missing."

"Your fault, the newspapers say."

"It was a long time ago. The council dismissed that article as idle gossip. If they thought there was any truth to it, they would have sent me away."

"So, they know about the old library, then? About the flood? About the boy you left to die?"

I felt my blood run cold.

You could run, you see. You could run fast, and you can run for a long time, but unless you run forever, eventually your secrets will catch up with you. I stared at the man who continued babbling about things he knew nothing about—things he should know *nothing* about—and felt something I'd only felt before in flashes. Hate. I hated him and the words that just fell from his mouth. I wanted him to stop. I wanted him to die.

I could feel the prickle of energy gather on my fingertips. Targus did, too, because his eyes glanced down quickly and I could see his own fingers moving, creating the beginning of a shield-spell. "Maybe the tabloids were right," he said with a smile. "Maybe you killed him after all. You seem like someone who would, Rosha Tar'elian."

"What do you have to gain if we sell our businesses?" I asked. "Who the hell are you to think you could blackmail my family?"

"I'm not blackmailing them. I'm blackmailing *you*."

"I'm calling your bluff. Whatever information you have is second-hand. Someone else told you. And if you don't tell me who—"

I knelt on the ground and picked up a rock, pretending I was casting a spell. If he knew I was a mage, it might make him rethink.

I threw the rock at him. My aim was perfect. It struck his forehead.

"*Child*," he repeated, as if I'd chucked nothing but a balled-up rag at his face. "Did you think that would hurt me?"

In the distance, I heard barking dogs, followed by shouting. I remembered the guards. They always had a mage with them at least, an Eheldeth-sanctioned bearer, and I had no desire to meet them. Flushed with shame, I turned and ran. Targus tried to grab my arm, but I slipped through his fingers like the wind. I reached the alley.

I hoped Targus was as smart as he seemed and would keep his mouth shut. If what he wanted was for us to sell our business—*legally*, then he would gain nothing turning us over to the authorities. Even just having one criminal in the family, especially people with bought citizenship like ours, might be enough for them to seize all our assets. Now I relied on the twists and turns in the district; I took every corner until I felt like I'd travelled far enough to lose them.

Eventually, I decided it was safe enough to head back to the shop. It was now completely closed, all doors locked, no lights. Glancing over my shoulder to make sure I wasn't followed, I went back to my family's house.

It felt strange walking alone on that road in the dark. Back when I was still in school, I would visit during summers and between semester breaks, which meant I often had to take the airship alone. I'm not sure why the idea of returning to my family should fill me with so much shame. I suppose because deep down inside, I knew their expectations. They were here because of me. They had to flee Jin-Sayeng because of me. And now here I was, nonchalantly stepping through the gate like I wasn't the ungrateful child who gave up on everything because it was— what, too hard? Because I could no longer stand being forced to do twice the work everyone else did just to get by.

In the presence of my family, every kind word Papa gave, every look of amazement from my brothers, would feel like a lie. *What are you doing, Rosha?* You're *the one they're using to tear your family apart.* You're *the liability. It's not like you need them. It's not like they need you. Just go your own way, like you meant to all along. Here's the excuse you needed never to see them again.*

"Rosha!"

I froze. It was Haro. He must have been waiting for me. Of course he would. He always did, back when we were younger. My first brother, as far as I was concerned, because he was Kefier's son and that meant more to me than if we actually shared fathers. I remembered how easily he used to fit in my arms, how everything made him laugh.

He got up from the steps.

"I got you something," I said as he came running down the path, because I didn't think I could bear it if he hugged me again. I still had the kites; I shoved the package into his hands before he could wrap his arms around me. "There's one for Ryo, too."

Haro didn't even look at them. "Mama and Papa and Portia's inside, waiting for you." He hesitated. "Are you…coming?"

I stared, a grown woman intimidated by an eight-year-old boy.

"Or are you going to leave?" he continued, like he could read me. Which really wasn't all that surprising, considering he was Papa's true-born son. "Are you going away again, Rosha? Mama said you might."

I might have, if he hadn't spoken about it. But listening to the tremble in his voice, I knew I couldn't break his heart just yet. "Not tonight," I finally said.

He broke into a grin. With a soft sigh, I followed him into the house.

The contrast between running for your life one moment, and then finding yourself in a well-lit common room surrounded by all the people you weren't sure you ever wanted to see again, was jarring. I think I'd rather have the former if it came down to it. I glanced at all of them, unsure of what to say. Mama was going through some papers on the table. Ryo was on the floor playing with wooden blocks, while Papa sat on the sofa, bouncing a baby on his knee.

I turned to Portia, who was coming from the kitchen with a plate of rice to set on the table. "Long day, huh," I said.

She gave a small, tired little laugh. She'd killed her first man today. At least, as far as I knew.

I turned to Kefier, took his hand, and pressed it over my forehead. My mother would have noted the deference was intended for her and not him. Kefier never cared for such formalities. If we were alone, I would have hugged him instead.

"Hey, Omer," Kefier said. "Meet your sister." He held the baby up to me. I didn't know what to do with it—it had been too long since the others. The baby gurgled happily, milk dribbling down the corners of his mouth. He looked like Haro when he was little, just squished in more places.

I waved at him.

"You want to carry him?" Kefier asked.

"Better if she helps me with the food first," Sume said.

Kefier gave me that look, the one that told me I had to keep my mouth shut. I sighed and walked over to help carry the pot of stew to the table. It smelled of peanut sauce and coconut cream. Kefier got up from the sofa and herded the boys to the bench.

We ate in silence, interrupted only by the sound of the boys inhaling the food like they hadn't eaten in days. I would have done the same if my mother wasn't sitting right across me. I hadn't eaten food like my family made it in years. It was as bad as Haro's hug, because it made me question the life I made for myself. If there was anything I despised the most, it was uncertainty.

"Rosha got us kites," Haro said, between bites.

"Did she, now?" Sume asked absently, reaching over to wipe a stray grain of rice from his face.

He grimaced. "Can we go fly them tomorrow, Mama? There's a great spot right up the hill."

"Can we?" Ryo repeated. It was startling to hear him talk so clearly. He couldn't even form intelligible words the last time I was here.

"We'll see," Sume said.

"Maybe I can go with you," Portia added.

"What about the shop?" Haro asked.

"I think we're closed for the week." Portia glanced at my parents. "We are, aren't we?"

"Haro," Kefier broke in. "Since you're just playing with your food now, do you want to get us some fireflies? We can sit out in the dark later before we set them free. I'm sure Rosha hasn't done that in years."

"Not much fireflies in Klossaka," I said. Or time. Some things you just never did alone. You could sit in silence by yourself, you can watch the stars or read, but a mindless task you shared with others just didn't feel right without them. Anyway, I wasn't a child anymore. I was long past such things.

Still, I felt a flicker of jealousy as I watched the boys scamper through the door. Portia finally let out a small sigh. "We didn't want to alarm them," Sume said as the door swung shut. "Haro's at that age. He'll ask questions and talk, and he has enough friends out there to make it difficult for us. What happened after the store?"

"I got him arrested." I pushed my half-eaten food away. "Mother, I think he was a mage." I hesitated. "I'm not sure I saw much of a connection of the *agan* in him, but he was very strong. It was—it was strange. I've never encountered anyone like that in my life."

"Shit," Kefier grumbled. "You should have sent for me."

"So you could crack his head open in the middle of the street for everyone to see?" Sume asked.

"It's better than wondering when he'll be back," Kefier retorted.

"He wanted you to sell everything," I said. "All the family's assets, in exchange for leaving us alone. He was trying to scare us. He probably sent that other one ahead to try and rattle Portia. Wasn't counting on her killing him, that's for sure."

"I don't understand," Kefier said. "He wanted us to sell them to *him*?"

"No. He just wanted us to leave the empire."

"What does he have to gain doing that?"

"I don't know," I admitted. "He wouldn't say. He was more interested in trying to scare me."

"This man knew your father and Hertra Ferral are connected," Sume said. "For him to have made the leap from *that* name to our store, to the questions he asked me…" She turned to Kefier. "He was very sure the boys existed. He just didn't know where they were. But Hertra Ylir yn Ferral's children—the real Ferral—are all dead. The old man was alone—it's why Enosh thought it was safe to steal his name in the first place."

"No matter how you look at it, this is all his fault," I broke in. "He stole a man's whole identity. That shouldn't be something anyone can just get away with."

"He did," Sume agreed. "I'm not going to defend his actions, but it was a long time ago, Rosha. Whatever we have now was built from scratch, under his real name. Hertra Ferral has no connection to this life anymore."

"We were talking about this other mage, not Enosh," Kefier finally said, a flicker of irritation on his brow.

Sume gave a small smile and placed a hand on his arm, squeezing it slightly. "We need to find out what this man wants. If it's just as simple as selling our properties, why bother with threats? This must be connected with Enosh's disappearance. It must be."

"He didn't say anything about that at all." I got up to open the window.

"If you ask me, he's gone and done something terrible, and we're dealing with the aftermath of revenge," Kefier grumbled.

"He promised he wouldn't keep secrets," Sume said. "He promised he would be honest about his business dealings with us."

"And you *believed* him?"

She took a deep breath. "We need transparency with each other to survive here. If we can't trust each other after all these years…"

"I can't hear the boys," I broke in.

They fell silent. Crickets chirped outside, but no children's laughter. There should have been—even when they were little, it was impossible to keep the boys quiet for very long.

"Did they go further down the hill for the fireflies?" Portia broke in.

"They know not to wander further than the fence," Kefier said. He handed the baby to Sume and bounded out the door. I was right at his heels.

We tore down the path, just as we saw Haro walking slowly back up the house.

"Thank the gods," Kefier said, grabbing his hand. "Did you go on the road? I told you a hundred times—" He paused, because Haro remained silent. "Where's your brother?"

"There was a man outside," Haro whispered. "He said he knew where Papa Enosh was. He said he was going to take us to him. I escaped, but Ryo wanted to go with him."

"Damn this," Kefier growled. "The dogs—set the dogs on his trail. Sume!" He charged up the house.

A deathly calm came over me as I turned to Haro, who was frozen there, his face wet with tears. He was trying not to sob.

"Did he say who he was?" I asked.

Haro swallowed. "He said his name was Hertra Ferral."

CHAPTER 13

FIREFLIES

The next few hours were some of the longest in my life. While Mother, Papa, and Portia went searching for Ryo, I sat in the corner of the boys' room with a sleeping baby in my arms and Haro on the other side. There, I listened to his story to keep him busy. They'd been outside catching fireflies, he said, just as Father asked. He caught a few already—enough to fill one jar. But there weren't as many as he wanted. He saw them flying just across the road, not even three steps away, in the grove of apple trees. He told Ryo to stay inside the fence while he went. That was when the man arrived, moving swiftly between them before Haro could do anything about it. The boy spoke in a soft voice. Out of all of us, I think he took after Mother the most.

"Ryo misses Papa Enosh," Haro whispered. "He wanted to see him. I told him not to, but he wouldn't listen."

Why would Ryo miss Enosh? I wanted to ask but didn't. I couldn't really recall his interactions with the boys. He was hardly around even when I was home—as far as I knew, both my brothers knew that Kefier was their father. They called Enosh *Papa* as an affectation both Kefier and Sume forced on them to keep the illusion that they were Enosh's legal sons, to preserve their Dageian citizenship. And Enosh didn't *like* children. He certainly didn't think much of me when I was young, and I was his trueborn daughter.

I tried not to dwell on how much had changed the last few years. "Let's go outside," I said. "Let's wait for them on the porch. Maybe it was just a mistake, and they found Ryo already."

It was a fool's hope, but I clutched onto it as tightly as Haro's hand on mine. We went to the porch. It was very dark—the clouds had covered the moon, and I didn't take a lantern with me. All three of us sat by the steps, watching the forgotten jar of fireflies on the grass. After what felt like forever, Haro got up to unscrew the lid, letting them free.

"Tell the heavens to bring my brother back," he said with all the conviction of an eight-year-old. He returned to sit beside us, pressing his head next to Omer's. He fell asleep himself after a few moments.

My parents and Portia returned with the dogs and no Ryo in sight. At the sound of their footsteps, Haro woke up. When he saw Ryo wasn't with them, he began to cry.

Kefier went up to scoop him into his arms. "Hush," he said against the sobbing boy's hair. "It's not your fault."

"I'm sorry, Papa," Haro whispered. "I'm so sorry. If I didn't let him go—"

"Shh. I'm the one who should be sorry. I should have been out there with you." I realized he was crying, too. My heart tightened. My family was hurting, and I wanted to make it all go away.

"I'm going to get those bastards," Kefier said, when he finally composed himself and Haro had fallen asleep again. "I'm taking a ship to Lon Basden in the morning with the other two. They'll be safe with the Boarshind."

"You can't expect mercenaries to babysit," I started.

"The assholes are free to try to get them from there," Kefier said. "*Then* I'm coming back with a dozen, and we're going to tear this city apart."

"It may not be for the best," Sume broke in. "The trouble we'll stir—"

"I don't *care*," Kefier snapped. "I'm done being careful. They've made it personal."

"They won't hurt him. They want something from us—they *can't* hurt him," I said. "What would happen if we did what they asked? Neither of you care about Enosh's businesses, anyway. Sell them. He's not around to stop you."

Kefier glowered. He looked conflicted.

"We can't," Sume broke in.

"Why not? At this point you can't seriously still care about money? About *his* money?"

"It's not about the money," Sume said. "The Gorenten…" She turned to Kefier, who swore under his breath.

"We technically *own* the Gorenten lands in the peninsula," Kefier replied. "The land we've built on, the farms, the fields. Enosh filed the paperwork and paid down a hefty deposit to legalize our settling there as soon as he was able. It's one reason the empire hasn't actively tried to go down south to reclaim them. They're more than capable of, given their history, even if the land is barren and useless and too far away to benefit them. But they like money, and so as long as we kept our end of the bargain, they looked away."

"Own," I repeated. "You mean—"

"As a company," Kefier said. "And the only way we get to keep it that way is if the owner—that is, Enosh Tar'elian—keeps his Dageian citizenship. Since he got it as a merchant, that means he needs to own property *in* Dageis *and* pay the required taxes to keep it. For the rest of his natural life."

"What happens if he's dead?" I asked.

"The condition passes over to his heirs," Sume continued. "Which is you, and then the boys after. And it will remain that way until the empire itself sees fit to give you a full citizenship on account of good service and exemplary behaviour, without the merchant guild's conditions attached. Which you could have gotten had you graduated as a mage under Eheldeth. The mage council's blessings would have overwritten the merchant guild's conditions."

My head was spinning. "This is—"

"I know," Kefier growled. "But that's what it is. The lives of several thousand Gorenten depend on this ridiculous arrangement. Any reason they find—*anything at all*—and they can seize the lands that rightfully belong to our people and throw them out again, just like they did hundreds of years ago."

The world suddenly seemed a little bigger.

The Empire of Dageis has only been around for a few hundred years. Before that, the nation and the islands around it comprised of a few nations—different groups of people who lived well enough on their own, dealing with the peculiarities of the continent in their own different ways. The people we call Gorent, my fathers' people, lived to the west of this, on a long strip of peninsula just off the coast.

The Dageians, so the story goes, came to the shores on ships as refugees, fleeing a civil war that wracked their own homes. The people of the continent welcomed them with open arms. And as the story often goes, the bond of friendship didn't last. The Dageians had superior weapons, and somewhere along the way, they learned to harness the *agan* and turn it against the people who freely sheltered them. They started taking over, working their way from the west all the way to the east. Along the way, the locals were driven from their lands to look for refuge on the barren, untamed islands—at least, those that weren't murdered or enslaved.

Absolutely nothing that hasn't happened elsewhere too, in some form or fashion. The Dageians taught this history with a wink and a smile. "There will always be war," Eheldeth keepers said. "Resources are finite. And in war, there will always be winners and losers." Most of the time, whenever they said *loser*, I would catch a few glimpses directed at me—me, the only dark skin in a sea of lighter faces. I pretended not to notice. They made it harder for you if you reacted, as if the only accept-able response to such words was gratitude. In their eyes, I was like any other Gorenten, the same people that cleaned their houses, made their ships run, and wiped their half-dead grandparents' bottoms so they didn't have to. The only thing I was supposed to say, hearing all this history, was "Thank you. You saved me when you didn't have to. Thank you for giving me a chance."

I had lived here long enough not to question what Kefier said. I should have realized it from the start. The peninsula where the Gorenten once lived was a land Dageis didn't want to touch for over a hundred years, for various reasons. Resistance from the south, from the Kingdom of Hafod, was pretty heavy, and the long, brutal wars had drained the land of any significant sources of *agan*. In short, they would gain nothing of value, so they eventually left it alone. And the south, wanting as much space between them and the mages of the north, were happy to leave it that way.

That left my fathers, both children of Gorent born in one of the islands overlooking the peninsula. Sometime in the last thirteen years, they slowly started helping Gorenten settle in small villages deep inside the peninsula. The Gorenten people, once happy to rely on magic as Dageis still does, were forced to learn how to farm and raise livestock blindly. I thought my family was simply doing their part in supporting the villages grow—I didn't know our status was the only thing stopping Dageis from putting an end to it. I didn't understand. I'd been down there before—the villages were thriving, but not doing much more than producing food for themselves. Simple folk poorer even than the wyrm-farmers of Ad Methas.

"Why would they even do that?" I said. "Sending people down there would cost more than anything they have to gain. Last I checked, rice isn't exactly a precious commodity for Dageian palates, and they've *never* expressed interest in trading with Jin-Sayeng or Gaspar. The empire would sooner jump off a cliff first."

"We can't risk the lives of people on a chance," Kefier replied. "There are children in those villages. Children who have never known a life outside of the farms."

"Dageis does nothing without the support of its citizens," Sume added. "In their eyes, as long as we are still law-abiding citizens—*one of theirs*—then any movement south will be questioned. Legally holding on to those lands is our best defense to protect the people."

"It's a whole damn empire," I half-whispered. "What chance do they have?" What chance did any of us? I glanced at my mother and then, haltingly, at Kefier, who hadn't said a word. I had seen the expression on his face when I told him I could never return to Eheldeth. He was piecing things together.

And yet, thoughtfully as ever, he waited until Mother had put the boys to bed and slept herself before he approached me.

"I know you're thinking of leaving," he said, after a few moments of silence. "Don't do this to me, my dear. Not now. Not ever. Not seeing you for years, without even a letter to tide me over…I can't go through that again."

I didn't answer. I could see he was walking on eggshells around me, too. We didn't talk anymore like we used to, not like when I was little. He was frightened of driving me away. How do you respond to the sight of a grown man absolutely terrified of you? I wanted to tell him he didn't need me, anyway—he had a family now, a life of his own, just as I had mine.

But I lied instead. "I won't," I replied. "I just can't sleep. Head to bed now, Papa. I'll keep watch. You need your strength for tomorrow. Maybe we don't have to do so much, and we'll find Ryo soon."

He didn't want to, I could tell. But the exhaustion was weighing down on him, reflected on the few lines there were on his face, so like my own, even though the blood we shared was at least one generation away. He stumbled back into the bedroom to join Mother and the boys.

When I heard him snore, I packed my bags. There were two things on my mind now, bigger than all my other concerns. The first, of course, was to see if I could find Ryo myself. I wondered if the city watch would have caught the stranger from yesterday—his unnatural strength didn't seem to come from spells, but if they were, the mages would have found him easily. If I could talk to him, he might give me clues on Ryo's whereabouts.

Once I found my brother safe, I would fake my death.

It was a big leap. Downright impulsive, to be honest. *As long as we are still law-abiding citizens,* Mother had said, years too late. If the authorities caught me now, they weren't just going to lock me up for a very long time. Chances were they would drag my family and their citizenship along for the ride. The empire could be petty like that—shrewd, manipulative, vindictive. And the only solution, as far as I could see—the only thing that would give my family a chance to breathe—was to die.

CHAPTER 14

TRAVELS OF THE DEAD

I knew it sounded dramatic. If I was still in Klossaka, I would have called it downright ridiculous. But the last few days in Kefier's company brought back memories of my childhood, and the last few hours made it impossible to deny. My family's choices had made me miserable, but there was joy there, too. No matter how much you turned everything upside-down, the fact was it would have been a lot easier if they were horrible people. If my brothers had been terrors, and my mother a touch more snippy. If Papa hadn't loved me so, so much that for a time it was my whole world, and I couldn't want for anything else.

Even after Enosh formally recognized me as his daughter and we had to live with him, Kefier still tried to spend time with me. He'd frame it as a way to catch *his* breath, because there was only so much of Enosh he could stand, and he wanted to spend a few days as far away from him as possible. So, he'd take me out to sea, first on a ship that would take us to Sen'senal, the one city still standing in Gorent, where he would introduce me to elders of our people—the ones too stubborn to move to the peninsula—and showed me the abandoned village and the beaches where he grew up. He would show me the ruins of villages Dageis had destroyed, including his own. Ashes and skeletons and broken dreams. "We find a way to survive because we must," he liked to remind me. "But it would be nice to thrive too, don't you think? To be given every chance in the world to succeed. I mean, *look* at you." It was clear he thought of me as a diamond plucked from the dust. Out of ruin and destruction, a gift; a child in defiance of an empire who believed it was its destiny to conquer. I could never find it in my heart to correct him. In many ways, he was right. If I had grown up anywhere else, I wouldn't be half what I was.

Sometimes we would row around the islands on a boat, just the two of us, where he would regale me with stories from his childhood, half-forgetting they were stories from mine, too. There was something special about spending so much time with someone that they run out of stories and begin to repeat themselves. It's not the stories you listen to anymore but the way they tell them, the sound of their voice, the details they might have missed those first few times. I would carry that with me forever—Papa's voice above that roaring sea, while I sat there thinking *this broken land made you, too.* And I would be hard-pressed to know anyone with a heart as big and strong as his.

Thinking of saying goodbye forever was painful. Remembering *why* it would hurt. I have never made it a secret that I always thought Papa deserved better. He deserved more than that spot under Father's shadow, and the love of the woman who—for all her shortcomings—loved him back. To *be* with her, to be seen as more than her brother-in-law and lover, to be able to call his sons his own. I couldn't give him any of those things, but I could still protect what little he had the way he always protected me.

I made my way through the city in the early hours of dawn. Maybe it was just the after-effects of what happened the night before, but something about it felt off. It was too quiet. Even the seagulls, normally roaring across the sky at those hours, weren't around.

I went to the precinct to ask about the man they arrested last night.

"You mean the gentleman found cheating on his wife?" the woman at the desk asked.

"I don't think so," I replied. "This was a suspected stowaway. You took him from the docks, near the mill."

"We didn't take anyone else last night, and certainly no one from the docks."

I felt my ears ring. Were they lying? No—there was no reason for them to lie. The woman at the desk looked friendly, and as far as they knew, this was a benign incident, absolutely not a danger to the public. I thanked her and went back out. Taking a deep breath, I took the road back to the docks.

I'd just barely passed the market before I realized that something was very wrong. It was still early enough that the vendors were just getting started setting up their wares and bringing in fresh fish and other goods from the ships. But the fact they were doing so, without officials hanging around, was odd. Dageis took things seriously and yet here we were, as if nothing had happened, as if the city watch hadn't brought in hounds last night.

I reached the old mill. It wasn't roped off. Labourers were lining up to go through the gates to start the day. One waved at me.

"I'm looking for someone," I said.

"Does he work here?"

"I don't know," I ventured. "Did anything happen here last night?"

"I'm not sure we know what you mean, miss," her companion piped up. "We're just starting our shift."

I took my leave and went around the back, back to the alley I'd taken the night before. A drainpipe was at the far end. I saw something sticking out—a hand, both pale and yellowing under the sun. I knew without even looking that I'd found my stranger and he was dead.

For a few minutes, I tried to hold my breath in turns so I could find the courage to touch him. Eventually, I dragged him from the pipe and into the alley. His face was all grey and his body was stiff. I didn't know enough about dead bodies to guess what that meant about how long he'd been dead. Inwardly, a part of me wondered if my mother would know. The weird part about him was he had no stench. Did someone cast some sort of spell to stop the decay? Perhaps it took longer for bodies to smell—it had been a cold night, after all.

I focused on patting his pockets. I found a thick bracelet made of silver, engraved with a number on the flat part, as well as a purse filled with coin. Both went into my pocket. The last item was a blank piece of card, small enough to fit in the palm of my hand.

I walked away from the body to hold it against the light. That did the trick. The ink began to appear, forming letters. *Cato tan-Tarsius.* It gave an address for the capital of Drusgaya, in one of the richer districts up north, overlooking the sea. I stared at it for half a second. It wasn't much, but it was a start.

Drusgaya wasn't too far away. An airship would take me straight there. One of the wonders of convenience in modern Dageis, though it came at a price. In school, some of the professors—against the wishes of the administration—brought up concerns that the *agan* fabric was never intended for so many mages drawing on so many connections at once. A number of them disappeared soon after, which told the others not to talk about it again.

I bought a ticket and sat in the waiting station for the next one, which wouldn't be for another hour. A family settled in the row of benches across me—a father, a mother, and a little girl. She was carrying a rag doll the size of her torso.

"You're just going to leave without another word?" a familiar voice whispered behind me.

"Let's not pretend it doesn't at least make you happy, Mother," I replied. "You know very well what my presence does to this family."

Sume walked around the aisle to sit next to me. She handed me a small wooden box, covered with a piece of white cloth. I could smell the steam through the cotton.

"You didn't eat breakfast," she said. "And Portia did such an excellent job cooking. It's dried beef with egg and rice—your favourite."

I took the box and placed it on my lap. It was still warm. "Thank you," I said stiffly. I said nothing else. I didn't even look at her.

She seemed to hesitate for a moment, like she was thinking of leaving without another word. Eventually, she placed a hand on my face. Her icy fingers traced a line across my cheekbone and up the corner of my eyes. "Whatever you think of us or the things we've done," she whispered, "you should know you were always loved."

Tears stung my eyes as she walked away.

For the next few hours, I sat in silence, frozen to my seat. Eventually, I ate the food and debated throwing the box away. But I kept it in my pack like some sentimental idiot instead, even though it took more room than I'd hoped. Then I boarded the airship and thought about how cruel I'd been and how much crueler I had to be, because no matter what anyone said, I couldn't change the past.

When we passed the low-lying mountains and hovered over Lake Lasta, I made the pretense of making my way to the lavatory below deck. There, I pushed the window open with my elbow and jumped.

The advantage of being in the middle of nowhere was that it was unlikely you would get anyone checking for unauthorized use of a simple spell for miles and miles around. Triple that if you were plunging straight for the bottom of a lake. Even if I had shattered into a million pieces, I doubt anyone would notice I was missing—at least until the airship reached Drusgaya and they noticed my ticket hadn't been turned in. Then they would label my disappearance a suicide, which happened in Dageis more often than you think, for so many reasons. My parents would learn my fate, in time; I was hoping the people hunting for me would know at once. If they were as hot on my heels as I expected, they would. While I wasn't confident I could fool them for very long, it would at least buy me time.

Of course, it was a simple enough process for a skilled mage not to *actually* die. I didn't have the resources to create a portal that would take me all the way—such a blatant display would've had the authorities on me before I could blink. But I had adequate time to prepare something simple from the lavatory, using the basin of silver-treated water you were supposed to wash your hands in. After I jumped, it allowed me to open up a portal from right outside the window to the surface of the lake below, which softened the fall immensely. I took a few minutes to marvel at what I'd just done. I hadn't cast a spell like that in ages, and I was surprised it came to me easily.

Afterwards, I swam to the closest shore, which happened to be the little island in the middle of the lake. As I emerged from the water against the light of the setting sun, I remembered how Papa taught me how to swim. When everyone else was so concerned about making sure I learned to control my magic, Kefier focused on things that made me feel almost normal. "Why learn how to swim at all, Papa?" I remember asking him, and now I felt a twinge of shame that I would question him at all. He had it right all along—I couldn't always rely on magic.

Even the most skilled mages couldn't feed themselves out of nowhere, for example. People outside of mage families sometimes had no idea how it worked—they thought we could create nourishment from mere air. Trying to explain that what they called magic was simply a process of transferring energy, of drawing on your connections to create a semblance of power where it already existed in the first place, just not clear to the naked eye…well, it's enough to make people nod off in mid-conversation.

"You are not just your gifts," Kefier explained kindly, words that if it had come from anyone else, I would have reacted with enough anger to burn from within.

But now I knew what he meant. His lessons made it possible for me to build a fire to dry my clothes (I cheated and made the spark, but it would have been for nothing if I didn't know how to stack firewood), and catch fish, and not be frightened as darkness set in and stars rolled across the night sky. Well—I wasn't afraid, but I suddenly felt a pang of emptiness greater than I had ever known. I felt a lump in my throat. *You were always loved.* Of course I knew that, but I should have told her life wasn't that simple. Love couldn't solve everything, or I wouldn't be here.

The next day, I saw a floating piece of log on the lake, which I used as a boat and saved me the trouble of having to swim all the way to the mainland. I reached the fields, which were really nothing more than an expanse of pastures that would go all the way along the western side of this coast.

By noon, I was in the nearest town and paid for two nights at the local inn. It was better not to show up in Drusgaya right when they were discovering my disappearance. Two or three days, and they would have lost interest already. I learned a long time ago how easy it was to disappear when you were a nobody. While eating dinner, I caught a few glances thrown my way, but that was probably because I was a young woman, dining alone. A young man, braver than all his friends, tried to sit next to me.

I pushed my nearly empty plate away and got up.

"Hold on now," the man said, grabbing my wrist. "I was just trying to say hello."

"Hello yourself," I replied flatly. "Now if you'll excuse me, I need to get some rest."

"Maybe you need help with that." He blocked my path just as I tried to reach the stairs.

The simple exchange had already attracted more attention than I needed. I swore under my breath. When he made a grab for me a second time, I inadvertently let a lick of flame strike his palm, small enough that only he could see. His eyes widened.

"If you're a mage," he said under his breath, "where the hell is your pendant?"

I wanted to swear a second time. Every other city had its own rules, but here so close to Drusgaya, there needed to be a way to distinguish mages from the rest of the population. It was partly to give tourists and other visitors a sense of peace. Many of the places they came from didn't have mages who walked as openly as the ones in the Empire of Dageis did, and it gave them a sort of reassurance.

"I'm not," I quickly grumbled. "It's nothing but a trick." I pulled away.

"Of course, you're not," he said to my retreating figure. "Gorenten can't be mages. You're a mage-thrall at the very least, aren't you? A mages' helper? Where's your master, little girl?"

I cringed, but the tavern owner, the man who served me earlier, grabbed him by the shoulder. "We'll have none of that here," he said. "Out with you."

"You'll have the authorities swarming your establishment within the week," the young man replied. "Serving Gorenten—"

"There's no rule against that."

"She's a swamp witch. If you won't call the authorities on her, I will." He waved his friends over and stomped out of the tavern, his face red. I should have noticed how drunk he was.

I went to my room, my heart pounding. I should have also known better than to be rude; the last three years of relative peace and quiet in that small town, where I could call on Jehar anytime I needed to, had spoiled me. Things were different out here.

I heard a knock on my door and went to answer it. It was the establishment's owner. "Look," he said. "I'm really sorry about all that, but... he's right about the trouble. It's a week before the festivities, you know, and well...if you don't mind. There are other inns in town."

There was no sense in begging him to stay. I was tired, but I didn't want trouble, either. "I was just leaving," I said.

"Come with me downstairs. I'll refund your deposit, and tonight's dinner is on me."

A paltry offering, but it wasn't the worst he could have done. Many would have defended the young man. Others would have been the first to call the town guards. I held my tongue and nodded. He gave me a sheepish smile, like he wasn't just about to send me out into the dark night, out on the road where those men would be waiting for me. Despite what he said, I knew the nearest inn would at least be an hour's walk away. But he didn't want trouble, and my own didn't matter to him.

After I got my money back, I shouldered my pack and went on my way.

I learned this in Eheldeth a long time ago: you cannot change what people think about you, but nothing won't stop you from feeling like you could have done something to stop their cruelty. A teacher of mine once told me it was my blood in an attempt to explain away my tormentors. "Your people are attuned to the *agan* in a way that Dageians can only dream of," she said, as if the fact justified whatever they did.

I was sure the man's desire to humiliate me in front of an entire tavern was connected to that same fear. Or perhaps the thought of conquering me made him feel like he could conquer his fear, and that made him better somehow. Maybe people like him didn't think at all. The desire to find yourself in your treatment of the other must be in all living things, else we wouldn't waste so much time on things that didn't matter.

After the accident with Lord Talos, I spent the whole evening in custody. I remember little of it. I remember closing my eyes and refusing to even talk while the officials prodded me from all directions. "What's wrong with her?" they asked, a sea of faceless voices in the dark. "Is she deaf? Dumb?" *Stupid?* They crowded around me, wondering if they shouldn't just drag me to a mage who could strip me from my powers—a process that was as dangerous as it sounded, as it left many people in the same state as Lord Talos. A few wondered what a servant girl was doing in a manor unchecked, unwatched; those without proper Dageian citizenship, people from the lower castes, were often shackled to a mage as a mage-thrall if they so much displayed as a whiff of connection to the *agan*. I said nothing until Father arrived at the precinct to fetch me, with papers signed by one of his friends from the mages' council.

I remember feeling a pang of disappointment once he arrived, head lowered, that easygoing smile on his face. He was courteous to them at every opportunity. I didn't understand. I was in there because I defended him in the first place—because I hadn't allowed a man to disparage his name and ruin his reputation. I expected him to defend me in turn. I wanted him to go in there and show them what a grave mistake they'd made—I wasn't just some servant girl, I was *his* daughter. My father, for all I hated him, was at least a Count. Didn't their titles mean something? The very structures that made them treat me with disdain were the same ones that gave my family a measure of power, no matter how miniscule. I wanted them to shake in their boots once they realized their mistake and take back every demeaning word.

Instead, my father treated them like *we* were the ones who erred. He smiled at all of them—the guards, the officers, the mages who had come to examine me—and repeatedly apologized for the mistake. If they had given him room, he would have grovelled. Right outside my cell door, I caught him exchanging pleasantries with the woman who had pushed me in, who had called me "so dirty, she *must* be a mage-thrall." He even complimented her hair. I felt like I would rather rot inside that cell forever.

He took me back home in silence.

"You're not going to tell me to control myself?" I asked, outside the gates to the mansion. By then, the party was over; the entire great hall was abandoned, with only empty tables and chairs to mark the night's festivities. I caught Kefier waiting for me by the path and longed to run up to him instead of standing out here with the man whose only contribution in my life was his seed. Kefier would have given everyone back at the precinct a piece of his mind. He would have made them pay somehow.

"What's the point?" Enosh replied. A question for a question. He liked mind-games, though I wasn't sure if that was what was happening.

"You didn't scold them," I said. "Lord Talos *attacked* me."

"They'd never believe it. Lord Talos is a distinguished guest, a harmless old man. You're…you."

Even at that age, I knew what he meant. "That's bullshit."

"If you don't stop with that language, I'm going to put an end to you spending time with your uncle's mercenaries. You need to learn to be civil, especially around these people. You don't want to make them think less of you than they already do."

"You know it's bullshit. You spend most of your days getting people to believe the most outrageous things. That you've bartered trades you've never touched, or personally know people you've never been in the same room with. You're a bullshitter, Enosh Tar'elian, and the one time you got the chance to tell the truth you made them believe I'm just some dumb waif of a girl who didn't know any better."

"Did you?" he asked.

By now, Kefier, who had heard the argument, was walking towards us, arms crossed. He had been told not to interfere with my father's authority ever since he came back into our life, which I think he tried to do most days. "That's enough, you two." Words that were surprisingly calm for him. "It's dark, and the neighbours will talk. Get inside."

"They treated me like an animal," I whispered. "They didn't talk to me. They talked *at* me. Never once stopped to ask what happened. Everyone else at the party they spoke with—they never asked *me*."

"Someday you'll learn that the world runs by its own rules and not your desires," Enosh said, before he turned to glare at Kefier. "You spoil her too much," he added.

Kefier rolled his eyes and let him walk by. Once upon a time, I got the sense that he would have struck him. Now they just let everything boil underneath, a layer of filth underneath our seemingly pristine, affluent lives.

Years of living in Dageis hadn't done much to soothe the anger from that night. If anything, it had only made it worse. I could feel it starting again as I left from the inn, like an itch that wouldn't go away. It heightened even more when I reached the first bend of the road, right under the darkening sky, and saw the man from the tavern and his friends appear under the moonlight.

"Hello again," the young man said.

I didn't reply this time. He knew what he was doing. He had threatened to call the authorities on me, in public; if I tried anything now, there would be no escape. They'd hunt me and find me and any chances I had of saving my family would disappear into thin air.

"Now that you've had time to think about my offer, I was hoping you've changed your mind," he continued. "What do you say?" He glanced at his companions, who all waggled their eyebrows and elbowed him.

I closed my eyes. *A little spell, then. Not enough to hurt him. Just a touch to frighten him.* But it would be risky. It might just aggravate him more. And I would give them enough reason to investigate me, an outlaw mage just suddenly appearing out of nowhere in a town beside the lake where another had disappeared. It would make all my hard work for nothing.

"Well?" the man asked. "Don't tell me you've forgotten how to talk?"

Let him scream at you. Let him get tired. Enosh was right about this one. Even when they treat you like an animal, you have to be the one to show them how to act like a human being. It's your only way out.

He lifted his hand to strike me.

"Leave her alone!" a voice called from the other end of the road.

CHAPTER 15

DRUSGAYA

I felt my heart constrict. It was a woman's voice, which meant little. She could just as easily sell me to the authorities as these men.

She approached on a horse, the kind of hulking animal more suited to pulling carts than riding. The cloak over her back barely hid the scars running along like rivulets on her face, as if she'd survived a mauling from an animal the size of a bear at least, maybe bigger. Her skin was the same colour as mine—darker, even. Another Gorenten, perhaps—there was a tinge of my fathers' accent in hers.

"Mind your own business," one of the men said. "Unless you want us to turn you in, too."

The woman got off her horse. There was a sword on her belt. The men, seeing it, just laughed.

"Oh, no wait," my tormentor said. "Don't laugh, gentlemen. She might just be one of those warrior princesses. The kind who are better with the blade than you, even if you out-muscle her and outnumber her three to one. Let's tremble in fear before her highness, before she decides to take off our—"

The woman took a knife from her belt and stabbed him between the shoulder blades while her back was turned. "You bitch!" he snarled, whirling around to strike at her.

She jumped out of the way. "It doesn't take a fighter to know you're more talk than sense," she said. "That's a tiny wound, if you must know, and quite far away from your vital parts." She pretended to lunge for his crotch, and he fell backwards with a scream. She smiled. "Now you can go running to the precinct to report you've been assaulted by two,

116

vicious women, or you can try to beat us right here, in front of the whole town. Even three to two and you might still have a chance."

I felt a trickle of sweat and turned my head. Indeed, the commotion had attracted enough attention from the inn we just left—several people were gathering along the streets.

The men spat and plodded away.

I realized I could breathe again. The woman sheathed her knife and tapped me on the shoulder. "I was in the tavern earlier," she said. "And so were those people. Anyone could have told you those men were waiting for you out here. Good thing they gave us all a show. With any luck, the guards will dismiss them for troublemakers."

"Thank you," I grumbled under my breath.

"Oh, don't thank me yet. We have to get out of here in case the guards *don't* dismiss them."

She led me down the path, her horse snuffling behind her.

"What's your name?" she asked, after a few moments of silence.

I suppose that was the polite thing to do. I coughed. "It's Rosha," I said, without even really thinking about it. Inwardly, I wondered if that was another mistake. I should have given her a fake name. But there was no chance at all I would ever remember to respond to one, and then she'd know I was lying, and then…

I realized she was holding out her hand. "Aren't you listening?" she asked. "I'm Nasuha Lang'rabay. Suha, for short. It's nice to meet you, Rosha."

I took her hand, giving it a half-hearted shake.

"You're born here, I suppose."

I shook my head.

"Oh. I thought, given your lack of accent—"

"Jin-Sayeng, actually," I said. "But I haven't been there in a very long time. I grew up here. Maybe that's the most important part."

"I see. I'm from Sen'senal."

"Are you a citizen?"

She gave me the sort of grin that told me I'd made a mistake. Not just that, but that she found my mistake infinitely more hilarious than she was letting on. "I'm a mercenary," she said at last. "Travelling the world, offering my services, sleeping under the stars."

"In other words, you're homeless."

She lifted an eyebrow.

"My stepfather is—" I said, before stopping myself again. *You were better at acting in Klossaka. Maybe just stop talking.* "Tried his hand at that," I finished, lamely. "He wasn't very good."

"It's a hard gig. People don't seem to mind hiring Gorenten, but they certainly don't like *paying* them, either."

"Why are you alone?" I asked. "It would make sense to have companions, wouldn't it?"

She smiled again.

"Sorry," I grumbled. "If you don't want to talk about it, then…"

"I'm what you call someone who has fallen on hard times," she said. "I'm not overly crazy about the idea myself, so yes, we don't have to talk about it at all."

A signal not to talk was just about all I needed, and we fell silent as we walked to the end of the road. At the intersection, over to the road leading down to Drusgaya, she finally turned to me and said, "You don't want to talk, but clearly you're travelling alone. I'll walk you all the way home. I can't let anything happen to you—it'll be on my conscience."

"It doesn't have to be."

"You really didn't grow up in Gorent," she said with a grin.

"What do you mean?"

"An observation. Your tone of voice. You take pride in being able to handle yourself, and you dislike the idea of letting someone else take care of you." The grin widened. "A Dageian thing, the illusion of self-sufficiency. A myth. No one can live on their own, not really. One way or another, you end up needing others, and the sooner you accept that, the easier it'll be."

I cleared my throat. "I'm going to Drusgaya."

"As was I," she replied. "That's settled, then. We'll travel together, and if you don't want to feel indebted to me—well, then I'll happily let you buy me breakfast in the morning. What do you say?"

I got the feeling she wasn't going to let me say *no*, so I nodded. As we walked, I wondered if my fathers had ever passed down the wisdom of the words she'd just uttered. If we weren't meant to be alone, why send me to Eheldeth at all? Why force me to grow up in a land where loneliness was my only protection?

Nasuha knew the roads well enough. Even as the evening blanketed the hills and fields around us, she seemed confident in pressing on until we grew weary. We stopped at a small inn, which she remembered served a great poached egg on a bed of wet noodles in spicy sauce. They served it to us early in the morning, at her request. The egg yolk was still half-cooked and spilled on the noodles with one poke. Peanuts, pork rind, and fried baby shrimp were sprinkled all over it as garnish. I felt a shred of regret when we finally had to leave; I wouldn't have minded staying another night there. The surrounding fields were peaceful. If I ignored the looming silhouette of the city in the distance, with the constant coming and going of airships and the perpetual grey smog that hovered on the horizon, I could almost pretend I was back in Klossaka.

An hour onto the road, the illusion of an idyllic countryside fell away. Now carriages rolled past us, and coachmen screamed at us to stay out of their way. Nasuha screamed right back at them, calling them names in half a dozen languages. She almost looked like she enjoyed it. One carriage eventually stopped for us, and Nasuha stomped towards the driver, who jumped off the seat.

"You no-good bitch!" the driver scoffed. "You mannerless madwoman, you—"

"You spineless, saggy-balled, slack-jawed bastard," Nasuha barked back, before drawing the man into a tight hug. "Sarus my old friend, they still let you run these routes?"

"Of course they do," Sarus laughed, the pretend frown on his face having literally turned upside-down. "Who else knows these roads better than me?"

"No one else, I'd say! I recall the time you knew it so well; you took a dirt road up the mountain straight into a nest of wyverns. Didn't you get those merchants killed?"

"I most certainly did not. One did, however, lose all his hair, but in my defense, most of it was gone already."

"Ah, my mistake. An oversight."

"That happens in women your age."

She punched him in the gut. "And this happens to men your age, so why don't we take this on the road? We can catch up on the way to Drusgaya."

"You mean to say you want another free ride?"

"Free? Oh no. I have my horse, see?" She turned around and gestured to where I stood beside Stormy, her gelding. "But Rosha here would probably prefer to ride in an elegant coach instead of walking on this dusty road, and she can pay, can you?"

"I suppose if she has to," I sighed.

She tied Stormy to the back of the coach while we settled inside. She wasn't kidding about its elegance—it had the kind of faux opulence that suited the middle class who wanted to move through the roads but couldn't afford their own horses. Leather seats, polished wooden arms, and doors and windows you could close for your own privacy.

Of course, Nasuha preferred to have it all wide open so she could chat with her friend. Her face was animated as they spoke of other acquaintances and old times. I figured from their conversation that Nasuha was merely a frequent customer who had occasionally made bad decisions and dragged Sarus along for the ride. She didn't seem to think it was a big deal that she once used his coach to flee the authorities, which landed him in jail for a good two days; he didn't seem to hold a grudge. As they talked, I noticed the sun shining on Nasuha's scars for the first time. They covered most of her left forehead and part of her eyelid. Where there wasn't a scar, the skin had a ridged quality, like it had been burnt.

She noticed my attention, and I turned my head away way too slow. "You can ask," she said. "I don't mind talking about it."

"Let me," Sarus broke in from the driver's seat. "It was her father. She had a mark on her face, from a disease she got as an infant. He was afraid it meant she would grow up to be a—what's that word?"

"You wouldn't remember," she teased. "It's a Gorenten word. Roughly it would translate to a *Lost One*."

"What is that?"

"Your elders never told you?"

I shook my head.

"The Lost Ones are children cursed with two things: a connection to the *agan*, and a lack of a soul."

"How do you lack a soul?"

She shrugged. "That's just what the legends say. These children lack humanity and seem to serve a purpose not their own. Some say they're minions of the Gorenten Fire God, who has been banished to the bottom of the ocean. When enough of them have been born, they will work together to break him out of his prison and wreak havoc onto the known world. Well, my father believed I was a Lost One, and he threw me to the dogs to be rid of me."

"She didn't die, though," Sarus said, almost proudly. "Old bitch just crawled out from beneath that pack and toddled on home like it was nothing."

"My mother found me, actually," she replied. "I'm not sure I could *walk* much yet. But I do like your version better—I think I'll steal it."

"Your father feared a tale so much that he was willing to kill his child for it," I said.

Nasuha shrugged. "I turned out all right, didn't I?"

"Where is he now?"

"Back in the village."

"They didn't punish him for that?"

"My mother never told them." Her face tightened, and I realized I may have strayed too deep into a pain too personal to talk about.

"I'm sorry," I mumbled. "I shouldn't have asked."

"What mattered was she told me," Nasuha said. "She could have continued with the lies that everyone else believed. Now I tell others. I'm not going to repeat the lies. Why should I? The truth hasn't hurt me."

"Gorent is…"

She held up a hand. "If you were going to say *backward*, I would advise you to stop right there."

I shook my head. "I wasn't going to."

"In many ways, I don't blame them for looking away," she said. "It has been centuries since the islands of Gorent have seen anything resembling prosperity, and it's worse these days. If the Dageians aren't razing our villages and blaming us for the deed, our settlements seem to find ways to destroy themselves. A drought one day, a firestorm the next. Wind, flood, disease, monsters…tragedies occurring one after another at a rate that can't be normal, and yet not often enough that people are willing to pack up and leave yet. Somehow, we've learned to accept the unacceptable, and pretend we're better than that. They're dead lands, yielding bitter people." She pointed at herself with a flicker of a smile on her lips.

"Now let's go back to the time she drove this coach straight off the docks," Sarus cheerfully broke in. "Because *that, that* was uncalled for. By Dorsin's beard, you take your eyes off this woman for one moment…"

Nasuha clouted him, laughing. "We're almost at the city. Where did you want to go again?"

I gave them the address I had seen on the card.

"That the sorcerer's shop?" Sarus asked. "Cato tan-Tarsius."

"He's famous?"

"Pretty famous," Sarus said. "His establishments cost an arm and a leg, but I hear he can do some really amazing enchantments. An armour coated in oil that'll deflect flames for thirty seconds…"

"Which isn't very impressive if you've ever been around fire," Nasuha drawled.

I thought it was, though. A spell like that was difficult to pull off, and it would have to be attuned to the wearer, like most enchantments of that sort. You couldn't just throw enchantments on a dozen breastplates and sell them like fried cakes from a stand. And it took a prestigious sorcerer to be even allowed to run a business like that deep in the heart of Drusgaya. Accidents like Lord Talos's would be far more common otherwise. I heard you needed to have passed your final exams with two mistakes or less and pay through the nose for either bribes or fees, depending on your tolerance for waiting.

I must have zoned out while thinking, because I suddenly noticed Nasuha snapping her fingers in front of me. "We're here." She pointed across the street.

Cato's Enchantment Emporium made my store look like a roadside stall. The building took up an entire block, from one corner down to the park. I quickly noted that it sold more than what it advertised. The first door led to a café, thick with the scent of the whiskey-infused coffee that had recently become popular out in the west. Jehar hated the stuff; he said it tasted like soap.

"You're going to be all right here?" Nasuha asked.

I gazed with trepidation at the giant sign over the main doors. "I suppose you don't just walk in there and ask to talk to Cato," I grumbled.

"You've never been to Drusgaya, have you?" She looked amused.

"Once, when I was little," I said. "But not in a long time." My parents didn't want to take me. Better to keep me away from trouble, they figured. Drusgaya was where both the mage and merchant guilds sat and was home to the emperor. Enosh thought it held too many ghosts, too many memories, for him. But then, was there ever a place in the world that didn't? The man made chaos everywhere he went.

"If you need company for a little longer…" she began.

"I think I'll be fine," I said. "Thank you for your help." I dug into my purse and handed Sarus payment for the trip. He took it with both hands, giving a toothy grin.

"Until next time, then," Nasuha said, shaking my hand. She looked like she wanted me to ask her to stay.

But I didn't know how I was supposed to do that. It's not that I minded the company—a part of me even enjoyed it, I suppose. I had never been around another Gorenten near my age. The children back in the farms didn't count—they all saw me as Enosh's daughter, which meant most didn't want to spend time with me for fear of getting in trouble. Their mothers or fathers would warn them about accidentally hurting me, which was the last thing they wanted to do to the child of their benefactor.

On the other hand, I hated company when they got in the way of me hearing my own thoughts. Nasuha was definitely one of those people —the sort who got fidgety if I stayed quiet too long, who thought she could drown out the awkwardness by making more noise. Jehar had been the same too, come to think of it. The more I kept my mouth shut, the more *he* talked, so I got into the habit of saying nonsense just to ease his nerves. It was the rare person who understood I could like their company without having to make a big fuss about it. Papa knew that, and so did Ivy.

I went into the store alone. A woman dressed in bright yellow robes greeted me with forced cheerfulness. I waved away her offer to help me look around and walked down a long wooden platform. There was a giant pond in the middle—a fountain, really, filled with lily ponds and fish. There was also a parrot with a yellow crest that bobbed its head at every customer. Just beyond the pond were glass aisles stocked with items of just about every kind. More than an enchantment shop, it stocked enough items that would make any merchant drool.

I wandered the aisles until I was bored. Only then did I try to find someone to talk to. I noticed someone following me—not one of the attendants, but a man in a grey uniform. There was a sword strapped to his side, a sabre with a leather hilt. I realized too late that he must work for the store as security.

"You haven't bought anything," he said. Accusation swathed his tone.

"I'm browsing," I replied.

"With all due respect, madam, I know what browsing looks like, and what you're doing…" He made a vague gesture at my direction. "Doesn't look like it."

"So, what do you think I'm doing?" I asked, turning to face him.

He looked slightly embarrassed, which lasted a full few seconds before he decided I had no right to make him feel that way and that it was my fault, actually, for putting him in that situation. "With me," he said. "Now."

I glanced at the door. I could make a run for it, but I wasn't much of a runner—chances were he'd catch me before I could take two steps in. And I didn't want to cause trouble, not if I could help it. I followed him to the back room. I almost balked here, but a woman greeted us.

"Gorenten, suspiciously walking around," the security officer said, all but shoving me forward.

"I was browsing. I told him that."

The woman waved him off. He scowled, but stepped away after a moment. "And you're probably right," the woman said. "But let's not rile him up. He's been in a terrible mood all day."

"I don't see how that's any of my business," I replied. "I can walk myself out."

"Go through the back door at the end of that hall," she said. "Keep you out of his hair." She winked, blonde curls on her cheek. I think she was convinced she was doing me a favour.

I knew asking to meet her boss wouldn't get me anywhere, so I decided to leave and come back later. I went out through the back door and imagined her sigh of relief as I closed it behind me. Maybe I *should* have taken Nasuha on her offer. She had it right, after all—she knew the city better than I did.

The back door didn't lead to the alley, as I first thought. Instead, it opened up to a small, fenced yard, with a gate at the far end. A little dog with floppy ears came bounding towards me, yapping. I crouched down, letting her sniff my hand. She gave it a cursory whiff before settling on my shoes. I guess she could still smell Daisy on them, because she seemed like she wanted to stick her nose between my ankles.

"Don't bother her, Bracken!" a man called, whistling to the dog.

She tore herself away.

"You," he said, pointing. He removed his gloves and approached.

I steeled myself, wondering what trouble I'd now gotten into.

"Are you the housekeeper Leida hired?"

Leida—the woman who just showed me the door. I paused, half-squinting against the light. The man in front of me was aging, with grey along his temples. He could've been anywhere from forty to his late fifties, a clear sign of either someone who knew how to take care of himself…or knew the right charms to make himself look better. I took one glance at his elaborate clothing, expensive-looking boots, and the fancy carriage that waited for him outside, and made a hasty decision.

"Master Cato?" I asked.

He nodded.

I wasn't going to have this opportunity again. I stood up straight and looked him in the eye. "That's me, sir."

His eyes flashed. I wonder if he thought it would be too insolent. "Excellent," he replied. He began putting his gloves back on. "The woman did something right for once. Come on, then. I might as well take you straight home. What's your name, girl?"

"Suha," I said without thinking.

He opened the door to his carriage.

ACT THREE

CHAPTER 16

THE SORCERER'S DOMAIN

My first day in Eheldeth was memorable for so many reasons. For one thing, it was the longest I ever had to be with Enosh. My mother was pregnant at the time and couldn't go. Kefier stayed behind to take care of her. She had argued against it, claiming she didn't need him there, but he thought I was old enough and that Enosh wasn't *entirely* incompetent. I highly disagreed with the latter, but nobody really cared what I had to say.

And so, I travelled with no one else but my father, and learned for the first time what it was like to want to stick my head into a beehive rather than sit beside someone a moment longer. I'm sure my father's associates had a different opinion. Around the right people, he was a brilliant conversationalist—charming, generous, patient. Around his family? Well, that was a different story altogether. As the head of our strange little household, he was expected to have the final say, and he took it for granted.

I felt invisible throughout the journey, a child who wasn't supposed to let her presence known unless asked for. Anything that inconvenienced Enosh was immediately criticized and shot down. *Don't call attention to yourself, Rosha. We're in the empire. Be polite. Be courteous. Thank everyone. Give respect and ask for none.*

I knew why I needed to do these things—knew after my experience at the precinct the power the empire could hold over people like me. But I didn't want to *accept* it. I was a young girl with the power to do magic in an empire that embraced the very concept, on my way to a school that offered to teach me how to better control it. I was supposed to be excited, not frightened out of my wits. I wasn't some weapon to be handled with care.

Except they treated me exactly as if I was a weapon, a monster waiting to turn on its master at the lightest touch. An entourage waited for me at the gates when we arrived, most of whom included mages that could probably incapacitate me with a single spell. The rest were armed guards. Firekeeper Ceres stood with them, golden-haired, beaming— standing prouder and taller than most short women were capable of. "Count Tar'elian," she said, reaching over to take my father's hands with a smile. "You honour us." But she sounded anything *but* honoured. *This child*, her eyes said. *We'll tame her for you. Don't interfere.* And who would argue with her? In many ways, she was the most powerful woman in the empire.

I was given the grand tour of the place with guards on each side— something I later learned wasn't standard for newly arriving students. The rest of them got to wander the grounds almost immediately after arriving. I was shown only a few places—the gardens, the great hall, the dining room, the library, the dormitories, and then nothing else. "Best get settled, dear," Firekeeper Ceres said when we reached the building where I was to be lodged. "Your father and I have things to talk about, and your first class starts tomorrow."

"Thank you, Firekeeper," I said, one eye on my father. I didn't want to give him a reason to complain.

He simply gave a curt nod and left. I didn't think I'd see him again. Most people would make it *clear* if they were saying goodbye, but Enosh never did. I've been told he wandered in and out of people's lives like a house cat, and even his wife and his brother were used to his absences. "He demands respect he doesn't give," Kefier had once grumbled under his breath. Which was ironic.

A little girl with crooked teeth greeted me at the common room of the dormitory. "Are you the new girl?" she asked. "I'm Berinda! I've been asked to take you around."

"Rosha." I glanced at my bags. "Where do I put these?"

"Oh, you can have any bed you want. The one next to mine is free!"

I would have preferred a quiet corner, but by then it was too late— she was dragging me halfway across the dormitories. I deposited my bag at the foot of the bed and watched as Berinda peered through the half-open window next to it. "The others are getting acquainted and playing ball outside," she said. "You want to come?"

I wasn't sure if I was supposed to. Father was still in the building somewhere, and I would get in trouble if I wasn't. But then a part of me asked *so what?* I nodded. She squealed and took my hand. I spent the better part of an hour learning names of people who were in my section. Berinda was in there, too, and Felan, that surly little boy who stood out in that group even more than me. He looked so thin most of the other boys could've probably snapped his bones simply by stepping on him. He frowned when they told him how old I was.

"She's nearly your age, Felan," one boy teased. "And Gorenten! Watch out, she'll probably catch up to you in no time."

Felan rubbed his nose. To the others, it was just a joke, but he took things like that seriously. He glowered at me without saying hello and walked away.

"He's rude, that little snot," Berinda said. "Got a big head because he's still supposed to be in prep school, but they realized he's much too talented or strong or whatever and sent him here at the beginning of the year. Half the boys tried picking on him to knock him down a peg, but he's a vengeful sort. Just stay out of his way and you'll be fine. Let him beat you once in a while."

"That sounds stupid."

"And don't let the keepers catch you talking like that," she added. "They *really* don't like it. Just be polite, and you'll get by."

Mirroring my father's words already. Later that day, before I could even return to the dormitories, I found out from Firekeeper Ceres that my mother had given birth to a stillborn baby. Enosh left as soon as he got the news, without even a word of goodbye. I felt like I was hanging on thin air, torn between my new life and my desire to go straight back home and grieve with my parents. I glanced at those magnificent gardens, with its cherry blossoms and apple trees, each full of pink and white flowers marking the beginning of spring. So beautiful, and the last place on earth I wanted to be.

The lessons on courtesy had stuck around all those years. I didn't have to think about how to answer Lord Cato's series of questions as we travelled through the city in his carriage.

"I'm very particular in how my house is arranged. Are you willing to listen to instruction and remember them all, step by step?" he asked, his legs crossed.

"Yes, sir," I said.

"You'll have to feed the dogs yourself. Their diet is also *very* particular, and I don't trust the stable hands with them."

"That's not a problem, sir."

"And cooking. I have a cook, but he's not here all the time. I trust you know your way around a kitchen?"

"Yes, sir," I lied, thinking about how Jehar would die laughing if he heard me.

"I want coffee on my desk every morning—no cream, no sugar, just all black. If I happen to be busy and I forget, take it away before it gets cold. I don't want to accidentally sip cold coffee. Do you understand?"

"Yes, sir."

He decided that was good enough and didn't quiz me any further. I'd been hoping he wouldn't ask where I came from and was relieved when he didn't broach the subject at all. Maybe it was enough to him I was Gorenten. Many of my fathers' people worked all throughout Dageis, and the reputation protected me from further scrutiny. It was almost convenient, as damned an arrangement as it was.

The carriage rolled into his mansion. I tried not to blink. Enosh had rented a pretty sizable place back in Lon Basden, but that was nothing. The grandeur of Lord Cato's place nearly took my breath away. It looked like the sort of building you could preserve behind a glass case and people would actually pay to see.

"Do you have a family, sir?" I asked. He had to. A place like that…

"I had a son once," Cato said listlessly. "But he left a long time ago. Now I'm alone." He glanced at me, an eyebrow quirked up. "Will that be a problem?"

"No, sir."

"Good." He opened the carriage door and stepped out, graciously helping me down, which told me he believed he was the sort of generous person who would treat even a housekeeper like a lady.

He led me through his gardens and into the main hall, which alone was the size of most homes in the empire. A long, curved staircase ran along the east wall, with heavy wood as dark as wine and polished to a fine sheen. Even the steps were polished—I didn't think anyone could run up them without fear of slipping. Two big dogs greeted us as soon as he closed the door behind him—a tall, imposing black wolfhound and a white and brown mastiff. Both waited politely while Cato hung his coat.

"You've met Bracken. This is Sunflower and Poppy." He greeted each dog by patting them on the head. "They eat morning and night. I'll show you the schedule. You don't have to worry about anything else but their food—the stable hands take care of the rest." He clapped his hands. "I suppose I should show you your room first."

He went into the hallway under the stairs. I followed, my eyes on the paintings that lined the left walls. I recognized a couple of artists—sar-

Kantel, Nel'din…painters that had made their mark on Dageian society a few centuries ago. Original ones cost a fortune. Enosh had a sar-Kantel hanging in the foyer of the house back in Lon Basden—just one, and he made sure to tell everyone to take good care of it. "It costs more than your lives," he joked once, which neither Sume nor Kefier cared for. He never made it again.

I was expecting a room in the servants' quarters the size of a closet, which was common enough in rich people's homes. But the room Lord Cato showed me could have been a guest room. There was a bed with enough room on both sides, four windows overlooking both the front gardens *and* the side orchard, heavy velvet curtains for if you grew tired of the scenery, a small desk, and a bookshelf. He scratched his chin. "I hope this suits you," he said. "There are other rooms in the house, but I thought you might like the one with the best view."

"Who else is in the household?" I asked.

He seemed taken aback by my candour, and inwardly I chastised myself. I was *supposed* to be a servant, and last I checked, servants didn't go around asking too many questions. But he seemed to decide it was benign enough. "My last housekeeper ran off with my valet," he said, looking somewhat embarrassed. "The other servants resigned afterwards. So apart from the stable hands, the gardener, the driver, and the cook, it's all you. And the dogs, I suppose." His briefest gesture towards them set their tails wagging so fast they looked like they would fall off.

"The cook doesn't live here, either?"

"The servants feed themselves, I didn't think it was necessary to hire a full-time cook with just me here. He owns a restaurant and comes by if I'm expected to be at home for a few days. Otherwise, I eat at the café. You'll have to make do with very little help, I'm afraid. But I'm sure you can handle it. Leida only hires the best, if she gets around to it, and it's not like there's much to do once you get the hang of things." He tapped his smooth-shaven chin, one that hardly bore the mark of stubble or a nick from a razor blade. "Well—I'll let you rest." He tipped his head towards the room and made a speedy exit. Of the dogs, only Bracken moved to follow him. The other two sat in the hallway and stared at me.

"I don't have food on me," I began. And then I sighed. "I guess you're supposed to be my chaperones. This is why he's fine leaving me on my own here, huh? I bet you'll follow me everywhere I go."

The dogs whined, tails wagging.

"Fine," I sighed. "Come on in."

They bounded inside the bedroom. Poppy, the mastiff, jumped on the bed and rolled over, her legs splayed in all directions. Sunflower was demurer and stuck her nose in the crack of the window so she could sniff the air outside.

I only had one change of spare clothes that hadn't totally been drenched by my misadventures in the lake, but knowing I could wash them here, I decided to indulge myself. After I cemented a lasting bond of friendship with the dogs by scratching all four ears, I carefully made my way out into the main hall. I reminded myself I was here to find my brother and father, not play housekeeper, and the sooner I unearthed information, the faster I could leave.

I had barely reached the staircase when Cato came tromping back down. "Forgot I had a damn meeting to attend to," he roared as he went straight for his coat. "You, girl. Are you any good with your letters?"

"I can recite Dalon y'n Cavalli if you'd like," I replied.

That gave him pause. He blinked. "Cavalli. Most people would have said Ranochi if they were trying to impress me."

"They would. But nobody reads Ranochi for fun."

"*You've* read Cavalli? At your age?"

I quoted the first page from one of Cavalli's books. I hadn't read it in years, but after that first line: "*The leaves of fall became winter,*" the rest came easily. There was once a time when that was all I had—nothing but the company of books while my parents screamed and fought each other over how best to raise me. You'd be surprised how books can drown out the sound of your world threatening to tear itself apart.

It didn't seem like he was prepared to pick his jaw up from the floor. He recovered easily enough as he tightened the cloak on his neck. "Go up to my office," he said. "The door's open. There are letters on my desk. Go through them. Make sure I'm not missing anything. Write them down on my calender, and then by Dorsin's Beard, *remind me.*" Without another word, he stomped through the door, Bracken at his heels.

I watched through the windows as he boarded his carriage. "I'm probably not getting paid enough to be the man's housekeeper *and* his secretary, am I?" I asked the other dogs.

They whined and nudged my hand.

"Let's go find something to eat first," I said. "Where's the kitchen?"

They recognized the words and were happy to oblige. Tails wagging, they bounded ahead, leading me deeper into the mansion.

CHAPTER 17

THE FIRST GHOST

I remember having lived in poverty long enough to be confused by the things rich people did, even after we moved in with my father and left all of that behind. Giant kitchens, for example, I could understand—big houses were often meant to hold plenty of people, and so it stood to reason you needed a sizable stove and oven and tables for food preparation.

I did not understand a separate room for dining, and then another one for tea.

I could write essays about Dageian tearooms. Actually, I must've done it in school once, to the ire of my classmates who took great pride in their families' elaborate tearooms, with its shelves of fine porcelain cups and dishes imported from places I'd never even heard of. Places that I'm convinced half the time their families made up just to sound even more sophisticated than the next. They would talk about chandeliers that took years to build or were made from the crystallized tears of some rare animal found only in the mountains of an unknown lake in the middle of an unknown country. If I ever made the mistake of staring at them in confusion, they would laugh amongst themselves, happy about that rare instance where they knew more than me. My ignorance of their lives was a weapon, and they wielded it with pride.

And of course, they didn't care about mine. Back in those days when I first started in Eheldeth, I might have longed for a bit of company, and I wound up telling them how extra rooms were too much of a luxury in Jin-Sayeng because the floor was just as good a place to eat if you kept it clean. I learned quickly that those sorts of stories made me a target.

"Only animals eat from floors," they'd say, in the same tone they did when they made fun of me for eating with my hands. When Enosh heard about the incident, he admonished me severely for it.

"Don't give them a reason," he told me under his breath. "They're just *looking* for reasons to treat you differently, Rosha. Don't hand it to them on a silver platter."

Speaking of silver platters, Lord Cato's tearoom was full of them. Golden ones, too. Some were affixed right to the wall, which meant they weren't the sort you ate from. He also had jars full of expensive tea, all lined up in a row on one shelf. The dogs avoided the tearoom, which told me they must've been scolded about being there in the past.

I closed the doors and continued on to the kitchen. The stove was cold, with no sign of firewood anywhere. I went out the back to the woodshed, and there was firewood everywhere on the ground. The shed itself looked like someone had taken a torch to it—the roof and half the contents were charred.

"Ah," I said. "The last housekeeper's departure wasn't amicable."

The dogs whined.

"Really?" I asked. "That's all you have to say?" I sighed. There really was no sense salvaging even the wood from the ground—last night's rains had left them damp.

I went back inside and went through the pantry. I found an old block of cheese. I peeled off the mold and then cut it into wedges, and then ransacked the rest of the contents while I ate. Apart from the cheese, he only had moldy potatoes, moldy carrots, and moldy apples.

"They left *and* cleaned him out," I said. "Impressive."

The dogs barked.

I went back upstairs and tested the rooms. Some of them were locked; the others just led to empty bedrooms. Eventually, I found his office. The dogs stayed outside the hall here, too, as if an invisible presence was blocking them from stepping inside.

Lord Cato's desk was a mess, the sort of mess that would get Enosh to pop a vein. Messy *and* successful—Lord Cato was certainly someone to envy. I wondered if there was a connection there somewhere. Did my father try to do business with the man and insulted him? Was Lord Cato trying to buy out competition?

I picked up the letters and meticulously went through each one. Most were bills for his various properties. Some were pamphlets from other stores. I placed those in a separate pile so I could go through them again—a rivalry could very well be the reason he was involved with my father. But as the names piled up, I began to have doubts. These other companies were bigger than my father's. Did these merchants turn up missing, too? He would have nothing to gain taking over a handful of small stores, which left my mother's theory on the Gorenten lands. Perhaps he was interested in them. Was he trying to build a store there? Of all places? It was in the middle of nowhere, and the Gorenten would be the last people on earth to pay money for overpriced Dageian goods.

The rest were invitations to various functions over the year. He had marked which ones he wasn't interested in with a big X on the envelope. Others had question marks on them. I kept the ones without marks and checked them against the calendar on the wall. I also noted the names and addresses of the letters. Some I recognized as prominent names from the merchant guild, and a bit of digging around got me to conclude that Lord Cato was a respected figure amongst them. A mage, sitting on the merchant guild instead of the mage council, was fairly common—it just meant his priorities lay with the economic interests of the empire instead of overseeing its magic (which by extension meant he preferred to make money over scholarly pursuits). And if I knew my father, who had to defer to the merchant guild's rules despite his own connection to the *agan*, it also showed disdain for the rules the mage council imposed on everyone.

It all took me longer than I expected, and by the time I realized it, it was already getting dark. I cleaned the room as best as I could and made a quick escape, trying to hide my disappointment from the dogs. I'd gone all this way and was nowhere even close to discovering this man's connection to my family, let alone how to help them. I tried to console myself over what Kefier had told me—if Enosh was dead, the conditions of his citizenship simply passed over to his heirs. They only took Ryo; if they wanted us all gone, they should have taken the other boys and myself. There was no sense in hurting either of them. They should still be alive.

But logic made for cold company, and when I crawled into the bed to sleep, a part of me hoped my brother had a bed just as warm and comfortable. Enosh—well, he could sleep in a cage for all I cared. But Ryo hadn't done anything wrong. He was six. He didn't deserve this. And the last thing I wanted was for my parents lose a child again. That first one had been bad enough, though I wasn't there to see it. Portia told me all about it—about the little girl baby, all dressed in white before they put her in a pyre to be cremated. She said Mother just sat near her window and stared at the sky for days. Kefier worked on the garden until he was exhausted, blaming himself for not taking Sume to the midwife sooner, or letting her walk at all, or any number of things. The doctors later told them the baby had a heart condition and there was nothing any of us could've done.

This wasn't like that at all. I knew there was something I could do this time, even though I didn't know what it was.

I fell asleep to my thoughts and woke up in the dead of the night to one of the dogs licking my ear. I got up, half-stumbling in the darkness. A low moan greeted me as I entered the great hall. It was coming from outside the door.

I glanced at the coat rack. Lord Cato's coat wasn't there yet, nor his hat. I knew from checking his calendar that he had an event for tonight. He was a single man, not yet too old, and if Enosh's parties were anything to go by, he wouldn't be home until well past morning. I turned to the dogs. The fur on the back of their necks was standing on end.

"Stay," I told them. I went to the coat rack and found a cane. It was a suitable size for hitting someone square in the eyes, if I found the right angle for it. Fighting was far at the bottom of the list of things I was comfortable with. I hoped the dogs would provide a suitable distraction.

I carefully unlocked the door and pushed it open. There was no one there, except the wind.

I turned back around, just in time to see a woman stumble into the main hall. I didn't know where she had come from. She fell face-first to the floor just as the dogs began to bark. "Help...me..." she gasped. I realized her face was torn to shreds, and so were her hands and wrists.

I dropped the cane and bent down to help her up. But then I saw that her whole side was bleeding. Someone had stabbed her in the gut.

"He's got people in the stables," I said. "Hold tight. I'm going to get help. Stay with her!" I told the dogs. I didn't even stop to grab a cloak for myself. I leaped over the first row of bushes and started running down the road.

I passed several fully fenced paddocks and at least three sizable stables, which told me Lord Cato kept more horses than he used. He probably bred them, from the looks of it. I should've known from the trophies lining an entire bookcase in his great hall.

There was a building at the far end, which looked like it provided lodging for his stable hands. The man barely fed himself, but would keep an entire staff on hand for his horses. It didn't really strike me as odd—I'd known worse from the days when I had to shadow Enosh at his meetings. One man had an entire house dedicated to nothing but sword replicas from all over the world. "Not the real thing?" Enosh had asked.

"Oh no," the man replied. "I would never. I'm too afraid of cutting myself by accident."

There was a single, flickering lantern from a window on the second floor. I started banging on the front door. "Help!" I called. "Help, please!"

"Who the hell is that?" a voice cried.

"Keep it down, some of us are trying to sleep!"

"Hey, it's the new girl."

"Go see what she wants, Mael."

There was a moment of silence. The door opened, revealing a sleepy-looking young man who was probably only a few years younger than me. He had the sort of wispy moustache that only a young man, hoping it would make him look older than he really was, would keep. "Yes?" he asked. He coughed. "I mean—do you need anything, miss?"

"A woman just walked into the main hall," I said.

He rubbed his eyes and blinked. "I'm sorry—could you repeat that?"

"She's hurt. I came here for help. I think she's been stabbed."

"In the main hall?"

"Yes."

"But there's no one in the house but you."

I resisted the urge to shake him. "Just come with me. I left her with the dogs. Do you have any bandages? We'll have to treat her wounds before we take her to the doctor."

He hesitated.

"Bandages," I repeated. "And get a carriage ready."

"She just *walked* in?" he gasped.

It took another few seconds before he finally concluded that I wasn't going anywhere if he didn't help. He shut the door and went to the stables, where he found a medicine kit they kept for the horses. He harnessed two horses to one of the lighter carriages from the yard, and we rode all the way back to the mansion in silence. It took much longer than I was happy with, and inwardly I was hoping the woman had found a way not to bleed to death all over the floor.

We got to the road in front of the house. I jumped off and came racing up the steps. The door was closed. I'd left it open.

I paused before turning one of the handles.

The main hall was empty.

Mael peered over my shoulder. "Where is she?" he asked. "I don't see her anywhere."

My heart was racing. I looked at the floor. It was clean. I could've sworn there was a pool of blood there when I'd left.

"I left her there." I pointed. "Right there. She was bleeding." I stepped inside and whistled.

The dogs came bounding from my room, wriggling from head to toe. "Where is she?" I asked, as if I actually expected them to answer.

Mael scratched the side of his cheek. He was still staring at me. "Uh —what did you say your name was?"

"Suha," I said. "I don't understand what happened. She was just here."

"I don't, either." he replied. He sighed. "Listen, miss…you think it was just a dream? We've got a few more hours before dawn." He yawned, glancing at the sky through the window. "Or hell, maybe an hour. Sleep's already ruined, from the looks of it. You want to eat breakfast with us? You probably got spooked, staying in this house all by yourself. Happened with the last girl, you know."

"The one who ran off with the valet?" I asked.

He nodded sagely. "She jumped at every little thing. Convinced the house was haunted, that she could hear things jumping on the roof all the time. And good old Elry, after he arrived, comforted her about it. That's how their relationship started, you know." He gave me an impish grin.

"No chance in hell," I told him.

He sighed. "Anyway, I really think it's just because the house is old. It creaks every which way. The old master's family has owned it for centuries. I'm sure you probably just saw the curtains or heard something. Like I said. Happens to the best of us. No one's supposed to live alone, least of all in a house as big as this."

He gestured, leading me back outside. I sighed and followed him, though this time, I allowed the dogs to come with me. They ran along the path behind the coach as we returned to the stables.

"Lord Cato said there were other servants who resigned," I said. "What do you mean she lived alone, too?"

"Well, he had assistants who would come and go," Mael said. "But Jaila kept the house, just like you did. There isn't much to do because the master isn't home very often. Between you and me, it's the easiest job ever if you learn his habits and which rooms to clean right before he uses them. The more invisible you are, the happier he will be."

"He didn't seem like that."

"You're new. He's being friendly. It'll wear off."

He let the horses loose into the adjoining paddock and then took me to the kitchens. It was still barely dawn, but I could already smell fresh bread. My stomach turned, reminding me I'd only had the piece of moldy cheese for dinner. An older man with a piece of cloth wrapped around his forehead was working the ovens. "That your new friend, Mael?" he called as we entered.

"It's Suha, the new housekeeper," Mael said.

The old man turned around, carrying two loaves of bread. He slid them across the table. "Still hot," he warned. He turned to me. "I'm Go-nir. You're Gorenten, girl. So am I!" He reached out to shake my hand. His grip was warm and strong.

"Your people are everywhere," Mael commented, tearing into the loaves.

"If you know where to look," Go-nir said, winking. "Sit down. I'll get you something better than the horse food Mael's having."

"What?" Mael grumbled, his mouth stuffed full of bread.

"I was saving these for the master in case he got home early, but it doesn't look like it," Go-nir said, showing me a tray of rolls. "Go on. They're stuffed with coconut jam. It's an old Sen'senal recipe."

I took one and grumbled a quick thanks as I took a seat across Mael. I didn't know what to think. The sun was rising, and the woman I'd seen was rapidly becoming a distant memory. Was it really just a trick of my imagination? But the dogs...the dogs had seen her, too. I glanced at them both. They were just sitting on the ground, their muzzles on my knee.

I broke the bread in half and took a bite. Sweetness flooded my mouth, and I remembered eating that same sort of bread way back when Papa and I would visit the Gorent islands. I really *was* hungry. The old man noticed, too, because he laughed. "You really should have come by sooner. You're welcome here any time you need company or food. These lads need three square meals a day. When the master's cook pays a visit, he only makes that weird food that only makes you hungrier."

"I can attest to that," Mael broke in. "He gave us his leftovers once. There was a whole plate with nothing but carrots."

"Cinnamon-glazed carrots," Go-nir said. "If I ate nothing but that, I'd start seeing things, too. Go on—put some fat on those bones. There's more where it came from."

I ate more than my fair share of the sweet rolls, which were all washed down with strong hot cocoa. My eyes stung when I recognized it was a kind imported from Jin-Sayeng. I could taste the smoke, fanned from fires made from coconut shells instead of charcoal. A pang of homesickness hit me, and I excused myself before I started bawling in front of these strangers. Mael offered to walk me back to the mansion, but I declined.

Lord Cato's empty carriage trotted past me as I returned. I swore under my breath and hurriedly made my way to the kitchen, remembering his explicit instructions to make sure he had a cup of coffee ready in the morning. I didn't want to get fired before I had the chance to discover his involvement in my brother and father's disappearance. The firewood was still wet, but as I had no other choice, I took my chances and stacked them in the stove.

It took an unbearably long time for me to get a fire started, and by then half the kitchen was filled with smoke. The dogs whined uncomfortably and watched me from the back door as I began perusing the kitchen shelves for the coffee. "I didn't even ask where he kept it," I grumbled. "Some housekeeper." I suddenly remembered the tearoom, and dashed down the hall, almost slipping on the mop in the corner. I could hear Lord Cato's footsteps upstairs.

I grabbed a cup from the ledge and turned to open the glass cupboard. Above the rows of tea were three or four jars of coffee beans. "I didn't ask what kind he liked, either. Or where the coffee grinder is." I could feel my chances of staying even a day or two longer slipping. The man was going to discover my ruse soon enough. What kind of housekeeper neglected the scant few duties she was given?

The footsteps, I realized, were getting closer.

"Lord Cato!" I exclaimed, startled by his dishevelled appearance near the end of the hall. "Did you have a good night?"

He gave an amused smirk. "It was a night, as nights go," he said. He glanced down. I was still holding the cup. "Ah, right, coffee. I was going to say there's no need. I need to run an errand in the city, and you might as well get some shopping while you're at it. You may have noticed the pantry is sorely in need of a few items, and I've noticed *you* brought little yourself. You do want to be comfortable in here, yes?"

"I—of course," I said.

"I'll have one of the stable hands accompany us to carry things for you."

I nodded again. I followed him to the main hall, where he whistled for the carriage again. The driver came by a few moments later, looking slightly irritated that he had to get fresh horses ready again. I would be, too. I glanced at Lord Cato, wondering. Did the man get any sleep? Where was he all night?

CHAPTER 18

THE MAGE AND THE
MERCENARY

I would have liked another few hours to wander the mansion alone again. I was already convinced the woman must have gotten up herself and fled the scene before I returned with help. She must have cleaned up the blood, too—that's what I would have done if I didn't want anyone to discover where I was. Or if she was too injured, someone else did it for her.

I knew the mansion would hold more answers than that carriage, where I sat across Lord Cato in uncomfortable silence. I didn't want to look straight at him for fear that he would start asking questions. A part of me also feared he would recognize me somehow. Not that he knew me—but if he knew my father, he would see the resemblance if he so much as squinted in the light.

Because there was no way around it: I looked like my father. When I was younger, it was easier to deny. I had the same skin tone as Kefier's, which didn't seem unnervingly dark until I had lived in Dageis for a few years, amongst people who were mostly lighter skinned than me. I used to believe I looked like my stepfather the most—that the father who didn't sire me imparted so much more than his temper and his fondness for sour fish stew. I always wanted to be like Kefier, with his generous heart and his incapability of bearing grudges, even towards those who hurt him the most. It sounded like a much easier way to live. To have the ability to attract people and then keep them and be content with nothing but their company. To know how to find peace, even when it wasn't granted to you. Perhaps if I had been more like Kefier, I would have visited home sooner, all bygones erased in the blink of an eye. I might have even stayed with Jehar. He loved me, and if I had been more like Papa, it would be all I needed.

But every time I looked in the mirror, it was Enosh's face staring back at me—that same, perpetually irritated brow, as if I was just waiting for people to disappoint me. That mouth, the one that could give a heartless smile better than a warm laugh. Those eyes—sharp, searching, always looking at everything that could possibly go wrong. I don't know what the gods were thinking, imparting such cruelty as to make me bear every flaw of the man I hated the most.

I must've told Jehar something similar the day I ended our relationship. It was a good few months ago, right after one of the festivals. I decided I had enough listening to people cheer and walked away in the middle of the pie-eating contest. He came running up to ask me what was wrong.

"Nothing." It was easier than telling him the truth. *The world, or me. One of us. Because none of it fits and I don't know where to go.*

"Then why leave?" he asked. "You know they'll ask what's bothering you. Everyone was looking forward to this celebration. If you leave now—"

"Then *you* stay," I said.

"At least tell me you're unwell. Does your head hurt?"

"Watching that infernal pie-eating made my head hurt, yes. I can think of a better way to use my time."

"And celebrating harvest with us isn't?"

I'd made a mistake, and I knew it. But I wasn't the kind of person who would admit to it readily. I swallowed, stared at him. His eyes flickered.

"Why can't you just be happy, Rosha?" he asked. "Why does everything have to be something you can study? People aren't books. You can't just discard them to the side when they come up empty. Even for just a few seconds, can't you just…be?"

"I was," I retorted. "And now it's over." I turned on my heel and left him on that road, grasping for an answer.

Ironic that I was now starting to miss him. I didn't think there was ever a chance that Jehar would understand enough about me to satisfy himself, but it was still company, and I occasionally appreciated the convenience. Another thing my father and I had in common, I suppose. It was why he left my pregnant mother in the first place all those long years ago. It wasn't for any identifiable reason. He just forgot she was there, and by the time he had started missing her, years had passed.

I swallowed. This *really* wasn't a good time to be thinking like this.

The carriage rolled to a stop, and we finally got out, to my relief. Lord Cato handed me a generous amount of coin for my purchases, and I went down to the market with Mael whistling behind me.

"Does Lord Cato have a lover?" I asked, long after we were left by ourselves.

"Not that I know of," Mael said. "Why? Thinking of applying for the position?"

"No." I paused. "Did the last housekeeper try that?"

"I mean, Jaila always did strike me as that type—"

I narrowed my eyes. "What type?"

He glanced away. "You know, the kind who tries to marry her way out of a bad situation. I mean, she might have tried something. I don't know. There's always gossip, and half of them aren't true. I've been with the master for five years—I know all of them very well by now. Anyway, it doesn't matter because she picked Elry in the end."

"Do you know where they went?"

"Not particularly. And there's probably no way of knowing. They disappeared. The master was *really* angry. He's gone through way too many housekeepers the last few years—hell, ever since his son left."

"A mystery upon mysteries," I grumbled. The man couldn't hold on to housekeepers and women randomly showed up in the middle of the night. "Did you meet the son?" I asked.

"No. I've heard about him, though. Sounded like a spoiled, sulky little man. I think he sent him off to be educated somewhere."

"He said he *left*."

"There was an argument of some sort. There always is with these rich folks. I guess when you're not thinking about money anymore, you find other ways to be unhappy."

I turned away from the conversation and focused on picking out the things I needed to buy. From the leftovers in Lord Cato's pantry, I deduced he appreciated having a steady supply of cheese, so I got two different kinds (I couldn't tell the difference) as well as an assortment of fresh fruits. Afterwards, I bought clothes for myself, just because I didn't want to go several days with only one set to change into.

As I worked my way through another aisle of stalls, I walked right into someone. I recognized Nasuha as I reached for the nearest wall to stop myself from falling.

"Rosha!" she yelped.

Mael heard. He stared at us both, eyes wide open.

"You've mistaken me for someone," I said in a low voice. I kept walking.

"But——" Nasuha started.

I glanced around. There were more people now than before, and if I knew anything about Nasuha by now, it was that she was perfectly capable of starting a scene. "Could you be a dear and pick up some blankets?" I asked the startled Mael.

"But there's plenty of blankets at home," he stammered.

"Buy. Some. Blankets."

He blinked, but the irritated look on my face finally did it. He turned away.

"What's happening?" Nasuha asked. "Did you meet Lord Cato? Are you——"

I grabbed her wrist, pulling her further away from Mael's direction. "I'm in his employ," I replied.

"Which means…?"

"He's hired me as his housekeeper," I said.

"Oh," Nasuha replied. She looked confused. "Was that what you wanted to do in the first place?"

"It doesn't matter. Look, I can't really be caught talking to you right now, all right?"

"Suha!" Mael called from one end of the stalls. "Do you want these ones?"

An amused glint crawled on Nasuha's face. "Well," she said at last. "Now it gets interesting."

Somehow, I managed to distract Mael with yet another errand while Nasuha and I shared a plate of potstickers from one of the food stalls. "Let me get this straight," she said, after I told her what had happened the last couple of days. "You didn't *intend* to enter his services. You just wanted to talk to him. But he thought you were the servant he's looking for, and you decided…not to correct him?"

"I thought it gave me a better opportunity," I said. "If I asked him questions, he could always lie. I might discover whatever he's actually hiding."

"What the hell were you going to ask him, anyway?"

"That's private," I replied.

"You went there under a fake name. Under *my* name. You owe me the truth."

I sighed, poking one side of the potstickers with my nail. It broke through the skin, allowing a quick spurt of oily water. I picked up the whole thing and shoved it into my mouth, chomping down on scallions and mushrooms.

"You're delaying here, *Rosha*. Unless you want me to tell your friend—"

"I'm looking for my father," I blurted out.

Nasuha turned around on her stool. "Now we're talking. Your father, the Gorenten?"

"He's a merchant. He's been missing for months. Cato tan-Tarsius is the only lead I have, and it's gone nowhere. There's nothing about my father in his office, or his documents. I spent all of last night going through them."

"Uh huh, I see. Have you checked his basement?"

"What?"

"He must have a cellar of some sort," Nasuha said. "I would've gone down there first."

"You mean—to see if my father's tied up there or something?"

Nasuha nodded.

"*Why* would he do that?"

She raised an eyebrow. "Why not? Wizards get lonely, too. Is your father good-looking?"

"That's *not* what's happening here," I said, pushing my empty plate of dumplings away.

"I'm not hearing a *no*. He is, isn't he? If he had you young, then maybe he's now in his forties, with salt and pepper in his hair—"

"Would you be disappointed if I said he was fat and bald?"

"Is he?"

I sighed. "What are you doing, Nasuha?"

"Helping. Gods, Rosha, if you're looking for a whole man who may or may not be alive, you *always* check the basement."

"I haven't," I said. "I'm not even sure he has one. Half the doors in the house are locked. But people—if they are hiding in there—well, they'd need to eat, and I wasn't exactly given instructions to feed anything but the dogs. I'm pretty sure if someone else was there, I would have heard it."

"In a big mansion? Please, Rosha. Some of those walls are built to keep sound *out*."

"It's only been one day. Maybe if he leaves overnight again…" I took a deep breath, staring at the sky. "I don't know his schedule. It's hard to sneak around."

"If you're his housekeeper, then you'll naturally have to be at his beck and call," Nasuha said. "I have a better idea. How about I do it for you?"

"I don't see how I'll be able to sneak you in there."

"I'll get him to hire me."

"I don't think he needs a mercenary."

"You'll be surprised," she said with a wink. "Anyway, I have other skills. Does he need a new driver? Stable hand?"

"He already has a coachman, and more stable hands then I can count."

"If I get rid of one for you…"

"You sound pretty desperate."

She laughed. "I haven't had a job in over a month, and I'm running out of money."

"If you're resorting to blackmail—"

"Oh, sweetie, it doesn't have to come to that if you'll just help a friend out." She gave a broad smile.

I sighed again. "Let me think about it," I said. "As long as you promise to help me in return…"

"If your father is as good-looking as I think he is—"

"You just made that all up in your head."

"—then I'm definitely going to find him. That's a promise." She held out her hand.

With the nagging sense that I was going to regret all of this, I shook it.

Mael and I returned to the mansion on our own; Lord Cato, it seemed, had other errands, and was simply going to hire a coach to get back home. Bracken sat between us, a little uncertain about getting left behind. I patted her chin, wondering how much easier my task would be if she could speak. All she'd have to do was tell me what her master was up to.

Mael went off to take care of the horses, and I unlocked the main door and carted my purchases indoors. The other dogs met me, and I fed them from a pail of meat Go-nir had dropped at the front porch. Apparently, the dogs were to be fed in specific amounts in order: Bracken first, followed by Poppy, and then Sunflower. Go-nir warned me that Lord Cato could tell if I fed them wrong—something about the consistency of their stools or the smell of their breath. The man didn't look like he took much care of himself, but the dogs had to be pristine.

I didn't find it odd, to be honest. Enosh's quirks were worse. Portia once told me it used to drive her crazy until she just learned he was going to complain no matter what she did. It didn't mean she stopped trying—I suppose to stop trying would mean getting fired—but you just had to learn not to care so much about *why* he wanted things done the way he did. "I guess he makes sense of the world that way," Portia had mused. "That if those few things could go just right, then the rest would fall into place. It all starts with that perfect piece of buttered toast and that cup of tea, steeped just right. He won't be able to conquer the world if his toast is burnt."

It was stupid, of course. Was a crooked calendar on the wall going to determine if he got a business deal or not? But perfection as the antidote to an uncertain world—yes, I could understand that. More than I was willing to admit.

I carried the pail to the kitchen and doled out the required amounts anyway. I stopped questioning why Sunflower, who was the same size as Poppy, had to eat more, or why I had to crush two tablespoons' worth of eggshells into Poppy's dish, and followed the instructions precisely. After they'd eaten, I left them in the yard outside the kitchen and closed the door. I didn't want them following me as I explored the rest of the house.

I found a door leading to what I thought was the basement. It was locked, just like the last time, but something about what Nasuha said stuck with me. I knocked several times and then pressed my ear against the wood, trying to see if I could hear anything.

There was only silence. I glanced around, and then looked at the key Lord Cato had handed to me earlier. It was the only key I had. I stuck it into the keyhole.

It wouldn't turn, which I'd expected, but...

I made a spell. A heat-spell, nothing more. I was hoping a bit of magic in a famous sorcerer's home would go amiss—even if I left my mark on it, if nobody checked, nobody would ever know. I was also hoping to soften the key enough so it would fit the lock. It was a tricky solution. Many homes in Dageis had extra wards on doorways, and a sorcerer's home would surely have *more*. There was a chance I would set off an alarm and get myself killed on the spot. But wards were also tricky things. You wouldn't want to accidentally be set on fire in your own house. Many of them responded to families—to people related by blood, or something familiar to the ward when it was created.

Since I was using a key that had just recently been in Lord Cato's hands, I could bypass any wards that had been placed in it. My gamble was rewarded, doubly so—the door creaked open, and I realized no spells had been erected on this door. I probably had no need to be cautious, anyway. Most people didn't go around putting up wards *inside* their homes.

I took a lamp and slowly made my way down the steps. The stairway creaked, probably from my very breath alone—I could feel the house shift with every movement. I watched the flames dance on my hands, elongating my shadow on the wall. Rot and mold clung to my nostrils. I sucked in my breath and held the lamp aloft, half-cringing at what I was going to see there.

The light flashed across the room, deepening the shadows even as my eyes adjusted to the scenery. No bound man or forgotten meat locker lay waiting for me. The basement…was nothing but a warehouse. Old furniture was piled in the corner. Cobwebs hung from nearly every crevice, thick enough to smother. I slowly approached the furniture and realized one was a child's bed without the mattress. There were other children's things, including an old, half-rotting cradle. At the foot of the bed were about three boxes of old books, all covered in a thick blanket of dust. I couldn't even read the titles without sneezing. There was nothing of interest in them, anyway.

In fact, there was nothing else in that whole basement—just old things and someone else's forgotten memories. I went back up the stairs and quickly closed the door. I locked it, pulled the key out, and went back to the main door to put the key back the way it was. I'd just finished molding the key to the lock when I heard footsteps behind me. I turned to see Go-nir with a sheepish look on his face. "There's someone looking for you," he said. "Said her name is Rosha, and that you needed help…?"

I swore inwardly. "I'll go talk to her," I said.

"The master doesn't like it if you have company," he said. "His patience, after Jaila…" He wrung his hands nervously.

"I know. Let me take care of it." I dashed up to the path leading to the gates.

CHAPTER 19

THE MERCENARY AND
THE MAGE

Gods, the woman couldn't *wait* an hour. Go-nir opened the gates for me, and she all but hopped in, an impossibly wide smile on her face. She'd ditched the travelling clothes and was dressed like a common peasant girl, out for a stroll. Even her sword was nowhere in sight.

"Hi, *Suha*," she said. "You really did well for yourself! To live in Lord Cato's house? Imagine—"

"What are you doing here?" I asked.

"You said there'd be a job for me." She glanced at the confused Go-nir and winked.

"I said there *might* be…" I began.

"Well, you might forget." She winked. "I know how forgetful you are, *Suha*."

"Why does she keep saying your name like that?" Go-nir asked.

"Because Rosha's an idiot," I said, realizing too late what I'd just walked into. Her grin grew wider. I sighed.

"It's a big mansion," Go-nir commented. "We *did* use to have more than one housekeeper at a time. But it's just been one problem after another, and…"

"Well, Suha can vouch for me," Nasuha said brightly. "We grew up together. Didn't we, Suha? Way back in Sen'senal?" She elbowed me.

"Really?" Go-nir asked, leaning on the broom he was carrying. "You don't say. Who's your family?"

"I grew up *here*," I hissed.

"Pretty clear from your accent," Go-nir said. "So why is your friend lying?"

"I met her a while back. She needs a job, but no one would hire her. She's incompetent—"

"Hey, now—" Nasuha began.

"—in just about everything but housework," I continued.

Go-nir narrowed his eyes.

"Look," he finally said. "Regardless, it's going to be the master who'll have to make the final decision. I'm just saying he probably won't be too happy if you have visitors coming in and out at all times."

"This will be the one and only time," I said.

"Come on, Grandfather," Nasuha added. "You're a kind, generous soul. I can tell. And also extremely handsome, I'm not going to lie."

She said the last part in the local Sen'senal dialect. Even though it was clear the old man knew she was flattering him, he let out a long sigh. "You children. Don't get caught. I don't know what time he'll be home. I'll try to rattle the gates extra long when his coach comes by. If you stay nearby, you'll be able to hear it."

Nasuha laughed, taking my hand.

"So?" she asked when we were alone. "Did you check it?"

"I went to the basement, yes."

"What did you find?"

"Nothing," I said.

"Did you check anywhere else? It's a big mansion."

"It's big, but not endless. There's clearly no one inside those rooms, and not in the basement. Whatever I saw last night—"

She glanced at me. "What *did* you see last night?"

"There was a woman here," I grumbled. "She was wounded. Looked like she was about to die. She collapsed on the floor right there." I pointed.

Her eyes widened.

"She disappeared before I could find help for her," I said.

"Then she must be hiding someplace."

"Where?"

"I don't know, but a woman doesn't *just* scamper out of here. That yard is very big. Unless you saw a ghost…"

"Ghosts aren't real," I said.

She laughed. "You live in an empire that runs on magic. Ghosts could be very real."

I whistled for the dogs. "Well, since you look like you really want to help, we might as well start with the yard." I hoped we'd be done by sunset. A part of me wondered if it was wise to look further or if it was better to give up now. Living people needed to eat, needed water, needed shelter. If Lord Cato truly was hiding something out here, it wouldn't be alive.

I felt a chill descend on me, crawling over my skin. *No*, I told myself. No. I wasn't going to think that. I wasn't going to think of anything dead, let alone my little brother.

I should probably admit that I'm not fond of little children—never have been. When girls my age were playing with dolls and rocking them to sleep, I was busy with books. The world outside didn't interest me as much as getting lost in facts or myths, and I always felt there was more to life than just plopping out babies and making a big fuss over them. I was free to think like that for years, as an only child.

But then, the stillborn baby. Neira, they'd called her, after the grandmother I've never met. Apt for the sister I never laid eyes on, whose grave I've never even visited. I learned this all from Portia, because no one spoke about her when I came home that summer. Mother had been heavily pregnant when I left and when I returned her belly was flat and she'd grown thin, haggard, like a candle that had gone on burning too long. It felt strange that no one wanted to talk about it. As if I'd come home to different people than the ones I'd left behind, and somewhere out there my parents were waiting for me with a happy, rosy-cheeked little sister, all bright and beaming the way dream-figures always were.

It was the first time I learned that grief isn't always mourning someone you loved. I couldn't understand at first why my parents acted the way they did. They didn't know that baby—she died before she could take her first breath. In many ways, she was a stranger, while I was the daughter they'd been raising for years. Why couldn't they have thrown a smile my way? I thought maybe they resented me, because they finally had a chance to have a family for themselves between the two of them, the way they never got to with me. I was the daughter of a man they both barely tolerated, the thorn in their backsides, the thing that stopped them from becoming whole. Because of me, they couldn't form their own family and have the life they'd always wanted.

But it wasn't about me at all. It was the absence of what could have been—of that same, happy family I thought waited for me after I was done with Eheldeth. I could feel the shadow of what could have been following me around like a sulky hound, which made me actually glad when I could finally return to school. There, I became busy with learning how to control fire spells while reading all about what happened to mages who *couldn't*. It was easy enough to forget time when you were busy, easy enough to forget sorrow when you could fill those quiet spaces with the mundane.

By the end of fall, when the rains were beginning and the wind had started to howl like wolves bereft of a pack, Papa sent me a letter, apologizing for that cold, lonely summer. "I wanted to take a trip with you and your mother to Gorent," he had said. "We were going to visit one of those islands I told you about, with the white sand and the blue water. But they've been expecting the baby in Sen'senal, and I couldn't bear having to break the news to the elders. Forgive me, Rosha. We haven't done right by you. Forgive me."

I cried after reading that letter. He was the one who lost a child—why apologize to *me*? Only then did I realize that I, too, was grieving. Grieving because for all the love he gave me, I couldn't make his pain go away. I could've been his—all those years he spent raising me wouldn't have been wasted only for my real father to find us and take back the woman he loved anyway. He would've seen his daughter grow up instead of burying her on her first day.

Haro was born the next summer. I didn't like children, but when Papa first handed him to me, I felt his tiny heartbeat against mine and knew without a shred of doubt that I would die for him. You see, I do know about family, even if they all accuse me otherwise. I hadn't been the best at telling them, but I understood at the very least it meant not wanting to see my parents bury another child.

Nasuha and I searched the grounds as best as we could, letting the dogs run through the loose leaves and sniff through the undergrowth. I choked down the fear of stepping on something or having one of the dogs return with a bone or two.

But whatever I was dreading didn't come to pass. We found a well in the yard, filled with soil, and nothing more. "He didn't kill anyone," I said at last. "He couldn't have. It makes no sense. Why would he?"

"People do crazy shit all the time," she ventured. Her eyes were on the old well. I knew what she was implying.

"Not a man who could build the business he did," I countered. "No —he didn't dump someone in there and bury the evidence." I pressed my foot on the well. "It's packed deep. This thing's been covered for years. There's grass and moss."

She crossed her arms. "You'd be surprised. The more powerful they become, the more infallible they think they are."

The dogs glanced in the distance, and I followed their gaze towards the gate. Go-nir banged it shut, twice, which told me the master was home.

I gestured for Nasuha to stay hidden in the trees as I came out to greet him. My heart was pounding. *My brother isn't in the well,* I told myself. *Neither is my father. They're not buried out here at all.* And yet I couldn't quite bring myself to believe they weren't here. I didn't know where else to go.

"Coffee," Cato told me as soon as he got out of the rented coach. He paid the driver and dismissed him with a wave. Go-nir held the gates open, waiting for the coach to ride past.

I bowed and ran off to get it done. This time, knowing where everything was, I picked the beans that smelled the most pleasant and brewed a cup. I carried it up the stairs carefully. He was already in his office, bent over the papers I'd arranged the day before.

"You went through all of this?" he asked.

I placed the cup on the table beside him. "Yes," I replied. "And I jotted down your appointments in your calendar, like you asked."

"I didn't ask you to sort them out."

I didn't answer at once. My father hated it when you got defensive immediately, and if Cato was anything like him, he was the same way. I waited for him to get up and read his calendar. "Where did you grow up?" he finally asked. He fixed me with an angry glare. "Don't lie, girl. I can tell when people lie."

"I've been all over the continent," I said. "Jin-Sayeng. Lon Basden. But I've spent most of my life in the heart of the empire."

"And you haven't been in the city long."

"No."

"I got that when you didn't know where you wanted to buy things. Almost everyone who's been here long enough has opinions on the best marketplace."

Joke was on him—I've *never* had an opinion on the best place to shop from. It used to drive Jehar insane, because he figured he could take me around Ad Methas, and I'd take care of the rest. Except I preferred to stay home, where I could hear my own thoughts. I hated crowded marketplaces, and I hated having to make decisions on things that made no difference in the end. White cheese, yellow cheese, cheese that tasted like it had been left in a dumpster for five weeks—if it staved off hunger, I didn't care. Besides, every time I was in the market, all the conversations—all the hustle and bustle and vendors screaming at would-be customers and everyone else screaming back—would burrow into my skull like a hundred bees.

"Tell me the truth, Suha," Cato continued. "Tell me why you're really here."

I blinked. "I'm sorry?"

"You're not a housekeeper. This is your third night here and I've yet to see the railing dusted. The dining table is as dirty as I'd left it—I could paint the whole shoreline on the damn thing." He turned around his chair to face me. "Come clean. I'm lenient. The sooner you tell the truth, the better it will be for both of us."

Damn it, Rosha. Clean the place. Of course. Would it have killed you to pick up a rag? Ah—right. Because I thought the couple of tasks he'd left me with had been enough, because it's not as if I'd ever thought to keep my own place clean, let alone a whole mansion. I don't believe I had ever dusted the inside of my cottage—Daisy's often-wagging tail kept most of the dust out of sight.

I felt like there was a lead weight around my tongue. "Jaila," I found myself saying. "Jaila's family sent me. I'm looking for her."

His face, which I had only seen as placid before, twisted slightly. His jaw tightened. "She hasn't returned home, then," he said. "I figured she would have gone straight back."

Damn if I knew. "I only know what they told me," I continued. "You said she ran off with the valet, but—"

"You think I lied?" His voice had barely risen, but I thought I could feel the ground tremble.

"It's possible *she* did," I said, trying to keep calm.

"It doesn't matter. You came here, you lied, and you've been snooping around my house. Grounds for dismissal under most circumstances." Cato snapped his fingers. "Well, did you find anything?" The irritation had turned into fury, as if every word he uttered was only proving to make him angrier.

"No, sir."

"You damn well didn't!" he roared, sending the cup flying across the table. It smashed against the wall, spilling hot coffee on the floor. "Because it's not my damn fault the woman would rather be a thief than earn an honest day's pay. Did they tell you that when they sent you? That Jaila *stole* from my coffers?"

Silence followed. I could hear the dogs whining from the other side of the door. They knew their master's temper, probably feared he was mad at *them*. I wanted to tell them they didn't do anything wrong.

I watched Cato pick up a rag and walk towards the coffee spill. He wiped it and dumped the rag into a wastebasket. Then he picked up the broken clay, shard by shard, and dropped them after the rag. Afterwards, he got up, straightening his clothes. He ran a hand over his hair, which had stuck out slightly when he was yelling. He looked almost embarrassed. "I apologize for my outburst," he said. "It's not as if you've done a deplorable job. The house is still in order, and the dogs seem to like you."

"I didn't mean to lie. I came to question you. You assumed I was the housekeeper, and I simply…didn't disagree. I've just been waiting for the right opportunity. You don't really allow me to get a word in." It was my turn to be irritated. It *was* on him.

He made a sweep of his hand. "I'll think about what to do with you later."

"You still need a housekeeper," I said. "You can't dismiss me till you've found a replacement, and I'm sure you want to find out what happened to Jaila and everything she's stolen, too. I'll hand over any information I come across. Whatever you want to think of me, I was *not* her accomplice. I wouldn't be back here, otherwise."

"You do not get to make demands, girl."

I took a deep breath. "I still need a job," I continued. "I was going to find one in the city. I kept the truth from you, yes—but you didn't ask until now. I had no desire to fool you. I told you—for all I know, it was Jaila who lied to you. Perhaps she didn't *run* off with the valet. Perhaps they both worked together to fool you. There must be a reason she didn't come home. Perhaps she's still hiding something." I didn't realize I could talk so much while lying—I risked tripping on every word that fell out of my lips.

He chewed over what I said. "Go," he finally said.

I waited a moment. "Am I fired?" I asked.

Outside, one of the dogs barked.

"Until I find a replacement," he said with a sigh, "you can stay."

I made as close to a curtsy as I was capable of. "Thank you, sir," I said. It took all of my energy not to slam the door behind me.

The encounter left my heart pounding. I went straight for my bedroom, letting Sunflower and Poppy through first before I shut the door and locked it. Before I could catch my breath, the window opened. I saw Nasuha's face peering through the crack from outside.

I had forgotten all about her. I pushed the window up the rest of the way. She slipped over and fell on the floor. "This room is gorgeous," she exclaimed, jaw agape. She got up. "And you're supposed to be a *servant?*

Gods. To have as much money as this bastard. Think of what you could do. Think of the possibilities."

"You need to leave," I stated. "Lord Cato knows I'm not who I said I was. I've given him a different story, but he'll find the truth out soon enough. Sooner, if he sees you here."

"I don't see what difference it would make. We'll tell him what we told Go-nir."

"I'll be in trouble."

"So?"

"I'm serious."

Nasuha gave me a look of concern, one that quickly changed into a lopsided grin. "You've never been in trouble your whole life, have you?" she asked. "I thought you were that type, but I didn't want to presume."

"You're already presuming too much," I said.

"Back at that tavern, with that man? I would have knifed him then and there. You—you're the kind of girl who's kept her head down her whole life, hoping it would just all go away in time."

"You don't know anything about me," I grumbled.

"I know enough." She stretched out on the rug beside the dogs. They seemed perfectly happy with her company and curled up next to her, tails wagging. "I'm going to close my eyes for just a few minutes," she said. "That door is locked securely, right?"

"I guess it is."

"And he hasn't gone in here at all since you've slept here? Hasn't gone creeping about the house, looking to take advantage of a poor, innocent young woman? Ah, well, if he tries anything, I'm here." She gazed at the ceiling, legs crossed. "I don't think I've ever slept anywhere as nice as this. It's always been barns and floors. Inns with flea-infested sheets, if I'm lucky. You'd think you were a princess. A *servant*," she repeated, whistling. "I wonder what sort of room his children would have."

"His son's furniture is in the basement," I said.

She turned to me. "Did his son die?"

"I—don't think so. He said his son *left* a long time ago."

"Could still mean he died. What a remarkably mysterious person this rich man is. Maybe money gives you time for such hobbies."

"I didn't realize being mysterious was a hobby."

"I've seen it all," Nasuha said as she rocked her legs side to side. "The shit these rich people will pay for, and all because they're bored out of their minds."

Lavish parties, and swans made of ice. I felt a flush of shame when I remembered my father's balls, even though none of that had anything to do with me. I'd had childhood bedrooms bigger than this.

"In the meantime, back in the village where I grew up, we had to share whatever food we found amongst ourselves. Gorent gets terrible famines after hurricanes, you know? There are only so few places in the islands where you could grow crops, and most of that land is owned by the more powerful families. Those like mine don't stand a chance." She shook her head. "I'm sorry for talking. I get sentimental every time I see how much the world has to offer, the amount of money people would pay for something like a plate or *tea*..."

"He has a tearoom here," I found myself saying.

She laughed. "I'm not surprised. Many of them do."

"A whole cupboard filled with jars of all sorts."

"Probably imported from such exotic places, with names we can't pronounce."

"Ziri-nar-Orxiaro," I ventured.

"Yes! Ziri—I give up."

"Quieflain."

"*Really?*" She laughed, and then grew serious. "And then you have people like my little sister. We didn't have enough to eat, and she..."

I stared at the ceiling, waiting to hear the rest. I probably didn't need to. When I realized she was silent too long, I glanced down and realized she had fallen asleep.

I got a spare blanket from the closet and draped it over her. Overcome with exhaustion, I fell asleep not long after, my back against the open window.

In the dead of the night, I woke up to a hair-raising howl.

CHAPTER 20

THE MONSTER

Nasuha was already up. She was looking through the window, as calm and collected as if she hadn't been asleep at all. "How many dogs does he have?" she asked.

"Just three. A little one that follows him around, and those...two." I looked around for Sunflower and Poppy. I thought they'd left the room, but no—they were both wedged under the bed. "Such cowards," I sighed. "Your ancestors took down wild beasts, you know."

Poppy made a sound halfway between a whine and a yawn.

"I don't blame them," Nasuha said. "That doesn't sound like a little dog, and now that I think about it, it doesn't sound like *any* dog I've known."

"We checked most of the grounds. It's all fenced. What could get in?"

"I don't know," Nasuha said. "It's not like Drusgaya's the place to suddenly get bears or wildcats in the night. He's got a piece of paradise out here, but we're still in the middle of the city." She pushed the window up and stepped outside.

"What are you doing? Just ignore it."

"I have a bad feeling, like I'm being watched. I don't like it."

"You don't have to do anything at all. Wait until dawn."

She turned around and tapped the hilt of the sword hanging from her waist. "I think I'll be fine."

I swore under my breath and crawled out the window after her. She gave an amused grin as I landed on the dirt, barely avoiding the giant bush growing right beside the house. "I want to know what it is, too," I said when I caught the look on her face. "What?"

"You're worried about me." She gave a smug grin. "Like I can't take care of myself."

"You'll get yourself caught and then *I'll* be in trouble."

"Remember what I told you last night?"

"Yes, I get it. You got me. I've never been in trouble before." If you didn't count driving a man insane for attempting to throw a spell on me, and getting dragged to prison for that, or Felan, or dropping out of Eheldeth only to run an illegal business on the side. I sighed. "That howl. You've got a point. When I woke up, I thought..."

I paused, wondering if I heard something moving about in the dark. My skin felt like it was crawling.

"You thought what?" Nasuha asked.

"That it sounded human," I breathed.

Something flashed in the shadows. Nasuha drew her sword and lunged after it. Her blade caught nothing but leaves. She swore and spat to the side. "Too fast," she said. "It's..."

We heard the howl again. It was coming from the other end of the yard, too far away to be that same movement. Just as I was still trying to piece my thoughts together, something slammed into my side. I dropped to the ground, landing on my hip. I tried to get up and felt a spray of hot breath on my face.

I found myself staring into the eyes of a giant dog. At least, what seemed to be a giant dog at first glance. It was covered in black fur and stood on two legs, with tusks jutting through its mouth. It looked gaunt, a thing half-starved and rotting with every step.

That was about the limit of what I could observe. It tried to take my head off by snapping its teeth. I was able to avoid the first strike, didn't think I had the room to be so lucky a second time. But before it could come, Nasuha's blade struck it between the shoulder blades and it turned and went for her, moving faster than a creature that size had any right to. It looked like it was made of wind.

Nasuha braced herself.

"Don't fight it, Nasuha," I called. "It's way too fast for—"

I didn't even see the thing move. The great black shadow knocked her to the side. She screamed. It was followed by the sound of bone crunching through flesh. The creature was trying to eat her arm where it stood.

The howl came a third time, long and low. The creature threw its head back, its eyes searching the sky. And then it dashed into the trees, a thin shade with no substance.

"The sound," Nasuha groaned. "It wasn't making the howling sound. There's something else out there."

I ripped my sleeve and tied the cloth around her wound.

"Another second and you'd have lost your arm," I said. "We have to get back inside the house. If all this noise hasn't already woken Lord Cato up, it will soon enough."

"That thing lives here. I just know it. That's not an animal. It's a damned monster, *and I think there's two of them.*"

I swallowed. One monster was problematic enough. It moved too fast. Whatever it was, it must have been created with a spell. A creature could be carved from dead things, imbued with the creator's own life-force to give it the semblance of life. I'd read about such techniques—in fact, we took whole semesters on it, in a class called *Illegal Magics*. It was made specifically so we understood what we *weren't* allowed to do, and much of the class was designed so Eheldeth knew our stamp on spells like these. We never tried to make dead creatures ourselves, but we'd gone through the steps, even as far as imbuing the spell runes with our own blood. It would make it much easier to catch us in the future if we ever attempted them ourselves. Most students knew better than to even try, let alone a prominent sorcerer in the middle of Dageis's most populated city.

I couldn't really say. The creature looked nothing like what these things were supposed to look like. It didn't smell dead, nor did it have the listless eyes of creatures moving to the beat of a hidden master. I could have sworn I even saw it breathing.

A fourth howl now, with the same substance as the first few ones. The sound of it made my heart stir. I realized why I'd woken up to it.

The howl changed into a scream. I ran.

It was my brother, Ryo.

When my brothers were little, I knew all their games like the back of my hand. Every summer, I would come home and be an unwilling partici-pant to get them out of my mother's hair for the afternoon. They didn't really like playing ball like the boys at school, but they particularly enjoyed pretending to be hunters out in the backyard. And of course, you couldn't play *hunter* without prey. Ryo, being the younger one, always got the short end of the stick and would have to hide while Haro looked for him. One day, he got bored, and decided he was going to be a wolf.

Back then, Ryo was so little it never really occurred to him that *howling* made it easier for Haro to find him. But neither of us put a stop to it. It made my heart melt, seeing that little boy on his haunches, howling his heart away at the sky.

Now, hearing that voice in the wind was like dropping my heart in a pit of ice. I tore in the direction it was coming from, two parts dread, one part relief. I emerged from the grove into the adjoining field, an empty section overlooking some of the horse pastures. I saw the creature first—huge, slavering, its stench a stark contrast to the crisp, morning air. And then I saw the little boy.

I threw caution to the wind and set the creature on fire.

I hadn't carved a spell in the air with such vehemence or force for years—not since I was a child. They had warned me against it in Eheldeth. "Mute your powers," I'd been warned. "Be good at what you do, but not better." *Never give them a reason to fear you more than they already do.*

But in front of my brother's imminent death, I had no reason to hold back. I felt the rush of energy nearly sweep me off my feet, a torrent as strong as a raging river. It used to be that I had no control of it—the *agan* would flow through my body and out of my fingertips like a shout of anger. I couldn't channel it where I wanted it to.

The years of creating threads, of tugging at strings like a weaver at a loom, had done their work. The full force of the spell struck the creature's snout and curled up the fur of its head until it was entirely ablaze. It roared, making a mad dance to shake the flames loose. I went straight for Ryo, who was just as startled by my appearance as he was by the spell. I picked him up.

"Pull that," he said, pointing at the ground. I squinted. There was a metal ring, set deep inside the grass.

Nasuha got there first. She tugged, revealing a crack on the ground already wide enough for a little boy to fit through. The metal ring was attached to a large slab of stone. She pulled harder, muscles straining, and the crack grew wider, revealing a staircase. Ryo jumped out of my arms to scamper down. "Hurry!" he cried.

We followed him. "Help me shut it," Nasuha said, and I snapped back to my senses and helped her with the handle carved underneath the slab. We pushed the slab about halfway through before the creature bore down on it. The slab shook, and so did the ground around us. I felt like it would all cave on our heads.

"Get off, you!" Nasuha snarled. She stuck her sword through the remaining crack and grinned in satisfaction when she heard it strike flesh. The creature screeched and she removed the blade just as we slid the door shut. We heard it pace outside, snuffling as it tried to turn the slab over.

"It won't break through," Ryo said. "It tried before."

I glanced at our surroundings. We were in a cramped passageway, lit by a single torch on the wall. I turned to him and placed a hand on his hair. The smile on his face faded, and I saw tears in the corner of his eyes. "You found me," he said. I could tell he was afraid to hug me. He wanted to, though.

"Sorry I took so long," I croaked.

He shook his head. A poor joke, come to think of it. It had only been a few days—a week? I'd lost count. But to a little boy, it would have felt like forever.

"I'm guessing this is your little brother," Nasuha said.

"I'm Rysaran!" he chirped. "But everybody calls me Ryo."

"Nice to meet you, Ryo. I'm Suha. Well—" She got up, straightening her back. "*She's* Suha right now. I'm Rosha. Don't let anyone tell you otherwise." She winked.

He blinked in confusion.

"You didn't tell me your brother was missing, too," Nasuha said, turning back to me.

"Details," I retorted.

"Seems like a very important detail to me."

"The man who took you," I said, turning to Ryo. "Haro said he told you he knew where Father was."

Ryo nodded. "He lied," he said. "He didn't. He took me to the airship, even after I said I needed to ask permission first. When I tried to fight, he said he would hurt you all." He rubbed his eyes.

"What did he look like?"

He gave a description that made me pause. It was remarkably like my friend from the docks, the one I'd found dead. The one that had Cato's business card in his pocket.

"Are you sure?" I asked, when he was done. "Because I think I know the man you're talking about, and he's dead."

Ryo shook his head. "He wasn't dead when he made me go with him. He took me to this mansion. The gates were closed, and nobody answered, but he broke the locks and walked right in. He took me to a room in the house, and we waited there a very long time. I got sleepy. When I woke up, he was gone, so I escaped through the window, and then Jaila found me."

"Jaila," I repeated.

He took my hand and led us deeper down the catacombs.

. . .

We reached a cavernous chamber. Monuments marked the tombs, which I guessed were all tan-Tarsius's ancestors. There were candles all along the side of many of the tombs, enough to give the room a soft, warm light. A woman sat on the floor next to one of the monuments. Ryo dropped to his knee beside her. "Jaila," he said. "I found some friends, Jaila. My sister Rosha is here. She'll know what to do."

Her eyes flickered. Her pallid skin was covered in a thick layer of sweat and grime. Crusted wounds covered her face, the blood black and stinking with rot. I recognized the woman from several nights ago. "You," I said. "You disappeared before I could get help."

"You were going to get the stableboys," she gasped. "They work for him. They would have told him."

"You went there for me?"

"I heard rumours that he'd just brought in a new housekeeper," she whispered. "I thought…there was a chance she would…that you would help." She suddenly curled up to the side, shivering.

"That woman's dying," Nasuha said.

"Her wounds need to be cleaned. They're putrid." I turned the woman to her side. "She had a stab wound, too. What the hell is happening here?"

"He did that to her," Ryo said.

"Who? Lord Cato?"

"Elry," Jaila whispered.

"He's here, too?"

"You probably met him," she gasped. "Out there."

The creature. I shook my head. "I don't understand. Lord Cato said you both eloped. Everyone thought you both eloped. Was that just all a lie?"

"We were going to," she whispered. "But Elry…discovered something the night we were about to leave. Lord Cato had refused to give him his final pay, so he thought he was going to steal something from the mansion. Just to make up for it. Lord Cato caught him and punished him. He turned him into *that*."

"That's impossible," I said. "You can't—"

"I just saw you throw flames at that thing's face," Nasuha broke in. "I don't think you get a say on what's impossible or not."

"It's impossible because it's not *allowed*. Turning people into monsters —that's obscene, even for Dageis. The kind of spells that would even

162

make it possible would have tipped off Eheldeth. Not even a man as rich as Lord Cato would get away with it."

"You're a mage?" Jaila asked.

"By the Dageian definition? No."

"An *outlaw mage*," Nasuha said. "Well, well, well. The surprises keep piling up."

"Lord Cato did that to Elry," Jaila continued. "And he left me to be killed. But I got away. I'd always known about these tombs—Lord Cato asked me to clean it out once. I've been hiding here ever since."

"Jaila found me in the yard and took me here," Ryo added. "Then she thought she could find help."

"I went back out, and he gave chase before I could even slide that door all the way open," she said. "I ran all the way to the mansion and found a knife. He attacked me near the woodshed. I barely made it back inside in one piece. I trapped him in the basement, and then that's when you woke up and found me."

And I was the one who let him out from the basement. But I didn't see anything when I'd gone down there, didn't *hear* anything. The creature could move as fast as the wind—perhaps he'd simply swept past me without me knowing it. "This all happened…while I was here?"

She nodded.

"You must have been raiding the pantry, too," I said. "No wonder it was picked clean."

"A few times before you arrived. I could do it in the daytime then, when he wasn't around and there was no one at home. Sometimes I went to the stables—Go-nir always leaves food lying around, and I know my way around there without getting seen. But I couldn't do either after I got injured." She started coughing.

Nasuha rubbed her back. "She won't last long like this," she said. "Especially without food or water."

"You said that thing—Elry—he doesn't come out during the day?"

"I think sunlight scares him," Jaila gasped.

"And Lord Cato doesn't come down here at all?"

"He hasn't been here in years. He doesn't like it."

"All right," I breathed. I looked at all of them. "In another hour, when it's daylight, I'm going back out there. I'm going to pretend none of this happened. If we're lucky, Lord Cato heard none of that commotion last night. Is he a heavy sleeper, Jaila?"

"I don't know," she said. "I wasn't his housekeeper that long. I don't…know if I've seen him asleep. He keeps odd hours."

"Then I'll have to take my chances. Your wounds need to get cleaned. Do you have anything in the house for that?"

She nodded. "The kitchen. There are bandages in one of the cabinets. And a bottle of spirits."

I glanced down at Ryo, who was listening to the entire conversation intently. I wondered how much he understood. "Why were you howling?" I asked him.

"I knew someone was out there, running from him," he replied. "I wanted to give them time to escape."

"A brave thing," Nasuha said. "We owe you our lives."

He flushed. "Anyone would have done the same thing," he whispered, and I thought, *not anyone*. But Papa would have. And he would have been proud of Ryo for what he'd done. I thought about how I was going to tell this story to Kefier before realizing I couldn't. Especially after what I'd just done out there, I needed to stay dead. If somehow I was able to get Ryo out of here alive, he was going home without me.

CHAPTER 21

THE SECOND GHOST

When I finally left the tomb, the sun was high enough that it looked like the treetops were on fire. There was no sign of Elry anywhere. I returned to the mansion, where Sunflower and Poppy greeted me at the front door. They looked terrified, almost as if they'd had a worse night than I had. I spent a few moments petting each one. "I didn't *mean* to leave you," I said, to their doleful eyes. "But you were safer here, weren't you? You wouldn't have wanted to be out there anyway. He would have torn you to shreds."

They crowded against me, tails wagging left and right.

I found the pail of meat Go-nir had left and carried it back inside. I whistled for Bracken, but she was nowhere in sight. I placed the meat in her bowl anyway and left it on the table while I fed the two other dogs outside. I went back indoors to check the main hall.

Lord Cato's coat was still hanging in the rack. I wondered if he was in his office and took the chance. I made his coffee and buttered a roll of bread. I wanted badly to take food back to Ryo and Jaila instead, but I couldn't afford to be careless.

I tiptoed my way upstairs and to Lord Cato's room. I knocked, waited. When there was no response, I turned the handle and stepped inside. It was empty. I placed the cup of coffee beside the other from yesterday, which was untouched. I stepped back to survey the contrast between the cold, black liquid from the first and the steam from the second. I was trying to reconcile what bothered me about the last few days. The man was a merchant, and yet in the time I'd been there, I hadn't seen him do anything that remotely resembled the work I knew.

My father had been a different story. He would wake up early, it was true, but only so he could stay in his office for most of the morning and write letters. The rest of the time he would spend in the shop with me in tow, running through numbers to make sure we were turning a profit. The sort of business Enosh ran depended on tight margins—he'd spend silvers to make back coppers. A schedule was necessary to keep things under control.

In contrast, Lord Cato's habits seemed haphazard at best. In the last week, I'd seen no pattern. Yet the dogs and the coffee showed that he had one. Something had disrupted it. Was it my brother? He had Ryo in his custody, though Ryo never met Lord Cato face-to-face. But clearly Targus—or at least the man who resembled Targus—brought him here for a reason, probably on his orders. You would think if he had an escaped prisoner, he would have been more concerned about getting him back. It was almost as if he was unaware that Ryo was here at all. Perhaps Lord Cato was still rattled after Jaila and Elry's theft. That would make more sense—if you couldn't trust anyone in your own household, you'd be restless, too. Ryo said Targus seemed irritated when no one was around to welcome them into the house—clearly Lord Cato didn't plan for how to handle visitors when he wasn't around. The lack of a housekeeper must've been a pressing problem for a while.

I glanced around the room now, wondering if there was a better way for me to keep track of Lord Cato's movements. There had to be a place he was spending his time in whenever he disappeared without actually leaving the house. And since I had detected no portals or lingering traces of a portal-spell in the air, he still had to be here somewhere. A secret room in the basement? Or behind one of the locked doors? I had heard no noises all morning—the house had thick walls, but you'd think if he was here somewhere I would have heard the floors creak, at least. He had to have another office, one he kept in secret. He *must* have been spending most of his time there.

In retrospect, I shouldn't have said I was a housekeeper—I could have tried to get him to hire me as an assistant. Never mind that such a maneuver would've been difficult for me to pull off. I really was no good at lying, no good at pretending. Not even a week in and I'd already been found out.

I sank into the chair, thinking. And then I remembered the dog. Bracken, the one who never left his side.

I looked around. There were clumps of white hair on the ground where she'd shed. The other dogs never entered Lord Cato's office, so I could tell it was her. An idea occurred to me. I went downstairs to find the mop. I set it aside for now and turned to fill a basket with food from the pantry. I also found some bandages in the kitchen drawer and the bottle of spirit she was talking about. I wondered if it was being used for cleaning or to help the last few housekeepers throughout the day. Probably a bit of both.

But before I could take a step outside, noticed the gardener pruning the hedges. It probably wasn't smart to lead him straight to the tomb, or even appear to be going anywhere near it. At the very least, he would have an answer if somebody started asking questions.

The basket returned to the kitchen table. I spent the next little while cleaning the floors while the dogs watched me from the kitchen door. "I really should have done this sooner," I told them. "Some housekeeper, huh?"

Poppy barked.

"Bracken follows him everywhere," I told her. "Well, I guess you know that already. With the floors clean, I can start fresh. You see?"

She cocked her head to the side. I didn't want to tell her the other side of this plan—that it meant both she and Sunflower had to stay outside more often. I needed the floors clean, because later on, new clumps of fur could tell me where Bracken had been, and by extension, Lord Cato. It also gave Lord Cato a reason not to fire me.

The floors were nearly sparkling by the time I was done. I set the mop aside and looked through the window again. The gardener was gone. I went back for the food. Just as I touched the handle of the basket, someone knocked at the door.

I closed my eyes for a moment, hoping it would just go away. But then the knocking came again, angry, insistent. I walked back out to the main hall and took a moment to straighten my clothes. Was there blood on my sleeves? My dress? I glanced at the mirror to brush my hair aside, and then took a deep breath.

I opened the door and came face-to-face with a man. A stranger. A ghost.

"Good morning," he said, tipping his head to the side. "My apologies. The gate was open, so I just walked in. Is Lord Cato home? I'm his son, Felan."

It's hard to explain how it feels to see someone you last saw as a child, let alone someone you thought was dead. I guess it's like walking through a doorway only to have the door suddenly slam on your face. I had to fight myself so I wouldn't stare so much at him.

He was shorter than me when we were children. Now he was tall, nearly a good head higher, broad-shouldered. So scrawny he looked like he needed a few extra meals, but not slight. A head full of long, black hair, and a well-trimmed, black goatee. A man now, a far cry from the little boy that made my life in Eheldeth miserable. It was the eyes that were familiar. His eyes, and the expression in them, like the universe was something to be prodded and analyzed. It had plagued me for years.

But now, he was analyzing everything but me. I realized he was waiting for my answer and that he didn't recognize me. Which was strange. It used to be that every time he saw me, his eyes would light up with rage and something else I couldn't put my finger on. Envy, perhaps, though I could never see what reason a boy who was just as good as me would ever be envious. Now—well, now it was as if he didn't see me at all. True, I'd changed haircuts several times since—back then I couldn't be bothered with long hair and kept it closely cropped, no different than my brothers'. Maybe because he *chose* not to see me. I was a Gorenten girl in Eheldeth—now I was just a Gorenten servant. I shouldn't be surprised.

"I thought Lord Cato's son died years ago," I blurted out.

There, I thought. *You probably just blew your cover. No servant would dare talk that way.*

He shrugged. "Rumours," he said at last. "You know how it is."

I did. "I'm sorry," I said again, pretending like I still wasn't sure what to make of him. "I'm new here and haven't been informed. Lord Cato's son? You look nothing like him."

"I see deference is lacking in servants these days."

"A housekeeper," I replied. "His only one. And I can't just open the door to someone who pretends to be the master's son, just because he says he is. Especially when he looks nothing like Lord Cato."

"I take after my mother." He scratched the side of his face, as if the topic embarrassed him more than he let on. "Lord Cato, if you must know, is my stepfather. He married my mother when I was a little boy."

I didn't know any of this. But Felan wasn't really the sort of boy who talked to me about his life. It was strange to hear him say such things now, clearly. If he'd used a different name, I might have started to second guess it was him after all. "Lord Cato is…busy at the moment."

"Is there anyone else at home? Old Nana? Go-nir?"

"Go-nir is in the stables, probably," I said. "Oh, that's right. I guess he'll know who you are. I can't let you in until I'm sure."

He frowned. "That's understandable, I suppose…" he began.

"I'll walk with you." I closed the door and strode ahead, my heart racing. I wanted to run away, but I guessed that anything less than friendliness would just make him suspicious. He needed to see me as the housekeeper, nothing more.

Felan, I repeated to myself, trying to drown out my panicked thoughts. *No, of course he wasn't dead. If he was dead, they'd have taken me away.* They did say his father was powerful, and perhaps it made sense now that I knew it was Lord Cato. Why Felan always arrived after summer in lavish carriages with expensive-looking horses, or why his clothes were always made of fine material. Not elaborate, but deceptively simple that only people who *knew* about fabrics would know how much they cost.

And it explained why the keepers were always on his side. They treated me like a gnat threatening their favourite student. Now I knew why. He was a favourite for a reason. His father wasn't just rich, but powerful, and proximity to power was all the motivation some people needed. My father was considered well-off in many places, but he wasn't anyone of note. As a relatively minor businessman, he held no influence; compared to a man like Lord Cato, he was a fly on the wall.

Felan started walking faster so that we now strode down the path side-by-side. I glanced at him again. It was weird to look up to him, instead of down. Surely it wasn't that long ago. I knew I didn't look at him with anything less than disdain back in the day. Not because I hated *him,* not in the beginning, but because his presence meant everyone was wishing for me to fail. I *couldn't* be the girl with the highest grades, not when precious Felan, who was studying in Eheldeth on special circumstances, was there. A teacher had actually asked me not to study for an exam once, "Because we're sure Felan is going to get top marks," she said, "and you'll pass, no doubt about it. But maybe it's better we don't get questions."

"Questions?"

"About how we do our teaching here," the teacher continued. "Felan —they had to make a reason so he could come here at his age. His magic is highly potent. Lots of connection to the *agan.* A mage like that boy only comes along once in a blue moon. And he studies really hard."

"So do I."

"His father is *very* important, dear," the teacher said, patting me on the shoulder. "Let's just not cause trouble, all right?"

I thought her fears were overblown. I studied for that exam like my life depended on it and came out on top. Felan was a close second. Nobody said anything, not even the teacher who asked me to sabotage my own grades.

"Where is your mother from?" I asked, to break the silence. I felt as if I was going to start unearthing too many old wounds if I didn't talk.

"Genthal."

"From one of the islands to the north." Many of the nations throughout the northern continent had folded under the Empire of Dageis, but some stubbornly held on for centuries. Gorent had been one, before it was finally defeated, and its people were forced to flee to the surrounding islands. Agarenth—the nation the city of Genthal once belonged to—was another. I heard one of the reasons Dageis left its people alone was to serve as a reminder to the other nations what allegiance could do for them. Others say it was only because Agarenth had nothing to offer—that it was simply a barren land with a volcano in the middle, sporadic rice fields, and fishing villages.

I had long guessed Felan wasn't from a family that considered itself *pure Dageian*—that is, from that original wave that came from the west a few hundred years ago. His complexion was too dark. It was much lighter than mine, but the sort that would darken instead of burning under direct sunlight.

Go-nir was sweeping the path outside the stables when we arrived. His eyes watered. "Lord Felan?" he called.

Felan bowed. "Master Go-nir," he greeted.

Go-nir went up to embrace him. "My boy," he croaked. "You took your time. I thought I'd die before I ever saw you again. You didn't even write."

Felan didn't reply.

"Ah, well," Go-nir continued. "You're home. That's all that matters. Are you looking for your father?"

"She wanted to make sure I am who I say I am before she let me in," Felan said.

"It's her job," Go-nir agreed. He gave me a beaming smile. "Well, he is who he says he is. A man now, not a boy, and so tall. What did they feed you over in Sorna? You even got some meat on your bones! Let old Go-nir add some more to that. Will you have breakfast with us in the mess hall?"

"It would be a pleasure," Felan said.

"What about you, girl?" Go-nir asked, turning to me.

"I just remembered the stove is still burning," I replied. I turned around and started walking back to the house as fast as I could.

. . .

I was in luck this time. I couldn't hear anyone else in the house. I rushed to the kitchen to grab the basket and then back out towards the gardens, trying not to look like I was in a hurry in case someone saw me walking by, but trying not to dawdle, either. Time seemed to crawl. It felt like forever until I was back in the tomb.

"Do you know there's other passageways to this place?" Nasuha said when I handed her the basket. She dug through the items and handed Ryo the food. She also uncorked the bottle, took a sniff, and swallowed a mouthful.

"I hope that doesn't make you blind," I commented.

Nasuha made a smack of approval before sitting back next to Jaila. She was sleeping. Nasuha carefully applied a bit of spirits to her wounds before wrapping them back up with the bandages.

"The passageways," I began.

"Right," Nasuha said. "If you take that hall, it goes in deeper. I didn't want to leave these two, but it might be worth a look. I'm convinced we're not in the main entrance. Who builds a tomb and then makes it inaccessible? You can't have funeral parades through that passageway."

"After what we saw last night, I'm afraid to see what else he has hidden in here."

"Maybe it's your father."

I didn't answer her. She was probably right, but I wasn't sure I wanted to find out. I was still processing Felan's arrival. "We have to work on getting you all out of here first," I finally said. "Things have gotten more complicated. Lord Cato's son is home."

Nasuha looked troubled. "That's not good." She glanced at Jaila. "I know your body hurts, but your mouth works, I assume. Do you know anything about the son?"

Jaila grunted. "Only that he left for his own safety," she coughed. "He was a mage too, I think. Something about a disagreement with the father. But he was still young when he left." She coughed a second time and turned to her side. Her skin still looked damp, but she didn't look as bad as she did that morning. Maybe it was the light.

Ryo sat next to her and handed her some bread. When she shook her head, he broke off a piece. "Just try," he said.

She sighed and took it, more to oblige him than anything else. It looked like chewing hurt her, but then she asked for more. I took out a bottle of water and handed it to Ryo after. He helped her take a sip.

"A mage," Nasuha sighed, after Jaila finally lay back down again. "That certainly complicates things. Even trying to get out may be tricky."

And there's no way we can drag Jaila through there without someone seeing us. If it's the daylight, it'll be one of the servants. If it's at night…"

"Elry," Jaila murmured.

"One or the other," I said.

"We can get rid of one," Nasuha continued.

"Elry, you mean," Jaila said. "You want to kill him."

"Or trap him again, but yes, if it comes to that. Unless you think there's a way to save him."

Jaila glanced at me. No one said a word. We were all thinking the same thing. But then Ryo wedged himself between Jaila and me. "Rosha can find a way!" he exclaimed. "She's a mage, too!"

Her face grew bright. "Could you?" she asked. "Please? He made a mistake, but the man he was doesn't deserve this fate."

"Most of us don't deserve our fates," I said. "Only the gods decide, in the end. Better I don't get your hopes up over something that can't be done." I saw the disappointment in Ryo's face and got up to avoid having to look at it any longer. "Let's see the rest of this tomb anyway," I told Nasuha. "If there's any other monsters lurking about, we might as well flush them out."

She grinned. "I thought you'd never ask."

CHAPTER 22

HIDING IN PLAIN SIGHT

We walked along a narrow corridor, dug right into the soil. Roots had found the cracks through the stone and spread along it like giant spiderwebs, giving the impression we had stepped into another world altogether. I counted my steps, knowing the farther we went along that this was no longer a mere tomb. Someone, a long time ago, had built this passageway for another purpose. I couldn't see what for, though. Why build a passageway leading to nowhere? Was it an escape tunnel? There had been a few bloody revolts in Dageis's history, but none near Drusgaya except a few years back. This tunnel was certainly much, much older than that. One whiff of the muggy air made you feel like you'd fallen into the dredges of time.

"Where do you go when you do that?" Nasuha asked.

I glanced at her in confusion.

She gestured. "Like…that. It's almost like you disappear into your head and you don't realize I'm still *looking* at you and waiting for an answer to my question."

"You asked one?"

She sighed. "Yes. Yes, I did. I asked if you think Lord Cato will be back soon."

"I really don't know. But it's been the longest he's been away the last few days."

"You could convince Lord Felan his father wanted to hire me all along."

"What happens when Lord Cato comes home?"

"You tell him Lord Felan wanted to hire *me*. Both father and son don't get along, if I understand the story correctly. Jaila said it was all the servants could talk about when she first came here, and Felan has been gone for years. I don't think they'll scrutinize it if I keep out of their noses. It will make it easier for me to bring food and water to Jaila if this Lord Felan thinks I belong here."

"I think she's going to die," I said.

"Don't say that."

"It's the truth. We need to get her to a physician, and even if we can get her out of the tomb there's no way we can afford to pay for one." I cleared my throat. "I didn't want my brother to hear."

"I was really hoping you'd be able to pull healing magic out of your ass."

"That's not…how any of that works."

"Well, *I* wouldn't know, so enlighten me."

I paused. "You really want to know?"

"Your brother said you went to school for this. To *Eheldeth*. Do you… not really understand what that sounds like to me?"

"You think I can make miracles because of that?"

She sniffed. "It's what the rest of them would have you believe. He studied in Eheldeth, as if that would erase the welt from your face. Or forgive her for trying to kill you, she went to Eheldeth, you see? What's so special about that school, anyway? Only the best and brightest go to it, they say, but I've heard of talented mages who end up taking apprenticeships in sewer-cleaning instead."

"Dageis doesn't officially consider anyone a mage unless the mage council approves you. The rest are outlaws."

She clicked her tongue. "Well, then. The mage council's rules aside, you're a mage or you're not, aren't you?"

"You pay the tuition for Eheldeth, and go through the process, and write your exam and choose your path with approval from the council, or you're not," I said. "I'm…not one. You cannot officially call me a mage without adding the word *outlaw*. And the healing arts, whatever that might be, is training afforded only to those who actually graduate from the basics. I left before I even got that far."

"That's unfortunate," Nasuha said. "Why did you leave?"

I gazed at the shadows with a soft sigh. "I decided I'd had enough with letting other people decide what to do with me." I left it at that and focused on walking down the rest of that tunnel. We reached a small landslide before we could go much further, a break in the ceiling that had allowed a few loose rocks through. I supposed I could squeeze through the top if I had to, but I suddenly didn't have the energy.

"Let's work on getting you hired." I gazed at the rubble. "We can come back later."

She didn't even try to argue.

I have a recurring dream that persists to this day—of being back in Eheldeth, wandering the massive halls and grounds of the school. Somehow, in my dreams, they grow even bigger. The polished floors seem shinier, and the amphitheatre, if I ever passed by it, would resemble the gaping maw of a beast waiting to swallow me whole. I would stop at the threshold and gaze down, torn between diving into the beast's jaws or running away to save myself. It should've been a simple choice.

I say *recurring* but of course there are differences between every dream. Sometimes I will simply walk through those halls, trying to get out to the main gardens where Papa would be waiting to bring me home. Students block my path. Sometimes keepers chase me.

In other iterations, I'd be rushing *in*, trying to find a classroom to write an exam I had just learned about that day. Somewhere in the back of my mind, I knew I didn't study for it. And yet failing the test would be the final straw, a mark of shame. *Now I am everything they say I am.*

A book I was reading told me such dreams meant nothing more than guilt. Residual guilt over what *could have been* if I had stayed. Would I be something more than a shopkeeper in some forgotten corner of the world if I had kept a brave face and finished those exams? But it was hard to believe when the last three years had been some of the happiest in my life. Not perfect, of course, but it was nice having to answer to no one but myself. Until Kefier had come barging back into it, I would have gone on happily living the rest of it.

So why don't you go back? Just abandon this stupid ruse. You're getting nowhere. Why don't you just send Ryo home, and go back to yours?

Because *happy* wasn't the same thing as *content*, and I wasn't the heartless, selfish, spoiled brat they thought I was. I wanted to believe that, anyway. That I wasn't like my rich, privileged classmates.

I was still thinking about my family—particularly what to do about Ryo—when we found Lord Felan in the gardens. He was sitting on a stone bench with a book, one leg resting over the other.

"Is your father home?" I asked, gesturing at Nasuha to step aside.

"Not yet," he said, folding the book on his lap. "I would have thought he only went out for a short errand, but all the carriages are accounted for. Perhaps he went for a walk and got distracted."

"Or he took a hired coach," I said. "Since you're the closest to anyone here in a position to make decisions…"

"My father will disagree on that," Felan replied. "But go on."

"He's been meaning to hire someone new to help around here. He was going to wait until next week, but she's got nowhere else to stay, and, well…we do need the help." I now indicated Nasuha, who stepped forward and bowed.

"Pleased to meet your acquaintance, Lord Felan," she said. "My name is Rosha."

His eyes widened.

I'd forgotten our little joke. I turned to Felan, holding my breath, hoping if I kept quiet he'd forget to look at me and associate me with the name. *He won't know it's you. You've changed. He's changed. You hardly recognized* him, *didn't you?* I tried to ignore that I *did*, actually.

"Interesting," Felan said, breaking my thoughts. "Is that a common name for Gorenten?"

Nasuha glanced at me. I nodded, urging her to do the same.

"Why, yes," she replied. "In Sen'senal, mothers name their children Rosha *all* the time."

I wanted to throw a shoe at her. Anyone would have been a fool not to catch the irony in her voice. And yet perhaps a fool was what Felan exactly was, because he gave an absent-minded nod and then went back to the book on his lap. He turned a page.

"So?" I asked, after what felt like forever.

He glanced up again. "Did you need something else?"

"Can she work here?"

"Yes."

I turned to Nasuha, who shrugged. "Thank you, Lord Felan," she said.

Felan dismissed us with a wave, his nose still on his book. "Although…" he said.

I turned mid-stride.

"There was a girl I knew once with that name." He didn't look at me so much as gaze absently at thin air. Eventually, he shook his head and gave a small smile. "Never mind. It was a long time ago, and I'm sure she's moved on to better things."

I could hardly get out of there fast enough.

While Nasuha went to the kitchen to find more supplies for Jaila and Ryo, I made my way back to my room. Someone had let the dogs in, and both were sitting on my bed, tails thumping on their hindquarters. "You think *you* had a day," I told them. I took a deep breath, trying to calm myself. "I don't think he's lying," I continued. "He was never that kind of boy. Arrogant, rude, condescending, all those things. But would he deliberately be cruel to mislead me?"

Sunflower gave a quick bark.

"I know," I said. "I'm working myself up over nothing, probably. We have other things to worry about. Felan said Lord Cato hasn't been home, but let's see if we can disprove that. Have either of you seen Bracken?"

They perked their ears up at their companion's name but did nothing else.

"Useless," I grumbled. They barked, jumping from my bed to dart into the adjoining hallway. "At least don't mess up the floor!" I called. "If you see any long, white hairs, tell me!"

But we found nothing like that, even though I combed through the floor as well as I could. I mopped it all over again, as if to make up for all the times the past few days when I didn't, and then—because Felan walked through the hallway and gave me a glance that could've meant anything—I took another hour to wax and shine the surface with a brush. By the time I was done, the deep mahogany gleamed so much you could use it as a mirror.

Nasuha saw all of it and whistled. "You're taking this job seriously. I'm impressed. At least you have options when this whole outlaw mage thing stops working out for you."

"Felan is an old classmate," I told her under my breath.

She grew serious. "What?"

"He doesn't know it's me. At least, I don't think he does. But the name…"

"You should have told me this earlier," she grunted.

"It slipped my mind."

"Is it too late to change it? Say you meant *Roha* or something instead."

"That's only going to make him more suspicious." She sniffed. "Don't overthink it. People get us confused all the time."

"That doesn't really make me feel better. He can't know it's me, Nasuha."

"Why not? What the hell did you *do* back there?"

The dogs exploded into a flurry of barking and lunged at the kitchen door, though there was nobody there. But when Nasuha pushed the door open to let them out, they wouldn't place a single paw over the threshold. "Bunch of cowards," Nasuha breathed. "I've seen braver cats."

They wagged their tails sheepishly.

"They can probably smell Elry somewhere," I grumbled. "It's getting dark."

"Which means I should make my way back to the tomb to make sure those two are safe," Nasuha said. "Have you come up with any ideas on when to leave? Or are you just waiting for Jaila to die first?"

I glanced at her. "That's not—"

"Oh, come on. It's clear as day. You're waiting for her to croak because you don't want to risk ripping Ryo away from her, and you don't want to drag her around, either. Just admit it."

"You can't save everyone," I said.

"There you go. Was that so hard?"

"You can't deny the truth. Trying to save her might just make things worse for us."

"At least you're not a liar," Nasuha sniffed.

We heard a knock on the kitchen door. I glanced at Nasuha before carefully stepping forward to open it. Through the crack, I got a good glimpse of Lord Felan's face.

"Excuse me," he said, looking somewhat embarrassed. "Master Gonir just had food sent up, and it's…more than I can eat. Could either of you take the trouble to join me?"

I turned to Nasuha. "You go," she mouthed. She held up the basket of supplies for Ryo and Jaila.

I sighed and turned back to Felan's questioning expression. Refusing might make him ask more questions. "Of course, my lord."

He looked almost happy when I closed the door behind me to follow him into the dining hall.

CHAPTER 23

THE MONSTER AND THE
UNSEEING MAGE

My first morning at Eheldeth, I sat alone at breakfast.

Well, that part isn't entirely true. Berinda did sit at the same table, though she was more interested in chatting with the girls behind us. They were talking in-depth about a young mage from the city of Bardes, who had the fortune of being both a prestigious graduate of Eheldeth *and* a famous actor for some popular play. *The Courting of Enis,* I think it was called. They spent less time talking about the play than his gorgeous eyelashes and elegant jaw.

Felan sat alone, too, at the table right next to mine. After our introduction yesterday—though you hardly could've called it that—he refused to meet my eyes. He was stabbing his food listlessly, looking like the process of swallowing eggs and nibbling toast was a chore. In a moment of courage, I got up from my seat and approached him.

"Not hungry?" I asked.

He glanced at me, staring with his ridiculously bushy, black eyebrows. I had a moment of regret. Why did he look so appalled I was talking to him?

I noticed, too late, that the entire dining hall had fallen silent.

"The new girl's making *friends*," someone called.

I hesitated, before drawing myself up to look at the crowd. "Is…is that a problem?" I asked.

"You don't make friends with Felan," another chimed in. "He's too rich and snobby for the rest of us."

There was a murmur of agreement. I glanced at Felan, who wasn't even looking at anything, though it almost looked like the pile of eggs on his tray suddenly held a dazzling secret he didn't want to share with anyone. "Just go away," he grumbled. "Don't bring attention on me because you feel bad. Gorenten brat." He said the last part like he was pretending to whisper it, only it was loud enough for everyone in that room to hear. The message was clear enough. Even the pariah, Felan, was rejecting me.

Anger stirred in my chest, followed by a flush of shame. I remembered walking back to my table in silence, to Berinda and her friends who seemed just as embarrassed for my sake. They seemed to sit a little farther from me afterwards. They said nothing mean, but after they finished eating, they didn't stick around to wait for me either. I walked back to fetch my books alone, a scene that would replay itself a thousand times over in the next few years. When I glanced back, I saw Felan walking a few paces away, his head low, just as alone as I was.

Now here I was, following him into that massive dining room, towards a table that looked like it could seat kings. Felan had arranged three plates. "It's a pity Rosha couldn't join us," he said.

"She's got an errand to run," I said as I took a seat, all the while thinking *I wish you would stop saying that name.* It made me feel strange, hearing it on his tongue. Not the least of which was that he never really said it that way back in school. He knew everyone called me Rosha, but he insisted on saying my full name on the few occasions he felt inclined to. "*Kirosha,*" he always grumbled, making it all the clearer the distance he wished to impart. He didn't want to be familiar with me. He didn't want to be my friend.

The irony of it all now, sharing a meal with him. He actually took a moment to serve food on my plate. There were boiled potatoes and slices of seared beef, seasoned with garlic, pepper, and a hint of soy sauce. The beef was garnished with red onions, all lightly caramelized with butter. Only then did he take a seat himself, directly across from me so I had no choice but to stare at him.

I cut off a piece of meat and placed it in my mouth. My starving body was screaming for food, and I realized that I hadn't been eating much since Lord Cato had employed me. I took a sip of water to calm myself down.

"I've missed Go-nir's cooking," he said. "I'm touched the old man remembers my favourites."

"I thought Lord Cato has a cook," I replied.

He chewed thoughtfully before shaking his head. "He does, but mostly for when he's at home. Whenever he wasn't—which is fairly often, as you can see—he would have food sent over to me. But I was a small, sickly child, and Go-nir thought I needed good food. I ate with the stable hands as often as I could get away with." He gave a small smirk before turning back to cutting the meat on his plate.

"And did you always know Go-nir was Gorenten?" I asked, before kicking myself inwardly. *That's not how you jog his memory.* But I wanted to know why it had been so hard to make friends with me back then. If a Gorenten had all but raised him…

"I must admit, it never really occurred to me," he said.

"But you would think you would have thought of it, being from Genthal yourself. Your people, just like Go-nir's people, are outsiders in the eyes of the empire."

"I have never been to Genthal." His voice had yet to rise—to him, my questions were mere inquiries, and nothing more. "My mother always meant to take me, I thought, but she died when I was very young, and I could hardly recall any of the stories from her home. I am…very much Dageian," he added, with a crack in his voice. "Which makes it somewhat inconvenient when someone from Agarenth talks to me in their native tongue, expecting me to talk back. They often think I'm ignoring them on purpose. What about you? Do you speak Gorenten well?"

"There's too many Gorenten languages. Which one?"

He made a vague gesture. "I suppose whichever your ancestors spoke."

"A variant of it, which is too much like the Kagosh we're speaking to really be all that different," I said. "I can understand a few others, but whenever I speak, I sound like a little child, and so…the elders treat me like one."

"It must be nice to have *elders* in the first place," Felan replied. "The thought of trying to learn Agarenthen at all makes me dizzy."

"My father said the first trick to learning any language is learning about the people," I said. "People from different places think in different ways. If you simply try to swap words around in your native tongue, you're going to spend forever trying to make substitutions." Papa spoke more than I probably knew about, including the common Jinan tongue of Jin-Sayeng *and* the language from my mother's hometown. He never bragged about it, either. *It comes with the life of a wandering mercenary,* he liked to say. *Or at least, a poor one.* A barb for Enosh, who never bothered to learn any of the Jin-Sayeng tongues. Why learn when you could pay someone to translate for you?

"A wise man. Has your family been in Dageis for long?"

"Long enough." I started eating again, hoping the silence would be enough to distract him away from that thread of conversation. I really was hopeless at this.

"I used to think about asking Lord Cato to find the rest of my family," Felan continued. "My mother spoke of her father and sisters, and perhaps a brother. Nephews. Nieces. But Lord Cato was never interested in any of that. He wanted me to focus on my studies."

"In Sorna?" I asked.

"No, in Eheldeth."

"But you were in Sorna these last few years, weren't you?"

"Yes."

"Tell me about it," I said. "I hear it's got lovely weather there."

"It's temperate. Doesn't get as cold as it does here in Dageis. It was good for my lungs."

I closed my eyes for a moment, trying to keep myself calm. Of course. His lungs. His burnt lungs. *I ran away, left you like a coward. I was hoping you'd survive, and you did.* But the knowledge didn't bring relief. I saw him lying there in that soot, his tiny body curled up as if shriveled from the flames, blood around his nose. I should have tried to save him, even if I got in trouble, even if it cost me my spot in Eheldeth. Why did it matter anyway? It was never fated for me to finish my time there.

Steady, Rosha, I told myself as I reached for the glass of water. *Don't get emotional.* "That must be nice." I took another sip. "People must have a very different way of life there."

"They do. They mostly eat outside, for one thing, unless it's raining. The sun is always gorgeous, and the days are mostly lazy."

"Were you in the city?"

"The countryside," he said. "Father owns a vineyard overlooking the river."

"It sounds peaceful."

"Mostly, though the servants regarded me with suspicion. Magic is... outlawed in Sorna, you see. They let Dageians own property there, but they turn a blind eye on how it works here. They do not want you talking about magic. They do not want to *see* magic. The rest is a matter of padding the right pockets. So as far as the papers are concerned, Cato tan-Tarsius is a mere businessman, an expatriate who holds the proper papers to invest in and live there. But of course, the servants know better. And they certainly knew that the master's boy isn't exactly just there for his health. After all, they were the ones who nursed me back from—"

"Did you hear that?" I asked, abruptly.

He paused, knife in hand.

I wasn't just trying to distract him from musing about what had happened to him all those years ago. I really *did* hear something—a scratching on the kitchen door outside, too strong to be either of the dogs. It was followed by a howl.

"Are the dogs trying to get in?" Felan asked.

I didn't answer.

He placed the knife down. "What's the matter, Lady Suha? You look like you've seen a ghost."

I pushed my plate away. "How much do you know about your father's activities these last few years, Lord Felan?" I asked.

"I don't understand."

"Because there's a monster outside," I said, as calmly as a person could utter such words. "And we believe he made it."

Felan's response mirrored my words, though perhaps I shouldn't be surprised. He was that one kid in school who could withstand our class-mates' taunts without even blinking. "Show me," he said at last.

"Take a look for yourself, Lord Felan," I replied. "The monster is in the gardens. I've had a very…unfortunate meeting with him not that long ago."

"And my father never said anything about it?"

"Why would he?" I heard something crash and felt gnawing worry over the dogs. They weren't barking, so perhaps the beast hadn't found them yet. But then again, they didn't bark the other night, either. They had always known about the beast and were frightened of it. I had wondered why they cowered over every little sound.

Felan wiped his mouth with a napkin and got up. I followed him to the kitchen door. He opened it and the dogs came running inside. Without even looking at either of us, they disappeared into the great hall.

"Fierce warriors, the both of you," I drawled.

Felan held the door open.

"Don't tell me you're going to go out." I turned back to him. "You don't even know what you're dealing with."

"You're the one who told me to go take a look."

"Obviously, I was being sarcastic," I said. "That thing's dangerous. If you know how your father made it, that could help us figure out how to get rid of it. You realize these sorts of spells are illegal. The mage council will blow their tops off if they learn a member of the merchant guild, especially a mage who is still supposed to be bound by their rules, is involved in such activities."

"I've had very little contact with my father all these years. I couldn't tell you what he's been doing last week, let alone anything illegal." Felan glanced at the darkness, where the bushes rustled under a spray of moonlight. He kept one foot on the door. "How did you discover the thing?"

"I...was dusting the basement," I said. "It escaped from there."

He closed the kitchen door and turned the lock. Without a word, he began walking towards the basement. He tested the door. "Key," he said, holding his hand out.

I hesitated. I couldn't very well remold it for the basement door with him watching. My heart racing, I reached into my pocket and handed him the front door key.

He inserted it into the hole and turned. It wouldn't. "This looks like the wrong one," he said.

"Oh," I grumbled. "Right. I must have left it in Lord Cato's office. But that was days ago. I don't know if he took it."

"I know where he keeps the spare." He drew away, placing the key in my palm. I stared at it, my heart racing. *Too close. How long are you supposed to keep up this farce? You can't even pretend you like people. How will you pretend to be anyone but yourself?*

I regained my composure when he returned with a key ring. He barely offered me a glance and began testing all the other keys until he found one that would work. He opened the door and descended the staircase, where he stopped at the bottom.

"Please bring a lantern," he said.

I grabbed it from the kitchen, where I glanced at the window for a moment, thinking about Ryo and the women. Hoping they were safe. Hoping that thing wasn't busy trying to dig them out of the tomb. I returned to Felan, who took the lantern and waved it over the bottom of the staircase. "Just as I thought," he said. "There was a spell here."

"I didn't see a—" I began, before stopping myself. He didn't look like he heard me, because he was now bent over the faded scratching on the wooden floor. I could see the gleam of candle wax that looked like it had been scraped from the surface. I must have stepped on it last time and missed it completely.

"You see that?" he asked. He traced the figures with his finger. "Someone tripped the spell and turned into whatever that is outside."

"A spell that turns people into monsters. I've never heard of such a thing."

He looked at me quizzically. "You've worked in many houses whose owners can afford such expensive glyphs, I presume?"

"I...yes," I stammered. "But I thought glyphs that did permanent damage weren't allowed in Dageis, let alone in the middle of a city. I thought all trap spells are regulated." Adding *I thought* when I was pretty damn sure of myself was hard, but I couldn't jog his memory down that road. We used to have such long debates in class.

"You've forgotten my father is a high-ranking official holding a seat in the merchant guild."

"The mage council regulates magic, not the merchant guild."

"Money and influence greases wheels. He has clearances regular locksmith mages wouldn't have. I'm surprised he even entrusted you with the key. If he knew that thing had tripped his spell and was still around, then he would have gotten rid of it already and possibly re-armed the trap. Which tells me he's been so busy he's neglected the whole house, or whatever he's keeping down here just isn't that valuable for him to remember." Felan stopped talking as his eyes skipped to the half-covered furniture piled up along the walls. He remembered his things.

"I see nothing valuable here." I wanted to make it sound like I hadn't been snooping around there already.

Felan nodded. "Me neither." His jaw tightened. "I think he just didn't want to remember me and placed the spell there so he would never be tempted to go down here." He glanced back at me, as if remembering I was still there. "An old man's idea of a joke," he said lightly, though his voice was anything but.

I didn't have an answer. "The thing moves fast, like the wind," I said, trying to change the subject. "I barely caught a glimpse."

"Then how did you know about it?"

I swore inwardly. I'd forgotten I wasn't dealing with someone like Jehar, who would take my explanations at face-value. This was Felan. As a child, he was already somewhat of a know-it-all. With every passing year, it got worse, and he'd shown himself to be ruthless in the pursuit of knowledge and making it clear he was better than everyone else. And by everyone else, I meant mostly me. I didn't know what he hated more—me or the fact that I usually got higher grades than him anyway. Either way, he was the last person I wanted an interrogation from.

You've beaten him before. You can do it again. I considered telling him about Jaila, and then decided it wasn't worth the trouble. "I saw it outside," I said, trying to think quickly. "The servants mentioned they heard strange sounds beginning that same night. I guessed whatever strange thing I saw must've been it. Look, we can talk about the last few days all night, but aren't you going to do anything about this? This is your father's doing. That thing could be out there hurting someone."

"I don't know what you want me to do," he replied.

"Is there…someway we could reverse the spell? Turn it back to the person it was before?" If I had *known* there was a glyph on the floor in the first place, I might have made an attempt. All I needed was time enough to study the patterns and runes on the wood. "You went to Eheldeth. They must have taught you something like that."

"They did," he admitted. "It's a matter of going through the patterns and—"

"So do it."

"There is no chance I can perform the spell."

"Because you didn't finish your studies?" I asked. "Surely the officials will turn a blind eye if they know who your father is."

"Unauthorized use of magic is a grave sin," he agreed. "But more than that. I am incapable."

"What are you talking about?"

He held out his hands, and I noticed for the first time that his fingers were deeply scarred. I felt a wave of guilt run through me.

"I am incapable of magic. I have been blind to the *agan* for a very long time."

CHAPTER 24

THE UNSEEING MAGE AND THE MONSTER

F elan rising from the dead wasn't half as surprising as his confession that he couldn't practice magic anymore. In the empire, there were spells you could use to render someone incapable of practicing magic so as long as they remained in the vicinity of such enchantments. But permanently removing their capability of working with the *agan* was, in theory, dangerous, and therefore illegal. The thought was such spells could rob both target *and* caster of so much more than their magic. Eyesight, memory, the use of their limbs, their mental capacities. Furthermore, there wasn't a need for it in most cases. The capacity to practice magic was never a bad thing as far as Dageis was concerned. A child born with connection to the *agan* was a gift, elevating their families' status immediately if everyone was willing to play by the mage council's rules. Even if you weren't a Dageian citizen, it offered a chance for something better. Mage-thralls were useful to their masters and could rise above the common servant. The gifted nearly always got education, shelter, good food, because Dageis wasn't supposed to let potential magic-users just walk around unmonitored. Barring that—because of course not *everyone* had access to those opportunities—you'd be dead.

I mean, *I* was dead, wasn't I? Or trying to be, anyway. The damn empire offered few opportunities for outlaws.

I turned my eyes back to the floor, because I didn't want to seem like I was staring at him. The guilt, the one I had wanted to put behind me forever, was growing. Whatever happened to his magic had something to do with what happened to him when we were children.

"Aren't you going to ask how?" His voice was very low.

"I'm curious," I said. "But I believe we have other things to worry about."

"Ah, of course. The monster at our door. Well, I don't believe we need magic in the first place." He held up the key. "We just have to put it back where it was."

From someone who spent long years in Eheldeth, the man was practically speaking blasphemy. But it gave me a moment to breathe. As much as I wanted to know his side of the story from all those years ago, I didn't want him to reminisce *that* much.

"What's the plan?" I asked.

"Bait," he said. "Do you know what that thing eats? Fresh meat, perhaps?"

"Now that you mention it, I don't think I've heard any of the stable hands mention missing horses," I said. "Most of the dogs are accounted for, save for the one who never leaves his side. And your father doesn't keep any other animals around, does he?"

"He can't abide most other animals. He doesn't like the way they smell or the noises they make. That's a dilemma."

"I know it chases people," I said. "I could go outside and lead it back here."

"I would not ask you to risk your life. This is my father's doing, like you said. I would not put the responsibility on your shoulders." Felan carefully straightened himself and removed his jacket, leaving only his shirt. There were more scars on his bare arms. I had to struggle not to look at them.

"It's really fast," I warned.

He gave a small sound of acknowledgement and walked down the hall.

I held the basement door open, closing my eyes. *You coward. Why are you letting him do this? If he's incapable of magic, then he has less means of defending himself than you.*

I sucked in my breath, trying to focus on why I was feeling guilty. That thing that happened years ago—he started it, all right? I offered him my friendship and he responded with petty rivalry. He started it. That was the only thing that kept me sane all these years.

We think of time like we think of *agan*, flowing like a river from one moment to the next, as if every action we take in the present hasn't been predetermined by our decisions in the past. We do not simply drift by and leave things where we find them. Instead, we circle it like dogs, cutting ourselves on the jagged edges where they've already scarred us.

Six years. That was how long it had been. Six years since I made the mistake of skipping lessons for the day. It wasn't normally my habit. You didn't get top grades by skipping lessons, after all. But the day's classes led straight to the sporting events that Eheldeth held at the start of every winter. Everyone was expected to take part, no matter how bad you were at dodging balls or chasing them—the mage council badly wanted to show the rest of the empire that their students could be worthy physical specimens, too. Considering how a good percentage of Eheldeth graduates go on to serve with the Dageian military, it wasn't exactly a misplaced idea. I, however, had no desire to stand around and think up long passages in my head to pass time when I could actually be reading the books or working on spells for that semester's final project. And as far as worthy physical specimens went, I was a pretty poor one.

So I feigned a headache, the kind that made my classmates think if they insisted on dragging me to the events, they were going to go home covered in puke. I was left alone with a bowl of hot broth the cook sent up for me.

I made the pretense of staying in bed for another hour before I wandered the common room with a shawl around my shoulders and a thick book. Only then did I notice Felan. He must have pulled the same trick. He was lying on one of the sofas near the window, a wet rag on his forehead. He looked startled when I arrived.

"Oh, it's just you," he said. In those days, he was well on his way to surpassing me in height. Black fuzz, rather like what would be left behind if a caterpillar rolled around, covered his upper lip. "What the hell are you doing here?"

"I could ask you the same thing." I slumped onto the other sofa. There really weren't any that offered me more privacy, but I didn't want to give him the satisfaction of returning to my room. I made a great show of opening my book.

"So, *this* is why you're always getting such high grades," he grumbled under his breath.

"I'm sorry, were you talking to me?"

"You're always studying. Don't you have friends?"

"Refer to my first comment to you."

"I don't like people. I don't *need* them to be friends with me. But you —you're always around those girls. All they have to do is snap their fingers, and you'll follow them like a lost puppy even though you don't talk to them and they don't even seem to notice you exist. You just like sitting near them. You call *those friends*? You don't even have anything in common."

"Shows what you know."

"Ah, right. That's why you're all alone here. Because you have friends."

I snapped the book shut. "It's like you exist just to make my life a living hell."

"If you're so spoiled that you think the world revolves around you…"

"Is *that* what you think? Because I could have sworn everyone is always tiptoeing around *you* because of *your* powerful father, whoever the hell he is. *Oh, don't be mean to Felan because his father can break yours with his little toe. Leave Felan alone because his father can get me fired. Poor, helpless little*—"

He threw a pillow at me. It struck the wall.

I laughed. "Was that supposed to hit me? You were off by at *least* an arm's-length. It's a good thing they don't give out grades based on physical prowess or else they would have kicked you out a long time ago."

He scowled. Despite the moustache, he still looked like that same little boy who found an affront in everything I did. He got up and practically stomped out of the room. I picked up the pillow. Only then did I notice something had fallen out of his pocket. It was a silver locket, with a painting of a woman inside, which I guessed was his mother.

I thought about putting it in the boys' dormitory, and then hesitated. For one thing, I really wasn't allowed in there. And if I did sneak in, I wouldn't know which room he was assigned to, or even his bed. I also wanted to get back at him in a way that made him feel ashamed—to show him I was capable of kindness, too. I looped the silver chain around my wrist and went down the hall to look for him.

I caught sight of him from the balcony, heading down to the main gardens. I ran as fast as I could. Down the spiral staircase I went, and then through the small bamboo courtyard with the rock garden and the aviary. I called his name as soon as I reached the first row of cherry trees, but either he was purposely ignoring me or he couldn't hear me at all, because he kept walking.

He strode straight out of campus.

At our age, we weren't technically allowed outside of school grounds, but there also weren't guards posted to keep students in. Eheldeth is a collection of many buildings situated around tall spires. Students our age went to the Chrysanthemum House, where we would stay until our fourth year. Afterwards, we would be moved to the buildings in the heart of the university, where all lessons were designed to push us through the very simple—and very difficult—final exams. Some students don't make it to that step—no matter how much money their parents pour into tuitions and various "gifts" to the keepers and officials, there's only so much a lack of magical skill can do. Others run out of tuition money and have to transfer out to lesser colleges around the empire—a place that will get them ready for a career much less prestigious than what the rest of Eheldeth offered.

In any case, the Chrysanthemum House was at the northern tip, surrounded by nothing but cliffs and wilderness. The only way out is through the buildings in the south, where a child our age—especially in the bright red robes of First to Fourth Years—would stand out like a sore thumb. Then it was just a matter of dragging you back to your keepers and doling out the proper amount of punishment. If somehow you were lucky enough and got as *far* as the spires, well…I probably shouldn't use the word *lucky*. Keepers were known for their patience, because training budding mages is part of the job. The other mages in Eheldeth, especially those outside the school proper? Not so much.

But I didn't really have to worry about any of that, because Felan went north, into the forest.

Now my fears turned from visions of angry keepers swearing endless homework to bears and wolves and other wild things. "Felan!" I called once more, my voice hoarse from screaming. Were there dragons out there? I could have sworn some of the children said there were dragons on the plateau. The shadows between the trees seemed to close in, and I looked up in fear at the imposing branches, imagining faces carved into the tree trunks. I started running faster.

Keeping track of Felan was difficult in the suffocating embrace of that thicket, but eventually I stumbled upon an open field. There was an old, crumbling building to my left.

"Can you just leave me alone?" Felan snapped. The wind blew past us, carrying with it a hint of earth and rain and pine needles. "Three years you've done nothing but make my life miserable."

"Excuse me?" I replied. "You're the one who's been insufferable since I came. I tried to make friends with you, remember?"

"I don't need friends!"

"What by all the gods is wrong with you? I was just trying to be polite, you brat. I'm sorry I wasn't aware you didn't *need* friends, but now it seems all you want are enemies."

"The last time someone did that…" He lowered his voice. "Come on. 'Fess up. The other boys paid you to talk to me, didn't they?"

"Do you really think that's the only reason someone would talk to you? That's the worst case of self-pity I've ever heard. If I was your mother, I'd be ashamed."

"Well, she's dead, and it's not your responsibility to—"

The thunder cracked across the sky, followed by a torrent of the strongest rain I've ever experienced in my life.

I could still hear that rain. All I have to do is close my eyes and I'm back in that field, my eyes half-shut, the water coming down like a hail of rocks. And I can see him standing there, all alone—just another boy I could have been kinder to, the way I should have been with my brothers.

I guess a part of me had blamed him for being stuck there. Well—I blamed my father, but he wasn't around for me to pour out my frustrations on, and the next best thing was my rivalry with that arrogant little snot. He represented everything I detested about Eheldeth: the snobbery, the falseness, the way he got away with acting the way he did because people were afraid of his father. I couldn't just throw tantrums like that and survive. He openly argued with teachers, while I had to pretend to be polite.

But the truth was that he was just as alone as I was. Even more so, I had to grudgingly admit. Sure, everyone stayed out of his way, but there were other ways to torment him. And whatever they'd done to him in the months before I came to Eheldeth must have been bad enough to stick. He had no one, not even the people who let me sit near them to give me a semblance of normalcy from time to time. He had no one.

And now? I stood at that basement door, waiting for sounds from the darkness. If something happened to him, that would be it. He would die alone, as alone as he'd lived. I felt my senses spin. Eheldeth had taught me to keep myself alive and nothing else. It hadn't taught me how to take care of others.

I reached for a candle from one shelf and jammed it under the crack of the basement door to hold it open. Then I made my way to the kitchen, out the back door. Just as I walked past the woodshed, Felan came tearing through the bushes with the monster behind him.

I picked up a piece of firewood and flung it at the beast. It flew past Felan's ear and struck the beast between the eyes.

"Back inside!" Felan called. He was dragging his foot. His trousers were torn to shreds; blood splattered across both his legs.

"Go on," I said, picking up another log. "Close the door behind you. I'll distract him first."

He groaned. "Are you out of your mind? That thing is dangerous!"

"We'll die if you keep talking."

He groaned again. Maybe the wound was starting to hurt. He dragged himself up the steps. I waited for the sound of the door shutting behind me before I let flames lick the surface of the firewood. Flames danced over my flesh. It was slightly unpleasant because of the heat—contrary to popular belief, mages *do* feel pain and can just as easily burn themselves when conjuring fire as others—but it came with a touch of excitement. Working the threads of the *agan* for the second, third time after all these years felt like wading into ocean after years of not swimming. And I happened to be a *really* good swimmer.

The firewood lit up in flames. I threw the projectile at Elry's face again and watched in satisfaction as his fur caught on fire. I smelled singed hair and flesh as he roared in pain, trying to put the flames out.

"Stop!" someone called.

As Elry crashed his head into the bushes, Jaila appeared from the thicket, limping, her arms around both Ryo and Nasuha.

"Please," Jaila continued.

"What are you doing out here?" I snapped. "This is—"

"Don't hurt him," she said. "Please. Deep inside that beast…he's still the man I loved."

"You said you would save him," Ryo added. "Rosha, you said—"

I placed a finger on my lips. "This isn't the time," I said. "Go back inside. Hurry!"

The beast got back to his feet.

The kitchen door flung open once more. "Here, you foul thing!" Felan called, holding an entire hunk of ham in his hands.

Elry must've caught a whiff of its scent because he immediately leaped in Felan's direction, strings of spit dripping down his jaws. His foul breath filled the air with a noxious stench.

Limping, Felan led him straight into the basement before throwing the ham down the stairs. The beast tore after it. As it crashed down the steps, I pushed the basement door closed. It rattled as the monster turned to break it down, but Felan joined me before it could open again and quickly locked it with the key.

We collapsed to the ground, our backs to the door..

CHAPTER 25

THE SORCERER'S SECRETS

"Now," Felan said, after what felt like forever. He placed a hand over his knee. "Is anyone going to explain the rest of this?"

I got up and dusted my dress. "That's Jaila." I pointed at the pale, half-dead woman standing near the windows. "She was going to run away with Elry…" I pointed to the door, which the monster was still trying to break down.

"But he decided to fill his pockets first and tripped the spell my father had thoughtlessly cast as a joke," Felan finished. He closed his eyes for a second and rubbed his forehead. He turned to Jaila. "She needs to be taken care of. How long as she had these wounds?"

"A few days," I replied.

He held out his hand to her. "May I…?"

She reluctantly took it.

He drew her to him before placing one hand on her back, the other under her legs as he lifted her from the ground. She had lost so much weight in the past few weeks that it didn't even seem to take a lot of effort. He started for the staircase, but I pointed past it down the hall. "Take her to my room," I said. "It's closer."

He nodded. The others followed.

Under the bright light in the smaller space, Jaila's condition seemed even more dire than I imagined. Her breathing was shallow, and her skin looked paper-thin, dark veins spreading like cobwebs. She was filthy from head to toe. "Why haven't you brought her to a doctor?" Felan demanded, glancing at me and Nasuha in turn.

"I was hiding from your father," Jaila croaked.

"Why?" Felan asked. "If you had quit properly, he would have let you go, with a generous parting gift besides."

"How long haven't you been home?" she whispered. "That sounds nothing like the man who hired me."

"Even so—"

"You saw Elry. He would have done worse to me. I didn't want to risk it."

"My father must have forbidden you to go to the basement," Felan said.

Jaila swallowed before slowly nodding.

"Elry tripped a spell," Felan said. "That's all. My father wouldn't harm someone on purpose. All you had to do was *ask*." But even as he uttered those words, a shadow of doubt crossed his face. He drew his brows together. I couldn't watch Jaila any longer and turned around to make hot water and get some cloth.

When I returned, Nasuha was getting her undressed while Felan paced outside the room. I placed the bucket of steaming water near Jaila's head and began washing her while Nasuha pulled the covers up to her chin.

"Maybe she wants food," I said, glancing at Ryo. "There's some in the kitchen."

"I'm not hungry," Jaila replied.

"She hasn't eaten all day," Nasuha said.

"In that case, I'm going to town for a doctor," Felan broke in. He glanced at Ryo and furrowed his brow some more, though he didn't comment, as if he wasn't sure what to make of him. "The boy could go with me, in case my father comes back. I will say he is my...assistant." He looked doubtful.

"I'm Ryo," my brother chirped up. "I'm Rosha's brother."

Felan glanced at Nasuha. "I suppose that makes sense," he said, after a heart-stopping silence. "Can you ride a horse?"

"With my eyes closed!"

They shut the door and walked out. I let out a small groan and glanced at Jaila, who had fallen asleep. Her hand was hanging from one side of the bed. I picked it up and placed it over her stomach. "This can't be happening," I said. "Now he knows about all of you. What's to stop him from telling his father?"

"You said you knew him," Nasuha replied.

"Once, when he was little."

"What was his character like?"

"I couldn't tell you."

"Was he the sort of boy who would betray you behind your back? Can he keep his word?"

"I told you. I don't know," I said. "I didn't know him that well. He was...we were rivals. He *didn't* like me."

Nasuha squinted. "That's strange. Usually, you'd remember people you detested. Even more so than people you like. How can he not remember you?"

"It was a long time ago."

"How old were you?"

"I was fifteen. He was fourteen."

"It makes sense the other way around," she said. "Perhaps you wouldn't have recognized him—if he had shot up in height and deepened his voice and grew a beard. But you? Surely you look exactly like you did when you were fifteen.."

"Nothing about this feels right," I agreed. "And the master—he still hasn't returned."

"Good. His absence gives you more time to investigate."

"If only I knew where to start. I went here on a hunch. I found my brother at least, but I still don't know what it means, why he's here, what our enemies *want* from us. And I can't every well ask Felan. He couldn't even explain the spell in the basement. He said his father must have left the glyph there to stop himself from going down and seeing all of Felan's things. A spell, made from spite."

Nasuha sighed. "And who isn't capable of spite? If the boy and the father had a big argument, then it's clear enough for me. *Ask* him for his help. He seems friendly. Maybe he does recognize you and has simply decided to put your rivalry aside."

"I doubt it."

"Then what's your explanation for all of this?"

I heard a loud thud, as if something had landed on the roof. I turned to Nasuha. "Did you—"

"Loud and clear," Nasuha said. "That didn't sound like a bird."

"Maybe it's a very big bird."

She gave a shudder. "Don't start."

"After Elry, I'm willing to believe anything is possible in this house," I said. "I'm going to go look."

"Where, outside? Let me do it."

"Stay with Jaila, in case anything attacks her here."

I tiptoed out of the hall. The dogs were waiting by the staircase, but when I went to open the door, they didn't want to go outside. They stayed by the first steps, tail wagging slowly, ears laid back against their heads. They knew something I didn't. I wished they could talk. I shook my head at them and went outside. Not a single cloud covered the moon, so I had a full view of the roof. I half-cringed as I tried to search for a hint of a shadowy wing or whatever foul beast had decided to attack us now. But there was nothing. I circled the house twice, to make sure, my boots growing wet from the sodden grass.

As I was halfway through my last round, I noticed a light in one of the windows of the second floor. I squinted. I was sure that I hadn't left anything in the study, but perhaps…

No. It wasn't a light. It was the moon's reflection on the glass, done at an angle that it was making the entire window glow. But also, I noticed two other things: a movement behind the glass, and that the window wasn't on the second floor after all.

The damn house had an attic.

How could I have been so stupid? Of course, the house would have an attic. The house had gabled roofs. The staircase, however, only went up to the second floor, so I didn't know how to access it. I went to both ends of the landing, and then all the way to each far end of the hall. I noticed no trapdoors coming from the ceiling.

A burst of inspiration struck me. Grabbing a lamp, I went to Lord Cato's office, which remained as pristine as when I last left it. I held it aloft, watching the shadows cast by the dancing flame. My hand looked enormous against the beams.

Fake beams. They weren't part of the house's structure. I held the lamp higher and saw the deep creases between a section of beams, hiding a square indentation in the ceiling. I dragged a stool right underneath it and pressed at the very end.

The ceiling shook. It wouldn't open inward, but when I tried to shift it another way, it slid all the way down. As it struck the end of the ceiling, a ladder dropped.

"Well, that's convenient," I said.

I took the lamp again and went up the ladder. I could feel my heart pounding in my throat. After Elry, I wasn't sure if I had it in me to fight another foul creature. Part of me wanted to turn back now and wait to do this until morning, or at least take Nasuha with me. But I didn't want to wait. I still didn't know if Felan, truly, was on my side, and a part of me felt like he would turn if he found out what I truly came here for, never mind if he found out who I *was*. And what if Lord Cato returned soon? No—if this was my only chance, then I needed to take it.

The attic was bare, filled with nothing but dusty straw. But it was also much too small for the size of the house. I held the lamp to the side of the walls and saw another fake door. I pushed it open and found myself inside a large room, at least the size of the great hall.

The first thing that struck me was the smell of rot. Of death. I struggled to make sense of my surroundings, my eyes adjusting to the half-darkness at the same time as the lamplight flickered around me. I heard something scurrying in the distance.

"I've fought one beast tonight already," I said. "Let's get this over with. Come out, whatever you are!"

I held my breath, let a lick of flame drift from my hand, and made it float into the air, dissipating a few feet away. Just enough to frighten. Just enough so I could *see* up ahead.

The light revealed Bracken, half-shivering in the middle of the floor, tail between her legs.

I placed the lamp on the ground. "That's where you've been." I patted my knees. "Come on. Come here. There's a good girl."

She slowly crawled along the ground, tail beating against her hindquarters. I didn't know why she was so frightened of me. She wasn't before. Just a few days ago, my very presence seemed to make her indignant. I pressed my hand on her back and then along her chest. Her fur was dry, and her skin practically seemed to collapse around her ribs from dehydration. I picked her up, pressing her against my chest. She placed a paw on my shoulder, shivering.

"You need water and food," I said. "You've been trapped here for days, haven't you?" I picked up the lamp with my other hand and walked back to the main hall. I walked down the ladder, making my way back to the office. I badly wanted to investigate the rest of the attic, but I took care of the dog first. One of the dog bowls underneath Lord Cato's desk was filled to the rim with water. I placed Bracken on the ground and pushed the bowl towards her.

She licked it twice, still shivering, before darting up the ladder once more. Two or three rungs up, she realized she didn't really know how to go all the way and began to whine.

"Fine," I murmured, carrying her again. She seemed grateful for the assistance. We returned to the attic. There, she jumped out of my arms and made her way through the darkness. I held the lamp up to my face and followed her.

The smell of death grew stronger. It wasn't long before I discovered the source.

Above a pool of sticky blood, Lord Cato lay on the floor, white eyes staring at the ceiling. His throat had been slit open.

I placed the lamp on the ground. "What happened here?" I asked. "Who did this?"

She trembled, too afraid to even make a sound.

I swallowed my fear and walked around the body. The smell was not as terrible as I'd first thought, or perhaps I was getting used to it. The cool, dry air in the attic had delayed the body's decay. I tried to count back the days. He had only been gone two nights. I'd heard no noises in the house that would indicate Lord Cato had been through it in the last day or so, which meant he must have died the same night I discovered Elry.

To test my theory, I prodded Lord Cato's leg with the tip of my boot. His body was soft, long past stiffness.

"Couldn't wait until you told me where my father was, could you, old man?" I said out loud.

A flash of lightning through the small attic window suddenly lit up the room. I gave a yelp of surprise, nearly tripping over Lord Cato's body. A shadowy figure was seated on a chair in the far corner, a man, his face obstructed from view. The lightning flashed a second time, followed by a rumble of thunder, loud enough that the house vibrated for a moment.

The body tilted to one side of the chair before it carefully slid to the floor.

"Two dead men," I said. "You've had a rough couple of nights, haven't you, Bracken? Maybe we should go downstairs first. Then maybe I can get Felan to—"

The other body began to crawl to its feet.

CHAPTER 26

HIS MAJESTY'S VOICE

I felt an urge to do two things. First, I thought about jumping from the window, which was an impulse so unlike my usual nature it should tell you how much seeing that body move affected my state of mind. Next, I thought about throwing the lamp at the man's head.

I decided both would cause my death—one immediate, the other slow and full of burning—and took a step back instead. The man ambled towards me, and I stared in the blank, white eyes of someone so old, he looked like he belonged in a coffin. His beard trailed down to his belly, sparse and white. His face was as wrinkled as a crumpled piece of parchment. He opened his mouth, revealing cracked yellow teeth stained with a veiny black substance that smelled fouler than I expected.

His tongue flicked past his teeth, like he was trying to taste the air. He said something unintelligible and lurched forward. I thought he was going to attack me and darted to the side.

He walked past me, oblivious to my presence. Every step seemed to pain him, and he dragged one leg heavier than the other. He walked and walked until he reached the end of the wall, and then he kept walking in place. He seemed unable to comprehend the existence of a wall there.

I glanced down at the dog. She was still shivering, but she barely reacted to the body's presence, and its movement didn't seem to bother her at all. I felt like I wanted to jump out of my skin, and here this dog didn't even seem half as frightened.

"You know him," I said. "Has he been keeping the old man up here all this time?"

She whined before delicately making her way past the sticky blood.

The old man was wearing nothing but a nightshirt, which left the lower half of his body bare. She prodded the back of his left leg with her nose.

A nose as cold as that dog's should have made anyone react, but the old man kept walking, as if he was trying to tear a hole through that wall without actually doing any work. His arms hung useless at his sides.

"Here, Bracken," I called. "Let's leave him alone, now."

She walked back across the room, but she didn't come to me. I watched her walk past her master's body—it didn't seem to hold as much an appeal to her as he did in life—and made her way to the chair. She jumped up it.

Light flickered on the wall in front of her. I narrowed my eyes. No—I wasn't a wall. It was a curtain, covering something flat. A painting or a mirror of some sort.

"Emperor Cerknar," a voice called from the other side. "If you can hear me, Your Excellency, please respond. It's been days. We're worried something bad has happened to you."

Bracken barked.

"Did you say something, my lord? Please, Emperor Cerknar. It is imperative that you—"

I grabbed the curtains and pulled them aside. My last guess was correct. There was a mirror on the other end—a glass mirror holding the image of a man.

"My Lord?" he continued.

Bracken pressed her nose on the mirror, her tail wagging.

It was a magical mirror, one that drew on the connections of the *agan* to act as a semi-portal that allowed you to communicate to someone not in the same room. But for some reason, the man couldn't see through to our side. I watched Bracken follow his movement, her tail wagging slightly. He seemed oblivious to the sight of the dog right in front of him.

"So not only do you know this man behind us," I said, "but that one, too. Is that right?" I patted her head, looking deep into her eyes. If only she could talk back, my job would be a lot easier.

I placed her on the floor. She weaved between my legs, as if finally happy that after two nights someone was doing *something*. "Hello?" I called to the image. "Can you hear me?"

Silence.

I glanced at the room. *Agan* mirrors worked because of spells that had been etched into them, which was then attuned to another mirror elsewhere. I got up to check the back of this one and noticed a series of runes carved right at the base of the wood. But at least the first two had been chipped off, like someone had taken a chisel and just struck enough off to make it useless. But it was still connected to the mirror on the other side.

"Let's see." I looked around on the desk and spotted a nail protruding under the drawer. I pried it off carefully and began etching out the rest of the symbol for one of the runes. It was clear what it needed to be—I could still make out a faint outline of the symbol in the bottom. I didn't know the others, though. Eheldeth had no artisanship classes—you needed another few years in specialized trades to learn how to stick spells on inanimate objects, and most of those you learned as an apprentice at a shop.

But my quick fix must have worked, because when I said, "Hello?" again, someone coughed.

"My Lord?" a voice called. "Emperor Cerknar?"

I hesitated. I thought about saying *no, it's not, and Lord Cato's dead.* But a part of me decided against it. "Yes," I said, not really knowing why I did it.

"Thank goodness!" the man said, peering at the mirror. "Your Excellency, your mirror isn't working. I can just hear your voice."

I stared at the mirror, wondering what other spells were engraved on it. Surely, he would have noticed a woman's voice. "There's been an accident," I continued. "But if you can hear me all right…"

"I can, Your Excellency. Loud and clear. Can *you* see me?"

I tapped my fingers together and paused. "The image is a little blurred. I can't make out your face. Who are you?"

"It's me, Your Excellency. Pacano."

Pacano. The Emperor's Chancellor.

"Chancellor Pacano!" I exclaimed. "Of course. Excellent!" I didn't know if the emperor even talked like that. I didn't know what I was doing in the first place, or why Lord Cato had a mirror that was supposed to be connected to the emperor. But I knew I couldn't stop. If I did, he might wonder what was happening to the emperor, which might lead him to me, which would inevitably result in the mage council finally sinking their claws into my backside. I needed to find an opening for a speedier exit.

"Is everything well, Your Excellency? You said you had an accident?"

"Oh, I just…hit my head on the mirror, that's all."

"But that's—"

"I'm fine, I'm fine. I've rested since."

"You missed this morning's meeting. Everyone was worried sick. We were just about to send a delegate to the official palace to check up on you. We know you didn't like that the last time, but—"

"Everything's fine, Chancellor," I said, unconsciously making my voice deeper, which was silly when he didn't seem to know any better. "There's no need to send anyone."

"Are you sure? A physician from Drusgaya, perhaps, or—"

"I said I'm fine." I scratched Bracken's head. So the Emperor *wasn't* supposed to be in Drusgaya. I knew the seat of the government was in Teleres Palace, right at the western edge of the peninsula where the City of Drusgaya stood. I had assumed the emperor lived there. Perhaps he didn't.

"If you say so, Your Excellency," Pacano continued. I could see a line of doubt on his forehead.

"The last time you were here…" I began. *When was that? Where was that?* I wondered if it would be in character to sound like a senile old man. Last I heard, the emperor must be nearing a hundred. As my thoughts went down that road, my eyes drifted back to the old man in the attic, the one who was still trying to walk into the wall. The soft *thud* as his body hit the wood had turned rhythmic.

"Your Excellency, while I appreciate the candour, I don't believe we have time," Pacano said. He folded a handkerchief into two and dabbed his forehead. "The meeting this morning…"

"Ah, yes," I said. "The meeting. Give me a quick summary."

He picked up a pile of papers from his desk and rifled through them. "First order of business—Queen-elect Isobel of Hafod desires a meeting with you. Of course, it remains preposterous that such an insignificant nation thinks it is well within their rights to demand a meeting with His Excellency, but we're running out of excuses, and Queen-elect Isobel's anger can be inconvenient. Last week, it seems as if her ships have been harassing ours along the western trade routes."

Where you pick up Gorenten to serve you, claiming it's for the good of the land. Claiming our labour and magic will bring honour to our worthless people when all you really want are slaves. I felt a prickle of anger and had to pause for a moment to swallow it all down. Still, it wasn't enough. "Good," I half-whispered, before I could stop myself.

"Your Excellency?"

I scrabbled to think of an excuse. "You can add that to her list of atrocities. Have every sea captain file a report. Perhaps when we have enough, we can use that to silence her demands."

"An excellent idea, my lord emperor. The wisdom of the ages…"

"Yes, yes. Continue on."

"The Gorenten. The ones squatting in the peninsula south of Lon Basden."

I felt my skin prickle. *You don't even own those lands. Our ancestors did. After you drove them from it, you took what you could and abandoned them not long after.* It took all my strength not to say anything except, "What about them?"

"We've received another request to look into deporting the squatters from the merchant guild. They say they're inundated with complaints."

"What complaints?"

"Some merchants are interested in purchasing land down there."

I couldn't help myself. "But it's barren land."

"The merchant guild wants to discuss that. Their members believe those lands hold untapped potential, and that it's a disgrace that the empire has abandoned them to savages."

I bristled. "The Gorenten—"

"Oh, I know, Your Excellency. A figure of speech."

"Those lands…" *Watch your temper, Rosha.* "I believe they're nothing but farmlands. Do we not, er, have enough farmlands across the empire to suit these merchants' taste? Are they not satisfied with the weather? Or have we stopped pretending to tolerate the natives and have decided to harvest them in earnest?"

Chancellor Pacano hesitated. I swore inwardly, wondering if I had gone too far. I didn't know how the emperor spoke. My parents had never been the type to go down to the square in the few occasions Emperor Cerknar addressed the public, and even if they had, I would have never gone. The cares of Dageis mattered little to me. I paid as much attention to its politics as I did its entertainment, which is to say I didn't care for it at all.

"Some merchants have expressed interest in developing those lands as tourist attractions," Pacano said. "The Gorent islands are supposed to be beautiful. I have never been, of course, but they say the seas are as blue as the sky itself. Deep within its hills are waterfalls that drip over crystal-clear pools."

"Someone already owns those lands."

Pacano picked up a paper. "Yes. A few thousand acres, in fact, seems to be registered to a Count Enosh Tar'elian. A Gorenten, I'm told."

"A Dageian citizen?"

"So, it says here."

"Then you can't seize those lands from under his nose. You'll have to buy them. Do you know where this merchant can be found?"

"I will have to inquire, Your Excellency. There have been reports he staked those lands out without permission from the empire first."

"For you to know about them now means he filed the necessary paperwork afterwards and has been paying taxes and a mortgage for their retention."

"You're correct, Your Excellency."

I paused. What I was about to say next was risky, but I had to get it out there. "So instead of seizing those lands, how about the merchants just do what he did? Why hasn't any of them submitted development proposals on what to do with the parcels *they've* claimed, along with the application fees?"

"They've tried," Pacano said. "The mage council is blocking them."

"What?"

"Rumour has it..." He coughed and lowered his voice. "That Tar'elian received approval from within the mage council to carry out his activities, and this same contact is preventing the others from doing the same thing. We don't have proof yet, of course, but—" He coughed again. "The merchant guild is demanding an answer, including insisting that something be done about the people on his lands in the meantime."

"Aren't those his farmhands?"

"They're saying he's taking in refugees. Non-citizens. Harbouring illegals is a crime."

"Find Tar'elian," I said. "I want a meeting with the merchant guild, too. I'll hear their concerns personally. When's the soonest?"

"I'll...have to let you know tomorrow morning, Your Excellency."

"Thank you, Chancellor."

"As for the other things—"

"Good night, Chancellor. I'm exhausted. We'll talk in the morning."

"But Your Excellency..."

I dropped the curtains over the mirror, hoping that would muffle the sounds from my end. I watched Pacano's figure slowly disappear. The mirror grew dim, and the hum of *agan* on my skin slowly evaporated.

Only then did I get up. I felt like I was dreaming. *Somehow, you did it,* I thought. *You're one step closer to the answer.* The merchant guild—of course. *Of course,* the other merchants wanted a piece of the pie. No one had paid any attention to the Gorenten lands until my family resettled in it. But Enosh's attempts to officiate our presence there must have turned some heads. Had he been expecting less? Everyone knew Dageian merchants were sharks. I knew his disappearance had something to do with the gnarly old bastards. It had never been a secret that they detested the sudden appearance of a Gorenten merchant with big ideas and the results to back it up. Most of my father's parties devolved into pissing contests for a reason.

I stopped in front of the old man. He was still walking in a straight line, right into the wall. I touched his shoulder. It was knobby, cold. A chair would have felt more alive.

"Are you the emperor?" I asked. "How long has Lord Cato been holding you prisoner here? Did he kidnap you?"

The old man groaned.

I glanced around the room and spotted robes hanging from a hook on the wall. They looked like royal garments. "I assume Lord Cato would make you sit there and then—what? Make you talk? No. You haven't said a word this whole time. But clearly, you're not doing too well." I paused, spotting something on the back of his head, barely perceptible through the lace-thin white hair.

I reached with both my fingers to part the strands of it. The old man didn't even react to my touch. I saw a spell-rune embedded directly into his skin. I brushed my thumb over it, feeling a spark of energy. An image sparked in my head.

And then I backed away.

The man wasn't alive. He wasn't even dead. He was a simulacrum, a creature with no soul imbued with the qualities of life. We were told in our fifth year at Eheldeth that to make them in Dageis was a crime punishable by death.

So why was the Emperor of Dageis one of them?

CHAPTER 27

KEEPER OF FLAMES

I wanted to stay in that room and study its secrets some more, but then I heard horses in the courtyard down below and realized Felan must have returned. I reluctantly tore myself away from the simulacrum. There were things I needed to do first. I needed to make sure Felan didn't go looking for me, because I didn't know how much of a hand he had in this. If he was involved, I didn't want him to know how much *I* knew until I found the answers I was looking for.

The room needed to stay secret. But also, I belatedly remembered the dead body still lying there. *That,* I needed to get rid of. And the only way to do that was to wait for Felan to go to bed and then ask Nasuha for help.

I glanced at Bracken, who looked like she didn't really want to leave her master all by himself. I gave her a quick pat on the forehead. "I'll be back," I promised. I took her water bowl from the office and placed it next to her. She didn't look like she wanted any. I've heard some dogs would pine for their masters to the detriment of their own health and hoped she wouldn't turn out that way.

I cleared everything and returned the ladder back to the attic, and then I went back to my room. Nasuha gestured for me to move along—I glimpsed another figure inside. "The doctor?" I asked her. "Will Jaila make it?"

"He thinks she might," Nasuha said. "But she needs a lot of rest."

"She can get that."

"Not if Lord Cato returns," she whispered. "What are we going to do?"

"I think we don't have to worry about that right now," I said. "I'll explain later." I made my way to the kitchens, hoping I could find Bracken something to eat.

Felan startled me as I came around the corner. "I made coffee," he said. "Rosha's brother is cleaning out the leftovers. The little thing has an appetite."

I made a mental note to take Ryo aside later so we could get our stories straight. But for now, Felan seemed oblivious enough. I nodded and followed him, expecting we would take coffee in the kitchen. But he opened the door to the tearoom, graciously letting me walk ahead. There were two steaming cups already on the table.

I took a seat and wrapped my hands around the cup. It felt a lifetime since I'd last sat in front of Felan like this, and that must have only been three or four hours ago. Outside, crickets hummed, and I thought I heard the dogs scratching at the back door.

"I let them out," Felan said apologetically. "The doctor wanted us *all* out of Jaila's room."

"Jaila's room now," I replied.

"We can't really move her. You're going to have to find some place else. My room is probably more comfortable."

I looked up sharply. "What are you talking about?"

"I meant to say that I'll move my things, and you and Rosha can take it. The bed is bigger there. There is a small guest room at the far end of the hall that would suit me just fine."

"If you can find the key," I said, eyeing the key ring in front of us. It looked like there were more keys than doors in the house. Were there more secret rooms there? I wasn't sure I wanted to find out what else I would stumble across.

"Ah, yes. That might be a problem." He sighed. "Lord Cato…has grown secretive over the years. More vindictive. Sometimes I think I'm to blame."

"Why is that?"

"He was angry with my decision not to go back to Dageis. I was supposed to stay in Sorna only long enough for me to heal. There, we discovered that my connection to the *agan* had been severed. The things that used to come so easily to me…"

Felan looked at his fingers. I knew what he was looking for—the flow of *agan* that any mage could easily draw on and *see* if they should choose to see it. I felt an involuntary twinge of pain. To be blind to the *agan* when you have spent your whole life swimming in it must feel worse than losing a limb. Eventually, he picked up his coffee again and took a sip. "He thought I was exaggerating. He felt I was merely injured, like someone who had broken a leg. That all I had to do was wait for the bones to heal and then I could learn to walk again. He needed me, he said. There are plenty of mages in the merchant guild, but mages strong enough to be courted by the mage council and choosing to join the merchant guild instead are rarer than hen's teeth. He wanted me to follow his path, to bolster the strength of the merchant guild. But how could I? The very thought of trying to tap the *agan* stream again was painful. Lord Cato thought it was cowardice. He was once injured badly too, you know? In his youth, he and a group of classmates were in some accident in Eheldeth."

"The Six," I said without thinking. "I didn't realize…the Cato in those records was him."

"Yes," he replied, peering at me. "You know about that?"

"You don't live in Dageis and not know about that," I quickly said. "The Six were Fourth Year Eheldeth students who took their spell work too far. There was an accident, so I heard. With a dragon?"

"They had caught a dragon," Felan said, nodding. "A small one, but big enough to cause harm. Dragons are rare up north, and some mages in Eheldeth have always been interested in them particularly because they're supposed to be connected to the *agan*. Other nations have harnessed dragons—why not a nation as proud as the empire?"

"What need does Dageis have for dragons?" I asked. "The spells here are sophisticated. Lands who use dragons for magic are…considered backward."

"Strictly speaking, that's what the mage council believes, and there's probably a manifesto somewhere forbidding mages to do any studies on dragons given how dangerous they are. Look at Jin-Sayeng—they *dared* bring those animals into their own homes. Look how much that has cost them. But The Six didn't know any better. They were young. Rebellious. They caught the dragon somewhere in the south—paid a Gasparian merchant, I believe, and then they took it all the way to one of the spell rooms. In Eheldeth, students learn new spells in safe rooms—the kind that doesn't allow stray magic from unskilled mages to hurt others. Of course, there's usually a keeper on hand to make sure the students do nothing stupid."

"Which is what the Six did, I assume," I said. "I heard three died. The others were badly injured."

"Lord Cato was one of the badly injured ones. The accident nearly cost him his arm. They managed to save it. He said he couldn't connect to the *agan* without falling to the ground in pain. That it was like learning to walk again—he had to do it slowly, relearn every spell that used to come to him as easy as breathing. He thought I could just do the same, that it was only a matter of will. But it's not like that. I can't just push through this. There's just absolutely nothing."

"I can't imagine what that feels like." No monster lurking under the bed could ever fill me with as much fear as losing my connection to the *agan* completely.

"I wholeheartedly believe this extended absence of his has something to do with me," Felan murmured. "He must have known I was coming back. Must have locked half the rooms in this house to keep me away from it. I don't blame him. I spent all these years convincing him I couldn't stand Dageis, only to change my mind. He probably thinks I'm a hypocrite."

I stared at the coffee in my hands. *Not quite,* I thought. *He never left the house. He's still here.*

"When was the last time you spoke to him?" I asked.

"About two years ago," he said. "In Sorna. We had another argument about this same thing, and he decided to just never speak to me again. I thought he would come around and spent all of last year waiting for him to reply to my letters, but he never did. I came back here hoping I could mend our relationship. As much as I hated the thought of being around all this magic, a part of me…wanted to be near it, too. Like a damn moth hovering around a candle."

"You were close with him," I said in disbelief.

"As close a stepson could, I suppose. He was never affectionate, but after my mother died, all we had was each other. Solidarity in sorrow." He seemed to find something amusing about that and smiled absently from the corner of his lips.

"I'm going to check on Jaila," I finally said, removing the empty cup from the table.

"It's been a long night. You should go to bed, too."

"Soon," I promised him. *But first, we have to bury your father.*

"What the hell did you do?" Nasuha asked later that night, long after everyone else had gone to bed. I had locked the part of the attic with the simulacrum inside and dragged Lord Cato's body to the hall, pretending I'd found him there.

"I didn't do anything," I said.

"His throat is slit," Nasuha observed, turning the body over. She sniffed. "And he smells like he's been dead a while. But he didn't die here. There's no blood on the ground."

"Interesting." I didn't think she'd notice—Nasuha probably had more experience examining dead bodies than I had. I hoped the simulacrum wouldn't start walking again—I didn't know how to explain it to Nasuha if it walked right into us. I had bound its hands and legs with rope and left it on the ground in the hidden part of the attic, where it just slithered in one spot pathetically, like a slug in the bottom of a barrel.

"I wonder if this happened the same night I arrived," she said. "The body looks like it's been decaying at least a day or so."

"The same night we met Elry and Jaila."

"Could Elry have done this?"

"It's possible," I said. "But it's too clean. Elry would have torn him to pieces. Also—he's a mage. A good mage, from the sound of it."

"He's rich. Doesn't mean he's good."

"He should have been able to defend himself at least."

She lifted his hands, holding it against the light. "No wounds elsewhere. You're right. He didn't even try. Whoever killed him caught him off-guard."

"Perhaps it was someone he knew."

She nodded. "Do you want to tell Lord Felan, or...?"

"That's...what I called you about." I grimaced. "Is there any way that we...don't have to?"

Her eyes widened slightly. "This is his *father*."

"When he died, it was just the two of us here with him. It's going to look suspicious. He'll think one of us did it."

She nodded empathetically. "Right, and you know what's going to look even more suspicious? *Hiding the body*."

"We're not even using our real names here, Nasuha. It's a slippery slope to begin with."

She sighed and rubbed the back of her head. "How did I get into this?"

"You wanted a job, and you said—"

"Right, right. But now my would-be employer is dead so I'm right back where I started."

"Lord Felan will pay you."

"Unless he finds out I dragged his dead father to where the sun don't shine. Rosha—and I say this as gently as I can, because I've grown fond of you—you're out of your mind."

I stared at her for a heartbeat. "So, are you going to do it?"

She sighed. "Where do you want him?"

"In his family's tomb," I said. "That's where he belongs, anyway. Did you think I was going to ask you to dump his body in the river?"

"It's good to know you're not completely heartless."

"The tomb's closer."

She cleared her throat. "You want to grab his head and I'll take his feet, or do you have a preference?"

"Does it matter?"

"I don't really want him looking at me."

"He's dead."

"The eyes—"

"Then get his damn feet."

The absurdity of the situation wasn't lost on me as we somehow—slowly, and without waking anyone else up—got the body out of there. Right at the edge of dawn, we finally rolled the body onto the floor of the tomb. My arms were starting to hurt. I don't think I had carried anything half as heavy my whole life.

Nasuha wrapped him up in sheets as best as she could and placed him alongside the wall. "When are you planning to tell the son?" she asked.

"When I figure out what killed him," I replied.

"Do you think it's the same person who's keeping your father?"

"And took my brother," I said. "It has to be. It's the only thing missing from this equation."

"And are you close to finding answers?"

I didn't have an answer for her. She returned to our room bleary-eyed, swearing to sleep until dawn. I hadn't slept a wink all night and didn't really want to try now. I returned to the office, taking a moment to comfort Bracken who had spent the last few hours hiding underneath Lord Cato's desk. She hadn't even tried to stop us from taking his body earlier. It was as if she knew he was dead and was just going through the motions, trying to find meaning in their old routine. When I pulled down the attic ladder, she was right at my heels.

I returned to the simulacrum. It groaned, not really reacting to my presence anymore than it had before. I turned it over, wondering how Lord Cato controlled it. More to the point—why it was still moving even though Lord Cato was dead. The animation of simulacrums depended on the mage that made it in the first place. It used the same life-force, the same flow of *agan* that ran through the mage's body.

I'd made similar things when I was little, before we ever moved to Dageis. Children's games, back when I didn't know how dangerous such games could be. I used little dolls filled with sawdust and oil. The oil was stickier than water, which would have simply drained through the burlap doll skin and allowed me to play with the dolls as if they had invisible strings. I could make them run and dance with a flick of my fingers.

Even such dolls were illegal in Dageis. Mainly because it required way too much energy to move them about, and mages have seriously hurt themselves and others even with just mere party tricks. A simulacrum like the one in front of me could have had the empire confiscating all of Lord Cato's assets.

Unless the empire is in on it.

I searched the room, trying to find clues. It was bare, save for the robes. Whatever had been going on here hadn't been for long.

I felt the hum of *agan* on my skin and saw a flicker of light coming from the mirror.

"All right. I guess there's no point in waiting. Let's try this, old man."

I untied the simulacrum. It started trying to walk away again, but when I held its hand, it stopped. I gently guided it to the chair, where it flopped down without trouble. "Almost like he's done this before," I said, glancing at Bracken.

She trembled, looking away so only the whites of her eyes were showing.

I took the robes and fitted them over the simulacrum. As soon as his arms slipped into the sleeves, he assumed a look of total concentration, and the empty eyes seemed to gain a spark of life in them. I ran my fingers over the smooth silk until I found a bump on the back , revealing a lump of leather stitched into the fabric. A particular glyph had been burnt into it. The spell choice made me smile. It was familiar, from the runes to the patterns connecting them. "Now we're talking my language."

I pricked my finger on the side of the table, just enough to get a drop of blood out, and then placed my hand on the glyph. My entire skin began to warm, as if I'd walked into a stuffy room.

I felt my body drifting back, deep into the shadows where no one could see, even as I saw myself sit down in front of the mirror, where the simulacrum's body was. I pulled back at the curtains with the old man's hands. I could see Chancellor Pacano looking back at me. "Your Excellency?" he was saying. "Have you fixed the mirror yet, Your Excellency? Shall we send some mages over? I'm concerned for your health."

"Everything's fine," I said. My voice, at least from my perspective. The simulacrum merely opened its mouth, working its way around my words. I couldn't hear what *he* sounded like, if it was raspy, like a doddering old man, or strong, like an emperor. But Pacano must be hearing whatever he needed to hear. I got up, old man's knees shaking slightly, and drew the rest of the rune on the back of the mirror, completing the spell once again. A flare of light surrounded my fingertips as I sat back down in the chair.

"Ah!" Pacano said, his eyes growing bright. "At last, sir."

"As you can see, I am in perfect health," I said. "About what I asked you last night—"

"Yes, Your Excellency."

"Did you find Tar'elian?"

"No, Your Excellency. It seems as if he is based in Triassa, but the mages there say that he hasn't been seen for months."

Damn this. I was going around in circles. "Well, keep searching. No man just disappears like that."

"Of course, Your Excellency. But in the meantime, someone's here to see you, and she is most insistent that we—"

"Is that him?" a voice called. "Is that the emperor?"

"Calm down, woman. I already let you bypass all the procedures, but you—"

"I will not calm down and if you *dare* call me woman again, I am going to set your clothes on fire. This has gone on long enough." A woman sat in front of the mirror. I had to physically stop myself from bolting out of my seat. It was Firekeeper Ceres, head of Eheldeth and one of the most influential members of the mage council. "You were looking for Tar'elian, Your Excellency?" she snapped. "Do you want to explain what's going on with the merchant guild, or do I need to invoke the people's right to *demand* that you return to Teleres Palace at once, where you're *supposed* to be ruling from?"

For a moment, I wondered if my heart had stopped. It took me another moment to remember I was in the simulacrum's body, which was why I couldn't feel it in the first place. It wouldn't have felt all that different from my real body. The Firekeeper's voice had power over me like no other.

Firekeeper Ceres...where do I begin? Ever since I came to Eheldeth, she seemed to have taken a special interest in my affairs, always checking up on me to make sure I was studying and eating and sleeping and the gods know what else. It was partly because she was enamoured with my father which is—yes. I know. It confused me the first time I found out, too. She looked like she was coming on in age, but I'm sure she had better options. As one of the most powerful women in the land, she could do so, so much better.

Of course, I never really said such words to her, but I always *thought* it every time my father paid me a visit and they would run off together like giggling schoolchildren. And I think she knew I resented her somewhat, though not for the same reason she would have guessed. She probably thought I was jealous of the attention my father gave her. As if I ever asked for it! I *wanted* her to take my father away. I wanted her to remove him from our life, so Papa could be happy with Mama at last and none of us would ever have to remember we were related to one another.

But they had their own lives—an arrangement I would understand had it involved anyone else. Also, she was the Eheldeth Firekeeper, a position she had held for the last fourteen or fifteen years, well-respected, even adored by the populace. He did...whatever. It came as a surprise that she would dare barge into the palace for his sake. Why would she jeopardize her position? Out of fondness for Enosh Tar'elian, of all people? It wouldn't look good for a member of the mage council to be suddenly sympathetic to a merchant, *especially* if Enosh's own connection to the *agan* (sparse as it was) came to light. People would draw the wrong conclusions.

I hoped the confusion didn't reflect on the emperor's face. I cleared my throat and tried to refocus. "My health—" I began.

"I know about your health, Your Excellency," Firekeeper Ceres drawled. "Ever since the attack on Drusgaya thirteen years ago, it has been of utmost concern to *everyone* around you. Believe me, I recognize it. I sympathize with it. But it's been years, Your Excellency. You have moved around to more summer homes than a merchant with multiple wives. Your people have a right to know where you are."

I reeled myself. "And you—" I began.

You are not Rosha, outlaw mage, I told myself. *Rosha does not exist. You are Emperor Cerknar, immortal emperor of the greatest empire in the world. Put her in her place before she turns this over your head. Because if she finds out what you're doing...*

She could do a lot of damage. She had always been sympathetic to my family, but how much more if she realized what I'd been up to the last few years? Running an illicit business, practicing magic I wasn't supposed to, and burying a rich, important sorcerer without telling anyone. Her fondness for my father could only go so far. She'd be obligated to ruin my family.

"Have no right to question your emperor," I said evenly. "If you are so interested in Tar'elian, why not look for him yourself?"

"If I hadn't tried that already, I wouldn't be here discussing this with you," she said in a voice that could cut.

"Your interest in Tar'elian is interesting. If he is a merchant, why is he your concern? You're supposed to be managing the mages."

I saw her face flicker.

"Tar'elian's daughter is my charge, Your Excellency," Ceres said at last. "She was studying to be a mage in Eheldeth. She disappeared a few years ago without graduating."

"I see," I said carefully, still hoping my expression remained blank, neutral. "And you believe that this has something to do with *his* disappearance as well?"

"I don't know. You tell me, Your Excellency. The father, disappearing three years after the daughter, can't be a mere coincidence."

"It is a big empire. You can hardly expect me to keep track of everyone."

"Yet you were interested enough to open an inquiry in the first place."

I swallowed. The woman was tough. If this went on for much longer, I was going to implode.

"What do you really want, Firekeeper Ceres?" I asked, letting the irritation drip through my voice. If she wanted to, I could fight fire with fire. I'd done it often enough to her in the past—in long debates during lectures she'd taught, where I would get into an argument with her for the sake of, because I was angry at what I thought she was doing to my family. "Surely you didn't come here to waste all of our times so you could lecture me on the fate of two nobodies."

"Your Excellency—"

"Without Eheldeth, we wouldn't have mages with the necessary skills to keep the empire afloat. Why these frivolities, Firekeeper? Or are you trying to pull distractions on us, keep us from investigating something within your jurisdiction? Are you trying to cover up your own incompetence?"

Her eyes blazed. "This is a step too far, Your Excellency."

"I am Emperor," I said. "I'm allowed that step. I'm allowed to rip this whole empire apart and examine every crevice as I please. So, *talk.*"

"Return to the palace," she said, her voice growing low.

I scoffed. "I am not yours to command."

"Return to the palace, Emperor Cerknar, or else—"

"Or else *what?*"

A bright light flashed.

I was knocked back to my feet.

Without thinking about it, I flung the strongest shield-spell I was capable of as the room exploded.

CHAPTER 28

THE PALACE DISTRICT

I t took me a good minute to realize it didn't, actually—
everything inside the room, my limbs included, remained intact.
I had been propelled out of the simulacrum's body and back
into my own. *The bitch,* was my first thought. But I didn't have time
to dwell on it further. I doubled forward to press my fingers on the
glyph again and return into the old man's body. The force was
almost too much. It felt like a boulder had been dropped on my
head.

"What did you do?" I demanded, even as my surroundings began to
stretch in abnormal directions.

"Did you feel that, Your Excellency?" Firekeeper Ceres retorted.

"I can have you arrested for attempted murder of your own emper-
or," I snapped.

"I did nothing, Your Excellency." Her voice didn't even rise an
octave. "Only a flash spell. A small flash spell. Child's play. Hardly illegal." Amusement danced in her sharp eyes. "You, in the meantime,
threw a very powerful shield-spell to counter it. You have not done
magic for a very long time because of your health, if I recall. Perhaps
you've been exaggerating your condition."

"I—"

"I expect you back in the palace soon, Your Excellency," she said.
"Or else we will track down the source of the spell."

Could she? In Eheldeth, they told us they could. That there were
Eheldeth-sanctioned mages in every corner of the empire who just
needed the time a certain spell was cast, and they could find traces of it

lingering in the air. Surely the emperor would be able to call her bluff. If it was a bluff, I could ignore it. If it wasn't a bluff…

"Good day, Your Excellency," she continued, when I didn't reply. "I will be in the palace for three more days. I hope we have a chance to meet in that time."

She turned around, robes flapping in the wind.

I felt myself shake with anger. A trick. A stupid trick. She was right —any child trained to be a mage could have conjured the flash. I'd done it myself hundreds of times. I should have recognized it. Why did I overreact? I struggled to regain a sprinkle of dignity. "Chancellor!" I roared. "Arrest that woman!"

He looked back at me helplessly, mouth opening and closing like a fish. "I can't, Your Excellency," he gasped.

"Then find a way to stop her." I cut the connection abruptly, without waiting for his response, and found myself back in my body. The simulacrum was slumped in its seat, its head on the edge of the desk.

One breath, and then I tore out of that attic like my hair was on fire.

I've done it, I thought. I took it too far. I should have stopped when I still had the chance to walk away. Now—

I couldn't get the look on Ceres's face from my mind. I knew the woman wasn't someone to be trifled with. What was I thinking? I felt like screaming and crying and tearing my heart out, all at once. But I kept it in, bottled up, the way I was taught from the start, and marched resolutely back from Lord Cato's office to the new room I was supposed to share with Nasuha. On the balcony by the main staircase landing, I glimpsed Felan having coffee at the bottom of the steps.

He must have heard me. He inclined his head to the side without looking directly at me, and said, "I made an extra cup, if you want one."

I glanced at the cup he had positioned on the side table next to the railings. It was still steaming. "Were you just waiting for me?" I asked.

He shrugged.

I didn't think he'd *seen* me come out of his father's office, so I decided it was better to just accept the invitation now. I carefully made my way downstairs and took the coffee from the table. The movement kept me calm. I sat on the step beside him, feeling oddly self-conscious at how tall he was when we were right next to each other. The boy he had been was rapidly fading from my memories.

"You haven't been sleeping?" he asked.

I looked at him in confusion.

He gestured at my face. "You look worn out."

I briefly considered telling him the truth. *Worn out* didn't even encompass what I was feeling. But even though he no longer resembled the spoiled, arrogant boy I'd known, jeopardizing my family was the last thing I would do. I closed my eyes, overwhelmed by the silence, by the secrets I'd been keeping growing longer than the shadows under the sunrise outside. I never stopped to think about it before, but I had been alone for a very long time, and it was suddenly killing me. To talk freely with someone—to share my most innermost fears without judgment—was the stuff of dreams.

I peered at him through the strands of my hair and watched as he sipped at his coffee, strangely calm despite last night's events. A monster. An injured woman. *A dead father, though he doesn't know it yet.* I got the impression that very little bothered him these days—the look in his eyes held a note of self-assurance, as if he'd seen worse and lived to tell the tale, so why did anything else matter? I wanted to ask him how he had lived all these years severed from magic. When you consider a skill an extension of yourself for so long, how do you survive without it? I threw the shield-spell earlier because despite all the years I told myself I *couldn't* risk casting magic; I craved it as much as I craved the air inside my lungs. I couldn't even say I regretted what I just did. I could still feel remnants of the spell on my fingers. It felt more than good. It felt *right*.

Despite that, exhaustion seeped into my bones, and I fell asleep without realizing it. I had the recollection of leaning on Felan's shoulder. When I woke up, I was alone, but he'd removed the coffee cup and left a thin, woven blanket around my shoulders. I rubbed it between my fingers, wondering if I'd made another mistake. Was I making it easier for him to recognize me?

No, I told myself. *If he recognized you, things would be a lot worse. You did this to him. You know he could never forgive you. You haven't even forgiven yourself.*

I pushed all my worries out of the way and got up to check on everyone else.

Jaila wasn't dead yet, which was a tremendous relief. Her colour was marginally better and she even ate a bowl of soup Nasuha had prepared for lunch.

"I'm probably going to town later." I placed a hand on Ryo's shoulder. "I need you to come with me."

My brother glanced at me in confusion.

"In case you've forgotten, young man, I need to get you home," I whispered. "Your parents are worried sick about you."

"But Jaila…" he began.

"We'll take care of her here," Nasuha said brightly. "Don't you worry."

"I'll go borrow a horse and coach from Go-nir," I continued.

Nasuha grabbed my wrist before I could walk out the door. "Maybe it's better if I go with you," she said. "Jaila will be fine. If she was going to die, she'd be dead by now."

"You need to keep an eye on things here," I replied.

Nasuha sighed. "I'd feel better if you took my sword."

I stared at her. "What would I do with that?"

"You hold it by the handle, you see, and then you swing it."

I pressed my fingers over my forehead, trying to drown out the image of me comically swinging a sword around. "I meant—I'm not sure why you think it's necessary."

She grew serious. "A man was killed in his own home," she said. "Whoever did the killing knew about us. Knew about *you*."

I swallowed. "So?"

She reached under the bed and shoved the sword at me. It was a short blade, closer to a knife, the kind of implement they used to cut down brush and saplings to clear the way. "Humour me."

I shoved the thing through my belt. Likely I would trip and cut myself before I could ever defend myself with it, but the look of relief on her features told me not to argue. I wondered why she was so concerned. All the woman wanted was a few free meals and a roof over her head—a woman as resourceful as she was could get by, with or without me.

I went back outside to find Go-nir. He seemed to have taken a liking to me and didn't even hesitate when I requested a cart and a horse to myself. "You can choose between a really placid gelding or a spirited young mare," he said. I knew little about horses, so I picked the gelding. He whistled for Mael to go out to help.

As they were getting everything ready, Felan arrived. His long, shoulder-length hair was disheveled from the wind.

"Going out for a drive, Mistress Suha?" he asked.

I suddenly found it difficult to meet his eyes. "I need some things from the market," I said. "And for our…guests." I glanced at Go-nir and Mael, who as far as I knew remained oblivious to everything happening inside the house.

Felan caught what I was trying to say. "They will be taken care of," he replied.

"Please make sure they're not disturbed," I continued. "We don't need to bother anyone else—there's enough work with the horses as it is."

He nodded. "Of course."

"I'm concerned about our particularly rambunctious guest. Perhaps we need to find a way to…send him home."

Felan crossed his arms. "A difficult task, if his behaviour last night is any indication. He seems fond of my father's house."

"It's a wonderful house. Maybe there will be something in your father's books that will…enlighten us more about his…peculiar habits."

"I will try." He turned to the horse and cart. "Unless you could use someone to accompany you. It has been a while since I've been to Drusgaya's markets, but I remember a particular kind of chaos out on those streets. You probably shouldn't be alone out there."

"I'll be with Rosha's little brother. She wants me to take him home."

"Does he live anywhere nearby?"

"He lives in Triassa," I said, before I could stop myself. Falling into a conversation with him was *too* easy. But I supposed the piece of information wasn't the end of the world. "I'm thinking of putting him on an airship straight back, while paying the captain to ensure he gets there safe. He knows how to make his way back, I think."

"He seems so young."

"As you said. Drusgaya is chaos. They know him in Triassa. I'd feel a lot better knowing he wasn't here."

He cocked an eyebrow.

"Because Rosha's brother has grown close to me," I said quickly. "I'll —I'll leave you to the rest of your day, Lord Felan."

He gave an awkward bow and left me to take the horse and cart all the way back down to the house. It was a hot and lazy afternoon, just a little past lunch, and I was pleased to see everyone was as weary as I was. Nasuha was napping beside a sleeping Jaila, and Felan, of course—Felan still had to walk all the way from the stables to the house. I went upstairs to fetch the simulacrum. It was still on the desk where I left it, but when I touched its hand, it responded, standing up to follow me like any stooped grandfather subsisting on the charity of his grandchildren. I took the chance to bring him downstairs. Only Bracken could get close —the other dogs saw me and fled for the kitchen, presumably to hide. They looked like they'd seen the emperor before and had been punished for their curiosity.

I let the simulacrum clamber inside the cart and then covered it with several layers of canvas. As soon as I let go of its hand, it collapsed in a heap. With just a bit of rope, it looked like a bundle of hay. I left it there and returned to the house to pick up Ryo, who was still so sleepy he was rubbing his eyes with his fists. Last night must have been the first proper sleep he'd gotten since he first arrived at Lord Cato's house. How long had it been since he was taken? It was becoming easier to lose track of the days.

I explained my plan to Ryo: about buying an airship ticket for him and asking the captain to deliver him straight home. About how he needed to get help from one of the airship attendants in Triassa to get him back to Father's store. He listened carefully, and for a little boy, he really wasn't the sort to miss details because as soon as I finished speaking, he asked, "You're not coming back with me?"

I shook my head. "I still have things to do here. I still haven't found Father."

"Everyone's going to be sad again, Rosha," he replied. "Just like when you left school, and we didn't know where you were."

I turned my attention to the road, to the horse lazily clopping along the cobblestone.

"You can't possibly remember that," I said under my breath. "You were so little, Ryo. I'm sure everyone will be fine."

He shook his head. "I remember. Haro had bad dreams. Sometimes he woke up screaming about you."

"My life was never in danger. I spent the last few years setting up a shop, Ryo."

"Like Father?"

"Like Father, I guess," I grumbled.

"What did you sell?"

"Advice, mostly. Concoctions. Charms. Most of which don't work."

"But they said you were a *good* mage."

"Well, I didn't make most of the charms," I said. "They were second hand. It means other people made them, and—"

"I know."

I smirked. To the rest of the world, he was still a merchant's son, and my parents had done well preparing him for the part. "Tell everyone they don't have to worry about me," I continued. "Tell them…" I paused. Tell them what? As far as the authorities were concerned, I had walked out of that last airship straight into the lake. Papa would never believe that would kill me, of course, but the message was clear: leave me alone. Let me live my life. "Tell them to forget me," I said. "If thinking about me makes them sad, they can just stop, you know?"

His brow furrowed. I didn't think he understood. *Someday, you might. Someday. When you feel the need to rise above everything without the burden of others weighing you down. You'll thank me for this first gift, little one. You'll thank me for teaching you to let go.*

We reached the airship tower. There was a long line of people waiting at the station already. "I hope there's a seat for you here," I said. "Let's find a place to tie up old Pepper. I—"

Ryo was crying.

"Gods damn it," I grumbled under my breath. "This isn't the time." I couldn't think of anything more awkward than sitting next to a crying child.

He tried to choke down the tears. "I know."

"You can't let yourself get attached to people," I continued. "They're only going to disappoint you. If you do this to just about everyone—"

"But you're not just *anyone*," he whispered, his eyes sinking downward. "You're my *sister*. You're my only sister."

The gods should have granted you a better one. But I didn't say it out loud. There was someone coming up the road behind us, and I needed to move out of the way, or—

"Rosha Tar'elian!" a voice screamed from the cloud of dust.

I turned my head. I recognized Targus immediately. Targus, the scoundrel who'd been sniffing around my family back in Triassa. Targus, who looked pretty dead the last time I'd seen him.

"That's him," Ryo screeched beside me. "That's the man who took me!"

Without waiting for another word, I yanked the reins, urging our horse into the nearest alley.

CHAPTER 29

THE GARDENS OF TELERES

F irst things first: I regretted not choosing the spirited mare when I had the chance. My family's aversion to horses was yet again proving to be inconvenient.

I tried not to worry about it as I focused on navigating Pepper through the tight street. "We've got to lose him," I said. "Go to the back of that cart and see what we can throw at him, Ryo."

He nodded and heaved himself over from the driver's seat to the cart. "There's hay," he said. "Underneath this tarp—"

"Leave that alone," I snapped.

"And...oh! There's a pitchfork!"

"That. Hold on tight. When he appears—"

"Throw it at him!" he yelled, which told me that *when* was happening *right now*.

I flicked the reins, hoping old Pepper had it in him to gallop a lot faster than he already was. Behind me, I could hear Ryo fling the pitchfork into the air. He let a small cry of surprise.

"What?" I called back. "Did you hit him?"

"Right in the face!"

"Get back here before you fall off."

He was laughing as he clambered back into the driver's seat. I turned another corner. I couldn't see the airship tower now, but Teleres Palace was right ahead of us.

I swore under my breath. The roads leading to and from the palace were probably crawling with guards. We couldn't just dash by, looking like someone in hot pursuit, without attracting attention. We were definitely going to be stopped and searched, and if the palace guards real-ized I had wrapped up what appeared to be a corpse who resembled the missing emperor too much they were probably going to kill me before I had the chance to talk.

But if we slowed down, Targus would catch up to us. I wanted to speak to the man again, but not under these conditions. Not with my little brother nearby.

"Can you take the horse?" I asked Ryo.

His grin was ear-to-ear.

"I'm assuming you know how to drive a cart," I added.

"Haro and I stole Papa's horse one time."

"Bluebell? You mean Bluebell, don't you? The poor thing's blind in one eye."

"And just as slow as Pepper."

I didn't know how much faith I had in a six-year-old, but I had little choice. I handed the reins to him. "When you see the palace guards, tell them a thief was chasing you and your uncle. Tell them your uncle fell off."

He nodded, his attention fixed on the horse.

I placed a hand on the back of the seat and braced to jump.

"Rosha," he said. "Be careful."

I swallowed. "You too," I managed to reply.

He reached back to clasp my hand momentarily before returning to the road.

I jumped to the back of the cart and began undoing the ropes around the simulacrum. I tugged the canvas loose, freeing its head. "Ready, old man?" I whispered. I touched it on the shoulders. It opened its eyes. In broad daylight, they were a startling shade of blue, brighter than the sky.

We leaped from the cart just as it hit the next bend. The simulacrum, having no concept of physical space, simply rolled like a sack of rice. It hit the wall with a near-deafening *thud*. Had it been human, it would have been dead instantly.

I was able to recover much better—my arm caught the fall and I pushed myself up to chase after the simulacrum. Its head was bleeding. *Leaking*, more like it, with a foul-smelling substance that smelled almost but not quite like blood. There was more rot than iron to it.

But the simulacrum seemed unaffected. It jolted upwards the moment I took its hand. I wonder if transferring myself into it had attuned myself to it, because it naturally took my lead, even when I withdrew my touch. Obediently, it followed me into the adjoining street.

I couldn't see hair nor hide of Targus. I hoped he was smart enough to leave Ryo alone now, and that he wouldn't try anything out in the open. That was all I had left: hope. There was nothing I could do, not with the emperor at my heels. It was imperative I bring him straight to the palace before Ceres decided to launch an investigation on the shield-spell. The other spells I'd cast in Lord Cato's mansion might have gone unnoticed, but she would look for that particular spell at that particular hour, with the particular intensity she saw through the mirror. The mansion was *right* in the city—she could send mages to investigate almost at once.

And mages would mean they would find me. I doubted luck would be on my side again, like what happened with the bearers three years ago—these mages would answer directly to her and were probably a cut above the rest. Which would mean I wouldn't be able to find my father, but also spending the rest of my life in some unnamed dungeon. At *best*. An outlaw mage might have a worse fate waiting for her—tear her apart for research or feed her to wild animals. I had no desire to find out.

I tried to steady my breathing. It still wasn't too late. Ceres was giving the emperor time to appear in the palace. Which stood to reason that if I could *bring* him in, well…it would keep her at bay. It was good he was walking on his own now. So as long as I kept out of Ceres's sight, I could pretend to be his attendant. That left the problem of his speech, but perhaps I could imprint more behaviours into the simulacrum. I could get him to turn his nose at everyone across his way and instill just enough of a bearing in his demeanour to send people stumbling to their knees in his presence. You wouldn't need to talk to a man who evoked power. I just needed an empty alley, which at that moment seemed to be all but impossible to find.

I reached a small garden, which separated two sets of streets. One led to the busy marketplace. I paused to catch my breath. The simu-lacrum, evidently absorbing the environment with rapture, took a seat on the bench. The bleeding on its head had stopped, though there was still a streak of blood across its stubbled cheek. I bent forward to wipe it with my sleeve. "Some mess we've found ourselves in, Grandfather," I said out loud.

"Suha," Felan's voice cut through the din. I didn't even respond at first—I wanted to believe it wasn't him. But then he got close enough that I could smell his scent, which was rapidly becoming familiar.

I turned in panic. "Lord Felan!" I managed.

He gave a small bow, before glancing at the simulacrum. "Your Grandfather, you said?" he asked.

I allowed myself a moment to think. Emperor Cerknar, with his pale white skin and blue eyes, would have looked nothing like either of my grandfathers. "My mother used to take care of him before she passed," I said quickly. "He has a new caretaker now, but he still misses her company. I remind him of her, so we go for walks now and again."

If I was him, I would already be wondering why on earth my priorities had changed within the hour. But that didn't seem to occur to him at all. He simply glanced around absently. "Did Rosha's brother make it to his airship?"

"I hope so. I left him at the station." I hoped he wouldn't ask about the horse. I could lie about that too, but it wouldn't do much good if he saw it on the road half an hour later. I held my hand out to the simulacrum before Felan could open his mouth again. "Do you want to join us? We were just going down to the park. Unless you're busy?" *Tell me you are,* I thought. *Tell me you have more important things to attend to.*

"I would love to," he replied.

I tried not to show the disappointment on my face and led the way, the emperor's hand in mine. The simulacrum ambled after us without comment, feet shuffling in the dust. It made for a passable senile old man, and Felan wasn't even really looking at it. He seemed to be in deep thought as he strolled next to us, his hands behind his back.

"Is everything all right?" I asked.

"I was just thinking about my father," he said. "He still hasn't sent word. It's been too long. I'm getting worried."

"He must have just overlooked arrangements. As far as he knew, it was just his servants back home—certainly no one who needed to know his whereabouts."

Felan shook his head. "That doesn't sound like him. He'll want them to know what to tell unexpected visitors."

"He's never gone off for a week or two with a lover?" The gods know, Enosh did such things often enough.

"He's normally very discreet with his relationships," Felan said. "Such an excursion would be tagged as a business trip, and anyway, last I heard, he was still with a certain Lord Vazon, a man who isn't fond of me. He hasn't been in the empire the whole year, though—and my father isn't the type to run off on personal business and leave everything else unattended."

I filed the name away in the back of my mind. "You've...found nothing else in his office?"

He hesitated. "An attic," he finally whispered. "With my father's dog trapped inside."

I held my breath. I left Bracken up there because the presence of the dog without the master was indication enough that something wasn't right. I was hoping he could come to some conclusions himself, without me having to nudge him towards them and potentially reveal more than was necessary.

"She was making an infernal racket," he continued. "I found the stairs and let her out. Strange how she got herself trapped there, or why there's stairs in the first place. It was just a hollow space, like a hall. Not even big enough for storage. In all these years, I never knew it was there."

A simple statement, and yet it spoke volumes. It told me that he either hadn't spent as much time in the mansion as I thought, or they'd only moved there in the years after his accident. The don't-look spell Lord Cato had imbued on the door jamb worked on him. Without the skill in the *agan*, he was just as susceptible to spells as the normal populace. Mages could be fooled but might suspect they were being fooled—most of us could detect the faint stirrings of *agan* in the air, the sort that told us a spell was being cast somewhere. It broke my heart to see how easily the disguise worked on him. Most decent mages wouldn't fall for such a simple trick.

"Is the dog all right?" I asked.

"She's doing well, considering. I asked Go-nir to take care of her. My father goes nowhere without that dog, which is why I'm now worried."

You shouldn't worry. There's nothing more you can do. It's over. He's dead. I felt guilty. Did I believe the same thing, too? Enosh could be already dead, and all my efforts were a waste of time. I could just save myself the trouble, abandon the simulacrum in the side of the road, and run back to Klossaka, if I had a life still left to return to. Given everything happening, though, it was very possible I didn't. My family's enemies knew who I was.

"I must apologize," he said, which was when I realized I'd fallen deathly silent. "I know my burdens aren't yours."

I led the simulacrum to a park bench and got him to sit there. "Do you want a snack, Grandfather?" I asked.

To my surprise, it nodded.

"I'll be back," I promised.

I gestured to Felan, who bowed to the old man before following me.

I strode to the food stalls, thinking about the best way to ditch him. I couldn't let myself get distracted. As guilty as I felt about his father's fate, Lord Cato's activities were his own doing. I didn't even know how much of it Felan was aware of. He could be lying to me—he could have known about the old man and was simply pretending—but I doubted it. Even as a boy, he wasn't a good liar. He couldn't even pretend to *like* me.

Which meant his newfound consideration was as genuine as they came. I sighed, paid for a packet of roasted chestnuts, and offered him some. "What do you think about accompanying us to the palace?" I asked. "Grandfather always liked to walk by the edge of the river there. Unless you have more important things to do…"

"It would be a most welcome distraction," he said.

I wondered if I liked him better as an arrogant little shit.

Teleres Palace had undergone quite a few renovations over the years. Once, it was surrounded by four towers, all of which functioned not just for defence but as conduits for the palace mages, for whatever purpose they considered necessary. One at least also served as an airship dock for the high-ranking officials.

But one of the towers had since been destroyed during an attack on Drusgaya and another made inert. From out on the road, all four appeared non-functional, as if they simply just blocked all the remaining connections to the *agan* to prevent another catastrophe from occurring. Last I heard, they had reinforced the ocean-side docks instead, and were thinking of moving the towers over to one of the islands across the sea. I didn't know the rationale behind it—Dageian politics never interested me much, and it all felt so very far away when I was living in Klossaka.

This, at least, was what I knew: while the palace itself was inaccessible, the plaza where the emperor often did his speeches wasn't. I could take the emperor up there, in the middle of the outdoor amphitheatre and conduct an emergency speech to keep Firekeeper Ceres happy. I would also have to form some sort of mandate to prevent her from investigating the source of the shield-spell—they couldn't really *pry* into those details without a reason, and if I removed that reason, I could render all future investigations on the emperor's whereabouts impertinent and illegal. It was a long shot, but it was the only way out that I could think of. I just had to get rid of Felan first.

He was being irritatingly obtuse. Even Jehar would have taken my *"Yes, sure, accompany us,"* to really mean *"Please don't."* Of course, I had years to teach him that my tone of voice and expression made all the difference. Felan, in the meantime, took it at face value. It had been refreshing the last few days, but now I wished he would just take the hint. If I told him to leave now, would he become suspicious? Would he get angry enough to dig through my lies?

I stared at the river as we walked along the paved path. Some mess I'd gotten myself in. I couldn't even blame my parents for it—I went here of my own accord. Perhaps if I displayed more prudence in my actions…but prudence wasn't exactly a skill that kept you alive if you walked out of Eheldeth the way I did. Outlaw mages don't evade the law forever for a reason, at least if you believed Eheldeth texts. They get complacent, they start taking risks, they let fear overshadow the reality that they have to learn to be two, three steps ahead of everyone just to get by. When the very act of surviving was hard enough as it was, adding your family's survival on top seemed like a doomed endeavour. But it wasn't in me to give either up. As difficult as things were, I had to see this through.

"Come and sit on this bench, Grandfather." I gestured to one under the tree. "You can see the river from here."

The simulacrum obeyed. His movements were becoming so much more fluid now. I placed the bag of chestnuts in his lap. He picked one up and chewed it thoughtlessly. I didn't want to think about what happened to the food once it entered his system.

I turned to Felan. I took his hand.

He stumbled after me in a daze.

We didn't talk for the time it took us to pass by the cherry grove. By then, the emperor was a dot by the riverbank and the sun was a pale red disk sinking slowly on the horizon. I had little time left. It was now or never.

Drawing on what courage I had left, I turned to kiss him.

CHAPTER 30

THE EMPEROR OF DAGEIS

Given what I knew of Felan, I expected the action to shock, even embarrass him into running away. Felan as a boy was easily frightened, and so arrogant that the idea of sharing space with me always seemed to be beneath him. A kiss should have thrown him off his guard, at least.

Felan the boy definitely wouldn't have taken my hand and squeezed it tight. He didn't that night in the field, when the rain came, each torrent hard enough to feel like shards of glass were falling from the sky. It was so loud I couldn't even hear myself think. We sought shelter in the crumbling building, which you could only get in by climbing through the window. When I tried to reach back to pull him up, he slapped my hand away. I stumbled backward, falling into a pile of rubble.

He finally clambered in after me, his elbows scratched from the attempt. "You're bleeding," I pointed out.

"Stop pretending to care," he snapped.

"Oh, believe me, I have better things to do than waste time pretending to care about you," I said. "It was a fact. You're bleeding. Maybe you should stop it if you don't want to pass out."

"Scrapes don't kill. Someone as smart as you would know that." He pointed at me with his finger. I think he was trying to prod me with it.

I slapped his arm away. "Since we're out here being honest anyway, you might as well admit it. You hate me, don't you?"

"Obviously."

"But not because of anything I did. No—you hate me because I took away the one thing that made *you* special. If not for me, you would be the only one ahead. Ridiculed, envied, terrorized, yes, but at least not one of *two*. I hate to break it to you, Lord Felan, but the thing that makes you special is the very thing that made me miserable all my life. It's hard enough growing up to be a mage, let alone a mage in a non-magical family. But to have so much skill even the mages who know what they're doing are *scared* of you…"

"Don't flatter yourself," he said, walking past me.

"You know it's true," I told him. "You know everything we learn is to make it easier to control us. They want a record of our skill, a pattern of our abilities. They've got samples of our blood, our hair, even our damn toenails. You and me—they've got their eyes on us for a reason. Did you honestly think the lessons are for our own good? You don't think they're teaching us to perform magic only in certain ways so they know *exactly* how to stop us if we ever stray? If you don't see them building that cage around you, you're more foolish than I expected."

He didn't want to listen to it. Maybe he knew all those things already. He started walking into the next room. Outside, the rain was getting stronger.

"Felan!" I called, as he disappeared into the adjoining hallway. I didn't want to chase after him. If I had my way, I would have been happy if he walked into an open pit and never thought about him again.

Now here I was, kissing him. An action that should have ended the moment I started it. But he didn't know me as Rosha, and perhaps that was my mistake. He didn't know he hated me and had more reasons to hate me still. His lips met mine and his hands went up to encircle my waist and I felt a momentary flush of desire, things I shouldn't have felt given who he was. It was more pleasant than I cared to admit.

I tore myself away before I got too distracted. My eyes were on his shoulder. I couldn't look him in the face. If his thoughts were clear on his expression, I didn't want to know, and I didn't want him to glimpse mine—of the shame and guilt mingling with this new, confounding, unexpected, *inconvenient* thing.

"Suha," he began, his cheeks red.

"My lord, I didn't…" I made a great show of stumbling over my words, turned, and started running.

He chased after me this time. When we were children, it was the other way around. I'd gone after him, against all my inclinations, against all sense, and made things worse. Always, somehow, I was making things worse. And I would stop it if I could, but I didn't know how. All I could do, all I could ever do, was to press on, even if I brought everything crashing down with me.

We reached the edge of the embankment. In the distance, palace guards were blowing their whistles, screaming for us to stop.

I stepped into the grove of trees, drew on the *agan*, and disappeared.

A portal, right under the noses of the palace guards—some of whom might be mages themselves—was more than foolhardy. It was dangerous. I was counting on them blaming Felan for it. He was a lord, he had power—he could endure the inquiry. I was also counting on the fact that he wouldn't talk. The kiss would have confused him.

After all, it confused *me*.

For very skilled mages, portals were an easy feat for short distances if there was an unimpeded path between where you were and where you wanted to go. It was even simpler when you only had to transport yourself. I re-appeared beside the emperor in the blink of an eye. The spell had drained my energy, which meant I wouldn't be able to do anything remotely similar for at least a few hours, if not days. Which was playing with fire because I still needed to jump into the emperor's skin, and I could end up wearing myself out. But I didn't have time to worry about the details. I took his hand and carefully led him down the path to disappear into a crowd feeding the swans by the side of the river.

We were too far away for me to tell if the palace guards detained Felan. I decided to assume they did. "Let's go to the amphitheatre, Grandfather." I patted the top of his hand like nothing was amiss. "You always loved the architecture, didn't you?"

He opened his mouth, as if he actually intended to answer. I felt a flash of fear. This thing was becoming more human the more I interacted with it.

There was a staging area in the back of the amphitheatre, a small building with a locked door. I detected a hint of a spell trap, something similar to the one in Lord Cato's basement that poor Elry thoughtlessly stepped into. A protection, probably, to prevent an assassin from breaking in and lying in wait for a hapless official, because the staging area was conveniently set up with a window offering a clear view of the podium. But a thought occurred to me. This wouldn't have been the first time the emperor had to address a crowd from here, and if Lord Cato had been responsible for controlling him all this time, then the staging area *must* have served as his own hiding spot.

I directed the emperor to place his hand on the knob. I didn't even have to coerce him—I merely pointed. He obeyed, as easily as if my thoughts were his. The door opened. I felt a shudder in the air, the sensation of a tight string loosening, which meant the wards had somehow been undone.

I closed the door behind us as we found ourselves in a room with a single armchair next to the window and more doors behind it. I made the simulacrum open each one himself—each had a different ward. One was a closet with clothes for the emperor. The other had an *agan* mirror.

"I'm impressed," I told the simulacrum. "Lord Cato thought of everything."

The simulacrum nodded eagerly.

Trying not to let this bother me, I switched out the simulacrum into new robes and even took a moment to braid the long, white hair so he no longer resembled the tired old man I was leading around the park. He looked like an emperor now, dressed in the stiff-collared, buttoned-up uniform reminiscent of the Dageian military's, but in dashing red. There was a rune on the back of this one, too. It was the same one on the robes he had in Lord Cato's mansion.

"No crown," I observed. "Do you even wear a crown?"

He looked at me blankly.

"I guess you wouldn't, if you've been travelling around," I continued. I slid the ceremonial sabre into his belt. "Now, what do we do? Shall we alert the palace? We've already given them too much trouble." I pointed at the door with the *agan* mirror.

He stumbled forward. As he passed me, I touched the back of his uniform, and felt myself recede into the old man's body.

My body took a seat on the padded armchair while I drifted towards the *agan* mirror. I placed my hand on the runes. The emperor's body triggered them, and the mirror flared up, revealing a full view of the throne room.

I heard a commotion from the other side. Servants calling. I gathered from the chatter that only the emperor could use the mirror, and that perhaps his sudden presence in the palace was unexpected so soon.

"Your Excellency?" Chancellor Pacano's face appeared in view moments later. "What—how did you—"

"I'm here at the amphitheatre."

"You could have sent for an escort," he stammered.

Yes, that would have made a lot of sense, I thought. I filed the information away for next time.

"I wanted to take a walk," I said. "The fresh air can do wonders for your health. You should try it some time, Pacano. Have you seen your belly lately?"

He looked embarrassed and made a great show of pulling his robe over it in an attempt to hide his paunch. "You do look healthier than when you left, Your Excellency. But still—you could have sent word. We haven't had time to prepare."

"Tell Firekeeper Ceres I am here to make a statement," I said. "You have ten minutes to gather everyone. I'm starting with or without her."

"My lord—"

"Nine soon, Pacano. Don't keep me waiting." I snapped my fingers, cutting out the connection on the mirror. I shut the door of the building, re-igniting the spell to protect my real body from unwanted intruders, and then walked out into the world as the Emperor of Dageis.

Power, my father used to tell me, is illusion.

Way back in the day, Enosh used enchantments for many of his business deals, even when he didn't have to. And he did it carefully. Enchantments are like charms—so light they don't trigger an investigation if you're smart about it, though the mage council took them much more seriously. He could only pull the spell off with associates who weren't mages themselves, which wasn't a problem when he was setting up shop in the south of the continent where there were no systems in place to regulate magic.

But he later admitted, in one of those rare occasions where he saw the need to talk to me as a human being out of boredom, that he went through the rituals mostly for himself. Even if he had no intention of sparking the enchantment—especially later in Dageis, where the safest option was just not to do it at all—he'd set out the candles, he'd draw on the ground even if it was just an inert circle made by his finger in the dust. The ritual itself, not the spell, was his shield, his armour. He still needed to prepare. Needed to step away from his own skin to fully encompass another's.

"The first step is to fool yourself," Enosh told me. "Believe you are everything you want them to think you are."

"Even if you're not," I drawled.

"Do you really think I'm as charming as everyone says I am?"

"You don't say," I said, unamused.

"Because I'm not."

"Right."

"But I have to think I am."

"Is this going somewhere? Because if this is your version of fatherly love—"

"All I'm saying," Enosh said, with an exasperated sigh, "is that the world will think what *you* first think of yourself. It doesn't know you. It needs something to latch onto first, something *you* can supply. So I find a way to make the world see me as smart, capable, someone you can depend on and do business with…"

"You would still be you."

"Well, yes. I don't think you're quite following this conversation."

"No, I am," I said. "You are saying everything about you is made up. That you think the world can only accept you a certain way, and so you *change* yourself to suit its tastes. Because deep inside, you have no substance. How can you? This is a world that doesn't value us for who we really are."

"One doesn't equal the other," Enosh said, his voice growing stern.

"I beg to disagree."

"What I *am*," he continued, "is not enough for the world we're in. I'm Gorenten, Rosha, and so are you. Someday, it won't matter. Today, it does. Today, they will take whatever excuse they can to discount the things I've done and invalidate my accomplishments. A stray word here or there, a rude comment, and suddenly I am untrustworthy, unreliable, unworthy. It is easier not to see yourself as this person in the first place. It is easier to be someone you are not, to mold yourself to what you want them to see you as from the very beginning. And when you have that—you have power. Illusion." He snapped his fingers.

"It can't be that easy," I said.

He laughed. "You'd be surprised."

I didn't believe him then. He could have told me the sky was blue and I would have insisted it was red. But now…

I gazed at the crowd through the emperor's eyes and wondered how it was possible for so many people to be looking up at him in awe at once. A *sea* of people, waiting to hear what he had to say with bated breath. And all gathered within the space of a few minutes. It felt strange that deep inside him, I still felt like myself. I was still Rosha: Gorenten, Jinsein, outlaw mage. How could someone like me, a child who lived only because of the mercy and charity of others, now wear the skin of the most powerful man in one of the most powerful empires of the world?

I lifted my hand. The crowd fell silent.

"Chancellors, council, guild leaders," I said, gesturing at the row of people in front. Chancellor Pacano was there, and so was Firekeeper Ceres. I didn't want to directly acknowledge her—this whole show was meant to appease her, but we could keep that between us. "Citizens of Dageis." I turned to the rest of the crowd, most of whom must be palace staff, herded to fatten it up at the last moment. It would be embarrassing if the emperor addressed a scant few—the tabloids would roar over his perceived loss of popularity for weeks.

"I've come to address concerns that the Emperor of Dageis, has abandoned you. That he is off on some remote island, enjoying the sunshine when the rest of you are shivering in your homes, or sipping expensive wine while you bear the brunt of these lean years."

"Rosha—what are you doing by that ditch, Rosha?"

"I saw something, Papa. I think it was a fairy."

"You and your imagination. What did it look like?"

"It was blue, and it looked like smoke. Come with me to the alley, Papa, I'll show you…"

"Nothing could be further from the truth." I crossed the podium, arms outstretched. "I left the palace to see the empire and experience its hardships for myself. For too long, I have ruled behind a glass case, fed nothing but what I'm supposed to hear to appease me." A cough of discontent from one of the chancellors—I didn't stop to see which one. They all looked alike from where I was standing—polished, well-fed ants trembling at the feet of their god. "I've been given nothing but lies about the state of the empire. 'The empire is prosperous, Your Excellency. Your land is the envy of the world. You are a shrewd and wise diplomat, and your people thrive in every corner.' I ask you now—all of you sitting there, is this true? *Is it?*"

My voice rang through the crowd. No one dared answer. I saw fear in their eyes, uncertainty. The emperor had never spoken to them this way before. I knew I needed to dial down, I needed to step back. I just had to *show* myself here—Firekeeper Ceres would have been content with a nod and a wave. I didn't need to do this.

And yet…

"I have to leave for work soon. Come back home, Rosha, your mother's getting worried."

"It's just a little further, Papa. But not too far. Last time it disappeared into those flowers, and the bushes went up in flames."

"I'm a little worried how often this is happening, Rosha. Maybe you should… read less? Those books your mother borrows for you…"

"It's not the books, Papa."

"Then what is it?"

"I left the palace to see the empire. I wanted to see how my people truly lived, what governed their every day. I wanted to experience for myself the filth in the cities, the barren fields, the farms barely keeping everyone but those at the top fed. You. All of you." I stepped to the edge of the podium, as close to them as I could without falling off. "What runs underneath the surface of Dageis? What blood keeps it alive? Do you people even know?"

They stared, still afraid to answer. Refusing to answer.

"*It's magic, Papa.*"

"Magic," I said.

They waited. They knew what was coming. They should. None of this was new.

"Magic borne on the backs of the less fortunate. Magic pumped from the ground, leaving nothing behind but wasteland, unfit to nourish even hideous beasts. Magic taken from their rightful owners, people we turn into serfs, servants, *slaves*, even as we expect them to be grateful for the right to live here." I paused now, watching the surprise on some faces, the outrage in others. Only Ceres wasn't reacting. Her face was a stone mask. I couldn't tell what she was thinking.

"I've come to the conclusion," I said now, turning half a step so they didn't have to directly look at me, "that we need an investigation into the activities of the mage council."

A flicker now on Ceres's features.

"The state of disarray of the forgotten corners of this land does not match the reports sent by Eheldeth," I continued. "There are places they claim to be so unstable that they cannot afford to send mages to repair them. Is it a coincidence these same places do not happen to be owned by anyone associated with the mage council or their powerful friends? People still have to eke out a living in those lands. Not everyone can afford to uproot themselves. Is there a reason why Eheldeth has neglected them?"

I now placed my eyes squarely on Ceres. I knew I was making her sweat.

The silence continued.

"I am asking you, Firekeeper," I said, "how much has Eheldeth allowed to slip through the cracks. Or is it as simple as the fact that you've forgotten? You've forgotten what mages are supposed to do for the people. You've forgotten your abilities are gifts, given by the gods, not treasures to be sold to the highest bidder. Tell me if I'm wrong."

She stared back at me. There were only two ways to answer, and I had her either way. If she denied it, it was easy enough to find proof to silence her. Klossaka, for a start. The windmills. The barren wyrm-farms. The simple fixes that could have made the region prosperous and yet were somehow too insignificant for her mages to look into. And then, if I wanted to goad her further, I could throw the raids on the

Gorenten villages at her. Her entire council turned a blind eye on that, too.

But she was smarter than that. "You're right, Your Excellency," she said, her jaw held firm. It was difficult to faze the woman—I should have expected it. "I will...call for a meeting. If you have a list of these places..."

"I will not do your job for you," I snarled. I turned around and descended the podium, leaving behind a crowd still shocked beyond comprehension. I couldn't have made a bigger scene if I tried.

CHAPTER 31

ESCAPE FROM TELERES PALACE

I went to the building in the back, hoping I would get there before anyone caught up. My heart was pounding. I wanted to be back in my skin—to be Rosha once more, to be left alone with no one the wiser, unneeded, unnecessary, a nobody in the grand scheme of things. The things I'd said…weren't untrue, but there was a time when I could face the facts of it without getting angry. I didn't know why I was angry now. Because I was in a position where someone could listen? Because I'd convinced myself for the longest time that I was removed from such cares, because I didn't belong anywhere, and so I couldn't possibly care about anything beyond my survival?

But somehow, I knew I wasn't that person anymore. I couldn't be, not after what I'd learned about my family. Their lives were in danger because they chose to give back a little bit of the gift of my life to people who needed it more. Which made it all the more difficult because I knew nothing. I lived my whole life surrounded by people who tried to protect me from what I was, which meant for all the horrors I'd had to face, there was more I never had to find out. There was so much I never cared to learn. And now here I was, throwing spells in the wind, hoping something would catch on fire.

I reached the door. My hand went to the knob.

"Emperor Cerknar," a smooth voice called from the shadows. "A fine performance there. I would have clapped, but I was too busy trying not to wet my pants in laughter. The look on the Firekeeper's face…you can't buy that sort of entertainment anywhere."

I turned around. Targus stood behind a tree, the moonlight framing his form.

"What I'd really love to know," he said, "is who's behind that door. It can't be Lord Cato. We killed him four days ago."

I reactivated the spell traps.

"That—" he said, seeing the movement. "See, that's interesting to me as well. I was wondering why you'd suddenly launch an investigation on the mage council itself. You want to throw them off your scent, don't you? Because you're an outlaw and it's their job to put you away if they catch you. You realize it won't do anything. They'll scramble to cover their tracks, and then they'll send the throne a highly polished, highly fabricated report about how they're doing *everything* they can for everyone involved and now could you please just let them off with a slap on the wrist. Don't even think about lying about what you are. Only a mage can wear that thing, after all, and if you're not one of *them*..."

I turned to face him. "Who are *they*?" I asked.

He laughed.

"The mage council?" I demanded. "The merchant guild? Who is behind all of this?"

"You must be a child," he said. "Only a child would think so simply. As it is, I have no desire to exchange words all throughout the night. Open the door. If you cooperate with me, things can be very good for you. But first you have to hand over the emperor's skin."

"I won't do anything until you tell me why you killed Lord Cato."

His eyes flashed. "This isn't a negotiation!" Without warning, he lunged at me with a bare sword. Instinctively, I threw myself back, remembering too late I wasn't inside my body. The movement propelled the emperor straight into the door. The wards deactivated.

Targus kicked the door open.

I rushed back into my body and tried to run past him. He grabbed me by the neck. "You," he laughed, eyes flashing. "Tar'elian's kid! I should have known!"

I bit his arm.

He struck me with the other hand, loud enough to make my ears ring. I didn't hold back. I struck him with a blast of flame, conjured from the air near the palms of my hand, so strong it would've made most men drop me instantaneously. But he didn't. He simply dug his fingers deeper, as if the prospect of *fire* didn't faze him any. There was no touch of fear in his eyes.

I reached into my core and struck him again. Drawing on the *agan* could sometimes feel as if *I* was the one submerging myself in fire, and several powerful spells in a row—including controlling the emperor in the first place—made me feel as if my blood was boiling. Even mages sent into battle weren't expected to be endless supplies of projectiles. You could just as easily hurt yourself as the enemy.

But I didn't have the luxury of prudence. This time, Targus must have felt a sliver of pain. His fingers slackened. I pretended I was readying for a third blast, and he dropped me.

I struck back with empty hands and then dashed into the open field.

I didn't get far. I *did* overextend myself, because my knees almost immediately crumpled underneath my body. I tumbled forward, and I couldn't even spread my hands fast enough to catch the fall. My jaw struck pavement.

Stars swam in my vision. I wondered if I'd broken my neck and couldn't help but feel like I deserved it. It's hard to take the training out of a mage. If there was one thing Eheldeth had drilled into me, it was that carelessly tapping into the *agan* came with its share of consequences.

"Suha!" a voice called in the distance. Felan's.

I struggled to remain awake. Somehow, I managed to push myself to a leaning position, even though I wasn't sure if my head was still attached to my body. I forced my eyes open. I could see Felan in the distance, his mouth opening and closing. He must be saying something, but somehow, the words had faded. The ringing began again.

I felt the slash of a knife strike my ankle, hitting the bone.

Blood pounded in my head now. I turned around and saw Targus bearing down on me. "You're not going anywhere," he panted. "You're attuned to the thing now. Either you help me, or you *die*."

I tried to kick him off with my other foot.

"If I scream, the entire palace guard will be on you in a moment," I hissed.

"You won't scream," he promised. "You're an outlaw. Nothing they can do to me will match what they will do to *you*."

I kicked a second time. When he tried to pin my leg to the ground, I remembered the sword Nasuha had lent me and struggled to draw it. I wrenched it out of the scabbard, held it forward, and threw another flame spell across it, one for all its weakness still seemed to pull all the breath out of my lungs. I didn't even care anymore if Felan saw it, or the universe, or if it obliterated me so as long as it took Targus down with it. I was so exhausted I couldn't sustain it for very long—without the sword, it would have hardly left my fingers. But making the flames crawl down the metal was easier. I pushed them down as hard as I could until they blasted right on Targus's face.

It did nothing.

I felt the flames recede only to have him drag me along the ground to him. He struck the sword out of my fingers with a fist. Kneeling on top of me now, his teeth bare, I saw no trace of red where I'd burnt him. The skin should be raw, at the very least, if not bleeding. He smelled wrong, like burnt rubber instead of flesh.

His eyes flashed. Something in the angle of his face, or the shadows cast by the moonlight behind him, struck me as odd. I'd seen him before. Not just as a dead man in Triassa, no. More recently. Very recently, as an older man.

"You—" I gasped. "You and the emperor…!"

He gave a small smile. It was, indeed, the emperor's face, but younger—three or four decades younger at least.

"You're a smart one, Tar'elian," Targus said with a grin. "I'd really hate to kill you. I don't have to. Work with me and you get to live, and your family too. Your meddling has earned you that much. The emperor —all we need is the emperor. They'd use me, but I'm not the right age yet, you see."

"How are you alive?" I asked.

"You don't think the man you've been using isn't?" he demanded.

Before I could reply, I saw a rock appear over his head. It came crashing down on his skull. His body wasn't impervious to pain—he cried out and slumped forward. Hands grabbed his shoulder, pushing his motionless body aside.

I found myself staring into the eyes of the emperor. He didn't say anything, but he extended a shaky hand and gripped my wrist, pulling me to my feet.

Through the darkness, I saw Felan coming around the corner. "Gods," Felan said. "You leave me to talk my way out of the guards, and then…"

I gave a small groan.

His brow furrowed. "We'll deal with the rest later. We have to get out of here before the palace guards catch us."

I could only nod. Seeing my wounded ankle, he bent over to pull my arm around his shoulder. Together, we made our way to the riverbank.

Several things ran through my mind as I let Felan lead me away from the lamplights and into the shadows, where the only source of light was the reflection of the moon on the river surface. I wanted to flee, but I was unsure about putting weight on my foot. He knew I was a mage. An outlaw mage. I was at the mercy of the worst possible person in the world: the only other person who knew exactly how low I'd sunk. If he found out who I was…if he *recognized* me…

What reason would he have to help? He had no magic because of me. His entire life, all his prospects, ruined. And I didn't think he'd believe I didn't kill his father. He would blame me for the old man's death. People had jumped to worse conclusions.

We reached the spot under the bridge, near the gates. "They're still busy looking for the emperor," Felan said. He glanced at the simulacrum, which had obediently been following us this whole time. It was still wearing the emperor's robes. "Maybe we should get rid of those clothes. We don't want to draw attention."

"So they can find it in the river and think the emperor's dead?" I pointed out.

Felan swallowed. "Isn't he?"

"You said we have to get out of here first."

"We have to cross the river," he said. "But the bridge will be guarded."

I swallowed. "Across the water."

"You're injured."

"I can swim."

"Against those currents? You've got to be exhausted. A portal and then that fire-spell, all under an hour—"

"Yes, I know," I snapped.

His cheeks coloured. "Didn't look like you did."

"I'm going to swim," I insisted. "I'm Gorenten. It'll be fine."

I pushed myself off him and slipped into the river. My body felt weightless in the water. A fool's gamble, and most days I would have scoffed at my arrogance. But I *was* Gorenten, as my stepfather had drilled into me when I was young and he was teaching me to swim on the sandy shores of the lake. We were Gorenten, with the sea and its salt in our blood. I was also Jinsein, with blood from people of the island of Akki, who boasted similar claims. I might as well have been born with gills. It would've been shameful not to know how to cross a river only ten or fifteen arms' length at its narrowest point. If anything, it was the easiest thing I'd done all night.

I came up to the other side and stumbled forward. Felan's concern wasn't entirely unfounded, however. My arms were now trembling. He emerged from the water a few moments later. His face fell at the sight of me shivering. "You're going to kill yourself," he said.

"Grandfather," I began. "Where is he?"

"The emperor, you mean?"

I swallowed and nodded. It had disappeared in the black night.

"I didn't stop to check if he could swim," I whispered. "I—"

There was a splash. The simulacrum appeared farther down, where the current had swept him.

"Did it…just walk across the bottom?" Felan asked. His voice seemed more pensive than shocked, which didn't really surprise me. He *would* find it more interesting to wonder about a simulacrum's entire existence than worry about preserving his own. In some ways, he was still very much like he was as a boy.

"It doesn't need to breathe," I said. "The other one…the one that attacked me…didn't need to, either."

"But it felt pain. It lost consciousness."

"The person controlling him…must have felt the shock. It must have cut the connection. He can't feel pain, but whoever was behind him could."

We heard hooves above us, followed by wheels. "Rosha?" a thin voice squeaked.

I swallowed. "Rosha isn't here," I called to Ryo. "It's Suha."

He appeared around the bend, astride on Pepper's back instead of in the driver's seat. He'd somehow lost his shoes. "Suha…" he began, as if just remembering the farce. "I've been looking for you. There was a commotion, and people were saying the emperor's missing, and…"

His eyes jumped from me to Felan to the emperor standing behind us like a watchful shadow. He swallowed. He was smart enough to know something else was going on and that he had to hold his tongue.

Felan bent down to pick me up. We were both drenched from head to toe, and his nearness was the closest thing to warmth I could find. My head spun as he assisted me up the bank to the cart. The emperor simply walked behind us, following my lead, all the way down to how I sat. I felt bone-weary and wondered if the simulacrum's state had anything to do with it. I could still feel a thread of connection between us—more than just a passing thought.

Felan got into the driver's seat. Ryo gladly handed the reins over to him and leaped across to get to me. He settled down beside me as the cart made its way down the road. Ryo looked up, and I placed a finger on my lips. He shook his head and leaned over to hug me. "I thought the worst," he whispered. "I heard them say there was an outlaw mage in the park."

I didn't answer. Of course, my brother knew what I was. Was this what they talked about at home, around the dinner table? Rosha the disappointment, Rosha the criminal. I felt that old anger return. To refuse to allow them to chain you was breaking the law, and my six-year-old brother knew it. If anything, it was all he knew of me.

Why did he come back then, hand in mine, head on my shoulder? Why was he *worried?* "You shouldn't have gone looking for me," I whispered into his hair. "We'll be in trouble, and——"

"I know."

"We can't afford more trouble."

"I know," he repeated. "You said be quiet, right?" He furrowed his brow, black hair half-covering his eyes, and he suddenly looked so much like my stepfather I didn't know what to say. I could hear his voice now, could see him standing there, arms crossed, the way he always did whenever I would denounce my father. *Family is family, Rosha, even when we don't want it to be. If we don't belong with each other, where else? The world is cruel enough as it is.*

I always told him what I felt about that: to be beholden to family is much crueller than anything the world could throw at me. I still felt that way. You shouldn't have to bow to family if they were hurtful or abusive, you shouldn't have to worry about their happiness at the expense of your own. But I also felt a flicker of longing, a passing fancy that would have made me laugh if I wasn't also cold and exhausted. For a moment, I wanted to close my eyes and then open them again to find myself back home. It didn't matter where—Triassa, Lon Basden, as long as I was with them. I wanted to sit next to the hearth surrounded by my brothers and my parents, listening to them talk and argue. I wanted to see the lines on my mother's face fade whenever Papa made her laugh, or Papa take her hand and kiss it, or carry my brothers on his shoulders the way he used to carry me. Enosh could even be there, too, pretending to look useful, having insults levelled at him by my mother or Portia, all while saying he would leave soon while somehow staying the night. A family set on its ways, with more problems than most. But Papa was right about one thing: if we couldn't belong to the world, we could at least belong to each other.

If you told me going back there was all it took to make this end, I would have said yes in a heartbeat.

CHAPTER 32

WHAT THE CRYPTS KNOW

F elan took the longest possible road to get back to Lord Cato's
holdings. Despite the years, he hadn't forgotten Eheldeth's teach-
ings. The presence of the *agan* lingered on the mage, especially
strongest after casting a spell. It was like falling into the sea—you needed
time for the water to dry off. I needed to wait for it to disappear so I
would be undetectable to most except to the most skilled mages.

Of course, that left us to travel out in the open while mages thun-
dered down the street looking for an emperor and an outlaw mage. It
helped I was half-asleep through most of the ride back.

Somehow, we got back to the mansion without trouble, just as it was
starting to rain. Nasuha and Go-nir met us at the gates. No one said
anything as I was helped down. There was talk of taking me to Jaila's
room, but Felan insisted on bringing me to his. He didn't want to disturb
her.

Nasuha was the one who stripped me out of my wet clothes and into
clean robes. "I'm not going to ask what happened out there," she said,
when she realized I was wide awake.

"I wouldn't know where to begin," I croaked out.

She pointed at my ankle. "You're lucky. The cut barely missed the
ligament."

"You should have seen the other guy."

She gave me a curious glance. "Are you trying…to tell a joke?"

"Jokes, I believe, are ruined when you try to explain them, Nasuha."

Someone knocked on the door. Nasuha went up to open it.

Felan stood outside, his hands folded behind his back. "She and I need to talk," he said. "Alone."

I felt myself grow ill. I considered asking Nasuha to stay, but before I could sit up, she was already walking away. Felan closed the door behind him before pulling out a stool. He sank into it.

"It's been one thing after another," he said.

"Tell me about it," I sighed.

"That thing," he said. "The old man. It went straight to my father's office the moment we arrived. The others think it's a guest, so I've let them believe it so far. It tried to get into the attic, so I let it. It's just standing there in the middle of the room, staring at the wall."

"Targus mentioned I was attuned to it, and…"

"Start from the beginning," he said, growing more serious.

I sighed. "The old man is the emperor."

"I assumed as much. After the guards finally left me alone, I saw him talking on the podium, and…" He narrowed his eyes. "You. That was you, wasn't it? His voice. It sounded like yours."

"It couldn't have."

"The emperor said things I've never heard him say in all the other times I listened to him as a boy. We know how things run in Dageis. Nobody likes to speak about it, let alone the emperor. He's always said things that *sound* good to the right people, and never the truth."

I shrugged. "I was trying to cause problems for Firekeeper Ceres."

"Why?"

"Because I made a mistake," I said. "There's a hidden room in the attic, with an *agan* mirror connected directly to the throne room in Teleres Palace. I was investigating the attic and then…used the simulacrum by accident." I had to pick which truths I could tell him, and which lies would cause the least harm. "It triggered a connection. Firekeeper Ceres was there, demanding the emperor show himself since he hasn't been in court for months. She threw a spark and I…overreacted. I threw up a shield-spell for protection. It wasn't necessary, but I wasn't thinking."

"Don't blame yourself. Firekeeper Ceres is wily. I could've warned you not to pick a fight with her."

"She threatened to have it traced if the emperor didn't show himself. Which would lead her to *me*."

"So you went up there to fix your mistake," he said with a small nod. "Because you're an outlaw. Don't even think about denying it. A sanctioned mage wouldn't lie after I'd so brazenly admitted to having lost my magic. And she would have certainly had more prospects than a mere housekeeper, even if it is for Lord Cato."

Felan wasn't going to give me a way out. I nodded. "Yes."

"All right. Now—" He placed his shoulders on the bed so he could look me in the eyes. "Tell me the rest."

His gaze reminded me of our kiss, and I immediately glanced away, flushed. "The rest," I began.

"That thing, the attic…"

"This is *your* father's house," I reminded him. "I didn't put those there."

"He didn't tell you about them? He hired you for a reason. You…an outlaw mage."

I could see how that would look. I shook my head. "He didn't know my…status."

"Then—"

"He hired me because I was there," I said.

He drew his eyebrows together.

"I'm Gorenten. He made an assumption. I didn't correct him."

"Does that work often?"

"More than you realize." I looked at him intently now. *He's not lying. He really doesn't know me.* He couldn't. The girl he hated was just another rich man's child. The woman in front of him was a Gorenten servant. That, on top of his injuries and his exile in Sorna, must have made the years between us into a blur.

"That must be convenient," he replied, not realizing his mother's people were just as prone to such mistakes. A lie Dageians tell you. All citizens are the same, except when they're not. But then how was he supposed to know? Lord Cato was the only family he knew, and I doubted the man had any clue about the reality of the land his people had occupied for hundreds of years. In the brief time I knew Lord Cato, I didn't see a man who would have thought much about the woman he married.

"I know nothing about your father or why he had the emperor in his attic," I continued. "I was hoping you would, but I didn't…know if I could trust you. You'd just arrived."

He made a soft sound. "Do you trust me now?"

"I don't know." I wrung my hands together. "Should I?"

"It would be wise not to," Felan replied easily. "My father is both mage and merchant—an important figure to both councils, no matter which way you look at it. He is easily one of the most powerful men in the empire. Not a boast, Suha—a fact. An outlaw mage in his household will not be overlooked. If you're not caught tomorrow, he'll take care of you himself. As his son…" He swallowed. "As his son, I'm obligated to turn you in."

"Well, there you go. You answered the question yourself." I meant to speak as matter-of-factly as I could, too, but I noticed bitterness lacing my tone. It was unsettling. I wasn't in a position to feel anything about this man. He shouldn't even be here.

"I didn't. I said I'm obligated to. I didn't say I would."

"And why wouldn't you?"

"Because…" He turned away, his cheeks growing red.

"I kissed you so I could escape with the emperor," I said frankly. "You know that, don't you? You're old enough to know that, surely. It meant nothing."

He muttered something under his breath.

"We don't know each other long enough," I continued. "Three days, by my count. I would like to know if you're playing the white knight, currying favours with his father's servant in the hopes it will lead to something—"

"That's not it!" he snapped.

"—because *that* would make the rest of the truth extremely conflicting for you."

"What truth?"

"Answer my question first."

"You want to know *why* I'm not going to turn you in?" Felan asked, a note of exasperation on his voice. "That's not exactly the kind of question you'd expect anyone to answer honestly."

"I want to hear it from your own tongue," I said. "Let me judge the rest."

He shook his head. "I don't know what answer you're looking for. But the truth is simple. I wouldn't. I was trained as a mage—I know what happens to mages who practice magic of the calibre *you're* practicing outside the law. An inkling, anyway. It's enough to give me no desire to subject anyone to such a fate. But you can't expect me to ignore this, either. I'm going to give you everything you need to get out of the city. Every moment you spend in Drusgaya is a disaster waiting to happen. You shouldn't have even come here."

It was tempting not to say anything. To simply agree and then let him engineer my escape from this mess. But my father would still be missing. My family would still be in danger. Nothing would change. My freedom wasn't worth their demise.

"Three days you've known me, and you're already lecturing me," I said instead.

"That's not what I'm doing." I recognized the same flare of impatience on his brow that marked most of our interactions in the past. I knew I should stop.

But somehow, I wasn't in the mood to let him off easily. "Then what?"

He sucked in his breath. "This…this isn't going anywhere."

I shifted my legs from the bed so I could get up. He tried to stop me.

"No," I said. "I can walk now. I need to show you something. Like I said—there's more to this."

"You tossed a lot of spells out there. You need to rest after all of that. We all do."

"After what I'm about to show you, rest will be the last thing on your mind." I stumbled off the bed and towards the door. With another sigh, he turned to follow me.

I didn't want to trust Felan, but I *had* to tell him about his father. He had expressed a desire to help me. I couldn't ask him about Enosh without revealing who I was, but I could perhaps manipulate him into investigating everything. He'd have the power to make inquiries. *Tar'elian's kid*, Targus had said, like it was something he talked about at dinner parties. Dig deeper, and I knew I would find the threads connecting my family to all of this. I could make Felan do the digging himself.

I took him down to the crypts. My thoughts died the moment I pulled back the blankets covering Lord Cato's corpse. The shock of his grief on Felan's face felt like a spell, thrown at him out of nowhere, unexpected, unwanted. Unavoidable.

"My lord," Felan said softly, sinking to his knees beside the body. "Oh, my lord. No. Not like this. I came too late." His head touched the soft soil near the corpse's shoulder.

I took a step back. I wanted to run away—I shouldn't even be there. But I also got the feeling he would want answers eventually, and my absence could be seen as an affront. I had no desire to add to his grief.

But was my silence making things worse? Was I supposed to go to him, place my hand on his shoulder, offer a word of comfort? What could I say? I'd never lost a parent. I had more parents than anyone could ever need, and it wasn't as if I could offer to trade Enosh to replace the one he'd lost.

"Suha," he said, breaking into my thoughts.

I approached him carefully. He had recovered from the shock long enough to examine the body. It was still caked in blood—Nasuha and I had no time to clean it—all congealed around the stab wound on the belly.

"Who did this?" he asked.

"The man in the park," I replied. "He all but confirmed it."

"How long ago?"

"I believe it was the night before you arrived," I said.

He shook his head, the shadows wearing down his expression. "Hours," he gasped. "Mere hours. If I had come sooner...if I hadn't stopped to *eat*..."

"Next, you'll berate yourself for breathing. Be reasonable. You had no way of knowing."

"We haven't talked for two years," Felan said. "Working up the courage to travel here wasn't easy. I was going to tell him I've agreed to return to Eheldeth. If that was what it took to repair our relationship, to get him to talk to me again, I was willing to risk the pain and the humiliation."

"But you don't...have the ability anymore."

His face tightened. "I know. But I could get tested. Consult with the keepers. Ask them for help. I wanted to do *something*, anything to make Lord Cato happy. All he wanted was I try. These last few years...I didn't even want to go back to the empire at all because the thought of being near so much magic, without *seeing* or feeling any of it..."

Felan swallowed, his hands quivering. He looked at them now, at the empty air, where long strands of *agan* that would hang like webs between his fingers if he was still as he been. *I*, who could still see, could detect nothing but a faint glow if I tapped into my connections, but every living thing had that. You wouldn't know he ever had the gift at all, let alone enough of it to make the Eheldeth keepers wary of him.

"I understand," I said.

"It would be like having a parched throat while watching others drink around you, knowing they could never offer you a sip."

"I wanted to help you when I saw you being attacked in the palace last night," Felan said. "I came running when I saw that man chasing after you. I forgot I couldn't do a damn thing. I don't even have a sword, and even if I did, I wouldn't know how to use it. Magic was all I had. And then I saw you cast fire and then...I remembered. I stood there. Filled with rage at first, because of what you hid from me. I suspected a portal when you disappeared in the woods, but I was willing to believe any other explanation if it meant..." He looked down again.

"What?"

"That I could spend more time with you." He shrugged, as if that last sentence was a stray thought. "Anyway. The rage quickly disappeared. Left something worse behind. Envy."

"You are envious of an outlaw," I reminded him. "It's a terrible fate. Every time I cast magic, I carve my own doom. I'm in the same situation as you."

"No. Not exactly. You can still cast magic, and when you do, don't tell me you don't enjoy it."

"I could," I replied. I gave a small smile. "I'd be lying."

Felan turned to his dead father. "I have to report his death. It won't be long before the authorities turn up at the door, anyway. Three days is too long. He would have missed half a dozen important meetings by now. Is there any chance we can pin this on an outlaw mage anyway?"

"What do you mean?"

"The man who attacked you in the palace," he said. "He *could* have been a mage. He would have definitely been acting outside the law."

"I don't think he was." He was a damn simulacrum. But I didn't want to tell Felan anything until I was sure.

"He *could* have been," Felan repeated. "Let us stick to one story. This: an outlaw came to kill my father three nights ago. He dropped threats. Disappeared. We were afraid for our lives, so we kept quiet. Do you understand?"

"Yes."

"Who else knows about you?"

"Only…Rosha," I said. "And her brother."

"Remind them their silence will be rewarded." He got up, looking much more aged than his twenty-something years. I couldn't even remember how old he was supposed to be now—I'd lost track of time. He graciously allowed me to walk up the stairs first, simply so I could place my hand on his shoulder with each step. I didn't want to accept the help, but I wasn't sure I could make it out of there on my own. I more than over-extended myself back there. Eheldeth could do an entire semester on what such foolhardiness could do to a young mage, with me as the shining example.

Out in the palace gardens, we were greeted with Go-nir's piercing whistle.

"My lord," he said, running up to meet us. "There's people at the gates."

"Mages?" Felan asked.

He nodded. "Two men," he said.

"Not the Firekeeper," I whispered to Felan's ear.

"I'll take care of this," he said. "Please, take Suha back to her room. I will inform them of my father's death and the assassin."

"No," I replied. "I'll go with you."

"Suha—"

"I'm done hiding," I said. "Either they know me, or they don't. Take me with you."

He was too worn out to argue. He gestured with a sweep of his hand, and I followed him out to the garden.

The mages were both strangers to my eyes. But I realized my mistake as soon as they introduced themselves.

"I'm Bearer Lontas," the senior of the two said with a nod. "We're here to ask questions."

The bastard had caught up to me at last.

CHAPTER 33

THE BEARERS

S itting beside Felan during the inquiry offered protection in plain sight. The mages could detect *agan* in the air, and it wasn't even a day since I'd cast those spells. I would still reek enough of it to give most mages worth their salt pause. However, because every living thing is connected to the *agan* in some way, it responds to the presence of other beings. The stray bits left over from my spellcasting would naturally drift over to Felan, simply by virtue of him being alive. To a skilled mage, it would look like we were both glowing, with no indication of the source. It was a fundamental truth that made hiding in Dageis as an outlaw easier than in most parts of the world. Someone who can see the *agan* might know a mage was there, but not how many.

I was counting on that small thing to shield me. I wasn't counting on coming face-to-face with a shadow that had haunted me for years.

"My lord," Bearer Lontas said, interrupting Felan mid-sentence with a sweep of his hand. He was a thinly bearded man with black hair and remarkably yellow eyes. Most heavy users of magic had eyes that lightened over time. Putting a face to the name was more than unsettling. Of all the mages in the world, why did it have to be him? I didn't think he recognized me from all those years ago—he didn't exactly *see* me, the same way I didn't get a chance to see him—but hearing his voice was like walking into a nightmare. It took all my strength not to fidget in my seat.

"I can't help but notice…" He gestured at Felan, hoping he would fill in the gaps himself. What a man chose to lie about could say so much, and I knew they must have all the information they possibly could on Felan already.

"The glow?" Felan asked, before I could make the mistake of interrupting. "You do know I was studying in Eheldeth, of course?"

"It says you dropped out. You should not—"

"Involuntarily," Felan continued. "There was an accident in my youth, and I've been unable to control my connections since. I was hoping Eheldeth could offer a solution. I've only been back in the empire for four days."

"You did not report when you docked," Bearer Lontas said. "You should have filed a report to the mage council immediately."

"My father," Felan said, "is a member of the merchant guild. I was hoping the report could be filed directly by him, to members of the mage council sympathetic to our family's troubles. As far as I was aware, his decisions over my future take precedence. You understand that his disappearance made it difficult for me to plan accordingly. The glow...I cannot stop the glow. I must still be drawing from the *agan* involuntarily." Lontas had no way of knowing the truth.

"Such ailments can be dangerous," Bearer Samran added. Compared to Lontas, he was unremarkable. Shaved head, shaved beard, a bit of weight around his edges. His eyes were brown and green, which could have been natural. Some mages got Eheldeth over with and then went for years without casting magic, simply because they were never skilled at it in the first place and were more afraid of it than anything else. I pinned him as one of those. I wondered if he was with Lontas at that inn three years ago.

"As I said, I was doing the best I could given the situation." Felan crossed his arms. "This outlaw mage in the palace—you must have also seen the report I filed with the palace guards."

Samran paused, looking through his notes. "There is no record of that," he said after a moment.

"I'll tell you what I told them. I was taking a stroll there with my... with her," he said, indicating me with a nod of his head, "when we heard a portal appear behind us. She's never seen magic before and fled."

"The portal is mentioned here," Samran mused. "So you think you saw him?"

Felan shook his head, in the same instance I said, "I did."

He chewed the side of his cheek.

Both bearers turned to me. "Who are you, exactly?" There was no recognition in their eyes.

"I'm Lord Cato's housekeeper," I replied. "He hired me a few weeks ago."

"Why, exactly, were you strolling with Lord Felan in the park?" Bearer Lontas asked.

I pretended to look away. "I didn't know *that* was illegal," I grumbled.

"If you're hiding anything from us—" Samran started.

"Intimate relations—" Felan broke in, his face redder than the rest of ours.

"It's not illegal to spend some time with your boss's son, is it?" I asked.

Lontas coughed. "Unprofessional, maybe. Ethically wrong."

"I didn't say I was a good housekeeper," I countered.

"I guessed that the moment we walked in here," Samran said, eyeing the dusty cupboards.

"Could we get back to the matter at hand?" Felan asked.

"You've embarrassed him," I said. "You're one to talk about professionalism."

"Just describe this man," Samran said, looking like the entire conversation was causing him great physical pain.

"About medium height." I held up my hand over my head, showing exactly how tall Targus was. "Blue eyes, brown hair. He crops it short. Clean-shaven, though that could change." *Could it?*

Lontas scribbled something down in his notebook. Or perhaps he was pretending—I caught him glancing at Samran. "About a million people in Drusgaya alone could fit that description," Lontas finally said.

I crossed my arms. "That's not my problem. That's yours."

"If you could give us something more distinctive, perhaps, like the colour of his skin, or…"

"I'm not going to make up a person for you to arrest," I countered. "His skin looks a lot like yours, if you want to know. If that happens to fit almost everyone in this damn city, I don't see why I have to worry about it."

"Blue eyes, brown hair," Samran said. "Most regular people look like that. Hardly sounds like a criminal to me."

"You don't think *regular-looking* people commit crimes every day?"

"This presents a problem," Lontas said.

"Again," I repeated, "it's not mine."

"This man killed my father, gentlemen," Felan broke in. "I'm not of the mind to discuss how much better it would be if he had decided to make himself easily identifiable. Of course he didn't. Assassins blend in, they don't stick out. Make yourselves useful and find him. In the meantime, I have a funeral to plan."

Both bearers gave each other a look. Eventually, they got up, somehow remembered Felan was still part of the hegemony, and managed awkward bows in his direction. They eventually left, stumbling through the door of the tearoom with the awkwardness of men who had felt like they wasted their time. I felt a flood of relief at seeing Lontas turn his back. I knew it would be rude not to see them out, but I didn't want to risk walking away from Felan and having them see the blue glow on just me. They could take it as an insult if they wanted to.

"They're going to pin it on some poor soul," I said, as soon as they were gone. "Someone intelligent enough to kill Lord Cato in his own home won't be caught by a couple of bumbling bearers easily."

"I admit that's not what I'm worried about," Felan replied.

"It should be."

"We have to get you out of here first." He absently began to clear the mugs from the table. I watched him carry the bucket outside and wondered if he even had servants in Sorna. He must have lived alone at some point. Did his disagreement with his father include withdrawal of the man's support? Perhaps his newfound humility had something to do with how he'd been forced to live the last few years. There were many ways to break the talented.

I heard a noise outside. It sounded like a howl. I whistled for the dogs, but none of them appeared.

Then I heard a scream.

I grabbed the doorframe, pulling myself out from the chair, and limped out after Felan.

There was a dead mage in the garden, slumped over the fountain. His throat was ripped open. I recognized Bearer Samran immediately. His body was still twitching, blood spurting from the veins of his neck. It seemed almost absurd that I was just talking to him moments ago.

I heard the creaking of hinges and turned my gaze to the side of the house. The cellar doors were wide open, flapping against the wind.

Cellar doors.

The basement had cellar doors.

The idiots had let Elry loose.

I heard the scream again. It was coming from the street. I bent down over Samran, grabbing the staff loose from his stiff hands. He wouldn't need it anymore. Using it for support, I started running.

The main doors flew open before I reached the gates. Nasuha must have heard the screams, too, because she came tearing after me. "Is everyone else inside?" I called.

"Your brother's with Go-nir, and Jaila's asleep. What the hell is happening?"

"The bearers set Elry free."

"Why would they do that?"

"Because they knew we were hiding something and were idiots enough to snoop around."

We reached the street, just before I narrowly avoided stumbling face-down into the storm drain. I saw Felan standing right behind the bleeding figure of Lontas.

"Keeping a magical creature within city limits is a violation of Dageis's laws," Lontas gasped as we came within earshot. His whole left arm was ripped to shreds—it was a wonder he could talk straight. "So the gods help me, if that thing is *agan*-wrought, you'll never see the light of the day again, tan-Tarsius!"

"My last name is Cartos," Felan corrected. "If there's anyone you should be questioning about this, it should be my father. I told you. I only arrived three days ago. That creature—"

We heard a howl from the rooftops of the closest building.

"That murderous creature is loose in a city full of people," Lontas hissed. "Someone has to pay! My partner is dead because of this!"

"Then open up an inquiry on *Lord Cato's* activities," Felan said. "He's still a mage, which means he's under your jurisdiction. Something foul *is* running loose in Drusgaya, and a mere beast is the least of your worries. An outlaw mage attacks the palace the day the absent emperor decides to make an appearance? What are *you* hiding?"

"The mage council wouldn't sanction anything like this."

"Then—"

Elry's snout appeared from the edge of the rooftop in the building across. He snapped his jaws around Felan's arm before I could reach them. His mouth closed with a sickening crunch—Felan groaned and fell limp. Grinning from ear-to-ear, the beast dragged him up before disappearing into the adjoining ledge, where the damned Dageian architecture—with its elaborate swoops and nooks and crannies—all but hid them in the shadows.

My stomach turned. No—I couldn't have done this to him again. I didn't just lead him to another disaster. He'd somehow survived the first time I dragged him to death's door. To have it happen a second time...

"You!" Lontas called behind me. "Woman! Servant!"

"I have a name," I snapped, anger rising through my pores. *No*, I reminded myself. *Not anger. The agan.*

He backed away.

"Your glow—" he began.

"So what about it?"

"There are no gifted mage-thralls in Lord Cato's employ. If he's hired someone like you, he should have informed us. Unless—"

"I'm an outlaw, too," I said. There was no point in hiding it anymore. Magic had shaped my life, even when I couldn't use it.

He pointed at me, his finger shaking. "You're to turn yourself in at once, or else—"

"I thought it was the creature you were worried about. Make up your mind, Bearer Lontas."

He made a grab for me.

Before his hand could even get close, Nasuha stepped between us, her sword making a small half-circle in the air. She pressed it against his neck. Moonlight glinted off the bare edge, yellow on steel.

"Is it true what they say about mages?" she asked. "If I stab you hard enough, will you bleed blue?" She inclined her head towards me. "Go after Felan."

"He's—"

"Don't give him up for dead yet," she said. "He's tougher than he looks. Go now!"

As if it were that easy. I didn't know where the beast had gone, and I could hear nothing on the wind. And Bearer Lontas had gotten something wrong. The creature couldn't be *agan*-wrought. You only used the term on creatures that needed the *agan* to give them life. Elry used to be human—his essence remained human. If Felan was as he had been, with as many connections to the *agan* as he did, I might have been able to sense his general direction. But the air felt blank as any cool night, as empty as most of the nights of my life. I couldn't even feel Lontas behind me.

My body trembled. I knew I shouldn't be standing in the first place, not after pushing myself to the limits last night. A few hours of rest wasn't enough to fill the well, and I was going to risk injuring myself further. You don't want to know what happens to mages who recklessly ignore their capabilities time and time again. There are rifts in the farthest corners of Dageis that used to be mages.

But I wasn't going to leave Felan if I could help it. However fast I went after him last time wasn't fast enough. I remembered pausing as he went down that hallway, rolling my eyes as I ambled after the stubborn boy with his pompous face and abrasive temper. I'd spent the last few years wondering if another moment sooner would have changed his fate. Would I have reached the library before that stranger did? Could I have somehow stopped the attack that— unbeknownst to me at the time— saw his own magic being ripped out through his eye sockets and into the stranger's own hand?

I thought I'd last seen the creature heading west, though, which was right past the mansion gates. A faint voice called from inside the yard. I recognized Jaila. She was leaning on the stone column of the arch.

"The church of Endros," she gasped. "He'll be at the church."

"What do you mean?"

"If there's anything left of him inside himself—and I think there is— that's where he's headed. We were supposed to meet there before *that* happened to him."

I looked her over. "If you're well enough to be walking," I said, "perhaps you should take Ryo and get out of here. There'll be inquiries shortly, and I don't want you or him involved. Ask Go-nir to hide you somewhere. I'll find you when I can."

"Miss," she began. "You're not...you're not going to kill him, are you?"

"He may not leave us much choice," I replied. "You saw what he did to the mage in the gardens. If he wasn't capable of murder before, he certainly is now."

"Miss..."

"Jaila, I don't know. If he attacks me—if he's hurt Felan—"

"He's not some spry, foolish young man," Jaila said. "He has a family that needs him, too. Children. A daughter. He went to work for Lord Cato for her sake in the first place. He said there were threats on her life. He thinks Lord Cato made them. He wanted him to leave her alone."

I stared at her. "What do you mean?" I asked. "What do you mean he worked here for *her* sake?"

"He thought her life was in danger. He thought Lord Cato was responsible, and he entered his service to find out more. He didn't tell me anything else."

I could feel my thoughts colliding. *No,* I managed to pull out of the mess. *No.* But it had to be. Everything was starting to fit.

What the hell have you done now, Enosh?

I turned back to the street.

"Don't kill him," she repeated, those same damned words.

CHAPTER 34

THE MONSTER AND THE MAGE

The thoughts spun in my head with the reverberation of a string wound too tight. Elry. Elry went to work for Lord Cato for his daughter. Was Elry my father?

I pushed them away. Nothing changed that he was a monster, that Felan was in danger. I stumbled through the doors of the Church of Endros, a massive temple built around an open alcove that served as both altar and offering pit during service. Endros was the Dageian deity of prosperity and trade, and almost every rite associated with him was a chance for merchants to rub elbows and create illicit deals on the side. His priests and priestesses were nearly always high-ranking merchants themselves, though you were supposed to give up worldly possessions to be ordained.

But Dageis was a land of ironies. Freedom laced in glass shards, comfort swathed in iron nails. I had never felt that as clearly as I did when I strode through the empty hallway, from where I could see the alcove immediately from the antechamber. A shaft of moonlight streamed onto the stone of the altar, bouncing all over the surface of the loose coins on the floor so that the room was filled with seemingly endless sparkles. Elry stood in the middle, haunches fixed squarely on the coins like a dragon roosting on its hoard. Felan was still in his jaws. He looked dead—his skin was unnaturally pale, and his limbs flopped like a ragdoll. With his eyes closed, he looked like the boy in my memories.

"Elry," I said, planting the staff in the soil in front of me. I tried to remain calm.

He gnashed his teeth, a movement that transferred into the hunk of flesh in his mouth. Fresh blood poured out of Felan's arm, streaming down the already dried specks of red on his skin. I thought I caught a movement of his lips. Perhaps it wasn't too late, but I needed to get the beast to drop him first.

Just like I should have tried to get that stranger to drop him in that night in the library. Hindsight. Back then, self-preservation won over, and I stayed at the edge of that doorway, watching him dangle in the air, the stranger's hand on his face. Blue light filled the dark room, deepening the shadows lurking between the bookshelves. I could have run straight into them and interrupted the stranger midway through the spell. But I was too afraid, too afraid to even breathe. I was hoping the stranger wouldn't notice me—that they would suck Felan dry, discard him like an empty husk, and then just simply walk right on by.

I was just a girl, and I didn't know then what I had to learn the hard way—that we cannot pretend we are as alone as we feel. It is appealing to be responsible for nothing but your own actions, a single stick bobbing in the river. I didn't want to be stuck in those ruins with Felan. I wasn't the one that made him run to the woods in the first place and I certainly didn't start the argument that made him want to flee. My only mistake was not walking away when I had the chance.

But I was the only one there with him. I could have done something. Then maybe he wouldn't have been so hurt and maybe he wouldn't have been shut off from his magic completely.

I didn't. And it changed nothing, because the stranger saw me, anyway. A single moment of not understanding how our fates are intertwined, how the decisions we make are not contained in a bubble.

If I made a mistake once, I could still forgive myself. We're human, we make mistakes. One of Papa's many lessons. But to make it again, with the same person? My stepfather would weep.

I took a step back, drawing on the connections of *agan* inside me and focusing it on the gnarled piece of wood, carved from oak and etched with runes that amplified connections and made magic so much easier to cast. The ground shook. The beast watched with gleaming eyes and slavering jaws.

The blast came from the ground, knocking him off his feet.

The quick burst of magic felt like needles running up my nose and through my skull. I kept my hands around the staff, focusing the last of my strength, drawing the *agan* from deep inside my body to channel it through the ground. *One more, just one more.* I felt blood drip down my left nostril, but I was too afraid to wipe it off. Removing my hands from the staff might weaken the spell. I couldn't risk that. If this last one didn't work, I wasn't sure if I could do another.

My head pounded. Through my darkening senses, I saw Elry drop Felan. Blood dripped into my mouth as I rushed forward.

I didn't even get close. Elry recovered and lunged. He seemed to have forgotten about Felan and was now pouring all attention on me. I turned, barely managing to protect myself with the staff. His jaws snapped around the wood. He bit down, shards of wood splintering between his teeth. With his Bearer's stipend, you'd think Samran could have afforded better equipment.

Of course, criticizing a dead mage would not increase my chances of survival. Evidently not happy with crunching on oak, Elry gave chase once more. I led him away from Felan's unmoving body to the edge of the church. I took the steps leading up to the second level. He crashed into the pew behind me, knocking wooden benches aside and tearing into them with his teeth. I didn't know why he wasn't exhausted yet. He had to be.

I reached the second floor, where more benches were gathered on the mezzanine. I thought I could make it to the edge of the railing and then trick him into falling off the side. I realized quickly that my idea was conceived during a rapid loss of blood and a sharply diminishing state of mind. He didn't follow me up the staircase. Why did I assume he was going to follow me up the staircase?

I heard a creaking behind me, the sound of chains rattling. I turned and saw Elry hanging from one of the chandeliers that swung from the ceiling around the open alcove. He leaped towards the terrace and crashed into the railing a few paces away. I tried to run, but he swiped at my legs. I fell to the ground.

Elry approached, eyes gleaming, hungry for the kill.

"Elry," I said, testing it. Nothing. He continued to circle me, lips drawn backward to reveal his bloody fangs.

I swallowed.

"Enosh."

A flicker of recognition. He looked like a dog who had heard his master's footsteps and wasn't sure if he was supposed to run to them or away from them. But it told me everything I needed to know.

"Father."

He opened his mouth, and for the first time since I'd seen the beast, he struggled to form words.

· · ·

265

The memory of the first time I met my father is covered in haze. I can only gather bits and pieces, most of which Enosh supplied himself. I remember standing in an old warehouse, a shed for storing rice and flour. It was cold—so cold that my skin, where it wasn't covered by my robes, felt sharp to the touch. I'm sure I was in the middle of casting a spell, because I usually associate that haze with drawing on the *agan* more than I should. I felt like I was a hundred different things at once. I was nothing but a doll—a limp, lifeless thing propped up by strings, relying on the intricate machinations of a master I couldn't see.

I remember the look on his face. He knew of my existence only about three years before, but it was the first time he laid eyes on me, too. He looked frightened. Now, I'm sure the prospect of having to be responsible for *anything* alive would have been enough to make Enosh wet his pants, but this went beyond that. He looked like he didn't want to know what to do with me: a child so young and yet already working her way through spells like a fish through water. I couldn't see what was wrong with it. If you had a gift, why not use it? I was born to the *agan*—I never had to try very hard to draw out the blue glow in just about anything. When I was a child, it was all I could see, all I could breathe. I played with it the way other children played with sand.

Later, I learned it was because he was a rogue mage himself—if not exactly the kind Eheldeth feared the most, the ones who stole its secrets and left without so much as a by-your-leave. The look of fear came from the understanding of what I was about to face. "The world is not kind to gifted Gorenten," he told me once. "You should know this by now." We weren't defined by our accomplishments, but by the things we couldn't do, the heights we couldn't reach, the strictures created by a world convinced we were incapable of achieving what the rest are allowed to dream of. It wasn't a matter of being capable of more. It was what the world did to us for even trying.

The worst part of it all was that he was right. Fourteen years later, here I was, just as much of an outlaw as he had been. Worse. I don't mean this as a boast, but my father was never so skilled in the *agan* that he had to be careful. He restricted himself to charms and inert spells— don't-look and other environment-altering effects to mask whatever idiotic thing he thought would get him ahead. Nothing he'd done in all the years I'd known him had ever impressed me. I used to think he was nothing but a witch, no better than the role I was forced to play these last few years.

I was different.

We all think that, don't we? Who of us doesn't think there is something in us, a quality that could make the world stop and pay attention if we could just find a way? I think that's why I hated Enosh. I hated that he forced me into this cage, not realizing it was never as easy for me as it was for him. Imagine having all that power. Imagine having the capability of turning dust into gold, of reading about a spell that would take experienced mages years to learn properly and then executing it on your second or third try. Imagine being told you had to wrap yourself in chains instead, submit yourself to rules not made to protect you but to protect others from you. You had to be less because the world had no room for you to be whole.

I decided none of that mattered that night. Seeing Enosh standing there, trying to return to his senses, a man who could have been a mage reduced to no better than a beast, made me ill. For all that I hated him, I hated Dageis even more. No matter what they tried to do to me, I was still…what I was. All the power lying dormant inside my veins was still mine.

I placed my hands on the sides of his face. The blood continued to pound in my head as I tentatively drew out the faint connections inside of me, and what I knew lay inside of him. If his name could bring back a flicker of humanity in his eyes, then he was capable of more. We were family. Our connections ran deeper than blood.

My eyes watered. Blood dripped down my nostril again, pooling in the creases of my lips. I swallowed the taste of iron and slipped into the *agan* stream, deep inside of him.

I swam in a haze of images, conversations spinning left and right before they finally faded, leaving just the one. There, I found myself staring at my reflection on the windows of a carriage I was just getting out of. I realized I was peering into Enosh's own memory. What appeared to be Enosh. I could tell it was him; another person might not. One blink and he looked like any man you could find in the street, someone down on his luck. He was at the gates of Lord Cato's mansion, holding a flyer in one hand, pointing at what was written on it. "Elry," he introduced himself. "My name is Elry." Go-nir was there, shaking his head, unsure of what to make of him.

I didn't know why he risked a high-level enchantment when he was walking right into Lord Cato's home. One look at him and the man was sure to decipher that he wasn't who he said he was, that he was hiding something. But near the stables, before he entered the first row of fences,

I saw him discard the pendant that triggered the spell behind some bushes. I glimpsed him through a puddle.

He looked…the same, but not quite. He now looked like the Enosh I knew, but with a rugged brown beard, flecked with white, and closely cropped hair that looked like it had never seen a comb in its life. Go-nir introduced him to the stable hands, and then later, Jaila, and it was like watching how I entered that household myself. Drifting in and out so easily, because people like Lord Cato never thought twice about the people who kept them fed and cleaned so as long as they stayed out of his way. If he'd ever met Enosh before, he didn't remember.

The memory faded. I stood in the middle of a field of knee-high blue grass. Enosh crouched in front of me, in the same position the monster had been. He was still opening and closing his mouth, as if he couldn't decide between yawning or vomiting out all his internal organs.

I crouched down next to him. "I have to admit," I said. "This suits you much better."

He stared at me with bloodshot eyes.

"Ironic," he replied. "I came here to protect you. You shouldn't have come." His voice sounded weary. It sounded like he had been screaming all night, which was…apt. You didn't retain your physical self across the *agan* fabric, but people love to carry baggage, even when they don't have to. Likely he was unaware of it.

"That happens when you don't tell anyone your plans," I said. "Would a letter have hurt?"

"Letters get stolen."

"Talking, then. In person. When was the last time you visited your own wife and brother?"

"You'd say that! I've visited more often than you have in the last three years."

I started laughing. "You—*you're* not going to make me feel bad about this, Enosh. After everything you did to this family, you're the last person who has the right."

"It's amusing you think that *feeling bad* is the worst this has come to."

"No, I know. Walking away from Eheldeth—"

"So you could be branded a criminal. Yes. How was that, by the way? Did the idea come to you in a burst of inspiration? Did you think you were going to be an exception to the rule?"

"It is not," I pointed out, "exactly a crime to leave my studies. There are no laws explicitly forbidding it. It *would be* if I practiced magic again. It shouldn't have to be a problem if Eheldeth decided it wasn't a problem."

"You're smart enough to know people like us don't *practice* magic," Enosh said. "It's not a candle you can just put out any time you wanted to. Sooner or later, you were bound to slip."

"I didn't for three years," I replied. "I didn't until *you* got stupid enough to get caught and the family you don't seem to think much about had to go asking for *my* help."

"You don't seem to think much about that family, either."

"I left so they could be happy," I snapped. "I stayed away so they would have a chance to be what they had been before *you* came along and ruined it!"

"What makes you think they were happy without you?"

"Because I'm *yours*," I said, exasperated. "Don't you realize that? I will always remind them of the years you robbed from them. And they refuse to have me disown you because they think *I* still need you. As if I ever did! I was fine without you in my life. Walking away from Eheldeth was the one chance I had to prove that, and I was right. I don't need you. I never did."

He sniffed, staring blankly into the distance. "So we're the same, then," he said. "You and I. Like father, like daughter."

"Don't start."

He cocked his head at me with a lopsided grin. "It's touching. It really is. I'm a failure—"

"You're impossible."

"—and you're a catastrophe."

"I shouldn't have come for you," I said. "I should have let you rot slowly inside that creature until the mages came to drive a stake through your eye."

"The left, or the right? You know I'm peculiar about the left."

I shook my head. "Just...just drop dead, Enosh."

"If I do, then you've just wasted your time," Enosh said. "The mage council know about you. If they didn't think you were a threat before, they will now. So much for the three years, eh, Rosha? I told you. You were bound to slip. If it wasn't me, it would have been for some other reason, some other favour or helpless soul you couldn't turn your back on. Ah, no, maybe you're not exactly like me. That wanton display of magic? You still have too much of Kefier in you. That's why you came."

"You know what? I think they've already accepted you for dead. How about I never tell them about this and just go? Enjoy the last hour or so of your life, Enosh. The mages will put you down soon." I began walking away from him.

Three or four paces away, I heard him sigh.

"If you think you're going to stop me—" I started.

"I'm not going to stop you," he said. "When did I ever?"

I whirled around and opened my mouth.

"I thought," he said, "that leaving Eheldeth was just about the stupidest thing anyone could do, and I maintain that it is. No—don't start. It was. To think that you even *finished* the semester, instead of leaving at the start of it. Non-refundable tuition. You ever think about that, Rosha? I could have bought another house with that money."

"I'll pay you back."

"It's not about the money," he replied.

"Now *that's* a lie."

"It's not just about the money," he said, without missing a beat. "But flunking those exams on purpose midway through finals week is...I don't know if you thought it was going to make *me* look bad but let me tell you, you came off a lot worse there. When I finally arrived in Eheldeth, they were still talking about you. The girl who couldn't face her shame. Seven years of hard work, all gone in the blink of an eye. All because you hated me that much."

"It's not always about you," I said. "Please."

"Then take my advice," Enosh said. "Leave Dageis, when you get back out there. Lord Cato was inquiring about you for a reason. I thought he had something to do with why you left in the first place, but I guess I was wrong, which means his interest in you is even more insidious. I don't know what it is—I tripped the spell before I could get to him —but I believe he means to hurt you. Knowing the man, he's not going to stop until he's got you in his clutches. If he finds out you walked right into them—"

"You can drop the fatherly concern. It's not a problem anymore. He's dead."

Enosh paused. "You killed him?"

"He's dead. That's all you need to know." I sighed. "Go back to your body, Enosh. At least one of us should go home."

"My body is—"

"Go," I repeated, holding both my hands out.

Our surroundings yawned inside itself. Everything faded.

I found myself back in the physical world, my bones aching with the sensation of having fallen from a cliff. I struggled to stand. The beast was gone. Enosh stood in its place, dressed in the same rags, gaunter and more hallowed than he'd been through the fabric. I stumbled towards him.

Before I could reach him, a flash of light exploded around us. A figure appeared behind him, gloved hand grabbing Enosh by the head. Enosh tried to turn; the figure struck him with a fist. He crumpled to the ground, dead or unconscious—it was too bright to tell.

The light receded, revealing the figure's face.

"Targus!" I roared.

"You found your father," he said with a smile. "Too bad he's mine." He bent over and hefted Enosh's frail form over his shoulders. The weight hardly seemed to bother him—there was no strain in his muscles, no labour in his breath. "You poor fool," he crooned into Enosh's ear. "Did you really think you could stop me?" There was a mad light in his eyes, and I got the impression the words falling out of his lips were personal.

Targus turned back to me. "Now all I need is the emperor and *you*."

"You think I'm going to risk my life any further for this man?" I asked. "You must be out of your mind."

"No one's asking you to risk your life. But see, an outlaw mage cannot hide in Dageis forever." He pointed at me. "I'm offering you a chance to have a semblance of a normal life. A place where you can be safe *and* useful. Think about it. You can do important work—much better than anything you would ever get out of that pathetic shop of yours—and certainly much better than anything Dageis could have ever given you."

"You want me to control the emperor for you," I said.

"Of course. I told you. You're attuned to it now. Either you coop-erate with us, or we kill you. It would be too inconvenient to find another mage to attune it with, so I'm hoping to appeal to your sense of judgment."

"Who will I control it for?"

His face lit up. "If you want to find out, then find me at the clock tower in the northern ruins of Genthal, on His Holy Endros's Most Holiest of Days. Midnight. Don't be late." He turned.

"We're not through yet," I snapped. "Come back here!" I tried to reach for him and fell on my face. Too much magic. Too many spells. He knew, the bastard. My fingers dug into the soil. I wanted to pull it out from under him like a rug, knowing such a feat was impossible. In my state, I would wind up killing myself.

Realizing there was nothing else I could do, I screamed.

When my voice finally died with the wind, I heard footsteps above. My eyes tried to focus in the dark. I could see the moonlight still, and maybe what appeared to be the first traces of dawn, just painting splashes of purple across the blue sky. Felan drew closer, dragging his leg through the dirt. His hair was plastered to one side of his face, smeared with mud and dried saliva. His shirt was covered in blood.

"Rosha," Felan started. His face contorted.

"I'm—" I began. And then I realized what he'd just said.

"Rosha," he repeated. There was a knowing tone in his voice.

"You remember now," I said.

"The creature kept saying it. After you went inside it, its body kept repeating your name, like it was stuck in a loop. And then I realized where I'd heard it before. I realized why you felt so…familiar."

I grunted. "The damage to your memory wasn't permanent."

"Maybe I just wanted to forget." He turned his head to the side. "Is that all there is? Are you finally out of lies? Or are you hiding something else?"

"It's not my fault you didn't recognize me," I said. "I didn't even know you were Lord Cato's son. I didn't come here for you. I came here for my father. You saw him. Elry. Count Enosh Tar'elian. Is that enough explanation for you?"

He looked like he was in pain, and not just because he'd been half-mangled by my father. "But you knew me. And you lied to my face. Even after…everything, you still lied to my face."

"We," I pointed out, "were never friends, Felan. You told me that, a long time ago."

His face tightened. "You're right."

"I owe you nothing. You yourself told me it's not wise to trust you. Do you remember how we were? Do you remember how much you hated me?"

His eyes flashed. "I remember you left me to die. So much of that night is lost to me. But that rain—and that stranger. All my magic, gone. You can't imagine what that felt like, having someone take everything that made you who you were, everything that made you whole, and leave nothing but emptiness behind."

I closed my eyes. I could see the image he'd painted just as clearly, but there was no sense letting him know. I never wanted that night to define the rest of my life. Surely he should have come to the same conclusion. "So why did you think I should have been truthful?" I finally asked.

"You left me to die," he repeated. His voice sounded broken.

"You don't have to remind me," I said. "It's haunted me all these years. Do you want me to apologize?"

"What would that do?" he asked, almost calmly. "It won't give my magic back, would it?" It was a truth he must have wrestled with all these years.

"No," I agreed.

Felan turned to something in the distance. I couldn't lift my head to follow his gaze, but I saw his brow furrow. I heard shouting, and the air tingled a little with the sensation of someone drawing briefly on the *agan*. "And now the mages are here for you." He gave a soft sigh. "It's almost morning and I've yet to plan for my father's funeral. You should stay here. It's not as if there's anywhere you can go."

"A fitting end," I whispered.

"Goodbye, Rosha," he said. "I'm sorry it has to come to this."

I watched him walk away.

ACT FOUR

CHAPTER 35

THE FIREKEEPER'S PROMISE

Three bells, each ring spaced approximately thirty breaths apart, marked the beginning of winter (and school year) in Eheldeth. They came from the single tower set on the northern end of the gardens, a structure of which only half remained intact. An accident connected to The Six—the safe rooms were in the buildings across the yard. It was thought that their attempts to harness the dragon caused fissures in the ground that sank half the belltower. It was an easy repair, but the mages kept it there as a reminder of the damage reckless use of magic could cause. A tour of the ruins was always on the agenda for the beginning of each year. "Six Mages, Three Dead," was the chant. *Never forget. You are not gifted with the power of the gods simply so you can use it for destruction.*

And yet…

I lay there in that cell, covered with cold sweat and wracked with fever from the days of pushing myself to the limits, and could only think of how Lord Cato was *one* of the six. He should have been expelled. There was no doubt that he and his friends brought the dragon over with every intention of breaking the rules. His defense quoted his quest for knowledge, his desire to contribute to Dageian supremacy, all while neglecting to mention there are ways to do things the right way. The *right* way never occurred to Lord Cato. He did what he wanted and got off with a slap on the wrist. He was suspended for a week and then returned in time to finish the semester with flying colours. By the time he graduated, nobody brought up that he got three of his friends killed.

I knew, even when I was just a fledgling student in Eheldeth, that no such glory awaited me. It was baked into the lectures, in the side glances of the keepers who were assigned to keep watch because I was some sort of *special* student. "Rein yourself in, Rosha," they'd warn, if they saw me attempting a spell that was more ambitious than my classmates'. "You don't know what that will do."

"What if I do?" I remember retorting after the fourth or fifth time. I was sick of their badgering, sick of the insinuation I got as far as I did simply because my father had been seen getting *too* friendly with the Firekeeper. "What if I've done it before?"

The surprised look on the keepers' faces seemed to take on a life of its own. "Don't make such jokes," one said, erasing the runes on my parchment by writing over them, a spell that made them inert. "You can't possibly have."

"Making something *move* as if it was alive…is practically sacrilege," his co-keeper added. "It requires a connection to the *agan* amplified by organic matter. By *blood*."

"Blood magic is still magic," I replied.

It was true. There was no difference. Drawing on blood made it easier to tap into the *agan*, but the *agan* was life essence, a substance that bound us all no matter where you accessed it. Living to living, living to dead, soul to soul. Even sources out in nature—hidden deep within the bowels of the earth or flowing from a crevice somewhere—drew from the same fabric. I was always so confused why Eheldeth treated the subject of blood magic with horror. My own blood was right *there*. I wasn't suggesting I go take someone else's. But the way they reacted, you would have thought otherwise.

"We need to take you to the Firekeeper," the mages said in unison.

"I'm not going to talk to that bitch," I told them under my breath.

They weren't amused. They each tried to grab my arms. I broke free, slapping one mage away. By now the whole classroom had fallen silent. Everyone was looking at me. I knew I would be the talk of the entire school for the next week, the next month even. My only salvation was that by then, Felan was already gone, so my embarrassment wouldn't be as great as it could have been. Even so…

"I'll go," I finally grumbled. I got up, my face hot. Eyes followed me as I walked behind the keepers. They were whispering to each other. I caught traces of their conversation—words like *travesty* and *she shouldn't even be here* and *how can her family afford this place?* I held my tongue.

Firekeeper Ceres was busy at her table when they arrived. She waved them off, and then beckoned with her right middle and index fingers.

Like I was a dog who had to obey her command. I stood there and crossed my arms.

"You're as stubborn as your father," she commented, "with none of the charm."

"What does that mean?" I demanded.

"Whatever you think it does," Ceres said. "Sit, by Dorsin's beard. I don't want to be screaming at you from across the room."

I walked towards her and stopped behind a chair. "I can hear you fine from here, can't I?" I asked.

"You know the rules here," she said. "You know why they're important."

"You say it's to protect the citizens of Dageis," I replied.

"Magic runs Dageis. But it can also swallow it whole. These little… rebellions of yours…are becoming a frequent occurrence. I can't protect you forever. Every incident, every stray remark, sends a barrage of inquiries my way. I'm fond of your father, Rosha, I really am, but even that can't stop the whole wrath of the mage council when they find a reason to be done with you."

"I know I'm not wanted here. You've never had to hide that."

She shook her head. "That's not it. But your people—"

I slammed my hands on her exquisitely oiled desk. "You haven't even eradicated the Gorenten from this land. All the people who owned this continent before yours arrived—we practiced magic without your Dageian rules and somehow nothing swallowed us then. What makes it so different now? Because *you* say so?"

"I'm not here to pick a fight," she sighed. She picked up her cup and swirled the tea inside. "These are the facts, Rosha, nothing more. I know you find them unjust, but I didn't make these rules."

"You're upholding them. That makes you just as bad as the people who made them. You know they're unfair, and yet here you are telling me there's nothing you can do—that *unfair* is just the way things are." I balled up my hands and slowly straightened my back as I removed them from her desk. "I was promised a place where I could practice magic and not have to hide it like I did back in Jin-Sayeng. Believe me, Fire-keeper, I didn't want to go here. I didn't want to leave the only place I could ever call home. But they told me all the things that once held me back wouldn't exist in Dageis. The Empire of Dageis would give you everything Jin-Sayeng or Gorent never could. You didn't tell me I was exchanging one set of shackles for another."

She glanced at her surroundings—her office was luxuriously furnished—before glancing through the window, where we had a full view of the pond. Cherry trees fringed the edges of it. "Shackles?" she asked, with a note of amusement. "You must have been in some terribly gorgeous prisons before, child."

"You know what I mean," I mumbled.

"I don't."

I stared at her. She was a beautiful woman—slim, with hair that looked like golden threads. A chiseled jaw. Hips that had not borne children and never would. She once told my father (when she thought I couldn't hear her) that she spent enough time around children to never want them herself. She was voted Firekeeper years ago already, and then again, and was given the rare chance of being reinstated for a third run recently. Feats that were impressive for a woman her age. She couldn't have been more than forty-five—certainly not even fifty yet. I wondered what story she heard while growing up. What did her own elders tell her? *You could have the world if you just believed,* or *be careful, because the world will break you?* I know what mine did.

"You don't give me a chance to prove myself," I said. "I tell you what I can do, and you tell me *don't.* You lecture about danger yet do not figure out the means to circumvent it without stifling my power. Instead of helping, instead of guiding, you silence me."

"It's not an option if it breaks the rules."

"You don't stop to talk to me if it does. All you care about is telling me to stop. I can't draw attention to myself, I can't discover new ways to do things, I must only do what the others are doing—the same students who are only here because their parents could afford it, who can barely connect to the *agan* without their eyeballs popping out of their sockets. How do I build a future out of this?"

"Graduating Eheldeth alone is enough to secure a bright future for you. You can work in just about any industry. You can get a position in the building industry, or the sanitation department, or the airships... good, honest jobs."

"How am I supposed to excel?"

"I don't understand. You get high grades, Rosha. I was going to write a glowing commendation for you after you graduate."

"A commendation? How generous of you, Firekeeper. And yet you still refuse to put me on the scholarship track. You've never even brought it up."

She smiled. "Ah. So this is what this is all about. You know the scholarship track isn't necessary to graduate Eheldeth at all."

"The students you've earmarked as *worth keeping an eye out for,* the ones you personally introduce to high-ranking members of the mage council for mentorship so that their path is all but set after graduation will have a much easier time than some nobody leaving these gates with a piece of paper and a pat on the back." I took a deep breath. "Eheldeth's reputation as *the* only magical academy in this empire that matters rests solely on the shoulders of that track, Firekeeper. Outside of it, I might as well just be scrubbing pots by the dockside."

The patience on her expression was well-practiced. "The scholarship track is indeed a rare honour, but you know seats in it are reserved for—"

"Your best?"

"Those who are *best* capable of the rigorous demands placed on those who would bear the burdens of servitude. Eheldeth is not just a school, Rosha. We are the heart of the empire—we were established not just to nurture it, but to protect it from both outside and within."

"And how do you become capable for those rigorous demands, I wonder? Extra lessons, private tutors, special camps…you hand those out like candy to just about everyone but me. I've tried to borrow enchantments from the shop, and they deny me every time. Money can't be the object, because you know Enosh is more than capable of coughing it out. Let's talk about being the *best*, Firekeeper. You know I can cast circles around every student in my classes. You know I can craft spells so intricate they would think one of the keepers did it. You know we can sit here and discuss magical theory for a whole afternoon without me once falling asleep or losing track of the subject."

"You can be proud of those things," Ceres agreed. "But—"

"But they're not enough?"

"We have a system here…"

"I've asked around. It's all but impossible to get a title once you graduate outside of the scholarship track. To even become an adherent, a high-ranking bearer must commit to having me under his wing, and they've picked those students out last semester. The only thing I've got left are the exams for my final year, and I don't know how much harder I have to impress you with those. What's the price for your support, Firekeeper? Perfection? I'm thinking there's no way. What I don't understand is how someone who claims to be as concerned for my family as you are—sometimes *enthusiastically* so—"

"Rosha."

"I remember when you travelled with me and my father, Firekeeper. The walls are thin."

She coloured slightly. "To return to the matter at hand—yes, I understand you are an excellent student, Rosha. But you're raw. You require too much work to clean up. You read a paragraph of theory and then throw the rest of the book away. You skirt the rules whenever you can, and even if the result blows everything out of the water the process leaves your keepers uneasy. This isn't what has stopped you from getting on the scholarship track, but the seats are limited and there are others better suited."

"Are there?" It was taking all of my patience not to start screaming. "I know it sounds arrogant for me to say it, but I know what I'm doing. My record speaks for itself. Maybe I don't fit—I make it work anyway, and with the proper resources you know the kind of mage I could become. You know what I have done to get this far. You know I can go much further. Give me what you give everyone else." I said the last part slowly, softly. Hearing my own pleading was painful. Embarrassing. *I shouldn't have to beg.*

"We are." Her expression was earnest. She truly believed it. She truly believed I couldn't tell the difference between how they treated me and how they treated everyone else, that I hadn't seen their gazes skip past the best of my work to settle on those who fit better in their imposed boxes. And she believed it so well she even had herself fooled.

"Give me what other people of my talents get," I said, exasperated. "Or else are you telling me that no matter how hard I work or how well I learn my craft...even if I bleed for it, sacrifice sleep and time and my whole life, you will never give me a chance? You will never recognize I could be more? Stop clipping my wings, Firekeeper, and let me soar!"

Foolish, arrogant child, I thought as I slowly sat up in my cell to face Firekeeper Ceres as myself for the first time in what felt like forever. *How long will you believe you know better?* The years had barely left a mark on the woman. Glamour? Potions for the skin? It didn't matter how she did it— she was still beautiful, still a Firekeeper (nearing the end of her term now, but due for a fourth if rumours were to be believed). In the mean- time, I had grown up and proven nothing after all. My little shop in the middle of nowhere was hardly the sort of thing that could have made her regret she ever doubted me. Worse. I ran away and became a crimi- nal. The stories they tell about me in Eheldeth were not the sort I once dreamt about. Rosha, who thought she could do better. Rosha, the worthless rebel. Rosha, the has-been that never-was.

It stings to think you were once destined for greatness only to find out you are a cautionary tale at best. There was once a time I couldn't fathom such a possibility. But the last few weeks had proven I could sink deeper. I wasn't done failing.

"Hello Rosha," Ceres said, sitting down on the bench next to the cell. "How are you?"

"Just tell me when the execution is," I replied. "We don't have to pretend to be polite with each other. I'm not in the mood."

"Is that a joke?"

"Exile gave me time to work on my humour, Firekeeper."

"You have a long way to go." She held a piece of paper in her hand —she lifted it up to read it. "It says here you've been running a charms shop in Klossaka, of all places. Hardly the sort of place I would expect an outlaw mage of *your* calibre to be. Someone like you could have carved out a place in the underbelly of Dageis—there is always demand in Chylos for assassins. The best ones have made names for themselves. I expected you would end up like that woman, the Killer Rose. Thorn on My Backside, more like. Gods, I hate her."

"You still haven't caught her."

"The woman is insidious. For every three mages I send to Chylos, she kills one and incapacitates the others. I don't have an endless supply, you know."

"I wasn't stupid enough to go where I know you look," I pointed out.

"Even if it meant dying in obscurity? You butted heads with me all throughout your years in Eheldeth precisely because you felt like you deserved more. But the moment you get away…you hide out in Dageis's ass crack." I could tell she wanted to laugh but was at least polite enough to keep it inside.

I shrugged. "Enjoy revelling in the irony," I said. "You owe me the courtesy of answering my question."

"I don't. But *you* owe *me* the courtesy of answering mine. From the beginning, Rosha. Remember: I'll know if you lie."

I sighed. "Enosh was missing. I had a hunch that Lord Cato might know his whereabouts, so I made my way here and inadvertently found myself in his service. He disappeared one day. While I was looking for him, I stumbled on his body…and something else in the attic."

"The simulacrum," Ceres said.

"Yes. I guessed Lord Cato was using it to position himself as the emperor."

"I suspected something was off about the emperor for years," Ceres said. "Moments where he didn't seem *quite* right. His personality changed on a whim. Sometimes he was arrogant, callous. Other times he appeared thoughtful, willing to listen to my requests…only for him to completely forget what we talked about, mere weeks later. I thought someone was manipulating him, maybe even pretending to be him—which can be done through an *agan*-mirror in poor lighting."

"Only someone who had been Firekeeper as often as you would have made that observation."

"Perhaps. I'm not the only one who's been voted in more than once, which concerns me. That means the others were willfully obtuse…or just didn't care."

I almost laughed. "Why do you sound surprised? Dageis has posited the man as an *undying* emperor."

"We've been led to believe the emperor is a powerful mage who uses the *agan* to extend his lifespan—a skill one can only learn from ancient beings in the continent, the ka-eng. Your father was once convinced he was dead. During the Hafed war, when Drusgaya was attacked, Enosh claimed he saw the emperor's body in a pool of his own blood. Yet weeks later, he showed up to a public ceremony without a mark on him, as healthy as could ever be. When Enosh expressed his disbelief, I told him what they all tell us: the Dageian Empire has been built on the idea that its emperor is blessed by the gods. I always assumed the person who died in the war had just been a body double. That he is actually a simulacrum, controlled by one of its richest merchants, is deeply concerning." She rubbed her temples with her fingers. "I don't know what possessed you to take it this far after you discovered Lord Cato's body. You should have called for me then. You could have even called for me *after*, when you knew I was looking for your father, too. Instead, you used the simulacrum yourself."

"To stop you from discovering me."

She smiled. "My little trick worked."

"In case you've forgotten, I'm still an outlaw."

"You don't trust me?"

"You just admitted to tricking me. Of course not. And you sent bearers on my tail."

"That wasn't me, if it's all the same to time you. And I started investigating your father's disappearance long before you did. I didn't have as much success, but you know I hold your family dear in my heart, Rosha." Ceres cleared her throat. "Did you find him?"

"I did."

"*Did?*"

"He was taken, right before you found me in the church. They want me to give the emperor in return."

"Who is *them*?"

"They wouldn't tell me. Not yet."

She got up and tugged the cell door open. It wasn't locked. It swung outward easily.

"What is this?" I demanded.

"You're not in the mage council's custody," she said.

"What?"

She indicated the room with a sweep of her hands. "You're in a private home."

"A home *with its own dungeon?*"

"Look, I didn't want to ask how the owner likes to pass time. Let's not judge an old woman's quirks. It's her only spare room." I opened my mouth to argue further, and Ceres stopped me with a wave of her hand. "The point, my dear. Lord Cato was assassinated. Someone else wanted the emperor. Someone who *knew* Lord Cato was the most recent puppeteer."

I nodded. "That's as far as I understand."

"I'm afraid if I take this to the council… it will all be swept under the rug." She said it in a voice that took me by surprise. She must have noticed my expression, because she gave a grim smile. "But of course, dear Rosha. You didn't think *I* controlled all of the council?"

"Three times elected…"

She made a dismissive gesture. "That's nothing. I never openly defied them, so they enjoy having me there. To be honest, I would have stopped that first term, except…as I said. Too many aberrations. I suspected something foul was afoot, but nothing this deep. I must admit it's beyond my capabilities. What I'm *allowed* to do. I suspect the moment I start inquiring, I might end up the same way as Lord Cato. Maybe I'm wrong. Maybe this whole mess is sanctioned by the merchant guild, and the mage council has no idea it is even happening. I can't take that chance."

"You're Firekeeper."

"So was Lord Cato, for a time. Ah, you didn't know? In his youth, he sat on the mage council. He only transferred to the merchant guild after his first term was done—a thing the merchant guild was more than happy to embrace him for. Perhaps he's outlived his usefulness." She straightened herself and finally got up so she could look at me. "I need names."

"Why are you looking at me like that?"

"You wanted to a chance to prove yourself," she said. "Here it is."

"A little too late. I'm an outlaw."

"You keep saying. That's exactly what I need."

"What do you mean?"

"Controlling the simulacrum requires blood magic." She gave me a pointed look.

"Gods, you make it sound like I murdered children," I replied.

"It's not a far leap for those who find themselves blurring the lines, as you did. We do not do blood magic in the empire."

I laughed. "What do you call using mage-thralls, Firekeeper?"

"You know there's a difference," Ceres said. "Mage-thralls are kept safe from spells by their rune-tattoos. This is unfiltered, unbridled use of magic while imbibing on your own life force. It's dangerous."

"Lord Cato didn't seem to have those problems."

She sighed. "It's always the ones who ought to know better."

"And you're saying I don't?"

"I'm saying you always had the predisposition towards bending the rules, Tar'elian. Given who your father is—"

"Comparing myself to him will do the exact opposite of what you're trying to, Firekeeper."

She drummed her fingers along one of the bars. "How does Lord Cato get away with blood magic? Obviously, people in the council are involved, possibly a number in Eheldeth itself, because people were willing to *look* away for years. You do not know who *they* are, and I don't, either. But it's my job to know and to do that, I need someone outside the system. Someone I'm *sure* of, despite the fact that she hates me for a reason I have yet to comprehend." The edges of her lips tugged into a half-smile.

"Every time I practice magic, you can send mages after me," I pointed out.

"If we have a reason to suspect something happened in the vicinity," she said. "Rogue mages practice magic all the time and by the time we get there—if we even get there—they're long gone."

"Your trick—"

"A trick to flush you out. If you had been the real emperor, and not a rogue mage doing something behind him, you would have known better than to fall for it." She smiled. "No need to look so angry. Of *course* we tell the students differently. You have to. Consider my honesty a gift."

"You bitch."

"Don't get me wrong," she continued. "We're *good* at what we do, Rosha. Eventually, we do catch up. Even Miss Killer Rose can't outrun me forever. And the prospect is much worse for someone like you, who was already inside Eheldeth and decided to flout its rules. We can't have students walking into Eheldeth, learning about magic, and then walking out to use the techniques for their own purposes now, can we? It's not good for our reputation. So I'm giving you a proposition. A trade, if you will. You wanted an arrangement of this nature before—a chance for you to show me what you're worth."

"You want me to work for you, in exchange for my freedom."

She laughed. It was beautiful and jackal-like all at once.

CHAPTER 36

CHAINS OF EHELDETH

I shouldn't have been surprised by her admission that the mage council knew less about outlaw mages than they let on. If anything, I recalled she taught the class on magical accidents herself—a way for her to get to know students better, to profile them before they grew into power. She enjoyed pretending she could predict the children's temperaments even before they were aware of it themselves. I can imagine her going through a checklist, watching everyone's reactions to her lessons—this one needs an extra eye on her, *he's* harmless, that other will experiment and cause untold harm. And thus her conclusion that I had the predisposition to bending the rules. Not that it was much of a leap. Enosh had the same gripes.

Was that why she never recommended me for the scholarship track? I once expected it to be a given, considering how friendly she was with my father. It wasn't as if I would have embarrassed her; after Felan disappeared, I had the highest average grades in my entire section. It was difficult to become someone of importance in Eheldeth as it was, especially with the amount of nepotism going on—high-ranking officials giving precedence to their own offspring, or the offspring of their friends, or whoever gave them the right gift.

Connections made all the difference to a mage's prospects. Keepers formed the backbone of the school, which worked closely with the government and military to manage Dageian affairs at home. Bearers served wherever they were needed—to every corner of the empire and back, and even abroad. Adherents supported both. There were minor titles too, more than I cared to remember—the important part is that they were mostly open to students who graduated from the scholarship track because it came with the mage council's blessings. As far as I was concerned, there was no future elsewhere. I couldn't get excited over the prospect of public service...of cleaning gutters or mind-numbingly blasting *agan* into airship mechanisms over and over again. They were important jobs, to be sure, but they weren't for me. I wanted to work with the council, I wanted to be right at the heart of things. I was promised *magic*, the chance to solve problems with spells and maybe, perhaps, change the world. Perhaps it was too much to dream of. Perhaps my own ambitions weighed me down in the end.

Firekeeper Ceres was right. This was the closest chance I would ever get to fulfilling my dreams. I could help weed out the corrupt official. I wouldn't just save my father, but actually do something worthwhile and show her and the rest of her damned council how wrong they were to look past me.

All I had to do...was to be her dog.

Life couldn't have been more ironic if it tried. A part of me felt I would have been more at ease working for Lord Cato than for Fire-keeper Ceres. He, at least, didn't know *me*. He couldn't lord my entire past *and* my family over me. Ceres had everything that could ruin me, and I knew she would do it in a heartbeat if I so much as gave her a reason to. She posited the arrangement as a proposition, but I knew there was no room to reject her. *Prison* was the other choice. Maybe not death, but certainly a lifetime of obscurity. I hadn't even made a big enough fuss for notoriety. And if I rejected her and made it personal at the same time, there was no room for mercy, either. In the Empire of Dageis, you didn't become Firekeeper without a touch of ruthlessness.

They let me sweat the rest of the fever out for the next two nights. On the third day, I felt much better, which was all Ceres needed to have me outfitted and led out of there. She took me straight back to Lord Cato's mansion, which was now devoid of servants. Everyone was sent home under the guise of an investigation. Well—almost everyone.

Nasuha greeted us when we arrived.

"You need assistance," Ceres explained. "She seemed the most interested about you, so I had her investigated, and..."

"Investigated, she says," Nasuha drawled. She flexed her neck left and right.

"I'm sorry. I'm just very persuasive," Ceres replied, with a small laugh. I suspected she had Nasuha interrogated under torture, though you would never get her to admit it. "She knew what you were and kept it from the council, which makes her an accomplice, of sorts. Which works perfectly for my purposes." Without considering what else we might have to say, she gestured to us and made her way down to the crypts with the surety of someone who had been there before.

The emperor stood in the corner, arms folded beside Lord Cato's corpse as if it were a mummy itself. There was a rune on its forehead, drawn with gold ink. A powerful spell that rendered everything else on it inert unless the glyph maker—which I assumed was Ceres—said so. Which made Ceres's intentions all the clearer. I wasn't to be given access to it anymore, not without her permission.

She placed her hand on the rune. Blue light flooded the air between her palm and the simulacrum's forehead, and then the rune slowly disappeared, looking like it was being sucked straight into her palm. The light faded. The emperor blinked before carefully shuffling towards me. It stood a foot away, as if it was a soldier awaiting my command.

"Fascinating," Ceres said, placing a cold hand on my shoulder. "The craftmanship of this thing is unbelievable. So lifelike. Even when I know I am being fooled, I can't tell *how*." She walked around me before approaching the simulacrum.

"I thought you mages know everything," Nasuha interjected.

"No," Ceres replied thoughtfully. "No, we don't. That's why the Empire formed Eheldeth in the first place. This continent yielded so much treasure, but also more danger than the first settlers—"

"Invaders," I corrected.

"—bargained for," she continued, like I didn't talk at all. "Dageis cannot function without the scholars of Eheldeth. Everything we learn about the *agan*, all information about those connected to its strands, is filed away, to be studied by keepers for years. We say there are rules, but truth be told, the one rule you can only rely on is that *nothing is definite*. We will say that something cannot be done, and yet find out the next day that it has already, enough times for it to be embarrassing. You can claim that one cannot reliably create something living with the *agan* and yet..." She indicated the emperor with a sweep of her delicate fingers.

"That thing isn't *agan*-wrought," I blurted out.

She blinked. "Oh?"

I took the emperor's hand and showed it to her. The veins running through it were greenish, not bright blue. There were wrinkles in the folds of its skin. "Using the *agan* to craft something organic is like playing with clay. Have you ever known anyone so good they can recreate every crevice, every imperfection? Most people who have the capability won't —we all have the incessant desire to fix what can be fixed."

"An acute observation," Ceres said, falling back to her old patterns as my professor. I don't think she even really meant it.

I frowned, hating the tone. I dropped the emperor's hand and crossed my arms. "Whatever this thing is, I know this: it grows old. The man who killed Lord Cato—I believe he holds the key. He looked like a younger version of the emperor. The same eyes, the same features. And if he was being controlled by someone else—well, they were doing a good job, because I didn't see him break connection once."

"Interesting," Ceres replied. "This tells me you have no objection to what I'm about to ask you."

"You want me to bring the emperor to them," I said. "To trap them."

"Is that an option?" she asked. I couldn't tell if she was fishing for information, or purposely acting obtuse and knew everything already. Not that it mattered to me.

"This…Targus promised to release Enosh if I brought the emperor to a certain place in Genthal on Endros's Day. Which is a trap, too, because they've all but made it clear they need me to control the emperor. They need me, or they need to kill me. I'm attuned to the damn thing and until I'm theirs or out of the way, they can't use it." To show her, I took a step backward. The simulacrum swayed to the side and took a step after me.

"Interesting," Ceres repeated.

I frowned. "Is that all you're going to say?"

Her forehead creased. "What else do you want me to?" she asked. "It sounds simple enough. Go to Genthal. Bring the emperor with you. Something you are surely capable of. And Genthal is a wonderful place —all hills and fresh breeze."

"You're not going to get the answers you need if they kill me, and I highly doubt they have any intentions of just handing your lover over, either. If I have the predisposition to break rules, then he has the predisposition towards pissing people off."

A furtive smile. "Oh, I know."

"Targus seems to have a personal vendetta against him. I can't explain why. The only time I've ever seen someone *that* angry with him is when it involves his scorned lovers."

Ceres opened her mouth.

"If you say *interesting* again, I'm going to leave," I grumbled.

"You will get assistants," Ceres said. "I have no intention of sending you there alone." She snapped her fingers, pointing at Nasuha. "There's one. I'm going to gather the others. Look at you." She pinched my chin between her fingers. "I promised to take care of you. I already have. Your brother Ryo is on his way home with the best guards I can offer. Yet here you are, still looking at me like I ordered you to jump to your death. Why would I do such a thing?"

"I don't know," I said. "Because you're the sort of person who likes to?"

She tittered. "Do you know," she eventually said, a thoughtful note in her voice, "that Adherent Orsalian, who died in the battle of Drus-gaya during the war with Hafod, was my cousin?"

I paused. I didn't.

"She who gave her life for Dageis," she continued. "A hero of our times, for all of time. And I miss her—I still find myself making note of things I would say for her for the next time we saw each other, only to remember it will never be again. That sort of loneliness is...difficult. You want to say goodbye, but you can't because you don't want to forget them, either. Your father was close with her, too—amazing, considering both their temperaments. I believe it's why we've kept in touch all these years. Grief, when shared, is easier to bear, and people don't seem all that dead when you can talk about them with someone else who loved them as much as you did. And yet..." She gave a soft sigh. "Do you know how hard it is not to be overshadowed by such greatness?"

"I've never been in that position," I told her.

"I still love her, but gods, after everything I've done to be Firekeeper, nothing else seems to compare." She placed her hand on my shoulder. "Help me, Rosha, and I will help you. But you have to stop pretending I have it out for you. I'm not your enemy here."

Maybe Firekeeper Ceres was right about not being my enemy, but it was hard not to resent the hand feeding you scraps while pretending it wasn't. Hard to accept they were being so generous now, when nothing had changed except this time, they needed you. This time, for the first time, they had something to gain. *Here, Rosha—here's everything you ever wanted*, said with a smirk and a grin. I better be grateful. As if I hadn't heard such things all my life.

I boarded a boat bound for Genthal two days later, feeling like I was dragging shackles on both my ankles. My circle was already waiting for me. *Some circle*, I thought bitterly. You couldn't even call it a *circle of mages*, which is what the term normally meant. Nasuha was a vagrant caught in the whirlwind of events. The second was Bearer Lontas, who had one arm in a sling and couldn't even offer me a glance, so intent was he on glaring daggers at Nasuha.

The fourth and last one didn't even come as a surprise. Felan sat the furthest away, his brow furrowed. Felan, the magicless mage. "She's sending us ahead," he said, by way of greeting. "She wants me to serve as your guide. I pointed out there must be a thousand more qualified, but…"

"But you're an accomplice in hiding my status," I said, "and thus easier to control."

He gave a small nod.

I sat beside him. My presence unsettled him, but the boat didn't give us that many options. I glanced to the other side, where the emperor sat from across us, a glyph on his forehead. It told me Ceres meant for us to wait for her on the other side, that we were not supposed to make a move until she'd said so. Even after making it quite clear how much of my life and future was in her hands, she remained uncertain of me. Wise of her, probably. Given half the chance, I would be out of there in no time.

"What are her terms?" Felan asked, breaking the silence.

"For assisting her, you mean?"

"I assume she promised something in return for all of this. You have never been the helpful type."

"She said *freedom*," I said, ignoring what sounded like a jibe. Not that I could have argued with the fact of it. "But there are reasons I believe it won't be easy. Either way, it's all in her hands."

Felan cleared his throat. "I am curious, if you'll indulge me."

"Ah. Chatting again, so casually? And here I thought we'd said our goodbyes."

He frowned and looked away. "I am only…wondering why someone like you had to go rogue at all. You have, from what I remember, every capability of graduating with flying colours. Graduating *at all* wouldn't have been a problem."

I shrugged. "Mistakes happen."

"Or is it that you thought merely graduating wasn't good enough for someone like you? Mistakes happen, and you couldn't have that. You couldn't finish your exams flawlessly and you'd run out of excuses—you certainly didn't have *me* to blame anymore—so you gave up. You always were the type to throw it all away because of one little imperfection." He couldn't hide the ice in his tone. Once, I would have jumped at the chance to retort. Now I just closed my eyes and let his voice fade in the background. I wasn't going to argue with someone I needed to spend the next few hours with. Genthal was easily a whole day's travel from Drus-gaya, and probably more. Even the Firekeeper, with all the power she held, couldn't possibly make travel easier.

In the distance, I heard something splash. I opened my eyes in time to see a gigantic swirl in the water.

"Is that tuna?" Nasuha called to the captain. She glanced at me. "We get a bunch down in Gorent this time of the year. It's a great time for fishing."

"Doesn't sound like tuna," Felan ventured.

"Doubt a rich boy would know," Nasuha said. "No offense, my lord, but—"

"I agree with him," the captain said, leaving the cabin in a hurry. He rushed straight for the sails. "I'm going to need help. You—" He pointed at Lontas.

"Me," Lontas repeated.

"The sails."

"You were paid to bring us ashore. We're not your crew."

"Well, I don't have one, and something's sucking the boat under-neath. We need to—"

Those were the last words out of his mouth before I heard a gut-clenching creak. It sounded like wood breaking, like bones being snapped in half. Something rose out from the water, something covered with black scales, complete with a white belly and enormous teeth. It cut through the boat in half, chomping through the floorboards until it exploded into splinters around its mouth. I didn't get much more time to admire the beast. We spilled out of the wrecked vessel like innards and went straight into the sea.

CHAPTER 37

THE FORGOTTEN ISLE

The myths of Gorent and my mother's island of Akki in Jin-Sayeng resembled each other in many ways. Both had versions of a story of how our people came from the sea. How the Moon God became lonely and went down to take a swim. And he was so beautiful the mermaids and mermen and even sea serpents were enraptured, so that when he left, they all followed him out to the shores to become people. Only he returned to the skies not long after. They inhabited the continent and the islands, unable to follow their god, unable to return to their homes.

"But it's why the sea is inside you," Kefier once said. "If you close your eyes and wait, you'll hear the sea calling your name."

I obeyed dutifully. "I don't hear anything," I replied.

"Nothing? Close your eyes tighter."

I shut my eyes deeper. I saw a glimpse of blue in the darkness, swirls of it rising like mist from the ocean at dawn. I felt it enveloping me and thought I heard voices. One was louder than the others. It sounded like a boy's, maybe a man's. It sounded like he was calling for help.

But before I could decide if it was real or something I was imagining, I heard wind and waves. Startled, I opened my eyes just in time to see Kefier removing a conch shell he had pressed over my ear. "I told you to close your eyes," he said ruefully.

"That voice…" I said. "It didn't come from the shell."

He didn't know what I meant. He never did. And I'd never told him that it meant the world he tried. And now…

I thought I heard voices again as I held my breath and fought my

294

way to the surface. It felt like the sea was whispering around me. Traces of nonsense—of gossip and half-formed thoughts.

I found myself on the shore, right underneath a blanket of stars. I crawled along the wet sand, wondering how far we'd gotten. We weren't even an hour off Drusgaya. Yet I couldn't see the shadow of the city on the horizon. I could see nothing but ocean around me. Had the others survived?

The air hanging over the shore glimmered, like a curtain dripping wet from the rain. The hair on the back of my arms stood on end. I was looking at the remnants of a spell. A protection ward, from the looks of it. It was rapidly fading, as if something had neutralized it. I wondered what it would have done otherwise. Covering an entire area with protection spells was an endeavour requiring the participation of multiple skilled mages, which meant it should, in theory, have been sanctioned by the empire.

I saw a soft glow at the farthest end of the shore, beside a rocky cliff. It was too dark to see anything else, so I followed the light, even though it was rapidly diminishing. I stumbled on a drenched figure, slumped in the corner in a sitting position. It turned its head towards me, revealing the emperor's face.

"Ceres's rune is gone," I told him, touching his forehead. "Is that what killed the spell?" I glanced at the sky again. It was possible. If the spell-veil was created by mages of the empire, then it would have been attuned to a select few, including Ceres herself. Anything carrying traces of the Firekeeper of Eheldeth would nullify it. She would have to reactivate the spell if she wanted to protect the area again.

"At least it didn't hurt you," I continued. Ceres's rune hardly left a mark on his skin.

The simulacrum smiled in response, a greeting that seemed almost child-like. It was strange how much more inclined he was to respond to me now. You would think he understood the conversation. I paused, wondering.

"Have you seen the others?" I tested.

The smile didn't disappear from his face. He merely nodded. There was no sign he understood me, but I felt at ease. Perhaps I was getting used to his blank-eyed stare.

"Let's go find them, then," I said.

He uttered gibberish, just before he gave the faintest indication of a nod. When I stepped away, he followed obediently.

We combed the shores for the others. I couldn't see much of anything except seaweed and sand. It was growing so much darker now, and I felt a flicker of worry. If there weren't other islands here, then it could only mean they all went down with the ship.

I decided to settle down for the night. It was cold, and my drenched clothes weren't helping. I found enough driftwood to make a small pile on the sand. I pressed my palms together, feeling the familiar sensation of heat on the surface of my skin, before I sent flames over the pile. The fire danced along the wet wood. I smelled seawater bubbling, and there was a brief flash of light before everything died down.

I swore under my breath.

"You're not doing that right," a voice called from the darkness.

"Felan," I greeted. "You're not dead."

He grunted and slumped down across the sand. He began to rearrange the kindling.

"They should have taught a class on this in Eheldeth," he said, offhandedly. "*Practical uses of magic.*"

I sniffed. "What for? Most students there don't need to light stoves themselves."

"True." He gave an ironic smile. "I had to, living in Sorna without servants, but by then I no longer had magic."

"I'm sorry," I said.

He turned to me quizzically.

I felt a flush of embarrassment, of shame. I didn't like apologizing. It was showing your weakness, admitting you'd erred, which in many ways wasn't the wisest thing to do around people who would use any opportunity to turn against you. If competence was the only thing you had to protect you, then you better damn well stick to the script. Apologizing to many of the children we grew up with was reason enough for them to tear me to shreds. I concentrated on lighting the campfire first, allowing the flames to carry all my emotions away.

"I'm sorry," I repeated. "For what happened. I'm sorry I left you." The words didn't make me feel any better, but I didn't say them for my benefit. I turned to gaze at him and wondered if I was merely imagining the shadow of pain on his brow. My apologies were useless. They couldn't change the past.

Felan gave a deep sigh. "It's all done, anyway," he replied. "As I said. Nothing will bring it back. You learn to live with it. Without it. My whole life today has been carved by this loss and it has so far proven to be…tolerable." His fingers hovered over the fire. He turned them in a circle, as if wishing the flames to dance to the motion. But there was nothing there, not even the slightest twitch.

We heard something screech in the distance. An owl, perhaps. "Do you know where we are?" I asked.

"I assume one of the islands north of Drusgaya," he said, his voice dropping the wistful tone. "We didn't get far. I hope the others are alive."

"Unlikely."

"*We* are."

"If they hit the shore before our good friend over there, there's a chance they would have succumbed to the spell-veil in the area. Those kinds of spells just obliterate people where they stand, don't they?" I nodded towards the simulacrum. "Ceres's ego saved us. Her glyph broke the spell."

"Protection spells are always so unsophisticated," Felan said. "They cause more problems than they solve. Father dealt with complaints on it all the time, and he stopped using it in his stores as a result. The one in his basement…with all my things…" He shook his head. It was still so hard for him to believe that his father was upset enough to put up a spell to stop himself from remembering his wayward son.

"I suppose the old man was fond of you, for all his faults." I stabbed the sand with my finger. Was I thinking about his father, or mine?

Felan frowned. "That makes me almost want to mourn him. I still haven't…shed any tears."

"Is it necessary?"

"I've been told it is," he said with a shrug. "The man was the only father I've known. I feel sorrow over his passing. I miss him. He was never affectionate, but we would have these long talks, and a part of me can't believe I'll never have them with him again. But I haven't cried. It makes me feel like a terrible son, the most ungrateful offspring there ever was."

"Don't fret over it. You get used to that feeling, too."

The screeching continued. He cleared his throat. "One of us should sleep. The other can keep watch."

"You go first."

"Are you sure?"

"I can protect us while it's dark," I said. "Who knows what else is out there?"

Felan frowned, but he didn't argue. He laid his head on the sand and turned his body to the side, away from me. He fell asleep quickly. Far from the spoiled rich boy I'd known, the one who might have balked at the idea of having to sleep on the ground. It dawned on me that the years I spent learning to live with the guilt of what I'd done to him, he was simply learning to survive.

. . .

Nothing attacked us during the night. Felan opened his eyes just as the faint rays of the sun stretched over the shores and twisted his head. "You didn't switch with me," he muttered groggily. "Why didn't you wake me up?"

"You looked like you needed sleep," I replied.

He wiped his beard. "And you don't?"

"It's how I got ahead of you in Second Year."

"By not sleeping."

"I skipped lunch, too."

He narrowed his eyes. "I see."

"Why is that so hard to believe?"

"I didn't say I didn't believe it. But we're not studying for exams now."

"My thoughts keep me awake," I said. "I don't know. I guess I like their company. Better than people, anyway."

"I can almost agree with you on that." He glanced at the dead fire. "We should explore the island and see if we can find a way off it. Maybe find something to eat along the way. I assume you're not opposed to eating."

We covered the embers with wet sand before we headed towards the woods. The simulacrum shuffled quietly behind us, giving occasional small grunts. I noticed he sweated under the heat of the sun, which was disconcerting. The thing didn't have any other bodily functions that I was aware of.

Felan saw it, too. "It makes me wish I tried harder to speak with my father, if only in the hopes he would have divulged some of this to me. It is fascinating. A creature that is alive, and yet isn't. I wonder if it would let us study it."

"Did you hear that, Grandfather?" I asked, craning my head to the side. "Would you mind if we opened you up?"

The simulacrum gave a terrified groan.

"It understands," Felan said.

"It's starting to," I agreed. "Which makes me wonder if at some point it won't need *me* to control it anymore. Will it just decide to walk off on its own? Be emperor by itself?"

"Or perhaps, since *you* are attuned to it, it's responding to your being. Your energy, your thoughts…the *agan* works because we are all connected by our life-forces, after all. May I have your hand?"

"I'm sorry?"

He held his hand out. "I want to check something."

I flushed before offering it to him. The nearness made me turn my head. I hadn't been that close to him since we kissed.

Thankfully, he didn't seem to think about it at all. He merely pulled my sleeve down. "Has your appetite increased at all since you first connected with him?" he asked.

"So much has happened that I've barely had time to eat," I admitted.

"As I thought. You've lost weight." He tapped the bone on my wrist and then slowly let go of my hand. "He must be taking sustenance from his handler."

"That must be why he was immobile when I first came across him. His previous handler was dead. Your father, I mean." I coughed. We had reached a clearing—a field where the trees had been deliberately cut down, leaving nothing but trunks in place. Some had smaller trees growing in the cracks—ugly, stunted things with yellow leaves. The grass was yellow, too.

A harsh wind blew. We crossed a small stream, past an outgrowth of bushes that gave me a better view of the rest of the field. There were holes in the ground, as if someone had gone digging through them. But someone schooled in Eheldeth would know better.

Felan said it before I could. "These are mage training grounds."

"Not for Eheldeth students, I'm guessing."

"It's probably beyond the scope of the regular curriculum. Students who graduate on the scholarship track are given years of extra training, after all."

He didn't really need to remind me. I glanced ahead. "Should we walk farther? It might be hexed."

Felan turned to the simulacrum. "Perhaps we can ask him to walk in front of us?"

"I won't risk him."

"He's not alive."

The simulacrum grunted.

"I believe we've hurt his feelings." I bent down to pick up a rock and threw it across the field. The rock bounced against something in the air before it burst into flames.

"All right," Felan said, after we were done being surprised. He bowed at the simulacrum. "I apologize, Grandfather."

"What's the point of having a training field so far away from Eheldeth?" I asked. "Getting mages out here would be inconvenient."

"Portals, perhaps."

"Portals. All the way out here."

"It would require an immense amount of power, but it's possible."

I shook my head. "By the time the mages get here, they'll be too tapped out to do much, let alone get back. No—the logistics make little sense. Firekeeper Ceres isn't the kind of woman who'd make such an oversight. Remember how she made sure the girls' bathhouse was well out of the boys' way?"

He blinked. Clearly it wasn't something he'd thought about before. "I shall take your word for it."

"During the reconstruction of the west wing, after the accident at the kitchens. You were there."

"I believe you, Rosha. So why would she have a training field all the way out here?"

"Either she hasn't sanctioned it herself, which I find hard to believe considering *her* spell made it possible for us to get through, or…" I trailed off, staring at the barren soil. "They've been doing illicit magic out here."

He didn't look convinced. "Right under Drusgaya's nose? There are plenty amongst the mage council and other high-ranking members of the hegemony who don't exactly agree with the amount of power the mage council has. I hardly think they'd let the mage council get away with practicing illegal magic so close."

"Maybe illicit isn't the right word, then." I bent over to pick up a handful of the soil and sniffed. It smelled acrid, with a sharp tinge that made me turn my head. "Powerful magic. The kind that would prove dangerous in the empire. They must have been studying them out here. That's the only thing that makes sense. Too close to Eheldeth, and you risk damaging the fabric there—especially with the spells the students make all the time. So they picked a place close enough to transport mages safely, but as far from Eheldeth as possible."

"Eheldeth must not have enough mage-thralls these days," he commented.

I let the soil drift through my fingers before turning to him. "What did you just say?"

"Mage-thralls," he repeated. "They're tattooed with runes to assist their masters, or their masters' mages."

I sighed. "Yes, I know. What did you mean about Eheldeth not having any? We saw them at school all the time."

"Not having *enough*," he said. "You can connect to your mage-thralls and let the excess *agan* seep into them. They can be both a source of power and a conduit for grounding."

"That's disgusting."

He scratched his head. "It's standard practice. If you have enough of them, they'll all receive just a little bit of the *agan*, which won't hurt them. And you'll leave the area unharmed. Not like this."

I struggled to maintain my composure. "Have you had that done to you, Felan?"

"I'm sorry?"

"Have you had someone *tap* you? To draw from you or put something in you, against your will? Like you were nothing more than an object, a beast of burden that can't object."

"I've…never thought of it that way before." He lowered his eyes.

"You wouldn't," I said. "I know Gorenten who do, though. I'm sure your own people have suffered the same fate. The Dageians never cared who they stepped on, so as long as they got to do what they wanted."

"There *has* been increased pressure over the last few years to reduce the number of mage-thralls in the empire," Felan croaked. He scratched the stubble on his face. "It might very well be why they've resorted to this. How the *agan* works is constantly changing, shifting. The keepers need to be on their toes. This here is not ideal, but…"

"It's ideal, if the alternative is to use people."

"Of course," he said. "I was thinking of it from Eheldeth's perspective."

"Or your father's?" I asked. "How much of Lord Cato's ideals have you picked up over the years?"

"I don't know," he admitted.

"At least you're honest about it," I sighed. "Well, perhaps we've cracked his thoughts open a little here. They need mage-thralls. Dageis cannot run without magic, and someone must have been pressuring Lord Cato to find a way, because that—you can't do that forever, can you?" I pointed at the field. "Sooner or later, you'll corrupt the whole place. It must be why he set his sights on my family. Why he wanted to use me to make my father give up his land. Perhaps Lord Cato meant to buy it after that. It would give him access to the Gorenten, and then…"

I didn't want to think about it further than that. I felt so much guilt that I could throw such words around without ever having experienced such hardships myself. Kefier never told me those stories, though I knew enough about his past not to ask. One time, the topic came up, and all he did was kiss me on the head and say, "What matters is you never have to be in that place. What matters is that you have a bright future ahead of you, Rosha. Whatever I suffered—whatever our ancestors suffered— is no longer on you." *But do us proud. Make it all count.*

"We have to get out of here," I said, gazing at the sky. "We're losing time."

Felan cleared his throat. "Then perhaps you should take a look at this."

He had walked along the edge of the field, all the way to two stone pillars standing between a clump of boulders. It was covered with moss, some of which had bristly, pink flowers.

The pillars hid a staircase, which went all the way into the earth.

"Do you think it's a shelter?" I asked.

"I think it leads to a portal," Felan said. "I told you."

The air hummed.

"Do we dare?" he asked, cocking his head to the side.

"Right after you," I replied with a smile.

CHAPTER 38

THE GATES

The stairs wound down into a spiral, each step made of springy wood that seemed to hold our weight, for all that it looked so rickety it must have been there for years. I picked up a stick outside and lit it as soon as the sunlight faded above us. Felan's face tightened the moment the flames crawled from my fingers to the piece of wood.

"I do understand," I said. "For what it's worth."

"I'm not so sure about that."

"After I dropped out, I couldn't use magic for three years. Not freely. Because the one time I did, it brought Bearer Lontas and his ilk right at my heels, and I didn't want to leave anymore tracks where I could help it. I was afraid of Eheldeth catching up to me. Afraid of ruining the life I'd built for myself. But it's not much of a life, having to hide, pretending to be someone I'm not."

"What did you do?" he asked.

"I ran a little store outside a small farming town."

"You?"

"Why is everyone so surprised when they hear that?" I asked, though I wasn't expecting him to answer.

"You didn't come off as the type. You had…dreams."

"Dreams die," I whispered.

We reached the bottom of the staircase. I lifted the makeshift torch higher, revealing not one, but three gates, all set against the stone wall. They were inert. Portals need a mage to maintain them at all times. Gates such as the ones we were looking at provided markers. A mage can't just create a portal to wherever they want. They need a memory of the area, a map in the mind so to speak. And memories, you must understand, are unreliable. It is easy to create a portal to a place a few feet away like I did back in the palace gardens. And most mages worth their salt can manage a portal even further—perhaps right outside of town—if they're careful about their destination. You lend your memory to the *agan* and the *agan* remembers for you. If the place is distinct enough, if you can remember every detail of your surroundings exactly, and if there's no one around to disturb it...

I tried not to remember the portals exam in Eheldeth. A prank gone wrong, yet it was enough to rankle my pride. I knew my worth as a mage —I knew my skills. I pushed the memory out of my mind and tried to work my way back to my knowledge of portals. I thought about how portals remain the most erratic means of travel available to a mage. The number of things that can go wrong vastly outweigh the benefits. Too many people have found themselves in the wrong place, and that's even if all their body parts remain intact during the process. Bad mages—and there are *many* bad mages—get themselves and other people killed trying to save money on coaches and airships all the time.

Whoever set up this place must have decided it was worth the risk. The gates help the spellcaster—they would have set up an area resembling the one we were standing on, with gates positioned the same way somewhere else. There would just be one key difference. I glanced at the ceiling, and then at the runes painted around the arches of the gates. I had no idea what that difference was.

"I can't use these," I said. "I could open up a portal and just transport ourselves back to the same spot."

Felan didn't answer. He was studying the gates intently. "The runes form instructions," he replied.

"Oh?"

"They're written in old Kagosh. Could you please...bring the torch closer?"

I approached him, holding the fire up so we could both read the text. "There's three destinations. The gates are painted on the other side."

"Red for Drusgaya, blue for Noraya, and green...for Genthal." He looked confused. "Why would they need a path to Genthal? It's not an airship route."

"No," I agreed. "The only way to it is by sea, right?"

"Or by portal, evidently." He touched the edges of the gates, still obviously fascinated by them.

"A portal you can only access with two mages, or if you have a lot of time to spare," I said.

"I don't know if that's true."

"Have you looked at a map lately? Do you know how far away those places are to here, let alone each other? It's going to take a lot of strength to use these portals in the first place, let alone go back and forth through each one."

He chewed his cheek thoughtfully.

"You're disagreeing with me again." I sniffed. "You never were good at portals class, though."

"No one is *good* at portals class, Rosha."

"I was." *Was.*

"They taught us the theories, but forbade us to use them on anything but rocks across the field. I believe the only time we would have been allowed to use them was for the finals." He gave a small shrug. "Well, you did them, I suppose. You did get to the end of the last semester, didn't you?"

"With or without Eheldeth, I've always known about them. I've done them since I was little."

Felan narrowed his eyes. "How?"

"I picked it up along the way."

"Whoever *let* you must be mad."

"You saw me make one. Did you think it was hard for me?"

"I did," he agreed. He coughed. He looked embarrassed, as if he would rather I didn't bring that memory up at all.

"Whoever built this wouldn't have intended it for regular students. I still think the keepers testing their spells on that field above us would have come here by ship. These gates…" I touched one, feeling it hum. It wasn't inert. There were spells hidden here, too. "Oh," I said.

"What?"

"The gates are also mirrors." I found the runes on one, activating it. I stepped back.

The grey, stone surface shimmered before disappearing, revealing a dark room on the other side. I squinted. It was too dark to see the colours on the gates. There wasn't enough light. But I could make out enough shapes to get a sense of the room beyond the mirror.

"That place looks familiar," Felan said. He furrowed his brow.

"I'd almost say it looks like your family's crypts," I ventured.

"I don't think so."

"Not any place we were in." I pointed to the edge of the mirror.

"You see the rubble? You'll find that at the very end of the tunnel, where we were the last time. We must be looking from the other side."

Realization dawned on his features. "My father was using this place."

"Seems like it."

"And so the portal to Genthal..."

I triggered the mirror on the far side. It showed a room with the same three gates set right against stone. Just like the instructions said, the back of each was painted green. Sunlight was streaming through what appeared to be broken windows.

"Something tells me we'll find ourselves in our intended destination should we choose to create a portal there," Felan said.

I gave a grim smile. "How convenient."

He turned his head towards me. "Are you up for it?"

I turned to the gates.

"You said you were good at—"

"Yes, I know," I snapped. I looked at the torch in my hand. One spell too much already. The spell I was looking at was a level I'd never attempted before. To carry not just me, but another body, across hundreds of leagues—a distance easily a fifth the span of the empire— was madness. Despite Felan's accusations, he got something wrong about how I approached spells. Being good at something didn't mean perfection. Sometimes all it meant was knowing the intricacies of a spell and your own body's limitations. Your own skill, or lack thereof.

I swallowed my fears. If I had more time to deliberate, I would have taken it. But Endros's Day was today, at midnight. I should have landed in Genthal hours ago.

"It's worth a try," I said at last. I walked around the room in a circle. Felan watched me like a hawk. That look of longing was in his expression again.

"Do you need time to prepare?"

"I'm just getting my bearings." *And my courage.* I tried not to think of that monstrous dog's head, snapping away on the exam floor. That had nothing to do with me. If Ivasus hadn't interfered, I would have passed that test with flying colours.

"Your skill in the *agan* always filled me with envy," he said, at length. He pressed his back against the wall.

"I could barely keep up with you on exams." It was funny how easier it was to admit this to him now. You would have never squeezed it out of me when we were young.

He tapped his heel on the ground. "Oh, the exams. The exams are different. Those just depend on how well you've prepared for them. I had tutors in the summer. But the spells. When it was time to cast them. You made it look so effortless, like you didn't even need the months we spent learning the theories. You just...*knew* what to do. I still remember the first time I ever saw you cast one. The fireball you made. The size, the intensity of the flames...I don't know if you noticed, but every student in the class was looking at you with their mouths wide open. I heard one of the teachers say most graduates couldn't have made one half the size."

"I wasn't paying attention. When you cast a spell, it's all that's on your mind. At least—all that's supposed to be. Maybe you were too distracted to do it properly."

Felan grunted. "Ah. And now suddenly I recall what was so irritating about you."

"I was going to say the same thing," I said. "I do know what the others thought. I know what the teachers whispered in the halls. Something that's always bothered me—not once did anyone ask themselves how they could do *better*. I was good at what I did because I was allowed to practice spells long before Eheldeth students learned *theory*."

"Was allowed? By the empire?"

"My childhood was spent outside the empire."

"In Jin-Sayeng, where talk of the *agan* is supposed to get you killed?"

"After that..." I drew a quick breath. "Before I came to the empire, I had other tutors. Tutors who weren't stingy with their knowledge, who weren't limited by Dageis's rules and showed me the full extent of what the *agan* can do."

"That sounds dangerous."

"Perhaps."

"Have you created portals like this before?"

"None of this size," I said. "Though I always wanted to."

He waited. I knew what he was thinking. This was the sort of thing I might have bragged about, the kind of *skill* I claimed to Firekeeper Ceres that I had so she would get me to pay attention. And I knew I had it in me, once. But it had been too many years.

I placed the torch on the ground, obliterating the flame and covering us in darkness. I closed my eyes and started the spell.

I slipped into the watery depths of the *agan* stream, deep within my consciousness. *The sea is inside you, Rosha. Just close your eyes and wait.*

Wait. Wait. Always, with the waiting. Waiting for Papa to come back from his work as a mercenary, or for my mother to fix things between them so we could go back to the way we were. Waiting for Enosh to go away. Waiting for the school year to end so I could have a semblance of normal, even for just a few weeks. Waiting, even when there is never enough time. It leaks like a punctured vessel and suddenly you're far too old to care about the things that used to make up your world.

I still think about what I could have been if things had been different. Probably I would be dead in Jin-Sayeng, a casualty of the war or the thing that caused it in the first place. But I assumed—as most of us do—that the best scenario is the only scenario there could be. We might have died, but we might have also escaped those harrowing events that shaped the lives of thousands. We could have found a home in the fringes of the empire, somewhere I could practice my skills in peace. Maybe we would have had to leave eventually…maybe we would need to go to Dageis anyway. At least by then, I would come in unhampered by its rules, harder to shackle, harder to control. I would have been whole.

I ripped through the fabric to create the portal. Darkness crawled through my vision, but I ignored it to focus on the few tendrils of light, rapidly fading before I could grab them. Deeper I went, like I was diving into the ocean, fighting the waves. My eyes watered. So much power, all the power that used to just jump along my fingers and that I could mold to my will like clay on a potter's wheel. Now it was threatening to swallow me, to submerge me, to kill. If I was smart, I would end it now.

But I remained convinced that I was simply out of practice.

The spell slammed into me, the impact of someone hitting the ground after they've been flung off a horse. I felt like my brain had exploded. Almost immediately, the half-formed portal spat me out.

I landed on the floor and felt the gates crumble. I forced my eyes open. Everything had turned to dust.

CHAPTER 39

GENTHAL

"That could have killed you," Felan said between the ringing in my ears. He was standing above me, not touching me, though he held both hands out, as if he wanted to. He still remembered Eheldeth's lessons. A mage reeling from a failed spell could still leak *agan*, and it was better to let them transfer the energy to just about anything else but yourself.

I didn't reply. I didn't think I could—my tongue felt like it was made of stone. I tried to get up and ended up falling to my other side. I landed on my chest. A web of pain erupted from my skull and climbed down my spine, spreading to my limbs. Even my fingers tingled.

"Rosha," he continued. "Can you hear me?"

My eyes flickered. I fixed them on him, though nothing else cooperated. He knelt down so I could see his face.

"This happened to you before, in the Church of Endros. Too many spells at once, you said. But this is *you*. It made sense if you had been any other mage, but two or three spells in a row shouldn't have left *you* incapacitated."

I tried to open my mouth. The movement caused me to shake, like I'd just crawled out of a frozen lake. I wanted to close my eyes and sleep it off, but I wasn't sure my body would let me do even that.

"What is happening?" he asked. "I know you said portal spells are complicated, but they're not *this* complex, especially when you've just been bragging how you've done them all your life. You look like you've overextended yourself. This is…" His eyes flashed. "Is this why you failed your final exams? All those spells you're supposed to cast, for one whole week—"

I shook my head. The movement made my eyes water.

"Then what?"

"Broke the gates," I finally managed. Gods, it felt like my tongue was on fire. I could taste blood, too. Clumps of it, like I had just consumed a mouthful of overcooked stew. Perhaps I should consider it a relief that I still had the sensation of taste.

"You did. You shouldn't have. There was a lot of *agan*. Did it just bounce off your body? I couldn't see." Felan swallowed. "What did you do?"

"Broke the gates," I repeated. "Can't get out."

"No," he agreed. He sat down beside me. "We won't make it to Genthal in time."

I stared at the ground. I could see it even in the darkness, just small lumpy shapes, covered in a sprinkling of ash. I tried to stick my fingers through them, hoping the cold soil might bring a measure of relief to the burnt feeling, but it felt like my mind and my body were working independently of each other.

Above us, on the surface, I heard the forgotten simulacrum groan.

"Your father…"

"It's all right," I whispered. "Won't be missed." Which was a lie. He would be. That was why they asked me to help look for him, after all. He was missed and so was I, for all that we seem to have brought nothing but suffering to their lives. At worst, family meant empty spaces where people ought to be. The lie didn't make me feel better. Wasted words, wasted breath. I shouldn't have answered.

Why didn't the spell work? I thought I'd eased the appropriate amount of *agan* into my body. It should have, in theory. Theories, always these damn theories, driven into my brain by Eheldeth like a wedge. It didn't used to be this hard. When I was a child, I knew nothing about theories. Working the *agan* was just something I *knew* how to do, as easy as the breath inside my lungs, the sea inside my veins. Unbridled power, second nature. I would think a thought and the spell would be formed before I could even find the words for it. Entering Eheldeth was supposed to have made me more powerful. That was the promise. The gilded empire, with all its riches and magic and wealth, should have only brought more chances for me to grow in my craft.

Instead…

"You are safe now, I assume?" Felan asked. "I can't see the glow, Rosha, but your breathing has grown steadier."

I nodded. Even that made it feel as if my bones were rubbing against each other, trying to get out of my body, hounds competing to squeeze through a single door.

Now he picked me up. I felt weightless in his arms. He carried me up the stairs, taking time with every step.

We fell back into the sunlight, where he placed me on the ground. I sank into the dead grass, still not quite trusting myself to move. Afraid parts of my body would fall off if I did. The simulacrum laid a hand on my shoulder, concern on its usually expressionless features. I noted its beard was singed, as if it had been set on fire. The fractured spell must have jumped on my connection with him and reached all the way back, though he didn't seem to bear any lasting effects from it.

"You need something to eat." Felan gazed at our surroundings. "The whole place is barren. I doubt there's any fruit-bearing trees in the vicinity. But maybe there's something on the shore. Shells, or edible…seaweed?"

"Edible seaweed," I choked. "You really don't know anything about the islands."

"There should at least be coconuts here."

"Don't leave," I said, turning my head until my forehead touched the ground. "Just don't…leave. I will be fine."

"You don't look fine."

"Don't need taking care of," I grumbled, trying to force the pain out, as if such a thing was even possible. But I'd been there before. I knew if I wasn't dead yet, I could drag myself out of it. I just needed time. "Just stay," I whispered. "I don't want to be alone."

"You're not alone." His voice was very soft now. Somehow, against my better judgment, it sounded almost soothing.

I finally closed my eyes. I didn't know if I was supposed to take comfort from it, but I did.

Sleep came easily. I slept for so long I felt as if I had died after all. I had the sense that the whole day passed us by, and then morning.

I woke to someone tapping my ankle. I didn't respond immediately.

Nasuha's face appeared, beaming down on me against the morning light. She looked pleased with herself. "There you are," she said. "Off causing trouble again, *ineng*?"

"The whale didn't eat you," I grumbled. "Damn."

"The advantage of tough skin. I told it I'd just break its teeth, and it listened." She prodded my arm. "Lord Felan told me everything. What the hell were you thinking?"

"It's what mages do."

"So the Firekeeper goes up and makes you her errand mage—"

"Outlaw. I'm an outlaw."

She crossed her arms. "Not from where I'm standing. She goes up and does this, and suddenly you think that gives you permission to cast spells left and right like you're not a criminal in Dageis's eyes? I gave you far too much credit."

"Maybe I agree with you," I sighed. "How did you get here?"

"A Gorenten fishing boat picked me up from the shipwreck."

"Did anyone else escape?"

"We lost the boat captain." She gave a wry smile. "And Lontas, unfortunately, went down with the fishes."

I read something else in her expression, one that told me it was better not to ask how that happened.

"Anyway," she said. "Our new friend has promised to take us all the way to Genthal, for a fee, which I'm sure our dear patron the Firekeeper would not hesitate to give."

"Not sure it matters," I replied. "We missed midnight."

"And you're just going to give up?"

"I didn't say that."

She scooped me up from the ground and onto her shoulders like a deer she'd caught for dinner. I didn't even try to struggle—she was too strong. "We *will* bring your father back. I have a feeling that thing will wait for you. You're the one in control here, Rosha, not him."

Swinging helplessly across her back, I wasn't so sure. But I kept my doubts to myself and focused on surviving the rest of that journey.

Steady winds and calm weather brought us to the port city of Genthal by the next morning.

Few cities in the islands surrounding the empire remain standing, and those that still do bear more than their fair share of scars from the mighty Empire of Dageis. Each has its own story. Kazfian, of the Shi-uin to the northwest, saw the Dageian ships on their horizon and mounted an *agan*-fuelled attack that ended with their whole island covered in ice. Sen'senal, in Gorent, was a small town forced to house thousands of our people as they fled the empire's assault on the peninsula. There are probably more I do not know about, cities shrouded in the cruel grip of time. History favours the loudest. If you wrote a book about each one, you would fill an entire library.

Genthal, of course, was no different. Look away from the majestic, cone-shaped volcano in the distance, and you'll see it the moment you dock on its shores. How can such a city so far away from Dageis—a city that was supposed to have its own history and culture—look so much like Chylos across the sea? The Dageians will have you believe their superiority caused that. "It's only civilization," they'll insist. "Things were bound to progress that way."

Which isn't true at all. The cities of Jin-Sayeng, for instance, do not resemble Dageis's in any way, and they are far from backward. The intricate network of dragon-towers, built to harness dragon fire for the good of the people, is a marvel worth singing songs about. What would have been a cold, harsh land became fertile fields that could grow rice and corn and all manner of fruit trees. Dragons were a little too much for Dageis's tastes, and they left those lands alone. But the others, the unlucky ones who landed right in front of Dageis's wandering eye, had to give up what was theirs.

Because why throw what was yours away to embrace something foreign? Why give up *home* for something strange and uninviting? No— the Agarenthen's culture was forced out of their hands, peeled off like a thief taking a doll from a child's closed fist. One finger at a time, pushed back, twisted, there, let it go, you don't need it anymore, see? *Let it go,* said in a voice both soothing and cutting at once, *and have this instead.* None of their temples, or their intricate bathhouses, or the monuments to their gods remained. You could stand in the middle of that dock and imagine yourself just about anywhere else in Dageis.

Behind us, I could hear tourists who couldn't have been there for an hour mumbling their disappointment. Their brochures promised calm, blue seas, white sandy beaches, and colourful, ethnic locals. But everyone who walked past us were dressed in Dageian clothes, just like we were. It made me glad such sights weren't common in Sen'senal, which is considered too far away for most Dageian citizens to be comfortable with. The sight of so many tourists, talking in loud, exaggerated Kagosh to the locals who could understand them perfectly well, looked like rot on a festering wound. It was hard not to see it that way. Papa could accuse me of a lot of things, but he couldn't very well accuse me of not listening to him. He hated Dageis even more than I did.

I turned to Felan to ask him what he thought and realized he'd fallen deathly silent. "Have you never been here before?" I ventured.

He nodded. "My mother spoke of it when my father wasn't around, but it's been so long. I don't remember much. I don't think I even remember her voice, or what she looked like."

"You don't have family here?"

"I wouldn't know." But there was a touch of yearning in his eyes.

We reached the inn where we were supposed to meet Ceres. It had a full view of the harbour, with an entryway made right out of part of a ship. A mousey-looking woman greeted us. She must have received explicit instructions about our arrival, because she led us straight to a private corner of the inn, where Ceres sat nursing a mug of cold beer. Her eyes flicked towards us, but she said nothing until the woman had left us alone.

Only then did she get up to slap me.

Everyone looked panicked. Nasuha was the first to speak up. "Unnecessary, Firekeeper. The delay wasn't her fault. And she almost killed herself trying to find a way here."

There was a flicker of shame in Ceres's expression, but it disappeared as quickly as it came. She flexed her fingers. "Leave us."

Nasuha frowned. I settled into the bench and nodded to her. She walked past the simulacrum, which stood silently against the wall.

Felan lingered.

"Lord Cartos," Ceres said. "Please." There was a firmness to her tone that Felan couldn't argue with. Eventually, he walked away. "There's one missing," she continued.

"Lontas," I replied. "He's dead."

"How convenient for you."

"I hope you're not implying I tried to escape."

"Isn't that what you do?"

I dragged her plate towards me. There was a bun there, which I picked up. I tore into it, stuffing pieces of bread into my mouth. It was sweet and buttery, filled with curry and beef.

She sighed. "I never did know what to do with you. When I became involved with your father, I didn't realize *children* were part of the package. He didn't look like the type."

"I'm not a child anymore, Ceres." I swallowed, half-choking on the food. The last couple of days had left me ravenous. Ever since Felan had pointed out that the simulacrum seemed to take sustenance for me, I was suddenly aware of my hunger.

Ceres pushed her beer towards me. I drank it gratefully. "You don't say," she said.

"Since we're on the subject of holding each other accountable," I said, after I had eaten and drunk enough to stop my head from spinning, "explain that island."

She straightened herself. "Ah. Of course. The damn glyph on the simulacrum."

"What did you expect would happen?"

"I was expecting the boat would take you straight to your intended destination, with absolutely no detours."

"Well, the sea had other ideas. What was that place supposed to be?"

"You're a smart girl, Rosha. Surely you have it all figured out." She tapped the table with her fingers. "I've never actually been there. Mage council pressured me to sign the papers, and I had my essence imprinted into the protection spells as a formality, but I've never gone. Never had the time."

"There were three gates, for creating a portal," I said. "One for Noraya. One for Genthal. And then a third, for Drusgaya—with Lord Cato's house as the marker."

"Is that what you tried to do?" she asked. "Make a portal?"

I drank the last of the beer and slowly nodded.

"And it didn't work?"

"I haven't tried creating a portal that far before, and I was trying to bring both myself and Felan over."

She blinked. "It's complicated, I know. But you throve on such complexities before. I would have expected, at the very least, that you'd be exhausted by the time you got here, but otherwise…"

"I'm here now," I quickly said. "We missed the meeting with Targus. What do we do?"

She placed a bracelet on the table. I recognized the same one I found on the corpse in Triassa. I picked it up, turning it to the side. *No*, I corrected myself. Not the same one. The number was different.

"I made the mistake of hexing the area before the appointed time," Ceres said with a sigh. "He knew, somehow. He never showed up."

"Smooth," I drawled.

She sniffed. "When I checked the next morning, *that* was left on the floor of the clock tower. I don't know what it means."

"Remember when I said I think Targus is a simulacrum, too," I said. "I think I saw another one in Triassa. Only *that* one died. He had a bracelet just like this, with different numbers."

"He's trying to tell you something," Ceres said. "Something to convince you to work for him."

"No," I grumbled. "I don't think that's it."

"Then what?"

I stared at the bracelet, at the maker's stamp in the corner, right underneath the number. The letters *HF*, set inside a plain circle. "What do you know," I eventually said, "of Hertra Ferral?"

CHAPTER 40

THE END OF THE LINE

Remember when I told you my father was a fraud?

A matter of fact, you see, and nothing more. I am not the sort of woman who throws such words around in anger. I have more important things to do, and petty grievances—even those that are warranted—demand little attention in my life. Count Enosh Tar'elian's past fortunes were not attached to his real name or status. His prior life as a merchant was stolen. Facts; nothing more.

He never told me why, even after he knew I'd found out. He didn't have to. As the years went on, I saw him struggle to gain a foothold as a Gorenten merchant; I had seen the frustration on his face after business deals turned sour for no reason other than the investors' distrust of a Gorenten enterprise. "It didn't used to be like this," Enosh once said, drawing an inert enchantment for glamour on the dust of his desk. Dealing as Hertra Ylir yn Ferral in the south, he could pass himself off as an elderly man, with white skin and grey eyes brimming with the wisdom of the ages.

"You know your father is very secretive," Ceres said at last, breaking into my memories. My question had struck her dumb for a few, uncomfortable minutes.

"He'd have to be," I replied. "His many, many lovers aside…"

She fanned herself. "Oh, I don't flatter myself on that regard. I know the type. If anything, that was always part of his appeal."

"That he could make you sick if you're not careful?"

"The experience."

I blanched. "Can we not—"

"Of course. Your mother *would* have raised a prude."

"The subject is about Hertra Ferral," I said. "I don't know anything about him. I vaguely remember someone saying he was Kag."

"As far as I'm aware, he was from one of the City-States." She turned the bracelet in her fingers, her eyes on the maker's stamp. "He wasn't a well-known merchant. The area near the City-States is rich in natural resources, and he mostly traded in ore. Iron. Gold. Silver."

"Were they involved in jewellery-making, too?"

"Perhaps."

"Did Father kill him?"

She turned to me. "You know he doesn't kill in cold blood."

"I *don't*. He's more than capable of murder. He's not really the sort who will get tangled up in a moral dilemma, is he?"

"Not the way you're implying. It's not that simple."

"He killed a man, and then stole his life. That sounds simple enough."

"He never told me any of this," Ceres said. "I had to do some digging around when I first met him, to ensure he is who he says he is. It was interesting to find out he wasn't."

I laughed. "And yet you chose to trust him, anyway."

"Hertra Ferral wasn't a citizen of Dageis, so it's not as if it was within my jurisdiction. What others do with the *agan* outside of our borders is not our problem. I did find it interesting how this rogue, untrained mage, who knew better than to openly draw on the *agan* inside the empire, had gotten away with pretending to be another man for years." She pushed the bracelet back towards me. "My sources tell me Enosh was apprenticed to the real Ferral. An arrangement with his old master, made not long after he left Gorent. There must have been an accident that forced Enosh to pick up and artificially extend Ferral's life —or else someone far, far more powerful than him in the *agan* helped him all those years. He's competent with enchantments, but he's not *that* good. Certainly not good enough to be as infallible as he seemed—the risks of what he did far outweigh any benefits. Remember, as soon as he could, he jumped on the chance to build a business around his own true name."

"Because of me."

"Not just you," Ceres said. "The man does cherish his own name. His legacy means to him more than coin, hard as that may be to believe."

"Oh, I can believe it. I stand corrected." I pointed at the bracelet. "It can't be a coincidence that these bear Hertra Ferral's mark. His business must have been involved with whoever's behind the simulacrums."

"Raw materials for the things, maybe." She scratched her chin.

"Except they're not *agan*-wrought. They're not inorganic."

She furrowed her brows. "I'm drawing a blank."

"You still need the *agan* to move the simulacrums. Complex spells run them—even more complex spells must have gone into building them. You said Ferral originally dealt in ore." I chewed my lip. "Is there featherstone near the City-States?"

"Of course. It's one of the places we had a trade agreement with back in the day. Featherstone is scarce in the north—I've been told the geography doesn't favour it."

"Or your mages used it all up when they first arrived," I said.

"That's just a theory."

"We can debate about it all morning."

"I'm sure you would love that, Rosha. But let's not get distracted."

I tapped the table. "Glyphs are more powerful on buildings made with featherstone, so if Ferral sold featherstone ore to Dageis, then perhaps…" I got up. "Check the records. See if there's any place featherstone is stored around here."

"You got all of that from a bracelet?" Ceres asked, with the barest flicker of amusement.

I coloured. "A bracelet with *Ferral's* mark on it. Our true enemy knows the connection between him and Enosh. We have to start somewhere, don't we? How about we start somewhere logical, instead of wasting our time knocking on every door in Genthal or whatever your original idea was?"

"I'm not questioning your rationale, Tar'elian. Only…"

"What? You really expected less from your best student?"

She quirked an eyebrow. "Best," she repeated with a smile. "Well. We still have to see about that."

"How much more do I have to prove myself to you, Firekeeper?"

She reached up to pat my cheek. Her fingers were cold. "Oh, my dear," she said. "You've only just begun."

Big words, coming from the woman who *scared* off our target with a badly concealed enchantment. If she had been more careful, perhaps all of this would be over already. But I knew I couldn't blame her forever. Maybe I would have made the same mistake, too.

We spent the rest of the day making inquiries, which Felan seemed to have the most knack for. Not surprising, I supposed, coming from a merchant's son. We found out featherstone had not been used in Genthal for a few decades. It made any spell you left on a building more powerful, but it also made them more unstable and was all but impossible to work with without losing people to its ill-effects. There were no warehouses storing featherstone for the masses, no factories for refining it, nothing that I thought would be so simple.

I felt the shard of frustration multiplying inside of me. I didn't want to return to Ceres with my tail between my legs. I didn't want to tell her I didn't know where to start.

While the others turned to finding lodging for the night, I made my way to the clock tower.

It stood just north of the town, overlooking a rickety stone bridge that crossed the brownest river I'd ever seen in my life. The place was a monument—a placard on the street indicated that a battle had been fought here centuries ago. Something about good Agarenthen, fighting beside their Dageian masters, against Agarenthen insisting freedom is the only way. Civil war, just one of many sparked by Dageian occupation. Such details escape me. I am good with theories, but facts fade in the background when I have no reason to hold on to them. Why remember anything beyond the truth? *The empire took what wasn't theirs.* That is all you need to know. The rest are distractions.

"Rosha," someone called from behind.

I turned my head to see Felan running to catch up. I sighed and waited for him.

"It's dangerous to be alone." He looked troubled by something.

"I think better when I'm alone."

"I know. This isn't the time, however."

"You're one to talk. I don't see Nasuha anywhere."

"You've let Firekeeper Ceres get to your head," he said at last, revealing what was on his mind.

I continued walking towards the clocktower.

"Everything she said, every action, every word that falls out of her lips...you saw it as a challenge, didn't you?" He swallowed.

"A challenge I can never win," I said in a low voice.

"Did you think she was testing you?"

"I used to think so," I admitted. "I used to think all I needed was to stop making mistakes. I could craft a spell better than our peers, but if the keepers saw a fault in it somewhere, then I would put it upon myself to do better, thinking it won't do. I'm starting to see the truth. I can never attain perfection, not when she doesn't see me the same way she sees herself. At the most, I…fascinate her. Just like my father fascinated her. She can't help it. She has lived in a world where magic is taken for granted every day. She was born to it—she can't imagine a life where she has to hide or withhold it or imagine how much better life would be if she wasn't *gifted*, because it would be a lot simpler."

"She worked hard to be Firekeeper several times in a row."

"I don't doubt it," I said. "I've seen how she leads the council. I don't doubt the woman deserves her position. In a flawed system, perhaps she remains the most qualified. But I also don't think she's ever thought she *deserves* less. She wanted it, so all she had to do was work for it. To see someone struggling to find their place in the world, to see that person make five steps forward and ten steps back—perhaps she sympathizes, but in the end it's all entertainment. And it shouldn't, but it makes me feel less somehow. I feel like I've squandered my gifts. I've wasted so much time trying to insist I belong in the first place that it's left me no room to do anything else. Everything I ever wanted shouldn't have to be this hard."

We entered the clock tower in silence. I wondered why I would open my mouth around Felan at all. Maybe because by then, I felt like I had nothing to lose. He'd seen me fumble with a high-level spell and had yet to drag me to the ground for it. Maybe he was just waiting for the opportunity, and I wanted to push him to the edge.

"I guess you do understand," he said, after what felt like a very long time. I remembered our conversation in the other island.

I gave a small sound of acknowledgement. I'd been so used to being miserable on my own I didn't think having company would feel different. I wasn't sure if it was better. You could be proud of your pain, too, and until then it was all I had.

We reached the base of the clocktower, where I should have met Targus last night. Nothing was amiss. I noted another placard on the wall. Felan was already reading it. I wondered if it was his first brush of Agarenthen history. He didn't speak like someone who knew anything about his native land. The imprint of Dageis was too strong on him.

I stepped behind him and read the placard over his shoulder. "Agar-enth had its own government for years after Dageis came," I observed. "Interesting."

"And yet they say it was the first to kneel."

"You do what you can to survive. Maybe sometimes you're rewarded for it." I pointed at the last paragraph. "It says Emperor Cerknar was here during the civil war. He was gravely injured during an attack on this very clocktower but survived with hardly a scratch. A wonder among wonders." I snorted. "Now we know better."

"But do we?" He made a vague gesture at the dates. "It's around this time that his reputation as an *undying* emperor started."

I turned to him. "You think it was the actual emperor, then?"

"Cerknar must have been an actual person once," he mused.

He was right about that. It was doubtful this scheme started with a simulacrum at the helm of one of the biggest empires in the world.

"What if he died here?" I asked out loud.

Felan's face twitched. "It's possible."

"The injuries they said he sustained—they didn't seem survivable. They used that to claim the emperor's strength, but what if they twisted the story. He died here, and they made the simulacrums after. Live, breathing dolls that can age. Where would they start? They would need a place far away from everything else, because it would require energy. A place where you can safely store featherstone if they've been using it to stabilize their spells."

I fell silent, realizing I had it. I'd seen it when we first arrived on the boat, dominating the horizon through the swathes of morning mist.

"The volcano," I whispered. "They must be near the volcano." I turned to Felan. Something had distracted him, and he was walking towards the door. "Felan—if there's a building or something near the volcano, perhaps—"

The door to the clock tower flung open.

"We've got you now," Bearer Lontas hissed. Two mages appeared behind him, flinging both fire and ice in my direction at the same time. I prayed to all the gods as I threw up a shield spell and shut my eyes as the walls crumbled.

CHAPTER 41

THE LOST ONE

"I knew it," Lontas said, as soon as the shaking stopped. He pointed a crooked finger in my direction. "I knew I'd seen you somewhere before. You're not just the girl who walked out of Eheldeth before she graduated—you're also that merchant's daughter, the one who maimed Lord Talos."

I lowered the shield-spell. Keeping it up was starting to make me feel as if my bones were shrivelling. "You're supposed to be dead," I said, staring at him.

"Your friend tried her best to kill me," he agreed. "Twice over. Tell her Dageian mages are hard to kill."

"I'm working for Firekeeper Ceres. If she finds out you've attacked me…"

"Firekeeper Ceres is in over her head," Lontas said. "It's about time the council opens their eyes. None of this was sanctioned. People like you shouldn't be out on the streets. I intend to put you down before I file my report on Firekeeper Ceres's incompetence. Certain people in the mage council will be thrilled to know she's not who she pretends to be."

"I'm not the enemy."

He smirked. "Imagine how much trouble we could have saved the empire if you were locked away from the very beginning. Lord Cato would still be alive."

"If you think that, then you're more naïve than I figured," I said.

His companions started towards me. He lifted his hand to stop them, before drawing a short sword from his belt. He swung it. "You need to be put down," he repeated.

"Crossing the Firekeeper is ill-advised," Felan broke in. "If you kill her—"

"They can punish me later," Lontas said easily. He charged.

I fled.

This Lontas wasn't a warrior. I used to watch my stepfather training, had seen him spar with his mercenaries more times than I could count. I knew what a warrior looked like. But it didn't matter if I couldn't defend myself—any fool with a sword could draw blood. In his eyes, I was nothing but prey. I thought about throwing spells in his direction, but whatever well lay within the man would be much bigger than mine. After the last few days, the very thought of drawing on the *agan* again filled me with fear and shame. He could deflect anything I could conjure. I wasn't the mage I had been.

I heard someone call my name from the far end of the yard. Nasuha appeared, sword over her shoulder. There was no time for greetings. I ran past her, and she stepped between me and Lontas. She swung her sword, striking his and sending it flying from his hands. Unfazed, he pulled up a shield-spell, sending sparks in the air as the sword connected. The scent of burnt steel filled my nostrils.

I watched as she stepped aside, allowing him to build up his shield. Strange—most people who knew nothing about how the *agan* worked would just beat at the shield, hoping to weaken it, maybe even break it. Which would be an effective strategy with a novice mage. But against a skilled mage, it was wasted effort. I don't know how a physical fight works, exactly, but for mages, it comes down to a matter of stamina. Back in Eheldeth, when they weren't telling us what *not* to do with magic, they were teaching us how to balance our energy.

Shield-spells were not meant to be kept up forever.

Nasuha knew this. Too many mages relied on intimidation to win fights, but it was suddenly clear such a tactic would not work on her. She stepped back, breathing slowly, conserving her own strength while Lontas sized her up. Whatever he threw at strengthening his shield would be for nothing. I could see the realization dawning on him, too. He was going to over-exert himself before she could break a sweat.

"You bitch," he said.

"You should have died when you had the chance," she replied.

"You didn't try hard enough to kill me." He grinned. "Stay out of this, and you'll be rewarded."

Nasuha's scarred face tightened. "You think I can be bought? You Dageians are pathetic." His hands shook from the effort of maintaining the shield-spell, and she lifted her sword, waiting.

"Someone like you," he said, trying to remain calm. "Surely you need the money."

"I am a Lost One," she replied. "I don't. What I *do* need is for you to leave this child alone."

"She's an outlaw mage," he hissed. "She needs to be put to justice."

"She's ours. Not yours."

"What the hell do you mean by that?"

His shield-spell sparked as he lost his connections. She struck. He tried desperately to throw more spells, trying to prevent her sword from striking, but it didn't work. The blade connected with his neck, spilling blood where he stood.

His corpse tumbled to the ground just as his friends caught up with us. "Two against two," Nasuha said brightly. "What do you both think about your chances?"

"There are others behind us," the mages said. "Our deaths won't mean a thing. Firekeeper Ceres will have to answer for protecting an outlaw mage, and she won't stand a chance."

Nasuha flicked the blood off her sword. "Take Felan and go," she told me.

"You can't fight two mages at once," I said.

"I can try."

"Why are you protecting me? Who are you? What did you mean by I'm *yours*?"

"Gorent's," she corrected. "A gifted child of Gorent, the kind that once made our kingdom what it was. If I'm alive after this, I'll explain."

"Tell me now, Nasuha."

She ignored me and laughed as she ran straight into the mages' path. Felan grabbed me before I could think about following.

"She's right," he said. "We can't stay here. We need to get out of town *now*. Let the Firekeeper take care of this mess. You came here for a reason, didn't you?"

He was right. Damn him, but he was right. I tore myself away from the battle, ignoring the burning and the thick blanket of *agan* enveloping the air. There was a time I would have rushed into the heart of it.

Ah, how the years could make a woman less than the girl had been.

Gorent coming out of the woodwork to claim *me* was an idea so outlandish, I couldn't come to grips with it. *Why now?* After years of struggling in an empire that couldn't even speak my name without getting it wrong, why *now*?

It wasn't a question anyone could have answered. Gorent was an ancient kingdom, a dead kingdom, its people pariahs spread far and wide. Certainly nothing Felan, who rode in silence beside me, could have shed any light on. He was wrestling with his own thoughts, too—the volcano in the distance, the heart of what *his* people had once called home. Neither of us even knew its name. We should. Our ancestors belonged to this land.

What are we without each other? Kefier's words, probably. He liked to speak of things I liked to forget, piling them away in the corner of my heart where I didn't think I would ever need them. But now I ached for his words. I ached for his company, for his stories, for the way he seemed to have an answer for all the parts of me I thought were missing.

"Do you think they will punish the Firekeeper?" Felan asked, after we reached a quiet stretch of road overlooking a swampy-looking lake to our left. A reddish cliff covered with bright green moss hugged the right. Our horses slowed down, none-too-thrilled with the prospect of trotting between the shadow of it. A loose stone might be enough to spook them.

"Not as much as they will punish us." I shivered, feeling something in the air, and my mouth had the sensation of dryness. Were we in the presence of a spell? I looked around, wondering if something was engraved on the cliff. "I'm sure she has the proper connections to get off lightly. Her family *is* related to the rog-Bannals, you know. They're well entrenched in the hegemony."

"As was my father," Felan breathed. "And that didn't stop them from having him assassinated."

I got off the horse and pointed. I could see a shadow right across the lake, something that seemed to fade between the gusts of wind. "Did you see that?" I asked.

He held his breath and squinted. "No, I'm sorry. I don't."

"You don't feel anything?"

"Rosha," he said, "I'm blind to the *agan*, remember?"

I felt a flush of shame. "It's so light that I thought—"

"There is nothing there."

I swallowed and pointed again. "There's something shifting in the horizon. I think it's concealed with a giant *don't-look* spell. Did they tell you back in the city where this road leads to?"

"A viewing platform," Felan said. "I just asked for directions to the volcano. It must be a popular tourist attraction." He cleared his throat. "How is it that you can see past the *don't-look* spell? Surely, they put it up to deter intruders."

"Then it must be that I'm breaking it," I said.

He didn't reply. The words sounded ominous already. I didn't really want to dwell on the fear that they knew we were coming. Perhaps having Enosh in their custody meant they had to attune the barriers to him, which meant they would allow me to pass. Would it be enough to break it for Felan?

"Perhaps you should stay back."

His face flickered. "It's…"

"Unsafe, I know. But I'll come get you if it isn't."

I could tell he disagreed, but that he also wasn't going to argue the merits of it. Without offering him another glance, I clicked my tongue, forcing my horse to traverse the swampy shore. Mud went up to the horse's chest, which meant my boots were drenched, but we made it to the far side without incident.

I couldn't see Felan through the brush anymore. I must have gone through the spell-veil already, because I could see the ruins of an old castle in the distance. It must have been the shape I glimpsed from the other side. Even with the volcano in the backdrop, it seemed substantial —a place that must have been important to the Agarenthen once, if the architecture was any indication. I left the horse tied to a tree and continued on foot. If I had to make a quick escape, I needed him alive, and who knew what waited for me inside the place?

The path leading up to the main gates was overgrown with moss and weeds, from which purple and white flowers had sprouted. I reached an iron barricade, which looked rusted and damaged beyond repair. The holes were bent from the outside, as if once upon a time, it had been assaulted with spears and swords. I imagined an over-eager soldier rushing to the front of whatever caused the castle to fall—someone who didn't think such an action could result in their death. In the quest for recognition, how many of us consider ourselves immortal? Or maybe they knew they weren't. Maybe they knew their immortality lay in that last rush, in that sliver of scar they made on the gate before an arrow took them in the eye. Our lives are finite, but our actions could last longer.

The fading sunlight skidded over the overgrown vines when I tested the gate. It wasn't locked, and the ease with which it swung inward told me there had been others here recently. There were footprints on the soil already, though a patch of rain had obscured most. I followed them into the vast courtyard, past three stone archways in the garden—all with cracked and faded yellow stone and overgrown vines. It lay directly in front of a structure that seemed newer, if the lighter shade of the white stone was anything to go by. It looked like a small chapel, large enough for ten or so people. A network of stairs hugged the walls, which led up to the roof. I spotted benches on two sides.

"You said you were going to get me," Felan called.

I sighed. "I wasn't even sure it was safe yet." I turned to him. He tentatively approached the entrance of the structure.

"The spell-veil disappeared when you went through. The castle was suddenly clear." He touched the stone.

"I suspected it was attuned to my father. Most attunements don't bother to discriminate between family members."

Felan nodded. "Yes. And Targus has had all this time to set up such spells."

I shook my head. "He's not a mage, remember?"

"I'm finding it hard to believe he's a simulacrum. From what little I saw of him in the Church of Endros, he seemed just like a man. And he had power. I saw him *leap* from the opening in the roof."

"Physical prowess," I said. "He had no connection to the *agan* beyond the ordinary. I would have seen if he did."

He frowned, and then took a step down into the chapel.

"Felan, I wouldn't."

"You'll see if there's traps, yes?"

No. Maybe. Before I could open my mouth, he shrugged and reached the bottom. I heard him swear.

I bolted down after him. The smell of old stone and soil filled my nostrils. The building wasn't a chapel after all. A stone tomb stood in the middle. A small quote was engraved on a headstone.

"*Here Lies What Cannot Die,*" Felan read aloud.

"It's him," I said. "The emperor."

"You don't say."

"I told you. He must have died here, and some of those in power must have viewed it as a catastrophe."

He still looked doubtful. "The man who sits on the throne is supposed to be Cerknar the Fourth," he said. "How old was he when he went to war against Agarenth?"

"It's your people, Felan."

"Regardless, he would have been an adult," he continued. "Did he hide for a few decades? Surely, they wouldn't have had simulacrums ready *then*."

I fell silent, thinking about his words. Wondering where I fit in all of this. "I think the answer lies inside this castle," I said at last. If my words had felt ominous earlier, now they were damning.

· · ·

This is what I wanted to say then, surrounded by those shadows and the gnarled remnants of an empire's past: *none of it had anything to do with me.*

I was there for my father, a decision I still questioned with every passing moment. If the empire was crumbling under the weight of its own lies, so be it. It was nothing to me. I owed the empire nothing. It wasn't up to me to fix it, and so I had no reason to discover its problems.

But as we stepped inside the main hall through a corridor lined with cobwebs and the pervading smell of rot, I wondered about all the people who must have thought the same thing. The same people who occupied this castle must have considered the Dageians' arrival as something far from menacing.

My thoughts dissipated when I saw the dark shape in the middle of the throne room. It was Enosh, lying with his back against the steps. His eyes were on the single shaft of light coming from the crack in the rooftop. I thought he was dead at first. He looked dead—the front of his shirt was drenched in blood, so dry it appeared black, and the bristly beard he normally kept trimmed was nearly all red. A long gash marked his chest down to his belly. But he shifted when he saw me.

"What did I tell you?" he said, his words coming out like a last gasp of air. "Too much like Kefier, you damned child."

I glanced at his injuries. "How are you still alive?"

He laughed slowly. "I'm not sure, to be honest. I feel like my guts are going to come tumbling out."

"Well, don't let me stop you."

"You didn't show up during his appointed time," he continued. "I thought for a moment you were smart enough not to fall for his tricks. I'm not sure if I should be happy to see you, or disappointed." He glanced at Felan. "I didn't realize you had a companion. Were you going to introduce us, or…?"

"I'm Felan Cartos," Felan said, taking him way too literally. I should have warned him about Enosh's penchant for sarcasm. "Lord Cato tan-Tarsius's son." He gave a gracious bow.

The smile on Enosh's face faded. "His son. You didn't take your father's name?"

"No, sir. I took my mother's."

"You don't have to *sir* him," I said.

"The boy knows how to pay respects," Enosh replied. "Unlike *someone* I know."

"Can you just save me the trouble and die already?"

He grinned. A trickle of blood dripped down the corner of his mouth. "I think I'd rather stay. Help me with the wound."

"I didn't study healing magic, old man," I said.

"Listen to this girl," he told Felan. "*Old*. Do I look old? Child—just come here and burn the wound shut."

"You're gifted with a connection to the *agan*. Do it yourself."

Enosh grimaced. "Not like you are. Not even close. Come and show off, like you always do." He leaned back, giving us a better look at his wound. I thought I could see the bone of his rib jutting out. "I tried, earlier, and almost passed out. I don't have the strength. If I ever went to Eheldeth, they would have kicked me out on the second day."

"Not the first?"

"Would have spent the first kissing ass. You know this."

I stared at the wound. I didn't really want to touch him. Even being near him brought back that old revulsion. I could never accept that it was this man that brought me to the world, that without his *contribution* I wouldn't exist at all. I wonder if life felt different for children conceived in love.

"Perhaps there's a candle somewhere," Felan broke in. "We can try to do it with a regular fire."

"You need it hotter than that," Enosh replied. His eyes shifted over to me. "Though I believe she'd rather watch me bleed to death, and perhaps I don't blame her." I didn't know if he spoke in earnest, or if he was being sarcastic again. You couldn't tell with him. I'm pretty sure none of his women even tried. He was what he was, to his detriment.

"I'm just trying to think of the best way to cause you pain." I crouched down beside him.

"Just warn me when—"

I pressed my hands on the wound and willed the flames to dance over his flesh. He roared. The smell of cooked flesh pervaded the air as I pulled away.

"—you're about to start," Enosh gasped, a thick layer of sweat over his brow. He let his hands drop to his side as he stared up at the ceiling again. "Gods, you really do hate me."

"It was oddly satisfying," I said. "Now can you get up?"

He reached behind him and grabbed the sheathed sword he always carried around, the sword I was fairly certain I'd never seen him draw in his life. He pushed the scabbard into the ground, using it as a cane to support himself. His legs shook, but I wondered if he was exaggerating the effect for my sake. I wouldn't put it past him. Felan offered his arm.

"It's fine," Enosh said, waving him off. He pressed both hands solidly over the hilt of his sword, planting it between his feet. "Lord Cato's son.

I suppose you know nothing about what's going on, or else she wouldn't be here with you. Is that right?"

He nodded. "Yes, sir. I arrived the night Lord Cato died. I haven't been in the empire for years. An accident forced me to drop out of Eheldeth."

"Since you were…" Enosh's face fell. "Oh. That's you. *Felan Cartos*. I knew the name seemed familiar. He's not dead after all, Rosha."

I glanced away. "I got the gist after the last few days."

"I didn't know you were Lord Cato's son," he continued. "The resemblance is…er…"

"I'm adopted."

"You can never tell if it's polite to ask that or not," Enosh stated. He wiped the sweat off his brow with his arm. "It's suddenly clear why he was looking for Rosha, in particular."

"Is it?" I asked. "He had all these years to express fatherly concern about his son's accident, and it took him three years until after I'd dropped out of Eheldeth to *start* making inquiries?"

Enosh frowned. "We should ask the son of a bitch who did this. Have either of you seen him?"

"Targus? No."

"That thing has a name?" He glowered. "I suppose you have to differentiate them from each other somewhat."

"What do you mean?"

"How do I explain this to children…" he began.

"Maybe start by remembering we're not anymore," I retorted.

"Well then," he said. "I suspect that thing isn't alive. Or at least, not the way you and I and I'm hoping Lord Cato's son here are."

"We know Targus is one of many simulacrums the merchant guild— possibly with the help of a few insiders from the mage council—has been using to control the Dageian government. That last part—"

"Hmmm." Enosh yanked his sword forward, without removing it from its scabbard, towards Felan's direction. Felan stumbled back.

"What are you doing?" Felan asked.

"I found out how your father made those simulacrums," Enosh replied, "and I'm not sure you're going to like it."

CHAPTER 42

THE PERVADING STENCH

Enosh took us down the corridors and up a narrow flight of stairs. I imagined it was for the servants—the doors were narrow, hiding passageways that allowed them to serve their masters without ever having to walk through the main halls. I couldn't tell what Felan was thinking. It almost looked as if he had walled himself behind a steel door. He must have learned how to do it, growing up with a man like Lord Cato for a father.

We reached another hallway, which was lined with doors. Enosh opened one. "I had a lot of time to explore while running away. That *thing* is relentless." He towards the shuttered windows. He pushed them open, letting a flood of light into the room.

There were dozens of beds in one side of the room, all lined up as if this was once an infirmary. The other side looked similar, except instead of beds, there were cots.

I glanced at Felan, and then turned to Enosh in confusion. "What is this?"

"Where they kept the Agaranthen women who carried the children they would grow into emperors," Enosh said. "From the records I found, they were last in use approximately…twenty-some years ago. How old are you, boy?"

"Twenty-one," Felan breathed.

"You're not saying he's *one* of these," I quickly said. "The emperor, Targus…they're all white-skinned, tall, blue-eyed. Felan is Agaranthen."

"That's why I said I was *hoping* that's the case," Enosh replied.

"And if Agaranthen women carried them, the emperors would all have Agaranthen blood," I continued. "They don't. Targus's hair is yellow. They should all have black or brown hair otherwise."

"The records are in the next room," Enosh said. "Perhaps you should go there and see. If we have time. And if you want to know." His eyes were on Felan.

Felan drew back, almost calmly. "Show me," he said in a low voice.

I fell in step behind him as Enosh led the way to the next room. There, Enosh placed a hand on my shoulder, stopping me from getting close to Felan. "What are you doing?" I asked.

His face assumed an almost thoughtful expression. "Do you remember when you first found out I existed?"

I shrugged away from him. "It was the worst day of my life. To find out the father I loved wasn't *mine*, that I came out of someone like *you*..." I let the silence fill in the gaps.

Enosh shrugged. He was used to my outbursts. "The person who told you meant to cut you to get to me."

"One of your women," I reminded him. "One of your many, many women, trying to get to you over me, over my own mother's corpse. Because *she* thought if you were going to try to make something work, well, shouldn't it be between you and her? Do you ever stop to think about what you leave behind? About the people who suffer for the choices you make?"

His eyes danced. "Every day."

"And yet—"

"I cannot take them back," he continued. "Believe me, I would if I could."

"It's hard to believe a liar."

His face twitched. "I don't disagree. But I'm not here to talk about past mistakes. I just wanted you to give him a moment. Give him a moment."

I watched Felan's face as he read over the letters splayed out on the desk in front of him. "You've read those documents?"

"I told you. I was bored, and our little friend had dropped enough cryptic remarks to make me curious." He took me aside, behind the walls where Felan couldn't hear us. "Lord Cato was one of the key figures of this operation, at least in this generation. He wasn't named, but I recognized his handwriting from the time I spent in his household. He ends with a sign..."

"With the looping *S*," I said. "Yes, I know."

He nodded. "He and a few high-ranking officials have an arrangement. Every few years, they vote in who gets to control the emperor—all seem to be members of the hegemony and part of the mage council or merchant guild. A secret clique, separate from the rest. Those who aren't mages could use a mage under their employ, with heavy restrictions. I don't know the details, only that it happens every five years or so. Lord Cato only acquired the emperor himself last year."

"What does this have to do with Felan?"

"As I said earlier, Agaranthen women carried the would-be simulacrums. They're grown in their wombs."

"Real children?"

He hesitated. "Almost."

"Then what?"

"They lack a soul."

I glanced back at the room. Felan wasn't one of those. He was a person—a boy with hopes and dreams, all of which I ruined.

"They're nothing but bodies," Enosh continued, noting my disquiet. "There are spells outlined in those documents. Perhaps you might have a better time deciphering them—it's gibberish to me. But I'm guessing the infants are placed in their bodies somewhat formed, and that they're *agan*-wrought—at least in the beginning. I believe a part of them contains a part of the real Cerknar's flesh."

"Blood magic," I breathed.

"Of course. There is enough indications in this castle that tells me they've refined this operation over the years. There are glyphs in various rooms, many inert. Other rooms are full of featherstone. A lot of magic has been practiced here, Rosha—enough to dent the empire's reputation if it ever came out. Something tells me they must have tried this the very first time with the emperor's own corpse, and it must have worked long enough until...well. Until he started rotting."

"Fascinating," I whispered. It all made sense now. I wondered how they were able to create children using the emperor's flesh. Perhaps they used an already-existing child as a vehicle.

Enosh cleared his throat. "You'd think so. You know, something tells me if you had stayed long enough in Eheldeth, if you had graduated and they had apprenticed you to someone from the hegemony, you'd be there with them. Complex, *illegal* spells sound like something you'd be good at."

"Like you wouldn't take the opportunity?"

He rubbed his chin. "Perhaps."

"Then maybe it's for the best that I will never be in that position." I turned around and went back inside the room. Felan was sitting on the floor with his back to the wall, parchment still in his hands. He didn't look up when I approached him.

"My mother was one of these women," Felan said. "Her name is on here."

I said nothing. I simply sat beside him.

He pressed his fingers over his forehead before looking at me. "They take Agaranthen women from all across the island and tell them they will bear children for the lords. I don't think they know anything about the procedure or what they are giving birth to. It only says they are compensated for it. Blood magic, for a bit of coin." He swallowed. "My mother…it says her body rejected the infant placed inside of her. That it must have done that because she must have been pregnant already. Pregnant with me. Lord Cato must have married her not long after. He fell in love with her…knowing what he was doing to her, and women like her. He fell in love with her in a place like this. It's…it's obscene. Did he even love her at all? Did he love *me*, knowing I've ruined one of his experiments?"

I took his hand. It was shaking, and I felt like he probably needed comfort more than my words.

"Thank you for being here," he said in a low voice.

"Rosha," Enosh called from the hall. There was a note of panic in it.

"Who we are today," I whispered, "is not all we could ever be."

He squeezed my hand. I think he didn't want me to let go. But I carefully dropped it before rushing outside, just in time to see Enosh dragging himself out to the end of the corridor.

"Quickly!" he roared. "He's—"

Something struck him to the side, sending him flying towards the terrace. I ran after him.

Enosh smashed into the wall before I could reach him. Cracks appeared on the stone where he hit it. I threw a shield-spell in his direction, stopping him from dropping to the ground to his death. Then I turned, because the split-second distraction was already a second too long. I held both my arms up and leaped back in time to stop Targus's blade from taking my head off.

The tip struck my arms, breaking the skin. Blood dripped down to my elbows.

He didn't even look like he broke into a sweat. "To think the daughter is as irritating as the father."

"Please," I said. I dropped my hands to the side and began to conjure fire in both my fingertips. My head pounded.

He smiled. "You know that's not going to do a thing."

"Not the fire," I said, my voice barely above a whisper. "But the inconvenience…"

His eyes widened as I let the fire grow, sending it out like a rope towards the ancient chandelier hanging over the landing. One tug, and the flames shattered, but so did the chains holding the chandelier to the ceiling. It dropped over Targus, pinning him to the ground. I heard flesh give in, followed by the snap of bones breaking.

I stood there, watching him struggle under the weight of all that rusted iron with fascination. I felt like a spider looking at a fly as it got trapped in my own web.

Enosh grabbed my arm before I could lick my lips some more. "Quickly," he said. "We need to get to open ground."

"Why?"

"Didn't you see what he just did to me? That's not a man. He's—"

The chandelier began to move. My stomach sank as I watched Targus carefully lift it from underneath, heedless of his injuries. With a roar, he sent it flying across the landing, striking the wall where Enosh had been pinned mere minutes ago. The remaining stone splintered, cracking the wall further—I thought I could see daylight behind the fissures.

The bloody heap that had been Targus calmly turned around. I realized Felan was still in the room where we'd left him. No—he was out of the hall now, staring back at Targus.

"Lord Cato's son," Targus said. "I thought it was you. We send our deepest regrets for his untimely death."

"You caused that untimely death," I broke in.

"*You* killed my father?" Felan breathed.

"He had grown careless," Targus said. "Careless, and greedy. Most of them turn that way in the end. It is an inconvenience many have come to rely on. Most days, it is useful. They used it to kill the emperor in the first place, after all."

"They?"

"Members of the mage council and the merchant guild," Targus said. "Always, the poisoned edges of Dageis's sword. It didn't take much to convince them then, either. A word here and there, and then the accident at the clock tower happened, and…"

"They killed the emperor while he was injured," Enosh interjected.

"There is no kindness in Dageis, not even when you're at the top."

His eyes fell on me. "Lord Cato was no exception. The man decided he would address the loss of mage-thralls by gaining access to the Gorenten peninsula. He has no idea what such an action would do to this continent. Dageis does not need more connections to the *agan*. Nevertheless, he began to look into your family and discovered you were the same girl who almost got his son killed. The interest in your family brought Enosh Tar'elian's name to his attention. He thought a mage he could extort—a rogue mage with an outlaw daughter—would prove to be more useful than an overly ambitious one. And so he had to die."

I frowned. "You…were protecting me?"

Targus didn't answer. Perhaps it was a stupid question. It had tried to kill me several times already, in addition to leaving my father a bleeding mess. "We were looking for your father," he said, turning to Enosh. "And he, in turn, led us to Cato and the simulacrum, which led us to you: a most unlikely and yet the perfect candidate to puppeteer the Dageian emperor. An outlaw mage, Eheldeth-trained and yet the very opposite of an Eheldeth dog. You see, we have been trying to find the right simulacrum for a very long time. This one, and the one who died in Triassa, and all the others we've found over the years, have been too young, and waiting for them to age out in order to replace the emperor will take another lifetime. The secret Lord Cato and his ilk have kept was difficult to track down. Your family has given us the key we've been looking for forever."

"Why were you looking for my father in the first place?" I asked. "Who *are* you?"

"Don't talk to this thing," Enosh broke in. "It's done nothing but *talk* the last few days. Trying to weasel its way into my brain, even as it kept me a prisoner the whole time. It asked me to consider killing *you* and attuning myself to the emperor instead."

"A father's wisdom can come too late," Targus observed. "A jest, Tar'elian. Don't you think your daughter can make the choice for herself?"

"She—" Enosh began.

"No," I said. "He has it right."

Targus smiled, bleeding wounds and all. "Control the emperor for us, Rosha Tar'elian. You have a good head on your shoulders. You've shown that the day you gave that speech in the palace gardens. Not even Lord Cato could have created such a spectacle."

"They voted Lord Cato as the emperor's puppeteer. Why would the others let me do it?"

Targus gave a short laugh, one that seemed to billow out of his lungs. "They do not know Lord Cato is the puppeteer. Their arrangement demanded secrecy, even amongst themselves. Only *we* know who, and he has four years left. You can stay for four years, too. Together, we can build a newer, better Dageis, one not built on the bones of those they deem less than they are."

"There are other mages you can use. You can kill me and assign someone new."

"We could," Targus said with a nod. "It behooves you, then, to give us a reason not to. We're not difficult to please."

"You're not seriously considering this," Enosh snapped. "These people are insane."

"Do *you* know them?" I asked.

His face darkened. "No," he said, after a moment.

I turned to face him. "You're lying. You do."

"They're…" He shook his head. "They helped me, years ago. Hertra Ferral. Assuming his identity wasn't easy, but I did it to get access to his funds. They told me it came without strings attached—they just wanted to help me out."

"You idiot. Nothing *ever* comes without strings attached."

"I was young," Enosh said. "I didn't know any better, and I felt like I had no other choice. Besides, everything I gained as Hertra Ferral I lost, anyway. I had to start all over again here, in the empire."

"Not everything," Targus interjected. "You paid the initial fees for the lands in the Gorenten peninsula you let your people settle in out of those funds, too. Your Dageian citizenship exists because of *us*. We helped you, and now we're giving your daughter a chance to be everything she ever dreamed of." He held out a hand.

I stared at it. "The only other prospect I have left is serving one of your women as an errand-runner," I mumbled. "I am an outlaw, either way. Why not pick the option where I have the most power?"

From across the landing, I saw Felan draw a deep breath, his shoulders visibly rising and falling.

Enosh shook his head. "Rosha. You don't know the people behind this bastard like I do. They're not opposed to blackmail, or extortion, or murder."

"Just like you?" I asked slowly.

He gave a small sigh. "Hertra Ferral was a long time ago," he breathed. "Rosha—you're not going to hand your whole life away just because of the mistakes *I've* made."

I turned my head from him. "Shows what you know."

"Now all we need is the emperor," Targus said.

"He's with the Firekeeper," I replied. "Back in town."

Targus's eyes flashed. "Go back and fetch it!" he roared.

"I can't do that easily. The Firekeeper has it in her custody. You're not going to pry him from her fingers easily."

"You foolish child. She knows everything?"

"Everything," I said. "And until you get rid of her for me, there's nothing I can do. I wouldn't be surprised if she's here already. She knew we were headed this way, and I already broke the spell-veil."

Targus roared, slamming his hand on the doorway. I realized there were runes etched on the side of it. The glyph began to glow.

The smell of burning filled the air, followed by an explosion down below. Someone screamed. Targus picked up his entire, mangled body, and began running down into the next hallway.

CHAPTER 43

THE BLOOD MAGE

I didn't move.

"What the hell did you just do?" Enosh asked.

"I told him the truth," I said. "He would have found out, anyway."

He stepped towards me, one hand trembling. I think he wanted to slap me. I stared back at him, daring him to. I wasn't a child anymore.

Enosh placed his hand down. "He has the whole place laced with spells. If he's re-enabled them all, even *your* friend up there could trip them. Boy!" he added, in a louder voice, turning his head towards the doorway. "I wouldn't move if I were you!"

Felan's face was ashen, but he carefully made his way down the steps anyway. "No one puts spells in common areas," he said sheepishly, as soon as he got to the bottom of the landing. "Rosha," he continued, turning to me. "That thing killed my father. You can't trust it."

"There are very few things in my life I can trust," I said, casting a critical eye on Enosh. "Maybe it's time I expanded my horizons."

The ground began to shake. I heard the screams again. It was clearly Ceres—a sound that told me she had stumbled into one of the traps. I felt my insides turn.

"That woman isn't perfect, Rosha, but she's never wished you harm," Enosh said. "Gods, if this is what it comes down to…" He tore his gaze away from me and limped through the doorway. I felt Felan's scrutinizing look for a moment before he, too, followed Enosh.

I stared at the ground. For the first time in my life, I realized my inaction was going to cause three deaths, at least. *Four.* A fourth voice was yelling from the farthest end of the great hall, followed by the sound of fighting. Nasuha must have been with Ceres.

Because from what I had seen of Targus, there was no way they were going to survive. The thing's power—whatever it was—went beyond mere strength. I couldn't see where it was coming from, but something told me it had something to do with the person controlling it from the other side. It had to be a mage for it to control Targus in the first place. Did the *agan* connection bleed through the fabric? It had to. But that power…which the emperor himself didn't have…it spoke of something else.

It was going to kill them all, and I still hadn't moved. I told myself there was no point. Targus was too powerful. How would I even fight it? I had perhaps a third spell left in me for that day, and I doubted it would do anything. I'd tried already.

I stared at the fresh flow of blood dripping down my forearms, the wounds I had forgotten in the last few minutes. I stared at it until I grew dizzy. A memory of my house in Klossaka flashed briefly in my mind. For all that it was the seat of my exile, I knew I treasured the place for a reason. It was mine, something I fought for, something I made for myself even if it meant nothing to everyone else. What did Eheldeth know, after all? Deny people a place in the world and they will make it for themselves, anyway.

The blood seemed to take on a shine of its own. I swallowed. I had my answer. My demise was written in the stars.

Closing my eyes, I placed my right hand on the wound on the left arm and used my own blood to channel the *agan*.

Sparks exploded in my skull. I made my way to the great hall.

Drawing on my blood did the trick. I could see the light emanating even from the ground, the faint wisps of *agan* normally undetected by all but the most powerful of mages. Even Felan and Nasuha emitted threads from themselves. Enosh's light was stronger, while Ceres was all but blinding.

She turned as I walked past her. She was down on one knee, panting. Her clothes were charred.

"Tar'elian," the Firekeeper said evenly.

I turned to her, expecting a reprimand.

She threw her staff towards me. I caught it in mid-air.

"Give him hell," she hissed.

I began to run towards Targus, who was floating in the middle of the room. His eyes sparked blue as I drew close.

"Have you changed your mind again?" he demanded. His voice

sounded like a roar inside of my brain. I felt a blast of heat, as if I'd been pushed into a kiln.

"Let them go, and I will do this for you," I said. "I'm giving you one last chance."

"Why the demands, Tar'elian? None of these people mean anything to you."

"I said one last chance." I drew on more blood, ignoring the sharp, searing pain in my wounds, and rushed him.

Blood magic was like flying while getting kicked in the head all at once. A perverse mix of fire and power and pleasure, balled up in a pocket deep inside your chest. The more you drew on your own blood, the bigger the well grew. Mages who weren't careful could fall into it. Mages who didn't stop would be obliterated by the weight of their own power.

I flung flames at him, bigger than anything I'd conjured in the last few weeks—giant tongues that threatened to set the whole castle ablaze. He moved with a speed that matched mine, but I didn't mind the chase. The staff and the blood magic helped, both things pumping life in and out of my veins. *The sea is inside you.* It always was, after all. If you were born to the sea, how could you ever lose it?

I slammed a fireball at Targus's head, knocking him to the ground. He recovered before he could ever fall properly. He pushed himself up and dashed to the corner of the great hall, towards the giant arches near the entrance, away from everyone else.

My head pounded as I gave chase. It felt like I was running down an entire street. Everything faded in the background.

As I drew close, he struck me with a blast I couldn't see—the same, hot wind that could've sucked the breath out of my lungs if it had hit me full force. I ducked, felt it slide over my forehead like a blade. The blood on my arms began to steam; the smell of my cooking flesh was like a slab of meat laid out on a bed of hot coals. I tried to shake it off as I released a shield-spell and jumped backward, my feet sliding across the cracked, ruined floor of the palace.

Targus smiled.

I took another step back, dropped the shield, and struck him with fire. Two spells, one after the other. Blood dripped down my nostrils. The sensation of floating in the air was rapidly fading, leaving only the pain. I knew I needed more blood, a fresh source. Should I pick up the debris we were leaving behind and cut myself deeper? It was too late to back out now, too late to stop. He had to go down.

"Look at you!" I heard Targus call. "You're falling apart!"

I tried to rush him head-first. He side-stepped easily, curiosity mixing with the rage on his features. "You can barely cast spells!" he cried. "They said you were one of the best students in your year, one of the most gifted that ever walked through those halls! They said your natural power was so strong they didn't know what to do with you! What's the true reason you didn't graduate from Eheldeth?"

I jumped on one of the glyphs engraved on the bottom of the columns, breaking it. Sharp shards of *agan* exploded in the air. The ground shook again. The spells weren't reacting to me, but they were still connected to the building. In the distance, I saw a column fall, blocking most of the hallway, trapping me with Targus.

He struck me with the back of his hand, sending me against the wall so hard my head and my shoulders were numb almost immediately. My senses darkened.

I had a flash of memory, of the night in that forgotten library. Of seeing Felan on the ground, unmoving, drained of his *agan* in a way I didn't understand. Of knowing I was next and forcing myself to leave him behind to save myself.

Of the stranger grabbing me by the shoulder, pulling me close. Whispering something in my ear. Turning me around to face those gleaming eyes in the dark. I couldn't remember what colour their eyes were. They gleamed—they must have gleamed. I recalled the feel of calluses on their palm as they pressed it on my forehead, followed by the sensation of being drenched in a vat of hot oil.

I remembered screaming.

"You're losing your sight," Targus breathed.

I said nothing. Even if I wanted to, I was coughing blood. The staff was the only thing keeping my upright. Gritting my teeth, I lunged at him again, not knowing what I could do if I reached him.

I heard someone call my name. Felan scrambled over the fallen column and headed straight for an untouched rune. I watched as he struck it with his hand. Again, it exploded. The shards cut his skin, sending long streaks of blood running down his right arm. His face remained calm as he held it out for me. I watched the red drip down his skin, rivers coursing down his sleeves. The smell of iron hung heavy in the air.

"Draw on me," Felan said.

"Don't be stupid," I snapped.

"Draw on me, Rosha," he repeated. "There's no time." He squeezed his fingers, letting more blood flow.

"I won't do that to you. I won't do that to anyone."

"Would you rather we all die here?"

When I didn't move, he grabbed my hand. I could feel his blood mixing with mine, the warmth of it. Blue light danced between the bright red.

I still wanted to say *no*, but my body had a mind of its own. It began to leech off his strength, his essence. Swimming in another's power when I'd all but exhausted mine felt invigorating. The ocean swelled around me. I felt a rush like nothing I'd ever known before and suddenly hated when I understood why the Dageians did this. The feel of pure power, so easily accessed without burning myself, was intoxicating.

As Targus drew close, I launched one last devastating attack. I saw the look of surprise on his face, as if he didn't think I had it in me. Why did he doubt it? Broken, I was still better than most. The spell obliterated him where he stood.

Beside the rubble, Felan stirred. "Rosha," he whispered. "Are you still alive?"

I nodded carefully. The movement felt like someone was jerking me with strings. Like my head would fall off if I did it some more. I stopped and rested my cheek on the dirt. The coolness of it helped with the headache.

"She did it to you too, didn't she?" he asked. "That stranger in the library attacked you with the same spell she used on me."

"She did," I replied, my lips cracking. I felt a trickle of blood run down my chin. "I fought back, so whatever she tried was cut short. I ran out of that place, and then…"

And then everything changed.

It began like a loose tooth, a slight wiggle here or there that would only give if you chewed on something hard. Simple spells were still easy. But harder spells eluded me.

The teachers never noticed. I knew the theories front and back and what I couldn't do, I could trick them into thinking I could. It barely affected my grades, though I found myself staying up longer, or practicing spells many times before any exams. It worked for a few years.

But then it grew worse. The spells sapped my energy. As the months wore on, I counted the number I could throw without becoming exhausted to the bones and found them growing smaller and smaller. From twenty or so spells, it dropped to fifteen, and then ten. By the time the finals came, I couldn't cast five spells in a row without feeling like my head would explode. I knew without a shadow of a doubt that an entire week of spells might not just drain me, but kill me, too. At the very least, without enchantments or help from elsewhere, I was going to fumble an exam in such a way that they'd have to investigate it. Exactly what happened during the portals exam.

If they'd gone through with it, they would have discovered the truth.

All those years, I made myself believe I walked away on purpose. On bad days, I told myself I let fear rule me; on good days, I truly believed it was because I was destined for better. Eheldeth didn't believe in me and would give nothing beyond promises—why should I have given them another hour of my life? If they couldn't give me the support I needed when I excelled, what more when I was struggling? What mercy was there in an empire that fed on the lesser without remorse?

I didn't explain all of this to Felan. I think all he had to do was look at me. He'd been there before.

"Don't tell them," I gasped. "Please."

"I won't," he promised.

"It could still come back. If Ceres finds out…"

"She will set you free. She has no reason to hold you in her custody any longer. If you are not a mage, then you can't be an outlaw mage."

"If I'm not a mage, then what am I?" I asked. "I'll be forgotten in some dark, dusty corner of the empire, worse than what I've been doing all these years. I'll be nothing, Felan. I can't be *nothing*. My whole family gave up their lives so I can be here. How do I tell them I've squandered their sacrifice?"

He grew serious. "Will you resort to blood magic to keep this up? What then, after that?"

"Please," I whispered, my voice smaller than whatever I felt inside. The euphoria was gone—all that was left was the hollowness of what lay ahead. "It's all I have."

CHAPTER 44

SYMPHONY OF THE LOST

I slept and dreamt I was inside Felan's skeleton, staring at his seared connections—at the knobbed ends of the rivers of *agan* that he could once slip through with ease.

I woke up and found myself in one of the beds on the second floor, where the women gave birth to the simulacrums. There were no mattresses—the bed underneath was made of bamboo—but someone had draped a cloak over my body. I took it off, noting how blood had leaked into patches, and stared at the wounds on my arms. Thick, black scabs had formed over them. Eventually, I turned my head—which felt like it had been screwed on backward—towards the window. The sun was high in the sky, which meant I must have slept for most of the night and morning.

The gravity of what I had just done to defeat Targus came back to me. The consequences of blood magic were unpredictable. There was a possibility I had made things worse for myself. I felt the urge to test it with a minor spell and lifted my fingers. But the fear stopped me from going further. What was I going to do if I couldn't conjure even the simplest spell?

I heard a knock on the door. "Rosha," Enosh's voice called from the other side. "Are you alive?"

I rolled across the bed and limped my way to the door. I opened it.

"Not in the mood for your jokes," I grumbled.

"You never are." He cleared his throat. "How are you feeling?"

"I've been better."

"Your colour has improved from last night, at least. Nasuha has the horses ready. You can finish resting back in the city."

I took a deep breath. "Did she say what she was going to do with me?"

"No," he admitted. "The battle sapped most of Ceres's strength, too. I didn't want to bring it up. Believe it or not, I'm not in the position to get the woman to say or do anything unless she offers it herself. That said, she lent you her staff. That must mean something."

"It meant we were all about to die, and she grew desperate," I said.

"We all do things when we are desperate." His eyes grew soft. "I feel like I owe you the truth, about Hertra Ferral."

"You don't. I'm just your daughter, remember?"

"You're my only daughter," he replied.

"That you know of."

He gave a rueful grin. "Fair enough. You're the only daughter I know of, and the only child I have that I have to live with, and I don't know if I can bear having you think the worst of me."

"Enosh," I said carefully, in case he missed what I was about to say. "I already do."

"And you're not going to give me a chance to improve it?"

I sighed. "I suppose you don't really need my permission to talk."

"I didn't kill Ferral," he said. "I was introduced to him when I was an apprentice merchant, and he readily agreed to mentor me for a time. During one of our private meetings, he died out of perfectly natural causes, and I realized I would be blamed. I sought help from this merchant couple, whom I long thought were Ferral's friends. They turned out to care more about his businesses than the fact that he was dead, and under their tutelage, I used glamour to impersonate him and carry on with his affairs as if nothing had happened. In exchange, I got access to his fortunes…which weren't what you would call vast, but they were a start. One thing after another, and then people just naturally accepted I was him because their memories were so muddled by the magical tampering."

"This couple," I said. "They're the ones behind Targus?"

"The man died a long time ago. The woman, on the other hand…"

"Are they Dageian?"

Enosh ran a hand over his head. "The man was. The woman…is Gorenten."

I blinked. "She—Targus—said she wanted me to control the emperor so we could build a better Dageis."

"She'd say anything to have gotten you to agree. Her lust for power drives her mad. It drives all of them mad. I know because I was there along with them. I always meant to get out of it, but…"

I took a deep breath. "I think I understand."

"When we started anew in Dageis, I did it under my name," he continued. "And I meant for it so you would inherit everything after I'm gone. Life is difficult, Rosha, but it's even harder when you turn around and realize your own children will face the same struggles. I wanted to lessen your burden."

"You couldn't," I said at last. "The burden can't go away. It just transforms."

He didn't reply, but he didn't disagree, either.

We went back down to the great hall, which still bore scars of last night's attack. Felan stood in the corner, arms crossed. He glanced at me while I walked by, but said nothing. At the far end, Ceres was inspecting what was left of Targus—the unmoving mass of torso with missing limbs. She greeted us with a slight nod. "I wanted one last look, to see if we can find any clues on his handler," she said. "You've all but burnt him to a crisp."

I glanced at Enosh, who kept his mouth shut. He wasn't going to tell her about the Gorenten merchant—not yet anyway. For the first time, I was of the same mind.

"We need to do the same to the emperor," I said.

"Why?" Ceres asked.

"Because it's dangerous. Targus's handler still wants it—who knows what else they will do to get it? If we get rid of it, we can say the emperor died, and end this."

She looked amused. "That will end nothing," she reminded me. "Especially since there are multiple versions of the emperor running around. Perhaps the one we have is the only one of the right age—but it's possible it isn't. And there must be plenty of others just biding their time. No. We can't tell the empire. Targus's handler and the people behind the emperor are not the same, and to find both we have to get right in the middle of things."

"We," I repeated. "I can't be your errand-runner anymore, Firekeeper."

"You would rather spend the rest of your life behind bars?"

I glanced at Enosh.

"Ceres—" he began.

She shrugged. "You see how she won't even give me a chance. With her grades, I could have done something for her after graduation. The scholarship track isn't everything. Instead, she treated the final exams like a joke. I can't undo what is written in Eheldeth's records. She knew that."

I didn't want to look at her while she was talking about these things, so I approached Targus's corpse and turned it with my foot. The body flopped to the side. I noticed a long scar on its back. It looked like a healed sword wound at first inspection, but when I looked closer, it was actually a rip, as if an animal had torn off a piece of his skin in the past and it had found a way to heal over.

"For as long as they think whoever was in charge of the simulacrum is still in charge, we have time," Ceres was saying behind me. "In the meantime, we have to find the members of this cabal. They've been fooling the empire for years. We can start with what's in these ruins. These Agaranthen women—they must be connected to the men who used their offspring."

"I will assist you, Firekeeper," Felan said. "Limited as my capacity might be."

"Tar'elian," Ceres added. I didn't know if she was referring to me or my father and turned to face her. She looked at both of us. "It's been a rough few weeks. Out of my misguided fondness for you, I will let you go home first."

"First?" I asked.

"You're still mine, Kirosha Tar'elian," she said. "Never forget that."

Beside her, Felan's face tightened. I knew what he was thinking. I could break free now, if I just told her. All I had to do was tell her. But I was more afraid of emptiness than I was of the Firekeeper of Eheldeth, even if she was one of the most powerful women in all the land. She was nothing to the emptiness. If I couldn't be a mage, what use was I alive?

I bowed my head.

And so, after all of that, I found myself home once again.

At least, that is how we expect our stories to end, isn't it? We dream of a future that holds none of the struggles or suffering our present day holds, and journey in search of it. The fortunate ones find something of value to bring back. Many others—those whose stories we hear less of—return only with sorrow and empty hands.

We come home, and we think it is the perfect time to stop. Let time stop—let me sit with this happiness a little longer. But just as there are no perfect beginnings, we cannot hope for a perfect end. There's a lesson in that somewhere, something about making the in-between count.

Perhaps the true value lies in the pursuit; what we want and what we need, always changing with the winds.

I can't say. I know only that after all my declarations of leaving it all behind, of letting my family believe the worst—an arrangement I might have gotten Enosh to agree with, if I was inclined to—I chose to come home anyway. I got to see that old road again, leading to that house on the hill. Ryo screaming at the top of his lungs, Haro nearly tripping on the footbridge near the ditch in his haste to greet us. Dogs barking, Daisy near-hysterical at the sight of me. Laughter. Tears. I saw Mother's expression drift between shock and relief, and then nothing else because before I knew it I was in Papa's arms and for a brief moment, our strange, impossibly difficult family was together again.

There, you see? The perfect end. *Whatever you think of us or the things we've done, you should know you were always loved.* It lasted a few minutes, minutes I counted with my stepfather's heartbeat.

And then I heard someone calling my name. I turned to face Jehar.

"Rosha," he greeted. He didn't look happy.

"What are you doing here?" I asked.

Kefier cleared his throat. "Let me explain. He—"

"No," I said. "Don't. Let *him* talk."

Jehar frowned. "I was worried about you. I decided to follow you."

"Because you didn't think I could take care of myself?"

His eyes narrowed. Maybe I looked worse than I felt, because he said, "Clearly you can't."

"It's touching you think so, but that's your opinion."

"My other opinion is that you should come home to Klossaka soon. Everyone's worried, too. Mother's been taking care of your store, but she said the bank's been there at least twice and she thinks they'll take it all away if you don't return to pay your bills."

It was jarring how I could hear those words and not feel anything. What would have once been devastating news now felt like a minor annoyance. "You shouldn't have come." I threw Kefier an angry look. "You shouldn't have entertained him, either."

"He was very persistent," Kefier grumbled.

"And polite," Sume broke in. "Rosha, you haven't even taken your shoes off yet, and you're already picking fights. Leave it alone for an hour. Dinner's ready. And Enosh…" She stepped up to my father, who —for what was probably the first time in his life—was speechless. She gave him a scrutinizing gaze, which seemed to make him wilt. But her expression quickly turned to one of pity and I saw her visibly restrain herself from touching his face. It suddenly struck me that she loved him once. "You look like hell."

"Well," Enosh replied with a small shrug. "I've been through hell."

She narrowed her eyes. "Which of your women did it this time?"

He coughed. "*This* time? There was nobody. You people always think the worst of me. I was trying to save Rosha."

"I ended up saving him," I replied. "Twice."

"Why am I not surprised?" Kefier asked.

"And he's lying again," I continued. "There *was* a woman. At least one that we know of. Father seduced her, and he got turned into a monster and…"

"Oh, excellent," Kefier said. "Go back over it during dinner. This is a story I can listen to all day."

"It's good to see you too, brother," Enosh scoffed.

They shuffled inside the house, one after the other, leaving me alone outside with Jehar.

"I heard things while I was looking for you," Jehar said, scratching the side of his face without looking at me. "It worries me."

"Thank you, but I am not *yours* to worry about," I replied. "Have dinner with my family, then go home. Tell your mother I'm safe. Tell her to let the bank have my shop. I can't pay for it anymore, anyway. I'll have to hand it over sooner or later."

"But you worked so hard for it."

"I know."

He drew a deep breath. "Is there anything I can do for you, Rosha? Please tell me. I still love you. Tell me what I should do, I'm begging you."

"You have a job," I pointed out. "Go back to it. The town needs you."

"I quit the job," he said. "They wouldn't let me take time off so I could go after you, so I told them they could go to hell. The mayor was furious."

"Idiot," I said.

"I know," he sighed.

I didn't have the heart to berate him further. I was beyond exhausted and after everything I had gone through, I didn't want to sour those moments with my family. I patted him on the shoulder and went back inside, to chatter and warmth and good food. I told myself the rest could wait.

Two days later, I found myself exploring the bay with just Kefier, on a small boat he'd built himself. He had named it after me, which all but told me how he kept himself busy during my years in Klossaka. It was a solid little craft made mostly of oak, and so pretty I felt a little terrible we were exposing it to salt water at all. But Kefier insisted the salt was good for preserving the wood, and besides, "You don't build a boat and not put it out to sea. It's just inconceivable."

"Since when did you start using that word?" I demanded, craning my head backward. I was sitting at the bow of the canoe, a position that meant I was in charge of calling out where we were going. He steered from the back.

He laughed. "I spend a lot of time with your mother. You're bound to pick up things."

I placed the oar on the hull so I could lean on it. We were drifting somewhere north of the city, overlooking a group of islands that looked almost like goat droppings floating at sea. "Papa…" I began.

"Hmm?"

I wanted to tell him then. I wanted to tell him what had happened those years ago, with Felan, and how I thought I was losing my skill in the *agan*. I would have if I was much younger. I turned the words over in my head and then decided I wasn't a girl anymore. I wasn't going to burden him with my problems. "Tell me about the Lost Ones," I said instead.

He looked surprised. "Where did you hear about that?"

"From someone who assisted me in Lord Cato's mansion," I said. "She said she was a travelling mercenary at first, and then later she defended me from the bearers who were trying to…bring me to justice. She said she was a Lost One."

"What's her name?"

"Nasuha," I said. "I believe her last name was Lang'rabay."

Kefier rubbed his jaw. "I'm not familiar with the name. Lang'rabay. It sounds almost like it's from one of the eastern islands."

"She said I was Gorent's," I continued. "Not Dageis's. She promised she would explain what it meant, but she disappeared when we returned to Genthal and I'm not sure if I'm ever going to see her again. All I can gather is that the Lost Ones are a myth of Gorent's—children born without souls but are connected to the *agan* anyway." I paused. What I'd just said sounded a lot like the simulacrums.

Kefier's expression turned to troubled. "It's more than that. The Lost Ones is also the name of an order established by King Elian of Gorent after Dageis set its eyes on us. The Gorenten Peninsula didn't hold the massive wells of *agan* that Dageis found valuable in its exploration of the continent, but we had a lot of children born with a connection to it. We knew, ultimately, that Dageis would find our own people more valuable than our land. The Lost Ones were supposed to protect those children from Dageis's clutches, by however means necessary."

I heard the seagulls squawking over us and felt a chill run over my skin at his words. "What do you mean by that?" I asked.

"They weren't opposed to putting our own children down, to keep Dageis from claiming them." He shook his head. "But that was a long time ago. The order was dissolved after High King Elian's defeat."

"She said her father tried to kill her because he believed she had the skill in the *agan*, but no soul," I said.

"You're not a child anymore," he whispered. "In this, you have nothing to fear."

CHAPTER 45

THE EMPEROR'S PUPPETMASTER

I stayed with my family for a month. To my surprise, Enosh stayed, too. We spent the days alternating between taking care of my brothers and trying to patch up the store and get it running. It felt like the shortest and longest month of my life, both at once. Trying to pretend we were a normal happy family, even though we knew it was the furthest thing from the truth. The calm before the storm. Ceres's words hung like a naked sword over my head, and I knew it was only a matter of time.

I was right. At the end of that month, I received a sealed letter, brought by a messenger in the mage council's robes, which she opened in front of me. Ceres's words rolled out of her tongue. I was to report to Drusgaya in two days. She also came with a purse with enough coin in it for my journey. I didn't want to accept it, but she didn't give me much of a choice and all but shoved the letter and purse in my hands.

I said my goodbyes, mostly for Papa's benefit. My brothers wept. It was strange—it wasn't as if I was going away for good. But no one knew what awaited an outlaw mage embracing her fate, and no one wanted to talk about the possibilities. My mother was holding on to the hope that since Ceres had known about Enosh and ignored his connection to the *agan* all these years, she would offer the same courtesy to me. But there was a simple difference. Enosh never walked out of Eheldeth. Enosh skirted the rules, but he never exactly broke them. I'd done it all, and more.

So the *see you later* somehow felt like a forever goodbye. I realized that as a grown up, I could never come home again. I more than left

Eheldeth when I walked away from it; I also left my childhood behind. Every homecoming henceforth would only be temporary. I had a life away from them now, even though I wasn't sure what it looked like.

My mother didn't want to say goodbye, and pretended it was because she had chores to do and a store that wouldn't run without her. Maybe she just didn't want me to see her crying. Only Enosh and Kefier walked me all the way to the airship.

"Just do what she tells you," Enosh said, as we waited for the ship at the base of the docking tower. "She's easy to please."

Kefier glanced at him, and he had the courtesy to look embarrassed. "We're here if you need anything," Kefier said, to change the subject. "Come back again, Rosha, all right? Always come back. Whatever you do, whatever you've become, we're here for you."

I kissed his cheek, and his cheek only, and went off to Drusgaya.

Ceres's mages were waiting for me as soon as I arrived in the city. Typical of her—she wasn't going to take any chances. These two were even more humourless than the messenger and wouldn't let me stop for anything, not even for a bite to eat.

I was expecting them to bring me to a nondescript inn somewhere, a place as cloaked in shadows as my existence. Instead, we got into a carriage, which took the road leading to the palace. My heart raced. Ceres wouldn't have gone through the trouble of procuring escorts if she meant to have me punished, would she? There were representatives of the mage council in every city, dungeons in each one. She could have just let me rot in the one in Triassa and saved herself the coin for my journey.

The carriage rolled through the main gates. We went past the gardens, in full view of the guards. At the front gates, someone opened the door.

Felan gave a bow. "Adherent Tar'elian," he said. "The Firekeeper awaits you."

"What?" I asked.

"Time is precious, Adherent. We can't keep her waiting."

I knew he was doing it for the benefit of those watching. I took his offered hand and got out of the carriage. The mages stayed behind, watching as we strode through the massive doors. We found ourselves in a lobby that could have been mistaken for a great hall—it was large enough to hold a wedding.

"Upstairs," Felan said.

I followed him in silence. We took the steps, down to a hallway with red carpet and crystal chandeliers. Even indoors, there was light everywhere—the chandeliers themselves used mage light. We reached the farthest end of the hall.

Felan knocked on the door. "We are alone, Firekeeper," he called.

The door opened. Ceres greeted us with pursed lips—hardly a smile, though I didn't expect much from her. She didn't carry a shadow of our battle with Targus—almost as if running into a trap that would have splattered her insides over the walls was an experience she wrestled with daily.

"Adherent?" I asked. "Are you going to explain this, or am I now allowed to file a formal inquiry through the council?"

"It won't go through," she admitted. "It's all for show. I doctored the records where I can, but I can't reach everything. You'll have to make sure no one looks into this any further than they have to. As far as everyone is concerned, you're just my assistant."

"Ah," I said. "Of course."

Ceres pursed her lips. "You look unhappy. Isn't this what you wanted? I could have made you an assistant without the title, but I knew how important it was to you, and so…"

"What's the catch?" I asked. "You wouldn't have gone through all this trouble to appease me."

She gestured towards the end of the room.

The emperor, the simulacrum, was sitting on the sofa, rune on his forehead. Ceres stepped towards him and placed her hand on the seal, breaking it.

Light flickered in the simulacrum's eyes.

"The Empire of Dageis needs its emperor," she said, "and until we can clean up this mess behind Emperor Cerknar, we have to dance along with everyone else. The secret council behind Emperor Cerknar can't discover we're onto their ruse until we can weed them out one by one and remove their corruption. I don't want to tear the thing apart in the hopes of fixing its attunement on another mage. I might break it more. I certainly would rather not kill *you* to break it free from you. As that despicable Targus said, we have a perfectly good mage behind it already, and I don't see why we can't use her." Now she smiled.

"You want me to control the emperor," I said. "For *you*."

"That's the idea. And in exchange, you get a title under your name, a healthy stipend that would make even your father pay attention, and the clearance to walk in and out of the palace to your heart's desire. So as long as you serve me, you can have everything you ever wanted."

For a moment, I saw the shadow of our secret on Felan's face. If I agreed to this, I was subjecting myself to more magic. What happens if I fail, if I am found out? How much further would I test Ceres's patience? If she realizes the emperor is attuned to a mage growing more useless by the day, she might decide to have me killed, anyway. However she thought this arrangement would go, I knew it wasn't bound to last.

But my hunger was bigger than my concerns. Always had been. Allow me to do magic, unbridled, and I would try even if it kills me. As both of them watched, I walked to the edge of her desk and picked up a letter opener. I cut my finger and placed the bleeding digit on the emperor's shoulder, activating the glyph. Heat pounded through my skull. I slipped into his body and found myself staring back at them through his eyes.

"Come, Firekeeper," I said in his deep, gravelly voice, now so clear to me it was like we shared one soul. "I believe my absence in this empire has gone on for too long. We need to show ourselves in court once more."

There was a proud, almost smug look on her face as she gave a mock-bow. "As you wish, Your Excellency."

I got up, feeling the simulacrum's bones creak. I walked past Felan and my own, unmoving, blank-eyed body, and out into the hall. People swung their heads to stare before belatedly falling to their knees in obeisance.

I made my way to the throne room and climbed up the platform, where the single, golden throne stood in the middle, framed with an image of the sun. For the emperor was the light of the most powerful empire in the world, and I found it beyond ironic that a mere child of Gorent would be the one controlling him. If I would be a fraud like my father before me, then let me be the biggest fraud of them all. I could take to this throne a lesson my people have known for generations: the most dangerous person in the world is not the one with the most power, but the one who has nothing left to lose.

I turned to face the crowd before slowly sinking into the throne. It felt cold, but comfortable. It felt like I belonged. I stared at the awe-filled eyes that would never give me the same respect or worship if they knew who I really was. I thought about all the things I could do to break them.

"Citizens of Dageis," I began, letting my voice carry the rest away.

THE STORY CONTINUES IN
BLOOD MAGE

ACKNOWLEDGMENTS

None of my projects would exist without the belief and unending support of people in my close circles—those who see them when they're still fleeting ideas and bones, and hold firm that we can turn that pile of dust into gold. For this one, I have my partner, Mikhail Villoso, my agent Hannah Bowman, and my good friend Quenby Olson to thank. As well, my eldest daughter Eirene has been a wonderful sounding board, copy-editor, beta reader, and just all around advisor—I hope I've made you proud.

To Tess Lina, whose out-of-the-blue email to me sparked the idea for this Kickstarter--hearing Rosha come alive through your narration was absolutely inspirational.

Beyond that, launching a project like this when I had no idea how to run a Kickstarter is nerve-wracking. Thank you to Merilliza Chan, Trish Isiderio, Kerstin Rosero, Amanda Bohannan, the folks at the Broken Binding, and everyone else who offered their talents to making this project shine. A special thank you to Intisar Khanani and Virginia McClain for holding my hand throughout the setup of this Kickstarter, as well as Anthea Sharp and her fantastic group for her wonderful support and cheerleading throughout the campaign process. Thank you as well to the Terrible Ten Writing Group for always having my back, and the fantastic B² Weird Bookclub for helping me out during launch. I also want to give a shout out to Lyssa Chiavari and the rest of the authors at the Snowy Wings Publishing Co-op for all their support.

Thank you to everyone who shared and pledged during the Kick-starter, including:

Tao Roung Wong
Rachel
Winnie Man

Erisnyx
Den
Kristine Paningbatan
Angela Boord
John E. Weglian
Paige Sullivan
Oliver
John
Jeff Ahlstedt
Jay
Shannon Tusler
Andrew Weldon

Marin Ito
Nelson Macabales
Alexis
Alexander Bundt
Kerstin Espinosa Rosero
Amenze
Sunny Side Up
Ashley
Christine Mclean
Mihir Wanchoo
JJ Brenner
Dave Bauhman
Greg Bergerson
Josefine Fouarge
Gavin Chua
Marie Goursolas
Nicolas Lobotsky
Steven Ede
Robin Hill
Jonathan Hamm
Richard Novak
Joseph Ryan Fontanilla
Damian Strzop
Dr. Charles Elbert Norton III
Austin Hoffey
Victoria
Katee Robert
Clephiro

Mrinal
Graham Dauncey
Ganesh Alwarappan
Anne Chesterley
Keith Alan Rothschild
Deborah Hedges
Travis
Josep Pisano
Louie Nuñez

Anne Shinoskie
kamalloy
Ellis
Kaitlin Mae Stubbs
Grant

Camilla Sutton
Grégoire Cotté
Joshua M Dreher
Alice
Alex Grande
Tyler Hise
Melissa Shumake
Deborah Hedges
Natalie
Manu Velasco

MG

AllanDLR
Michelle Wierenga
Kevin Kastelic
Zachary Amos
Amanda Tambacas
Matthew Witkowski
Winter Hart
Hilarie Anderson
Rowena Santos
paul
Eric DiCarlo
Kye Handy

Tamara Case
Johanna Olano
Adam Holcombe
Courtney Walton
Rhel ná DecVandé
Linz Nyre
Margaret Beldyk
Briana Forbes

Thordis Jensen
Julie Roehm
Meghan Newton
Jacob H. Joseph

Quenby Olson Eisenacher
Melissa Newcomb
Guerric Haché
Jason Aycock
Grégoire Cotté
Frøya
Nicolas Mandujano III
Cody Allen
Mackenzie
Paul Trinies
Elisa B.
Alex Grade
James Perkins
Tyler Hise
Kristen Bell
Samantha Endres
N. Scott Pearson

Joshua M Dreher
Katherine Shipman
Clair johnson
Oriene Shiel
Jes McCutchen

This project wouldn't exist without you. Thank you for your support of
an artist just trying to get by. It means the world.

ABOUT THE AUTHOR

Born in Daraga, Albay, K.S. Villoso writes speculative fiction with themes shaped by her childhood, with grim and grit inspired by both the streets of Manila, Philippines, and the wilds of British Columbia, Canada. Her books range from epic fantasy touched with the horrors of the aswang to long adventures through magic-strewn lands inspired by the engkanto. She now lives in BC with a pack of dogs and humans. When she isn't writing, she spends her days counting to when she can get lost in the mountains again.

ALSO BY K. S. VILLOSO

Legacy of the Lost Mage: Jaeth's Eye
Legacy of the Lost Mage: Aina's Breath
Legacy of the Lost Mage: Sapphire's Flight
Blackwood Marauders
Daughter of the Wolves
The Wolf of Oren-yaro
The Ikessar Falcon
The Dragon of Jin-sayeng
Blood Ties